Imagine Jade Gone

Published by Ulu Publishing
Paperback ISBN: 978-0-9914111-3-9
Hardback ISBN: 978-0-9914111-4-6

Envie: Cajun French, pronounced ahn-vee.
Meaning a desire, craving, a hunger for something.

PRÉCIS

The bayou holds terrors that can devour her alive.

After barely escaping a horrifying pack of hybrid mutants, all sixteen-year-old Jaden Lisette wants to do is put the episode behind her, especially now that her future includes the sweet and sexy Briz Nolan. But falling in love may not be their fate.

As Jaden battles her new living nightmares, an old adversary returns, intent on revenge. This time, every last ounce of her strength and courage may not be enough to save the ones she loves...or herself.

What Jaden learned:

1. Forgiveness must be earned.

2. Fear enables bravery.

3. Indian actor and film producer Shah Rukh Khan was right. *There is no right time and right place for love...it can happen any time.*

Praise for the award-winning novel
IMAGINE JADE GONE

"Imagine Jade Gone by Wray Ardan is the sequel to Sweet Desire, Wicked Fate. It's refreshing to see each of the characters grow and change by the end. It's not just one person's journey. Jaden is the type of heroine that you want to see succeed and earn her happy ending. Ardan creates a range of characters that aren't perfect, they make mistakes, but they learn and keep going. I sympathized more with Jaden than anyone, but by the end I understood Ava and Briz, and it was nice to see them all grow. Wray Ardan strikes the perfect balance between humor, family and romance with the classic horror elements. The ending is a complete surprise and took me off guard, leaving me desperately needing more of Jaden's story."
Readers' Favorite Book Review

"I was impatient to read Wray Ardan's second book, Imagine Jade Gone from the trilogy, Sweet Desire, Wicked Fate. It's just as gripping as Book 1, which I suggest reading first if possible. This book has never-ending, spine-tingling drama. The author's writing format continues its strong, imaginative flow that makes this story fascinating. The creatures' descriptions and their actions are very repulsive, but these make the story even more intense and thrilling. It's obvious a lot of time and inventive thought went into this book, and it connects to Book 1 so precisely. I'm still convinced that a horror movie can be made, now having perused two novels from Wray Ardan's Sweet Desire, Wicked Fate series."
Readers' Favorite Book Review

Imagine Jade Gone

Book 2 of The Sweet Desire, Wicked Fate Trilogy

Wray Ardan

*For my sister, Robin,
my most ardent cheerleader.*

PROLOGUE

JADEN

Jaden sniffed the air. A pungent odor filled her nostrils. Once again, she felt a glass pressed against her lips and a stringy liquid slide into her mouth. She smiled drowsily. At first, she'd found the taste and texture revolting. Large hands had to physically restrain her to get the foul solution into her mouth. She'd gagged repeatedly as it was forced down her throat. But now, she didn't mind as the drink pulled her from her dreams of Professor Dekle Thatcher, the brilliant grandfather she'd never known, and of his genetically engineered creations, the Mal Rous.

Ahh, yes, more, she thought, swallowing the savory, delicious interruption.

People swore the Mal Rous were monsters, that the Professor had been deranged to create them. But Jaden understood his devotion to the Mal Rous. Especially the one called Datura. After all, Datura's blood now ran through Jaden's veins; they were partly kin.

A vision of Datura dying flitted through Jaden's mind.

Was that because of me? She thought of the other Mal Rous: Anders, Tig, Esere, and Ivan. *Did I kill them all?*

She swallowed more of the thick liquid.

The glass emptied too soon. Jaden struggled to open her eyes as the coolness of the glass slid from her lips. She tried to speak, to demand more, but her mind dulled as unconsciousness stole her away.

This time, she dreamed her sister, Ava, was chasing her down a dim corridor lined with windows that framed the dark night beyond. Jaden looked back, then stumbled as Ava morphed into a creature with horns and fangs. Jaden moved to run again, then stopped. Glancing at her reflection in the window, she realized she had become a monster, too, deadlier than her sister. She turned and stared into Ava's fiery eyes. Jaden's eyes blazed hotter.

Confront the beasts that torment you. Then allow forgiveness to find its way. Unleashed from her mind, the words thundered down the hall, pushing against the walls and shattering the windows, the broken glass sparkling as it fused into rivulets of water. Jaden spread her arms and flew into the night. She looked down and saw Ava, no longer a monster, watching her.

Jaden's eyes popped open; the dream withered away.

Perspiration seeped from Jaden's skin. Blearily, she stood. Multiple hands pushed and pulled at her, forcing her back into bed. Voices tumbled around her, some badgering her to respond, others declaring she wasn't in her right state of mind, vowing they'd find a way to help her.

Jaden snarled and lunged as nylon straps were tied to her wrists and ankles, then fastened to the frame of the bed. She thrashed, struggling to get free.

The badgering voices returned. This time, they cooed

that Jaden would be all right, implored her to calm down. But Datura's blood and the feral Mal Rou instincts within told her to trust no one. Soon she found another glass pressed to her mouth, followed by two more. The concoctions within tasted familiar, not as pungent as what she'd been given before, less stringy.

Her body felt heavy. Had she been drugged?

When Jaden dreamed again, she found herself soaring above the bayou, smiling, the tips of her fingers touching the tips of a crow's wing. The cool air whispered of changes to come, promised that eventually the nightmare she'd been living would end.

"When?" she asked. Then a shrill voice called her name, and Jaden plummeted downward, knowing the nightmare lived on.

CHAPTER 1

JADEN

Surrounded by the early morning bayou, Jaden stood on the triplets' porch. The large T-shirt that served as her nightshirt hung loosely over her slim body as she leaned back against her boyfriend Briz's chest. Jaden felt she'd been transported to another world. A peaceful world. A sane world.

Briz's arms wrapped around her, comforting her. Jaden placed a hand on his and squeezed gently, confirming that he wasn't an illusion—that she was alive. When Jaden woke up this morning, after four days of drifting in and out of consciousness, she was unsure of what was real and what was not.

The sound of Hubs's boat rumbled in the distance. Jaden wasn't ready for this moment of tranquility to end. She felt calm and wanted the feeling to last.

She needed time. Time to be with her family. Time to be with Briz. Time for all of them to heal.

Physically. Mentally. Emotionally.

Somehow, they had all eluded death. The horrifying

version of her life that she had been living for the last few weeks was so close to being over that she could taste it.

Taste it...the words brought images of Datura and the other four Mal Rous to Jaden's mind. No doubt, with Datura's blood pumping through her veins, it was a trait of the mutant creatures that Jaden would have for the rest of her life: smelling and craving fear, tasting elation.

She touched the gauze taped over the wounds on her neck. Then lowering her hand, she let it hover over the stitches in her stomach, wondering who had sewn her up. Jaden drew her slender fingers together, then flicked them open, wanting to magically erase the memory of her shock when Datura had stabbed her, of when she had jabbed the machete into Datura, killing the small Mal Rou to save Briz.

Jaden faced Briz, guiding his head toward hers until their lips met. For a moment, passion replaced her feelings of anxiety.

Hubs's boat went silent.

Jaden turned toward the dock. A soft sigh passed from her lips as Briz kissed the top of her head. Resting his chin where his lips had just touched, the two of them watched Hubs come up the wood walkway to the house, nodding at them when he reached the porch.

Jaden was grateful for all the help Hubs had given her, her family, and Briz. If he hadn't brought her here to the triplets' house when Datura had first bitten her or brought her mom and sister after they'd been attacked, there was no telling where or what any of them would be now—fledging Mal Rous, mere shells of who they were when they'd first arrived at Belle Fleur. *Or dead.*

Hubs handed Briz a small package. His stutter was more pronounced than normal. "The f-fresh m-mushrooms f-from yer f-friend in W-Washington." His eyes filled with compassion as he regarded Jaden. Then he looked back at Briz, the lines on his face holding back a question. Not uttering a word, Hubs opened the screen door, and like a phantom, he glided into the house.

Jaden looked over her shoulder at Briz. With a shrug, Briz guided her back against him. Her head resumed its place against his chest as he wrapped his arms around her.

She had forgotten all about the mushrooms. Which seemed impossible. As far as they knew, a formula made from them was the only thing that would kill the Mal Rous. How could she not remember they were going to boil the little mutants in it until their bodies dissolved—it was going to be an added precaution in case they could seed and sprout back to life.

Mal Rous. Jaden thought of the nickname her crazed grandfather, Professor Dekle Thatcher, had given his creations. Mal, Latin for bad, evil; Rous, a play on the word rougarou—a beast from Cajun folklore, part human, part animal. Their scientific name, *Cerophagous Cautelosus.* Cerophagous was Latin for flesh-eating; Cautelosus, for treacherous, cunning. She cringed, knowing their blood now ran through her veins.

With the soft squeak of the screen door, she felt Briz turn his head.

The scent of Olympe preceded the woman as she padded her way toward them. During the time Jaden had spent with the triplets, she had learned the obvious and not-so-obvious differences between the identical albino sisters.

Olympe's scent was soft like a fading flower, motherly like fresh-baked cookies; the cadence of her speech was infused with the essence of the South. Her sister Isadora's accent was lyrical, not as strong as Olympe's; she smelled musky, rich as her vast book collection. While Tamara lacked warmth, she ran hot with a spicy scent and a biting tongue.

Jaden moved away from Briz to greet Olympe. The petite woman was wearing a blue bathrobe that was slightly darker than her pale blue eyes.

Olympe handed Jaden a large glass of her herbal brew. The mixture kept Jaden's system balanced, more human—less Mal Rou, less aggressive, less angry.

"It's yer original blend," Olympe said with optimism, stressing the word *original*. "We added some spearmint, trying to improve the taste."

"Thank you, Olympe. Thank you for everything." Jaden's voice was meek as she reached for the glass. She'd hoped to sound filled with lifelong gratitude; only her words came out like Olympe had just served her a cup of hot cocoa, not saved her and her family's lives. Jaden raised the glass to her lips. "I really need to give this stuff a name."

"How about *Envie* Tea?" Briz offered with a smile toward Jaden. Answering the question in her eyes, he spelled the word. "E-n-v-i-e. It's pronounced 'ahn-vee.' In English it means envy. But envie is Cajun...or is it French?" He looked at Olympe for confirmation. "Anyway, the old timers in town say it when they have a craving for something." This time Briz's smile reached his eyes. "I was thinking it was a good name because you drink it to stop your cravings for me."

Embarrassed, Jaden sipped the mixture, thinking, *Envie Tea it is.*

Briz and Olympe stood at her sides, reminding her of guardian angels—*or perhaps*, she mused, *they were guards, not guardians*. She wasn't ready to face her family, and they knew it.

Olympe turned and went back into the house. As Jaden and Briz walked over to the screen door, Jaden heard Olympe's sweet voice greet Brooke and Ava.

"Oh, good morning. I hope I didn't wake ya."

The triplets' living room was large and open. Normally, the sofa was placed in the middle of the room; it had been pushed closer to the entrance to make space for Brooke and Ava's cots.

"So is Jade...*finally*." Ava sat looking at Jaden through the screen door, with an expression that Jaden couldn't read.

Concern? Confusion? Contempt?

No.

Loathing!

Jaden could see that Ava's foot was wrapped with gauze —more bad news. How was she going to ask for forgiveness? She had ruined everyone's lives.

"Jaden, are you all right?" her mother asked.

Briz opened the door wide enough for Jaden to enter the house. It was clear he thought her moment of reckoning had arrived. It was time for her to face her jury.

Yep, guard, not guardian angel, Jaden thought. Briz's eyes were no longer smiling at her; he motioned with his head, signaling Jaden to go inside.

Jaden wished she'd just pass out and fall onto the floor. She wondered if she could fake it. Delay the inevitable for a bit longer. Probably no one would think it was odd—just another reaction to Datura's poisons in her blood.

She looked at her mother and Ava sitting on their cots. They didn't appear to be as bruised and battered as the day they were attacked by Ivan and Tig.

"Sweetie, please." Her mother's weak, concerned voice beckoned her in.

Jaden sucked in a breath of air like a boat sputtering out of gas as she tried to suppress her tears. "I'm, I'm so sorry," she mumbled. "Please forgive me for everything." Shoving her empty glass into Briz's hand, Jaden dashed off the porch into the yard.

Chapter 2

Jaden

Jaden expected someone to follow her, to escort her back to the house so they could have a nice long chat about genetic monsters over morning coffee. But no one came.

The ground was moist, soft under her feet. Keeping an eye out for snakes, Jaden went around the corner to the triplets' first home on the property—now it was where they created their brews, though the place was nothing more than a shack. The weathered gray structure leaned to one side, ready to collapse. Pieces of screen were nailed haphazardly over the termite-eaten walls; crooked door hinges were attached with wire.

Jaden looked through a grimy window. The rotting floorboards had been replaced with bricks. Two cauldrons sat on a stone fire pit. Above them, the ceiling had a vent for smoke to escape.

The sisters weren't into Voodoo as far as Jaden knew, but maybe her grandfather Dekle had been right when he'd written in his journals that the triplets seemed to be a little Wiccan. Jaden could imagine them at night, dancing outdoors, whistling to stir the wind, drawing down the moonlight, conjuring up spells.

A whisper of stuttering words drew her away from the window. Jaden peeked around the corner of the shack.

She could see Hubs on the porch talking with Olympe, a blue housedress having replaced her blue bathrobe. The two of them went back into the house. The sound of chatter swelled, then subsided, and swelled again. Everyone's words were muffled, though Jaden recognized the irritated cadence of her sister's voice.

With her jaw set, Jaden shook her arms like a prizefighter preparing for a match. She took a step toward the porch, but immediately changed her direction and went around to the back of the house.

Jaden looked out across the yard. It had no ending or beginning. She understood why the triplets had purchased this land; it was one of the highest patches of ground for miles and wouldn't flood every spring.

Jaden jumped as Briz's hands embraced the sides of her waist. She hadn't smelled his pheromones or sensed him walking up behind her. She smiled. Maybe she was less Mal Rou than she'd thought.

She could feel Briz's breath on her hair as he murmured, "Come on babe, everyone's waiting."

The clouds released a drizzle of rain on them as Briz placed a hand on her shoulder, encouraging her to return with him. Jaden wanted to go anywhere except back to the house. She pulled free of his touch.

"Jade...you have to do this." Jaden's muscles tightened at the sound of Briz's now firm voice. "Look, I've been here every step of the way for you. I'm...I'm not bailing on you now, but your family wants to talk with you. They've had a tough time, Jade. We all have."

He was right. With all they'd been through, he'd always been there for her...*always*. Her shoulders dropped as she exhaled.

Briz continued with his unsympathetic tone, "The other day, when your family came to, we told them everything. Well, almost everything."

Jaden wondered what Briz and the triplets *hadn't* explained to her mom and sister. Did they tell them how, if she didn't drink her Envie Tea, that she'd be aggressive, violent, lustful? She remembered the way Hubs had looked at her. Briz was leaving something out.

"And me?" Jaden turned to face him. "What aren't you telling me?"

Briz looked past her, the sounds of the bayou ticking off the seconds.

"Yeah, well..." Briz's gentle voice was back—but it wasn't comforting. "I guess now's as good a time as any." Jaden lowered her eyes and stared at Briz's T-shirt. "When Hubs brought all of us here, the triplets plied you with bottles of that *improved drink* they'd made for you, to balance your system," Briz said with light sarcasm. "At first, they had to force you to drink it. Then you started crying out for more, like you were addicted to it. Isadora went into the kitchen to get you another glass. She was only gone for a moment."

Briz's words were guarded, as if he was unsure of how much to share. "When she returned...you," he exhaled, taking Jaden's hand in his, "you had a pillow over your sister's face. You were trying to suffocate her."

Jaden's heart stalled, then spasmed as it labored to beat again.

"Ava wasn't aware of what was going on," Briz added in a pathetically reassuring voice. "She was still full of Tig's poisons."

Jaden could barely speak. "I, I'd never do that."

"No, you wouldn't." Briz's words swelled with sympathy. "But...Datura would."

"You mean Datura was here? She's alive? I thought I'd dreamt it."

"No, Datura wasn't here." Briz squeezed Jaden's hand. "Jade, you have her blood. She's..." Briz didn't finish his sentence.

Jaden felt nauseated; she knew exactly what he was going to say. After all, Datura had pumped more of her blood into Jaden. She pulled away from Briz. "What are you even doing here? I'm more like Datura now...like the Mal Rous, with the heightened need to harm others. Get away from me while you can! Before I try to murder you, too!"

"It wasn't you, Jade." Briz drew her into his arms as he whispered in her ear, "It was the drink."

"You're wrong!" Jaden stepped back. "You should leave. Go back to town," Jaden demanded, clenching her fists. "I don't want to see you anymore."

"Jade, you saved my life." Briz's tone wavered between annoyance and sympathy. "If it weren't for you, I'd be dead in that crate in your grandfather's cellar."

"Get real!" Jaden glared at Briz. "If it weren't for me, you never would have been in that crate. You never would have been captured by the Mal Rous."

"I'm not leaving you!" Briz reached for her. "You're still my Jade."

CHAPTER 3

ESERE

A dense pressure pushed against Esere's eyelids, forcing them to stay closed. Engulfed in darkness, gasping for air, he swallowed hunks of dirt. More filled his mouth as he attempted to spit it out.

The small Mal Rou's heart pounded as he realized he'd been buried alive.

He forced his fingers to move through the weight surrounding him and started to dig until his hands broke free from the earth. The damp air soaked into his leathery skin as he clawed his way out. Crawling from his shallow grave, he sat upon the fresh mound of dirt. His skin rippled over his bones as he shivered and stared into space.

"Where am I?" His throat was thick with particles of dirt. "How'd I get here?"

Had he upset Datura? Was this her way of punishing him?

"No. No..." He paused, spitting out pieces of mud. "I 'member bein' with the others and torturin' some man in a truck."

He looked at the dirt on his hands, the remnants of roots sprouting from under his claws. He reached up and felt sprouts on the tips of his ears, the horn on top of his head.

A smile filled his ashen-colored face as he considered what a truly unusual creature he was—that all the Mal Rous were. How clever the Professor had been, creating him with DNA from scorpion, Calabar bean, and vulture.

He and each of his four siblings had a unique blend of rodent, insect, newt, and poisonous plant DNA—most importantly tardigrade, and a tad of the Professor's own DNA.

The Professor had always believed the combination made the Mal Rous virtually indestructible.

Esere lay back in the hole and looked up at the sky, watching the clouds. As the rain washed the dirt from his skin, he could feel seed pods germinating in the core of his cells, pushing runners through his veins the entire length of his twelve-inch body—filling him with life.

When the movement in his veins diminished, he sat back up.

A secretion oozed from the tip of his chin horn. Slowly sliding his long tongue over his dry lips, he extended it down toward his chin to lap up the bitter drops of his scorpion venom. When the precious nourishment dwindled, Esere's tongue slithered back into his mouth like an eel into its den.

Esere looked out over the bayou as he removed hunks of dirt from his ears.

"I has been here before." Esere coughed, clearing his throat. He swiveled his head from side to side, taking in his surroundings. "Am I near the Professor's cave?"

Esere called out with his weak voice, "Datura, Tig...Ivan, Anders..."

He waited for an answer.

All he heard were insects chirring and buzzing.

His eyes moistened.

"I gotta find my family."

CHAPTER 4

AVA

Ava sat next to her mother on the sofa and watched as her sister entered the house; Jaden's movements were hesitant as she came toward them. Without a word, Jaden knelt in front of Ava and Brooke—despite of all their physical wounds, the three of them embraced. Surprising herself, Ava leaned her head onto Jaden's shoulder. Jaden's nightshirt felt damp and smelled of rain.

Regardless of their differences, they were family, and as her grandmother Jin would say, their lives were tightly knotted together like an Asian ikat weaving. Tears welled in Ava's eyes, but she refused to let the moist traitors escape. They nearly found their freedom as memories of her father's death when she was twelve years old came into her mind. How she and her mom and sister had embraced, and for one brief moment, the three of them had experienced a heartfelt connection.

A bond. Ava thought the word had an uncomfortable ring to it, like the words *helpless* and *powerless*. But right now, she needed to feel a sense of closeness. She hated feeling weak—being kidnapped, abused and traumatized would do that to a person.

Not to mention waking up in a strange house in the middle of the bayou, with identical-looking albino women, forcing you to drink some strange herbal concoction.

Ava felt Jaden turn her head, saw her give Briz a smile, as if Jaden wanted to include him in their personal, loving, supportive interlude of *we are family, we are a friggin' ikat weaving*.

Ava looked at Briz, then back at Jaden. An ache spread through Ava's chest as she pulled away from Jaden and their mother. She tried to cover the hurt in her expression, knowing Jaden would never care about her. Why should she? From the moment Jaden was born, she had been the enemy, forcing Ava to share the attention of her parents. Why would anyone form an alliance with the enemy?

Her entire life, Ava had done all that she could to distance herself from her younger sister. Now she swallowed back the bitter taste of regret.

"You only came in here because he made you."

Jaden shook her head. "No...no that's not true."

Her sister's timid voice was all it took to alter Ava's moment of remorse. Sneering at Jaden, Ava reclaimed her normal combative self. "You should be begging for our forgiveness you little fu—"

"Ava," her mother cut her off.

"What, Mom? She doesn't care about us." Ava let her anger roll off her tongue. "I really think it's okay to cuss in this situation. *Especially* in this situation!"

Ava stood abruptly and wobbled for a second on her bandaged foot. With her hands on her hips, she watched as Jaden cowered back.

"Because of you, this happened to me." Ava pointed to every wound on her body. "Do you even care that one of your monsters ripped a hunk of my heel off. I watched him lap up my blood from the cave floor. But why would you even notice?" She flipped her hand, gesturing toward Briz. "You care about him more than us!"

Jaden raised herself up; sitting on the edge of the sofa, she looked down at Ava's foot. "They...they aren't *my* monsters," Jaden said in a mousey voice. "I'm sorry, Ava. I screwed up."

"You should be sorry." Ava mentally ran through her list of reasons that Jaden would never be good enough for her. "I can't believe you're so dumb that you set them free."

Brooke reached over and rubbed her hand over Jaden's back.

"What are you comforting her for?" Ava glared at the two of them. "I'm the one that stabbed that hideous beast in the eye to save your ass. Every horrible thing that's happened to us is because of her."

"I am so sorry." Jaden gulped in a tear-filled breath. "But it...it's not *all* my fault."

"Not all your fault?" Ava laughed. She could see the little wimp's tears threatening to undermine her determination to defend herself.

"You...you p-pushed me out of the car," Jaden stammered. "You told me to, to go off and die. None of this would have happened if you hadn't made me so damn angry and then dumped me in the middle of nowhere!"

To die—the words hung over Ava's head. She waved her hand through the air, as if to push them aside. "What? You're blaming me for your stupidity?"

"I knew you'd never forgive me," Jaden muttered as she

slumped against the sofa.

"Forgive you? Forgive you—"

"Ava, calm down." Brooke rose and placed a hand on Ava's arm. "Sit back down—you need to stay off of your foot."

"I don't want to sit." Ava pulled away from her mom. "Why would any of us forgive her? She messed up big time, and you're coddling her."

"I didn't mean to set them free." Jaden straightened up; pursing her lips, her eyes crinkled. Ava realized Jaden was mirroring her own annoyed expression. "You told me you had sex with Briz, then kicked me out of the car when a storm was coming."

As her mother sat down, Ava saw a flash of awareness in her eyes. For a second, the sound of rain pulled Brooke's attention to the ceiling before she looked at Jaden, then at Ava.

"Ava, you had *sex* with Briz?" Brooke questioned with an exasperated sigh. "You told me Jade was upset because Briz had asked you on a *date*."

"Really, Mom! Aren't we a wee bit past that now? Because of Jaden, we were almost killed by depraved monsters." With her hands back on her hips, Ava glared at her mom before looking at her sister.

Bond with Jaden...what was I thinking?

"Ah, ma'am." Ava looked over at Briz, standing at the front door, taking everything in. "Since Ava wants this to be all about her, how she's the victim, you should know—I've *never* had sex with her. And I *never* asked her on a date."

"Butt out, Briz!" Ava raised her voice as the beating of the rain grew louder. "This doesn't involve you. This is my dysfunctional family's problem, not yours!"

"Doesn't involve me!" Briz jerked his arms through the air like they were exclamation points. "You've got to be joking! Being locked in a wooden crate for two days—saving *you* from that monster, Tig. I'm as much a part of this as anyone else here!"

He stopped gesturing and dragged both of his hands through his hair as he walked over to her. "We're all on the same side, Ava, but you don't see it. We have to figure out how to move ahead, and you're acting like a dethroned princess."

Princess. Ava flinched.

"You diss your sister all the time." Briz stood in front of her as if thinking his six-foot stature would be intimidating to her. "Are you even aware that Jade saved your mom's life? Our lives?"

Ava didn't look at Jaden, but she could feel her sister's delighted expression. Briz was defending her, so once again Jaden wouldn't have to fight her own battle.

"And are you aware none of us would have been in danger if wasn't for her, the immature twit! What's more, I'm not a princess!"

"Oh yeah, you are a princess!" Briz snapped.

"You didn't seem to mind when I was in your bed, did you!" Pleased with her response, Ava smirked and folded her arms under her breasts, propping them up, drawing Briz's attention to them.

From the corner of her eye, Ava could see the way Jaden was clutching the sofa cushion to brace herself as if the floor was moving. Knowing how much Jaden was into the guy, Ava figured that right now her little sister felt like seismic shock waves were moving through her.

While Briz wore a stunned, embarrassed expression, his eyes lingered on Ava's breasts. She smirked again.

He looked at Jaden, shaking his head.

"I slept on the couch, Jade. I let her sleep in my room when your mom was in the hospital—she didn't have anywhere to stay. The Mal Rous had broken into your apartment."

Briz looked back at Ava. "Christ, Ava. What is wrong with you? I would think that almost dying—twice in one week—would have changed you for the better. But you're still a manipulative, bitter, egocentric princess!"

"Stop calling me a princess!" Ava raised her hand, ready to slap him across his face.

Briz grabbed her wrist. His eyes creased, challenging her as he squeezed tighter. Ava let her hand go limp, and he released his grip.

Her shoulders sagged as she heard her father's words— the last friggin' thing he'd ever said to her—before he was shipped out to fight in some war and was killed.

For your mom's sake, take it easy on Jaden. Be nice to your kid sister. Don't act like an evil princess or the ultimate ice queen. No words of comfort, like, "I'm going to miss you." Or, "You're my little darling, my favorite daughter." He must have told her he loved her...? Why couldn't she remember hearing it?

Her eyes met Briz's scowl as his words admonished her. "Implying that we've slept together...telling Jade we'd had *sex*."

Ava took a step back as Briz threw the word "sex" in her face, like she was the last person in the world he'd want to be close to.

He was looking right at her. How could he not see her pain?

She glanced around the room. Violet, the diminutive, fairy-like Bellibone Ava's grandfather Dekle had created, was sitting on the piano, her broken leg in a makeshift cast. Supposedly, Ava's grandfather had created her by combining damselfly DNA with violet and pampas grass, along with her grandmother Elvina's DNA. Like Ava, Violet had Elvina's nose. Disgusted by the thought, Ava quickly shifted her attention to Hubs in his oversized chair, taking everything in.

Everyone was so charmed by sweet little Jaden that no one could see her. Ava. *If I scream loud enough, if I continue to withhold my love, will they bother trying to understand me?* Ava met Briz's gaze—there was a hint of compassion in his eyes—maybe he did see her pain. Or perhaps it was pity. That was worse. It made her feel vulnerable, uncomfortable. Ava raised her chin in defiance.

"You find power in hurting others, especially Jade." Briz took in a breath, the understanding in his eyes gone. "If you're going to dish it out, you'd better learn how to take it."

Ava stood taller, deciding to give everyone what she knew they expected from her.

"It was her stupidity that almost got us killed. I suppose you think it's funny...a big joke that she set the Mal Rous free."

"She didn't do it on purpose!" Briz shouted.

"Yeah, well, she did let them out, and from what you've told us, now Jaden's a she-devil just like them!"

Ava saw Jaden squeeze her mom's arm as if to say, "You're the adult, make them stop."

Before her mother could speak, the triplets raised their arms. Their voices thundered over the rain. "ENOUGH!"

CHAPTER 5

JADEN

Jaden looked over at the triplets, their stances solid, their postures straight as they reclaimed their home as their own. Next to her, Brooke's embarrassment was evident in her furrowed brow and downturned mouth. Jaden knew her mom was thinking what a pathetic excuse of a mother she must seem to the triplets. Jaden glanced across the room at Hubs; he had probably been a sweet kid. The triplets had no idea what it was like for her mom, raising Ava.

Tamara spoke first. With an edge in her voice, she focused on Ava. "We understand that you have all been through a lot. That your emotions might feel raw. But you've vented enough! You are done speaking to one another like this in our home. From now on you will be kind and respectful."

"*You're* lecturing me on kindness and respect?" Ava sat down next to Brooke. "I may not have been here long, but I've heard the way you talk to everyone. Do your sisters respect you, or do they just placate you to keep you quiet?"

"Stop it." Brooke reached over and turned Ava's face

toward her. "This is not how I raised you."

"You raised me to stand up for myself." Ava snapped back.

"Yes, but I did not raise you to be insolent and contemptuous." Brooke's fingers flared out, as if touching Ava had burned the skin on the tips of her fingers.

Jaden looked away as Ava glared at her. Clearly, her sister blamed Jaden for their mother standing up to her. For once in their lives.

"Missy, you have worn us out to the point that none of us cares how you feel or what you think." Tucking her maroon blouse into her denim skirt, Tamara walked behind the sofa and pulled Ava back against the cushions. "Shush up, or you'll be confined to the chicken coop out back with the rest of the cackling hens." Ava squirmed under the firm grip of Tamara's pale, white hands. "In spite of what you may think, the worst is over."

"Ouch!" Ava wriggled free of Tamara's grasp. "Leave me alone!"

"According to Hubs and Briz," Tamara continued as she straightened the patchwork quilt that adorned the back of the sofa, "three of the Mal Rous have been maimed. Now we—"

"Maimed?" Jaden interrupted. "I thought we killed the Mal Rous." Jaden's eyes darted from Hubs to Briz.

"We don't know for sure." Briz looked apologetic as he sat on the piano bench. "They appeared to be dead. Hubs wrapped their bodies up and stuffed them into your grandmother's old refrigerator. Datura had done a number on you, Jade—we had to get you to a doctor. Hubs took you to his Aunt Laura's house."

Jaden gave him a quizzical look.

"His aunt is Dr. Schilling. She used to be married to Hubs's Uncle Cape. She's the same doctor your mom took you to for the poison ivy. She stitched you up. No questions asked."

"Right now," Isadora's voice was decidedly calm, "our focus is on capturing the last Mal Rou and retrieving the one that is buried. Which brings us to you, Jaden.... When you are feeling well enough, and if Briz is willing, it would be good if the two of you could return to the Professor's cave."

Briz stared at Jaden as he said, "Okay."

"Not Briz." Jaden glared in reply. "He's going home. But I'll go."

"What?" Brooke sounded borderline hysterical. "No. Jaden, you are not going back to that cave!" Brooke looked at Isadora. "What are you thinking?"

"It's okay, Mom. Anders knows me; he thinks I'm one of them. I'll be all right." Jaden's voice wavered as she tried to sound confident, to convince everyone, including herself, that she would be fine. "And I have to get Esere's body. What if someone finds him?"

"No, it's not okay!" Brooke took hold of Jaden's hand. "One of them is stuck in a cave, the other buried in the middle of nowhere. No one's going to find them! I don't want you going back there." Brooke squeezed Jaden's hand. "I don't like it!"

"Brooke." Isadora clasped her hands together as she continued. "We are open to hearing other options." When Brooke frowned, Isadora added, "Dear, so you know, if you decide to let Jaden do this, we've made the same drink for Anders that Jaden gave to the other Mal Rous. Once Anders drinks the mixture, he'll be sedated, and Jaden will be able to capture him."

Or kill him, Jaden thought.

Jaden's mother slowly moved her head from side to side. Her voice was firm. "My daughter is not going back there!"

"If not me, then who, Mom? I'm the one who caused this mess. I'm the one that Anders knows. You can't expect Hubs to go."

Brooke glanced at Hubs. "What about the local police?"

"Mom, the police would hand them over to government officials. Eventually they'd end up with scientists that—"

Brooke's chest caved in, as if in defeat. She released Jaden's hand as she conceded, "Scientists that might be enthralled by the idea of recreating them."

"That's our rather general assumption." Tamara fixed her gaze on Brooke.

"I am sorry, Brooke." With a solemn expression, Olympe rested her pale hand over her heart. "We all are. But we can't just leave Anders in the cave."

Brooke stared at Olympe, silent.

"Mrs. Lisette..." Briz's eyes were on Jaden as he spoke. "I *am* going with Jade! She won't be alone."

"Well, all right then." Tamara stepped closer to her sisters as if to stand in solidarity. "*We* still feel the best option to destroy the cellular makeup of the Mal Rous is to boil them in Dekle's mushroom concoction. Since you..." Tamara briefly looked at Briz, then Jaden, "will be in the Professor's cave, it would be helpful if you could try to locate Dekle's lab records so we can recreate his Amanita Muscaria formula."

"What is so important about this mushroom formula?" There was a ring of challenge back in Brooke's voice. "Hydrofluoric acid would dissolve their bodies. There must be a source in New Orleans, Lafayette or Baton Rouge."

Tamara's head bobbed up and down, as if Brooke's idea

was settling in. Then her eyes fixed on Hubs.

"B-Brooke's right," Hubs said. "It w-would work. B-but it's mighty t-toxic. I'll ch-check around."

"What about the cave?" Jaden asked. "Is there some way we can seal it up? Destroy it?"

Olympe moved next to Hubs and placed her hand on his shoulder. "According to what Hubs here has read, unless exposed to moisture, salt caves will just seal themselves right up. As long as whatever government agency dug that there hole never returns, one day Dekle's lab will be consumed too."

"So, then, why can't we leave Anders in there?" The rise and fall of Jaden's voice contained a sinister hope. "There's no food or water. Won't he die soon?"

"Yes!" Brooke practically cheered. "My thoughts exactly."

"No." Violet met Brooke's gaze. "We can't take that chance. If Anders escapes, he *will* find us. And, we're all in agreement that if he doesn't escape, someday, some company might come along and decide to excavate the cave. If his remains are found, we can't be certain that they wouldn't use his cells to bring his species back to life."

"Jaden, Brooke, we can't let that happen." Isadora's tone was thoughtful. "Think of it like climate change. How you choose to live now, what you do now, affects future generations. You're doing this for them. So others will have a better life."

"Yes, I get it. But I'm still not happy about any of this." Brooke was rubbing her brow as if it were a worry stone. "If Jaden has to go to the cave, I'm going with her!"

"Mom—" Jaden's plead was cut off by her mom.

"I'm going with you!"

CHAPTER 6

ESERE

Ripples of heat rose from the ground as Esere made his way up the trail. Breathing in the faint smell of his siblings in the moist, hot air lessened the tension that had been clinging to his small body since he awoke buried in a shallow grave. He began to salivate as he picked up the fragrance of two humans, pausing to sniff the plants where their skin had brushed, leaving traces of their fear.

He inhaled deeply. "*Ahhhhh.*" The smell of the pheromones caused hunger pangs to rumble in his empty belly.

When he reached the mouth of the cave, he spotted the frayed remnants of two ropes and followed them into the bushes where they were attached to rusted stakes. Close by, a piece of rotting cable stuck out of the bushes and disappeared under layers of dirt, reappearing at the entrance. Digging it free, he held onto it as he stretched his neck forward to see over the side.

He cleared his throat and called, "Hellooo!" His voice bounced around the chamber below. "It's me. Esere."

He looked down at the smooth, slick ground—swearing as his feet slipped.

"I'm a dang *cooyon*...one stupid idiot!" Digging his toenails into the ground, he steadied himself. Phlegm pooled in his mouth. It had the bitter taste of his Calabar bean toxins seeping from his fangs; he swallowed, grateful the toxins didn't have the same effect on him as it did on his human victims.

"Hits 'em like nerve gas." He chuckled as a smile lit his face. "The Professor was a most brilliant man, usin' it in my DNA."

Esere scrabbled back up the incline, away from the opening. He sat on the ground, gripping the frayed rope, and mulled over what he was going to do now.

The shack—maybe everyone is there. Standing, he gave one more holler. "Anyone down there?"

He stared at the opening to the cave for a moment. As he turned to walk away, he heard a voice picking and scraping its way up the cavern walls.

"Esere? Esere, ya is alive!"

"Anders? Yeah, it's me," Esere drooled with excitement. "Is the others with ya?"

"I'm alone. Datura's gonna be mad as all get-out wit me. I let them girls escape—one stuck a knife in my eye and now it's shriveled all up. They cut the ropes so I couldn't climb outta here.

"What girls?" Esere asked.

"The ones that run ya over with their car," Anders rasped. "Don't ya 'member?"

"Sorta." Esere stroked his chin horn like it would help him call up the memory.

"We thought ya was dead, so we buried ya," said Anders.

"Dead! The Professor always said nothin' could kill us!"

"I know. But that were a long time 'go, and ya looked pretty dead. We thought maybe nowadays there is things that *can* kill us." Anders's voice sounded painfully dry. "Datura said the girls were Jaden's family, so we brought 'em here to torture for runnin' ya over. She was hopin' there'd be somethin' in the Professor's lab to heal ya. But we couldn't get the dang lock open. Yesterday, I got into the lab, but there weren't nothin' there to help me get outta this here dang hole. And nothin' that looked like the Professor had been there in one long time."

Esere stood there, looking around, thinking.

"Esere?"

"Yeah. I'm here. Just tryin' to figure how to get ya outta there."

"I'll try tossin' one 'a the ropes up; it's got a wood step attached to it that ya can catch."

"Nah. I'd have to get too close to the edge. Gonna find a long branch to reach over the side."

"Well, hurry on up. I is real thirsty. And hungry. There ain't nothin' to eat down here."

Most every branch was moist and flimsy. Esere settled on an elm branch with a nice kink in it and dragged it over to the metal stakes. Untying the short piece of rope from one of the metal stakes, he tied it to the end of the other piece of rope and attached the loose end to his ankle. Pausing, he listened to the bayou. The insects, and birds, the stillness between the noises. He'd always considered himself to be the most ruthless of the Mal Rous, at the same time, the most poetic.

"Anders?" Esere called as he yanked his foot to make certain the rope was tight.

"Yeah. I ain't gone nowhere."

Esere gripped the tree branch as he maneuvered closer to Anders's voice. "I is gonna hang this here branch over the side. I want ya to throw yer rope up high, so it catches on it."

With the branch in hand and his foot secured to the rope and stake, Esere laid flat on the ground with the side of his face pressed into the dirt. He shimmied over to the opening and held the branch over the edge. "Is it low enough?"

"I think so," Anders called up, grunting as he flung the rope. "Here it comes."

The wood rung of the ladder hit the branch, rattling Esere's hands. He dug his claws deeper into the bark of the branch. Anders tossed the rope again. Seconds later, he cussed as the rope fell back onto the ground.

A loud snarl was followed by a whooshing as the rope sailed up once more. Esere's arms jerked. He clutched the branch tighter as the rope caught hold of it like a hungry gator snapping at its prey.

"*Coo-Wee*," Anders called out. "Look-ee that. I'm gettin' myself on outta here."

Esere lurched forward as the weight of Anders's body tugged him closer to the opening—then the rope around his ankle slipped free.

"No, Anders! Get off!" Esere slid closer to the hole. "Ah, chi-it." He let go of the branch.

Esere heard the thud as Anders struck the cavern floor. The sloped incline continued to pull Esere toward the cave's gaping mouth. He released a high-pitched yelp when he saw Anders far below.

"Stop yerself from fallin' or we ain't never gettin' outta here!" Anders yelled as he scrambled out of the way.

CHAPTER 7

JADEN

Jaden emerged from the bedroom, dressed in the same clothes she'd been wearing for the past few weeks, though now both her capris and T-shirt were bloodstained, and the hole in her shirt where Datura had stabbed her was neatly stitched. Even though Olympe had washed her clothes, they felt soiled. What Jaden had been through couldn't be scrubbed out of them, no matter how many times they were put through the washing machine.

Jaden could hear her mom and sister talking with the triplets in the kitchen. Words like *contaminated blood* and *kill the last Mal Rou* drifted from the room and settled on Jaden's shoulders, causing them to slump.

She looked at Briz sitting in one of the wingback armchairs, the package Hubs had given him earlier open in his lap. Briz's vibrant blue eyes met hers, and he quickly stuffed the letter he had been reading into his pocket.

Jaden bit the corner of her lip, then looked back at the kitchen. Briz came over and took her hand. Jaden let him lead her outside to the enclosed garden.

Braided patterns of moisture ran down the screen that covered the structure. Spider webs clung to the hardware cloth that protected it from vermin like raccoons, squirrels and deer. Inside, they moved past hanging planters and raised garden beds filled with okra, collards, chard. Jaden's arms brushed against a large rosemary plant. The smell clung to her skin.

"They have everything," Jaden commented, looking at cantaloupes growing on a trellis, the small melons hanging like tiny ornaments.

The garden curved behind and attached to the triplets' "brewing" shack. Briz steered Jaden to the back of the structure, to what remained of its eave and stopped in a narrow space of shade. Though shade in Louisiana in the summer was just as warm as standing in the sun.

"Thanks." Jaden rested against the rotting wall. "I wasn't ready to talk with everyone."

"Yeah, that's what I figured." Briz leaned against the wall next to her. "Jade, everything's going to be okay," Briz reassured her, while taking in her pained expression. *"You're going to be okay."*

"Sure." Jaden looked at the spider webs up in the eave, their food trapped in silk cocoons. She wished she could trap all her emotions and problems in neat little packages like that and tuck them away until she was ready to deal with them. *Like never.*

She had survived the Mal Rous—now she had to survive Ava.

Jaden inhaled a broken, staccato breath. Avoiding her stitches, Briz gently pulled her to him and held her like he was ready for her to cry. But she didn't.

"Jade," Briz spoke over the top of her head. "Have you

considered that if you hadn't released the Mal Rous, you never would have found Violet, and she would have died. She was trapped under that tree branch—no food, no water. How long would she have lasted?"

Jaden hadn't thought of that. Something positive had actually come from this nightmare.

"Oh geez," she groaned. "I never thought to ask. Is Violet's leg going to be all right?"

"When they checked it yesterday, they didn't sound hopeful. Violet didn't argue when they talked about possibly having to amputate it. I think she's just happy her wings weren't damaged. Because of you, Jade, she's alive and in a good home." Briz tipped his head to the side and looked at Jaden. "I shouldn't have flipped out on your sister. You believe me, don't you...? That I didn't sleep with her. I wasn't even in the—"

"Of course, I believe you." Jaden ran her fingers down the length of his arm. "Don't fret." She grinned, realizing she sounded like the triplets. "Even on a good day, Ava's a handful." Jaden took Briz's hand in hers. "I was afraid to ask Ava what happened to her foot. Were the Mal Rous, like," Jaden cringed, "*feeding* on her when they were trapped in the cave?"

"No," Briz responded softly. "Anders bit a hunk of flesh from her heel when she and your mom were escaping."

Jaden flinched.

"She should be all right." Briz gave Jaden's hand a gently squeeze. "Do the two of you ever get along? It seems like you're always fighting."

What could she say? It was true. Jaden gave a slight shrug as she moved out of his embrace.

"You know, it isn't normal." Briz raised an eyebrow. "You fight more than me and my three sisters combined."

"I don't think it's all that abnormal. You just have a freakishly compatible family."

"Well, then freakishly compatible should be the norm," he stated as he stared at the garden. "It's not like my sisters and I don't fight with each other. But we also watch each other's backs. We don't belittle my youngest sister for being immature. She's young—of course she's immature. We've all been there—I'm still there."

"Not Ava. She was born mature."

"Mature, or with a defective superego?"

Hand in hand they stood, backs to the wall, the humidity and the sounds of the bayou enveloping their silence. Jaden thought about Briz's mom's theory, that *everything* happens for a reason—that there are no accidents in life, even if you stub your toe. Whatever reason Jaden had created this nightmare, whatever her "life lesson" was supposed to be, she was no longer going to let Briz be a part of it.

She tilted her head up at him. "I want you to go home today."

"I know you do—because you're dangerous to be around." Briz grinned as he looked down at her.

"Please," she begged, leaning into him.

"I'm not making any promises, Jade."

"Please," Jaden tried again. "It's enough already. Enough. I don't want you to be a part of this anymore. You must be tired of it all. I am. I am *so* tired of my life. Of everything that's happened...is happening."

"You're right. So am I," Briz said wearily. "This isn't exactly how I envisioned our relationship."

"I want us to be like normal teens," Jaden grumbled. "Go out on a date."

"A date, huh?" Briz gave a soft chuckle. "Where would you want to go on this date? Belle Fleur doesn't have a lot to offer."

"I don't know. A movie?"

"Okay." Jaden heard a lightness in Briz's voice that she hadn't heard in weeks. "Jaden Lisette, after everything is done and the Mal Rous's bodies have been dissolved, will you go out with me on a real date? Dinner and a movie?"

"Then to a make out spot," Jaden smiled up at Briz. "Belle Fleur must have a make out spot."

There was a glimmer in Briz's eyes. "Oh yeah. That it does have."

Jaden stepped in front of Briz. Reaching up, the fragrance of rosemary still on her skin caressed them both as she guided his face toward hers. He said her name, but as her mouth and tongue met his, his words stopped, and he kissed her back.

She pressed against him. The sensation of his soft lips made Jaden feel suspended in space. She ran her fingers through his hair as his hands slid down her back. Her knees felt weak...or *maybe it was his knees,* she thought.

"Jaden. Sweetie..." her mom's voice called from the porch.

Briz's lips slowed as he moaned softly. He lightly bit Jaden's lower lip, then raised his head. "Yeah, good timing, Mrs. Lisette," he said with a ragged breath.

"Good timing..." Jaden reached up and gave his lips a quick kiss. "I don't think so. I like it when you want me. Usually you push me away."

Briz took her hand. "I always want you, Jade. If I craved you more, I'd go insane."

Jaden curled her fingers around his as he led her out of the garden. Her eyebrows arched as her mouthed pressed into a thin line. *He'd go insane.* This was a first. A smile spread across her face. Never before had a boy craved her.

Before entering the house, Jaden paused. Her smile faded as she whispered, "I'm sure this morning was only the beginning for Ava; she has no intention of going easy on either one of us. It's going to be a long day...and night. Are you ready?"

CHAPTER 8

JADEN

The words wouldn't stop. Jaden tossed and turned in bed, as the day's conversations played on an endless loop in her head. It had taken until well after dark to convince her mother to stay behind and allow Briz to accompany Jaden to the cave. And to answer everyone's questions, all while apologizing every few minutes.

Jaden repeated, *Sleep, Sleep, Sleep,* until her repetitive words had slipped into silence, only to have exhausting dreams of Anders smelling her betrayal, knowing she was sent to kill him. She awoke with her skin moist with panic.

She stared into the darkness. When the faint glow of daybreak appeared, there was a soft tapping on her bedroom door. Olympe peeked in, making certain that Jaden was awake. Jaden raised her hand to acknowledge her.

It was time to go back to Dekle's cave.

Jaden dressed, used the bathroom, and was tiptoeing down the hall as Olympe came out of the kitchen. Olympe paused, placed her wrinkled hand on Jaden's cheek, and smiled meekly before disappearing into her own bedroom.

The concoction the triplets had made for Anders to drink was sitting on the kitchen counter. They had divided it into two bottles, each marked with a large A on the lid. Jaden just had to convince Anders to drink it. Jaden drank a glass of her newly christened Envie Tea, then slipped a full bottle of her brew and a flask of water into her backpack, along with the containers of Anders's drink.

With her pack hitched over one shoulder, she went into the living room. Standing near her mom and sister, Jaden studied their faces as they slept on their cots. "Forgive me," she whispered.

Slowly, she opened the front door, her mouth compressing as the hinges squeaked. She didn't check to see if the noise woke them.

Briz was on the screened porch. With sleepy eyes, he picked up his backpack with one hand while reaching his other hand out to her, and they went to the small dock where Hubs was waiting for them.

"G-get yerselves on b-board."

"Hubs, you know you don't have to come with." Jaden didn't see the point. She'd been there twice and would be able to find it again.

"F-feeling like I n-need to."

The boat cut through the mist that hung close to the water, keeping the temperature on the edge of tolerable. Within the hour, the sun pushed its long rays through gaps in the clouds, lighting up strands of Spanish moss. Soon, the mist would surrender to the heat and vanish.

Jaden sat facing Hubs. His hardened expression reminded her of a piece of petrified wood.

Briz reached over and trailed his fingers over her arm, causing her skin to lightly vibrate. Loud enough for only her to hear, he murmured, "Staring at him like that, you're going to make him more nervous than he already is." With the trace of a smile, Briz added, "You're making *me* nervous."

Jaden shifted her attention to the shore but wasn't focusing on anything. She just wanted her day to be over. The Mal Rous's bodies to be destroyed. To get out of town and never return. *And never see Briz again*, she thought sadly as she looked over at him.

She turned away as a silver carp shot up out of the water, inches from the boat. "It freaks me out when they do that. Do they ever land in the boat?"

"It's b-been k-known to h-happen." Hubs gave her a sideways glance. "We al-m-most there?"

"Yeah." Jaden leaned forward. "Hubs, we'll go to the cave while you wait on the boat."

Hubs reached down and picked up the bottle of calming remedy his mom had made for him. Jaden couldn't tell if he was grateful to be staying behind or not.

Twenty minutes later, Jaden motioned to where the land slopped upward. "We're here."

"The trail we made is further up," Briz said, staring at the shore.

"This one's easier. It's the one Datura and I took." She pointed farther up the hill. "Look, right there, you can see the trail." Jaden grimaced. "It's the one she forced Ava to make."

Hubs guided the boat next to the shore and jumped into the muck. He tied a nylon rope to the trunk of a tree, then hurried back onto the boat. Reaching into his pocket, Hubs pulled out his courage; it rested in his hand in the form of his friend Stella's small pistol. He'd said he'd use it if he had to. He wasn't going to let anyone else get hurt by the Mal Rous.

Jaden could see he was trying to hold his hand steady. She wondered if he'd ever shot a gun. Maybe it wasn't so wise for him to have brought it.

Briz made certain his hunting knife was secured to his belt. Then he removed a bottle of Non-Odeur, the triplets' scent-canceling mixture, from his pack and rubbed some on his arms and face. "Hubs, here." Briz handed Hubs the bottle. "I'll leave this with you."

In case Anders is wandering around the bayou, Jaden thought with a shiver. The Non-Odeur would stop Anders from being able to smell Hubs and Briz. Whereas Jaden... well, they wanted Anders to smell her.

Briz took a bandana from his pocket and tied it around his neck, to stop the perspiration from running down his back. Slipping on his pack, he jumped down onto the mushy ground.

Jaden handed Briz a fat coil of rope, then wrestled her backpack on.

"Hubs, will you be all right here...by yourself?" Jaden asked, climbing out of the boat.

Hubs nodded as he held the gun.

CHAPTER 9

JADEN

"Esere. He, he's gone," Jaden stammered, looking at the shallow hole in the clearing next to the trail. "But he...he was dead." Just a week ago, Datura had shown her Esere's grave. "Violet was right. The Mal Rous are indestructible." Jaden felt the humidity press against her as the contours of the bushes became shadowy images of Esere, watching them. She inhaled a deep breath to see if she could pick up his stench. Instead, the smell of the moist green bayou embraced her.

Briz stepped closer; as if reassuring himself of its presence, he patted the sheathed knife that hung near his hip, as they stared at the empty grave.

"I'll get one of Anders's bottles from your pack," Briz whispered as he unzipped her backpack. "We can open it and hope Esere gets attracted to the smell of the drink rather than us."

Jaden looked down at the shimmering water of the bayou peeking through the trees. "Do you think Hubs will be all right?"

"I hope so." Briz handed her the bottle, and they started back up the trail.

When they reached the cave, Jaden pulled her damp shirt away from her skin as she stretched her neck from side to side and looked for evidence of Esere, wondering if he was waiting for the perfect moment to attack.

Her attention shifted to Dekle's rusted sign. "DANGER! CONTAMINATED! DEADLY! KEEP OUT, by the authority of Belle Fleur County, Louisiana, U.S.A."

Jaden spat on the ground in front of the sign—blushing when she heard Briz chuckle. Giving him a tight-lipped grin, she stuck the bottle she was carrying into the side pocket of her backpack and looked at the entrance to the cave, feeling as if she was going to hyperventilate. It had happened to her before.

Briz fastened the rope to the rusting metal stake. It was time to follow through with another one of their poorly thought-out plans.

"Anders," Jaden called, standing near the incline. "Are you there? It's me, Jaden. Datura sent me to fetch you."

It should be easy, Jaden thought. Once he answered, she would drop his drink over the side and wait. As soon as he passed out, she would climb down and kill him. Jaden winced. She had never been a mean person, a revengeful person. Not until Datura had "changed" her.

When there was no response, she looked at Briz. He gave her a curt nod.

"Just get in and out as fast as we can," she muttered as she picked up the rope and inched down the embankment like a spider walking along the side of the cavern wall.

The darkness in the cave crept around her as she set her

pack down. Pulling out her flashlight, she scanned the space. The rope ladder her mom and Ava had cut loose and dropped to the cavern floor was lying in a heap next to a tree branch. Her light reflected off the walls—deep claw marks had etched an abstract pattern into the salt. *Anders had tried to escape*. She wondered if he'd succeeded.

Across from her, the two tunnels appeared to be matching gateways to the underworld of Hades. But according to Ava, Jaden was a she-devil. Nothing could harm a she-devil. Right?

The part of her that didn't want to find Anders called out his name in a hushed voice, "Anders?" Jaden removed his bottle from the side pocket. "Anders, it's me, Jaden. I brought you something to drink. You're probably pretty thirsty."

Jaden opened the bottle, her nostrils drawing tight from the stench of the brew.

"We caught my mom and sister," Jaden spoke louder, hoping her tone was sincere. She couldn't figure out why she bothered. Inside she was a wreck, and once he got a whiff of her pheromones, he'd know it was all a lie. "We're all set up to perform a truly gruesome ritual on them."

Jaden gritted her teeth, forcing her mouth into a strained smile in case Anders was in the shadows watching her, and counted the seconds as she waited for a reply. There was only silence.

Next to her, the rope jumped to life, and Briz made his way down. Jaden slipped on her backpack, and moments later they were descending deeper into the earth, the sound of their footsteps rising up the curved, slick walls of the tunnel as if whispering, "Shhh," in response to every loud breath they took. Hurrying past the cavern where her mother and sister had been held captive, they continued on to Dekle's laboratory.

The door was as wide open as Jaden's eyes.

Inside, the glow from their flashlights hunted for signs of Anders. Several of the jugs that had been on the shelves during their previous visit were now on the ground, broken apart. Jaden assumed Anders's goal had been to unleash more of his kind. But there was no liquid, no slimy residue. The containers had been empty.

The two of them searched every inch of the room, as if looking for clues to a secret treasure. A secret that only her grandfather, Professor Dekle Thatcher, knew.

Jaden looked down and saw that she was standing on a rust-colored stain.

Three feet away stood a refrigerator, once smooth and white, now a tarnished golden-brown. The same rusty color had seeped out from beneath the corroding device.

She stepped closer.

"What are you looking at?" Briz asked, shining his light on the same spot.

Jaden raised the beam of light up the wall, next to the refrigerator, and across the top. Briz moved his light steady with hers.

"It's a door jamb." Jaden reached behind the refrigerator and ran her hand over the decades of salt that sealed the door closed. "We didn't pay any attention to the refrigerator the last time we were here."

"Do you think Dekle's secrets are being guarded by the refrigerator?" Briz smiled as he lowered his backpack and flashlight to the ground. "Let's move this sucker," he said with zeal as Jaden removed her pack and set her flashlight on the lopsided lab table.

"You ready?" Jaden asked, gripping the back edge of the refrigerator.

"Yeah. Pull it forward on three. One...two...three."

Jaden wondered if the enthusiasm surging through her was her own, or if it was Briz's excitement, the smell of his pheromones, overflowing with his sense of adventure, masquerading as her own.

The antique appliance scraped and wobbled across the floor, leaving behind a trail of rusted hunks of metal.

"How can it be so heavy? It's not that big," Jaden grunted as she tugged harder, then stopped. "Did you hear that?"

"It sounded like glass bottles." Briz grabbed the refrigerator's handle.

"Don't open it." Jaden put her hand on his arm, remembering what her grandfather had written in his journal. "It's probably deadly toxins. More rabies virus."

"If it is, we can't leave it here for someone to find." Briz started to open the door.

"Wait," Jaden squeezed his wrist, "till we're ready to leave."

"Okay... So, let's try walking the fridge away from the wall."

With their hands embracing the back and curved front of the refrigerator, they seesawed it from side to side, inching it further from the wall.

The refrigerator shuddered: the corroded bottom gave way. Jaden jumped back as the refrigerator tumbled forward, vibrating the floor and clinking with the sound of glass bottles breaking.

"Well, that's that," Briz said as they looked at the appliance. "Doubt there are any bottles left for us to take."

Jaden's attention returned to the doorjamb—picking up

her flashlight, she traced her fingers over the bulge where a doorknob would be. "Check this out."

Briz removed his knife from its sheath and chipped at the large encrustation of salt on the knob. Hunks of salt broke free, revealing a tarnished bronze lock. "Whatever is in here, Dekle didn't want anyone to find it." Briz scraped the keyway clean. "Jade, hold your light closer." He tried to slide his blade into the opening. "This knife is too big. Do you have your knife?"

"Here." Jaden handed him her dad's old pocketknife.

Briz slipped her knife's blade farther into the keyway, but the lock was intent on staying locked.

"Maybe it's a sign." Jaden felt the rush of excitement and her sense of adventure fading. "Maybe the lock is protecting us from what's in the room."

"I think it's a sign that Dekle has hidden something in there that might help us." Briz handed her back her knife. "We should try to break the door down."

"What?" Jaden squinted as his flashlight briefly shone in her eyes.

"Well, yeah," Briz said as if she were dense. He ran his light across a lump near the top of the doorframe, and one at the bottom. "I'm assuming those are locks, too. It will be easier to just bust the door in."

"We can't break it down," Jaden replied, her tone mimicking Briz's as he went over to the oak shelves that lined the wall. "Let's just get out of here. We've already killed three of the Mal Rous without the mushroom mix. We don't need the formula to kill Esere and Anders! My mom said hydrofluoric acid would dissolve them."

"Jade, we think we've killed the others. And we don't know if they sell large quantities of hydrofluoric acid to just anyone that comes in off the street." He aimed his light back at the door. "We're here. We're so close. It doesn't make sense not to try to get in." Setting his flashlight on the ground, Briz reached for the bottom shelf. "We can use this as a battering ram."

"Yeah, right," Jaden challenged. "You've watched too many movies!"

"I'm serious," Briz said, tugging at one end of the thick, rough plank. "Come on Jade, you're strong. I could use some help here."

"I don't feel good about this. I don't want to know what's in his *secret* chamber." Jaden stood watching Briz wrestle the shelf into his arms, hoping any minute he'd give up. Realizing that wasn't going to happen, she snorted and shook her head. She dropped her stubborn stance and took a step in Briz's direction.

"Shit!" Briz dropped the plank and grabbed his wrist, his fingers splayed apart. "I cut my hand."

"I knew this was a bad idea." Jaden held her light over his bloody palm. "Why can't guys ever listen to girls?"

"Testosterone," Briz snickered. "My mom says it makes guys deaf to the female voice."

"Testosterone. Is that why you insist on helping me instead of running for your life? Your He-Man hormones drive you to kill the beast and save the little woman?"

Briz gave a chuckle, then grimaced as he removed a sharp piece of wood that was wedged into his palm. Pressing his hand to his shirt, he pulled his bandana off his neck and handed it to Jaden.

"This doesn't look good," Jaden said as she tied the bandana around his hand.

"It'll be fine." Briz reached down and picked up one end of the wood plank. "Grab the other end."

Jaden had never seen this obstinate, headstrong side of him before.

"Hit it high. Left. Right." Briz called out directions like a lieutenant in the infantry each time they thrust the wood plank against the door.

The impact reverberated through the cavern, through Jaden's arms and legs. Fine particles of salt floated down from the ceiling, dusting the two of them. Hunks of salt broke free of the door. Jaden could see Briz's bandana had slipped from his hand and was hanging on his wrist as his blood dripped onto the floor.

"Left. Right. Middle..." Briz directed over and over.

The door groaned in protest. Followed by a loud crack.

Jaden heard a dull, heavy thump from within the closed-off room. Then a noise thrummed in Jaden's ears. Setting down their battering ram, she asked, "Do you hear that?"

Briz didn't respond. Leaning against the door, he began to push. "I'm close. It's almost free. Hand me my flashlight..."

Jaden gave him his flashlight. As she picked up her backpack, Briz pushed open the door, and the thrumming in Jaden's ears grew louder.

As he stepped into the dark room, Jaden shouted, "NO STOP!"

But it was too late.

CHAPTER 10

JADEN

A frenzied beating of wings quickly drowned out Briz's screams of agony.

"NOOO!" Jaden howled. "*No. Not Briz!*" Her body jerked forward, then she was rushing toward her fears into the dark room.

Inside, her flashlight exposed the terror on Briz's face as his body thrashed on the ground. Jaden stared at the four dove-sized creatures attacking him. One was lapping up the blood on his hand while the others were biting him.

"Briz!" Jaden dropped to her knees. Discarding her pack and flaying her hands around, she swatted at the creatures with her flashlight, the light flickering over crimson drops of blood oozing from each of Briz's punctures.

"Leave him alone! Bite me, not him. Come after me." Jaden choked on her words, hitting one creature that resembled a giant hornet. She stood up. "Why aren't you attacking me? 'Cos I stink like a Mal Rou?"

One creature raised its head. Turning toward Jaden with mechanical movements, it flew up to her face—followed by two more. Jaden held her breath as they hovered in front of her, sniffing her. They seemed mesmerized by her flashlight shining inches from their faces. Jaden stared at the milky film coating their eyes.

They're blind.

Blood dripped from the beak of one, and the rows of sharp teeth of another. Their bird, fish, and bee-like mutated bodies glistened with slime; drops of a fluid appeared on the strands of hair that dangled from their underbellies.

All at once, they darted back to Briz, where a fourth one was thrusting its stinger into Briz's neck. The fine tendrils on their bellies burrowed into Briz's flesh as they nuzzled his bare skin before biting him.

They're hungry. That's why they've gone after Briz. They smell the blood on his hand.

Briz cried out. Then stopped. Jaden wondered if he'd passed out or given up. Kneeling, Jaden rubbed her flashlight over his cut, coating the flashlight's entire surface with Briz's blood, then used it to strike the creatures until they released their hold on him. All four of them came toward her—pursuing the coppery smell of blood and the glow of the light.

"Come on...follow me," her voice was shaky as she called to them as if they were one of the triplets' dogs. "That's right, follow the light, the smell of his blood. This way." Waving her flashlight, Jaden led the creatures through the main laboratory, into the hallway, then tossed the blood-covered light into the blackness. The creatures followed it as it rolled down the tunnel. Jaden hurried back into the lab and closed the heavy door.

The sound of whimpers in the other room gave her hope. However badly Briz was hurt, at least he was still alive.

Guided by the faint light coming from the other chamber, Jaden made her way back to Briz.

He was now squirming and moaning. Jaden felt his agony pump through her veins. There was a pulling in her chest, as if her heart were rejecting her soul. Holding her hand against her breastbone, she inhaled a deep breath.

"Save Briz. Just save Briz…"

She picked up his flashlight and looked around the room. Near the door, two wooden shelves lay on the ground. Was that the noise she'd heard? *They must have fallen when we were ramming the door.* Jaden's light settled on glistening pools of liquid and the shattered remains of earthen vessels.

"I don't see any more of those creatures." Her words felt hollow and worthless. "I want to get you into the other room, just in case." Jaden bent down, placed her hands under his arms, the stitches in her stomach pulling as she dragged him a couple of inches. His body stiffened as he cried in pain.

"You're too heavy. I can't move you without hurting you." She gently lowered him back down. Slipping her hand under her shirt, she felt the tenderness of her stitches, but didn't feel any blood.

Briz convulsed.

"I'm right here." Jaden sat down; cradling him in her arms, she longed to take on his pain.

When his body stopped convulsing and shivering, Jaden released him from her arms and slid away from his damp body. Shallow breaths of air struggled to find their way in and out of his open mouth. Using his bandana, Jaden dabbed at the bloody wounds on Briz's arms and legs.

"I'm going to get Hubs."

Briz stared into space, his eyes empty.

"Briz, can you hear me? Did you understand what I said?"

His eyelids lowered—and didn't open again.

"Your knife's right here." She placed it next to him, letting the handle rest against his fingers. "Just in case," Jaden said, knowing how useless it would be.

Right now, he couldn't even lift his hand. How would he be able to defend himself?

"I'm leaving the flashlight with you." The beam of light shone aimlessly across the room. "I'll make sure the lab door is closed tight."

She wanted to kiss his cheek, to stroke his hair—to comfort him. "I'll hurry," she promised, wiping the tears from her eyes. "Please don't hate me." Picking up her pack, she walked away.

Jaden retraced her steps through the dark main laboratory, inched open the door, and stepped into the tunnel. She strained to hear the sound of small wings frantically beating. Silence surrounded her. Closing the door, she skimmed her fingers over the wall, guiding her as she walked toward the glow of her flashlight that lay at the far end of the tunnel. She wiped the blood from its handle onto her hands, then rubbed her hands over the slick walls, but the slimy feeling and coppery odor remained.

Worried the creatures would find Hubs, Jaden climbed out of the cave and hurried down the hill.

CHAPTER 11

BRIZ

Briz had felt his body being tugged across the floor, the tiny particles of salt rubbing into his open wounds. The burning sensation had brought him back to consciousness. He'd heard a mumbling, heavy breathing, and weeping.

Jaden.

A pulsing hummed through her hands. *Adrenaline,* he'd thought, pumping through her as she'd pulled on his body. He'd been grateful when she'd stopped.

Then he'd felt her next to him. He'd shivered when she'd moved away.

Briz heard the door leading into the tunnel close.

And Jaden was gone.

The feeling of small serrated knives being thrust into his skin, burning into his flesh, hadn't subsided. Blood was dribbling from the punctures. He understood that something had been feeding on him. It had been more painful than anything Tig or Ivan had ever done to him.

He was cold. Very, very cold. He wasn't sure if he was in shock. Or if was he dying.

Unable to move, Briz was aware he was near the cavern they'd found Jaden's mother and sister in, the same cavern where he had told Jaden they'd have to come back for her family another day.

Jaden's voice had been shaky, sad, when she told him she'd hurry back with Hubs.

No, he'd thought, *don't leave me here like I made you leave your family. I can walk. Just give me a minute.* But he'd been unable to speak.

Briz opened his eyes. The room was pitch black except for a light shining on the broken ceramic jars. He thought of Pandora's box. His sister Hartley had read a book that claimed Pandora's box had first been Pandora's vessel, "a honey-vase, *pithos*, from which Pandora poured out blessings. It became a box in the late medieval period, when the word was mistakenly translated from *pithos* to *pyxis*. How was he remembering this now? *Walker...someone named Walker had written about it.* Only the broken jugs before him had contained evil, not blessings.

His brain felt hyped up on speed, his body lifeless.

He heard a noise. His thoughts scattered. Ignited by fear, pain swept through him. He wanted to pick up the flashlight, shine it around the room to see if there were more bloodthirsty demons. Then again, he wanted to turn the light off. He'd be safer in the dark. But he couldn't move.

His throat tightened; his skin tingled and itched. He was light-headed. Why hadn't he been more cautious? He'd been so wrapped up in finding the Professor's journals. Wanting to do what was necessary to keep Jaden safe. Keep his family safe. And the triplets, and Hubs, and Violet.

His heartbeat quickened, then slowed. His head jerked, then drooped to the side.

A light flashed over his face.

"Mum..."

It was his mom. Standing over him. How had she found him? Had Jaden been gone that long? Had she gone to town and brought his mom here to care for him? His mom knelt down and moved his hair off his sweaty face. She raised a container of water to his lips, encouraging him to drink. He took a sip; it felt like turpentine trailing down his throat, burning his lungs.

His mom screamed. Dropping the water, she sank onto the ground next to him. He helplessly watched as the flying monstrosities returned, and his mom squirmed from pain as they bit into her.

Briz heard a hiss and gasped. Tig's tongue was sliding across his face, snaking its way into his ear.

No. No. Tig is dead.

CHAPTER 12

AVA

Ava stared at herself in the bathroom mirror; running her hands over her creamy complexion, she saw the red welts on her wrists. "Thank God that wretched Mal Rou Tig didn't claw my face or bite into me." Her attention shifted to her clothes. Since the Mal Rous kidnapped them over a week ago, she'd been stuck wearing her frayed denim shorts and the T-shirt she purchased while her mom was in the hospital.

She eyed her fingernails. Even after multiple washings, they were still dirty. Ava turned on the warm water and worked at cleaning away the remaining bit of dirt. She needed to rid herself of all reminders of the horrible day when she'd been forced to dig a grave for Esere with her bare hands. She looked back at the mirror. The image of the teary-eyed, mousy girl looking back at her pissed her off. Jaden was the mousy crybaby, not her.

Ava turned off the water, dried her hands, and wiped away any possibility of tears, vowing that her anger would keep her strong. Safe.

Now, if she could wipe away the images of the Mal

Rous's hideous faces, the memory of when Ivan shoved her mother flat against the ground and pressed his fangs against her throat. Those visions would be with Ava for the rest of her life.

With her foot resting on the edge of the tub, she studied the welts and punctures on her ankles as she secured the bandage wrapped around her foot. Olympe had replaced its herbal poultice filling that morning.

Ava opened the bathroom door just in time to hear her mom say, "It's a hot one today."

She could hear the politeness in her mom's tone as it mixed with gratitude toward the triplets for all their help. Her mom sounded tired, frail from the events of the past week—filled with anxiety, over *baby* Jaden trekking off to dig up Esere, capture Anders, and dragging Briz and Hubs with her.

"I know ya must think this here heat is gonna do ya in. Ya should come visit between October and April. It's real nice then." It was Olympe's lilting cadence.

"Oh no!" Ava rolled her eyes. "I can tell the triplets apart by their accents now—I have to get out of here. I want to go home!"

Ava hobbled down the hall toward the living room. The fans were on high, and all the windows closed; the triplets kept the house sealed up during the day, professing it helped to keep out the heat. She stood watching her mom and the triplets—they were all engrossed in their conversation. Ava felt invisible and doubted they were even aware she was standing there. Her mom looked at the wall clock and sighed, then looked right past Ava and over at the wall of books.

Ava wanted to yell that Jaden wasn't the only one to be concerned about. That she'd been attacked, too. *The Mal*

Rous could have killed me! Her annoyance ping-ponged from her mom, to Olympe, to Isadora, to Tamara. *I'm probably scarred for life, physically and psychologically!*

"I was looking through those books there." Brooke pointed at the bottom bookshelf. "The one about the French writer, Olympe de Gouges, it says she was a feminist in the 1700s. And there's one about Isadora Duncan, the dancer, and another about Tamara, um..."

"Tamara de Lempicka," said Olympe. "Our mama was a fan of her art."

Brooke gestured toward Olympe. "And your mother named you after her favorite author?"

"That she did. Though everyone says my name, 'Olymp-ee,' until my mama's dying day, she pronounced it in the French way." Brooke shook her head, and Olympe repeated her name as she'd heard it from her mother's lips.

Ava thought it sounded like "Oh-lahnp." The "ee" sound was gone, the "p" at the end was barely audible.

"Though my papa, he never did get into the habit. He'd say my name both ways. Have ya met him? Dr. Whiting? He's our stepfather. Since we never knew our biological father, he's papa to us."

"No. I haven't had the pleasure of meeting him." Brooke smiled and turned to Isadora, then Tamara. "And you're named after the dancer, and you, the artist." Brooke looked down at her fingers. "Jaden was named after the jade stone." She held up her hand. "Our wedding bands are made of violet jade." Her mother rubbed her thumb over her ring, as if tenderly invoking the memory of her deceased husband.

"We were visiting friends in Ava, New York, when I got pregnant with Ava. I'd been trying to get pregnant for months..." Her mother's words faded.

Ava hated it when her mom shared that story. Like people wanted to know where her parents had had sex. Besides, it was demeaning; she was named after a town with six hundred people, while Jaden was named after a valuable gemstone.

Tamara sat up straighter; Ava met her eyes. Tamara looked right through her...or into her. Scratching the scars on her wrists, Ava looked away. She was stuck here in the land of the Swamp People with friggin' mind readers. No Internet, no phone, and her purse and everything in it was in their car in some dead cane field.

Ava went to the front door and onto the screened porch; sitting in a wicker chair, she leaned her head against the back. The humidity was sucking the energy out of her.

"We were nineteen years old when Tamara and I met Jack Kerouac." The words from the living room drifted through the slightly open front door in a faint, subtle Southern cadence.

Isadora. Ava gave a shudder, having recognized Isadora's voice.

"Jack Kerouac? As in the beatnik Jack Kerouac?" Her mom asked, surprised. "Writer of *On the Road?* The Beat Generation Jack Kerouac?"

"No way..." Ava said to herself. "Who knew the old broads had such a wild past?"

"How did you meet him?" Brooke asked. "I didn't realize Kerouac spent time in Louisiana."

"Don't go telling all our secrets, Isadora." Tamara's words stomped past her lips like a command. "It's no one's business! The past is the past, and that's a good place for it to stay!"

The topic of conversation immediately stopped.

Someone cleared her throat. Then Isadora changed the subject. "Ava resembles her grandmother Elvina."

"Yes, she does," replied Brooke. "I never met the woman, but from the photos I've seen of her, I can see the resemblance."

"Is she smart as her grand-pere Dekle was?" Tamara asked.

You bet I am! Ava roared in her head.

"She's a straight-A student," her mom's voice rang with a smile.

"She certainly has her grand-pere's temperament." Tamara had a smile in her voice, too. An obnoxious smile.

"What?" Ava glared at the door. "The woman doesn't even know me."

"Tamara, Ava's a good person," Brooke said. "I know she can be harsh." The room went quiet. Ava could hear people fidgeting, teacups clinking onto tabletops. Then her mom added, "I've done my best to teach my girls to be considerate, good people, but honestly, all you can do is hope that someday they'll remember some of the values you've taught them."

"Suppose so," Tamara replied.

"I know my sisters and I were a lot alike when we was in our youth. 'Till puberty came along," said Olympe. "It does have a way of changing a person. The good thing is, over time, most of us grow out of it."

"Just seems Ava can be quite a handful," Tamara added, determined to make her point. "She doesn't show much sisterly love toward Jaden. I suppose that's why when Jaden wasn't herself the other night, she was so intent on smothering her—"

Ava's breath caught in her throat.

"What?" Brooke yelped.

My Sister Tried To Smother Me?

"No...no, that's not possible!" her mom exclaimed. "Jaden would never do something like that."

"Well, it is not only possible—"

"Tamara, enough!" Isadora snapped at her sister. "Brooke, it was not Jaden, it was the mixture we were giving her. It was our wrongdoing. It never would have happened if we hadn't changed up the original formula."

Ava's eyes narrowed; her jaw clinched. Malice seared the air around her, burning into her thoughts. She would be stubbornly vindictive, unforgiving.

CHAPTER 13

JADEN

Jaden stepped out from behind a cypress tree. Her eyes opened wide as she stared at the gun aimed directly at her. "It's just me." Jaden watched as Hubs steadied his hands. She didn't move. "It's just me..." she said again, softer.

Hubs lowered the gun. Then quickly raised it toward the sky, following the path of a blue heron flying overhead.

"You okay, Hubs? Nothing came after you, right?" Jaden asked.

Hubs continued looking up into the trees.

"Th-thought I s-saw s-something earlier." His gaze shifted past Jaden. "W-where's Briz?"

"He got hurt. I need you to help me get him out of the cave."

"H-hurt?" Hubs's hands were shaking. He gripped the gun tighter. "M-Mal R-Rous?"

"No," Jaden squeaked, then cleared her throat. "We didn't see Anders. Or Esere."

"I t-thought Es-Esere was b-buried."

"He's gone," Jaden said quietly, not really wanting Hubs to hear her, to know that their lives just got more complicated. From Hubs's expression, he'd heard her just fine—and understood exactly what it meant.

"I'm th-thinking ya has w-wronged one p-powerful *bon coeur*, and th-they has p-put some k-kind of curse on ya. Isadora can m-make ya a *gris-gris* to k-keep ya safe." Hubs paused before adding, "B-Briz too."

Jaden's lips thinned into a straight line as she gave Hubs a nod, remembering she had thought the same thing the day she'd discovered the Mal Rous. She took a step closer to the shore; twigs snapped under her feet. Hubs immediately directed the barrel of the gun in her direction. Jaden didn't move. She exhaled as he lowered the gun.

"I'm just going to rinse off my hands," she cautioned as she crouched down next to the shore to wash Briz's blood off her hands and flashlight. When she stood back up, Hubs was drinking his calming brew.

As they started up the trail, Hubs asked, "W-what happened to B-Briz?"

Jaden picked up her pace as she filled Hubs in on what had transpired. She kept her voice low in case the flying creatures were nearby. In case Esere and Anders were stalking them. Behind her, she heard Hubs make a gagging sound. She turned around. Hubs's hand was covering his mouth—stepping off the trail, he started to dry-heave.

Jaden had anticipated that today's excursion would be challenging for him. That the memory of being attacked by the Mal Rous as a young boy would resurface. But last night he had insisted on joining her and Briz, despite her objections. And now here he was, smack-dab in the middle of the bayou, determined to overcome his greatest fear. Hubs straightened up, blotted the perspiration on his brow with his handkerchief and gave her a nod.

"Let's get this over with and get out of here." Jaden turned and started up the trail. "Fast. In one piece. And alive," she muttered to herself.

Jaden glanced back at Hubs; his feet were striking the ground hard, as if stomping on his fears, as he continued resolutely forward.

They were silent until her grandfather's "Keep Out" sign appeared. Jaden watched as Hubs scrutinized the foliage. Pheromones seeped from his pores. She could smell his fears hanging in the thick air, bullying him. Goading him to run away as fast as he could.

"I'll go first." Jaden wondered if Hubs would succumb to his urge to leave. She began her descent into the cave as Hubs looked over the edge of the incline, watching her disappear into the darkness.

"All right, Hubs. It's your turn."

When Hubs's feet touched the cavern floor, he stared back up at the shafts of light high above their head. "Like the g-glow of an a-angel. P-protecting us." Hubs pulled his flashlight from one of his pockets, then patted the gun in the other pocket.

Once they entered the tunnel, Jaden could hear Hubs pat the gun like clockwork every few minutes before flashing his light behind them, making certain they were alone. She found it comforting and unnerving at the same time.

"This is it." Jaden stopped where the downward slope of the tunnel evened out. Her light jittered across the salt-coated door.

"Briz..." she called as she stepped inside. "I'm back. I have Hubs with me." Her voice stretched ahead of them as they walked toward the second chamber. She paused to pick Briz's backpack up off the floor and repeated his name as she walked into the room. Kneeling next to his crumpled body, Jaden took his canteen from his pack, removed the lid, and tipped the container until water touched his lips. Briz didn't respond.

"Hubs..." Setting the canteen down, Jaden looked over her shoulder. "Hubs..."

Hubs was waving his flashlight around, as if drawing abstract patterns across the cavern walls, the collapsed wooden shelves, and broken vessels on the ground. "D-did ya f-find the rest of the j-journals?"

"What...?" Jaden glared, irritated by the question.

"De-Dekle's l-lab records?"

"What? No. I didn't. I didn't look." Jaden's heart pulsed with sadness and anger. What was wrong with him? Didn't he care about Briz?

"They'd b-be in s-some kind 'a m-metal b-box, right?" Hubs continued, sweeping his flashlight around the room. "W-we s-should look for them."

"I don't give a damn about the lab records! We have to get Briz out of here!" Jaden's voice was loud, cutting through the quiet that dwelled deep in the earth.

Hubs picked something up off the ground and slipped it into his pocket.

"Hubs, help me get him up!"

Hubs squatted next to Jaden and shined his light on the wounds scattered over Briz's body. Jaden heard Hubs swallow hard and hoped he wasn't going to start retching again. Instead, he began to sob.

Jaden's anger faded immediately. She could see him as a six-year-old being assaulted and battered by Mal Rous. They'd stolen his childhood. His voice.

She set her flashlight on the ground and wrapped her arms around Hubs and held him until he stopped shaking. When he raised his head, her shirt sleeve was damp from his tears. Jaden ran her hand over his cheeks and dried his face.

Hubs gave her a slight nod as he wiped his nose on his handkerchief, and their attention returned to Briz.

Jaden stashed Briz's knife and flashlight in her backpack.

Hubs handed Jaden the pistol. "J-just in c-case."

Her hands shook; she had never held a gun before. "It's locked, right? I can't, like, accidently shoot anyone?"

"Yup. Ya s-slide th-this." Hubs pointed at the manual safety lock, then turned off his light and slipped it into Jaden's pack.

Jaden put the gun in her pocket, then she and Hubs slipped their hands under Briz's arms and raised him up. With a grunt, Hubs hoisted Briz over his shoulders and positioned him like a firefighter carrying an injured person. Jaden grabbed her flashlight and the backpacks, closed the doors of the laboratory, and led the way, surprised at how quickly Hubs was able to move.

In the main cavern, Hubs leaned Briz against the wall, then took the end of the rope that hung down, looped it into a harness, and slipped it over Briz. After checking that his knots were secure, Hubs reached well past Briz and used the rope to climb out of the cave.

Moments later, Jaden watched as Briz rose, fishtailing from side to side until his body was dragged over the incline. When the end of the rope was tossed back down, Jaden turned off her flashlight—the cave's malicious secrets shadowing her as she ascended the rope.

When Jaden emerged, she saw that in the light of day, Briz looked worse than in the cave. Tears flowed from her eyes like projectiles as she untied the rope from the metal stake; leaning over the bushes, it was her turn to dry-heave.

They had made it to the boat and settled Briz between two of the benches when the sky darkened. Hubs handed her a towel for Briz's hand. She hoped it was clean. Jaden slid next to Briz and pressed the towel to his palm to stop the bleeding. As the boat moved forward, raindrops the size of pellets soaked their clothes and punctured holes in the blanket of green velvet growth that covered this part of the bayou.

With Briz's head resting in her lap, Jaden ran her fingers through his damp hair and watched the rain wash off the blood that peppered his skin. Whatever DNA Dekle used to create his flying creatures, it caused Briz's muscles to twitch.

Suddenly Briz's body tensed, and he twisted onto his side in pain.

"Can't we go any faster?" Jaden asked urgently, turning back to Hubs.

"T-this is f-fast as I can g-go here."

Jaden looked up toward the sky, letting the raindrops glide over her face, washing away her tears.

Soon after, when the clouds grew thin and specks of sunlight snuck through the tree branches, Hubs steered the boat into a wider canal where the green-black water was so clear you could see the bottom, and they were able to make better time.

Hubs was docking the boat as Jaden's mother and the triplets came down the walkway.

Jaden summed up the horrible situation for them in three words, amazed at their simplicity. "Briz was injured."

The triplets raised their hands to shield their light eyes from the sunlight.

"Injured?" Tamara exclaimed. "He looks like he's been rolled in barbed wire!"

CHAPTER 14

JADEN

Jaden moved the mosquito netting aside. As Hubs lowered Briz onto the bed, she saw rope burns on Hubs's hands from when he'd pulled Briz out of the cave. Hubs glanced at her. She was certain that he was recalling the time when he had brought her into the same room, covered in blood and unconscious, just two weeks before.

Jaden stepped over to the door, keeping out of everyone's way as they crowded into the small bedroom. She watched as Violet smelled Briz's wounds, trying to identify the odor permeating from his pores.

"Green tobacco," Violet said. "And something else. I don't recognize it."

The door knocked into Jaden as Brooke hurried in with a pan of water and towels. The triplets were busy stripping Briz down as he lay like a corpse at the morgue.

Olympe took hold of his hand.

Briz's eyes sprang open. He cried out, "No! No! Get off of me." He pulled away from Olympe, swatting his hands in the air as he squirmed to the far side of the bed. "Leave me alone."

Olympe looked at her sisters. "He seems to be hallucinating."

Isadora and Tamara marched over to Jaden. Grabbing her arms, the two women dragged her down the hallway, with Violet hovering close behind. Isadora's words were softer than her grip.

"We have to talk."

Tamara's words were damning. "What the hell happened?"

They ushered Jaden into the kitchen and sat her down at the table.

"What bit him?" Tamara demand. "Did Anders do this to him?"

"Dekle's laboratory door was open, and things were tossed around. Anders wasn't there. Neither was Esere." Jaden's throat constricted as they gasped.

"What do you mean, *neither was Esere?*" Tamara's pinched eyes prodded Jaden for an answer. "Your sister said Esere was dead. That they buried him! *You* said Datura showed you his grave."

"I...I know. But, but there was just a hole—like he'd dug himself out."

Violet pressed her fingers to her mouth, as if holding in the thoughts.

"What?" Tamara asked.

"Perhaps being buried stimulated his plant, and newt, and tardigrade DNA, allowing his body to heal." Violet's eyes grew wide. "The Professor was right. They are indestructible."

Tamara stomped over to the island counter; reaching up,

she grabbed her favorite pot for steeping cures down from the rack above the stove, then looked at Isadora. "What do you think?" The women stared at the drying herbs hanging from the ceiling. "I don't know where to start."

Tamara answered her own question. "Clean out his wounds first. At least the fever is fighting off any infections."

Isadora nodded, her glasses riding low on her nose as she thumbed through an oversized herb book.

The ceiling fan clanked loudly above Jaden as she rested her elbows on the table and cupped her head in her hands. *I'm so stupid! Why didn't I listen to Hubs when he wanted to look for Dekle's records? There might have been information that could help Briz.*

Jaden peeked at Violet from the corner of her eye. The Bellibone was sitting only a few inches from her on the kitchen table, looking like a damaged fairy doll. Seated on top of a miniature stool, her bandaged leg stuck out from under a small table that Hubs had fashioned for her.

"You never answered my question." Tamara's voice was like the cold metal of a crowbar, snapping Jaden's head up. "What bit him?"

"We...we were in Dekle's lab and found a door that was sealed and thought maybe Dekle had hidden his reports in there. We busted it open, and when Briz went in the room, he started screaming. I ran in and there were these *things* biting him. They didn't touch me. I think they went after Briz because he'd cut his hand and they smelled his blood."

"How large were they?" Isadora glanced up from her herb book. "Did they look like they had human DNA?"

"No. Nothing about them looked human. They were the size of a dove. Their pupils were just a milky gel—like they were blind. One's skin was smooth, slippery looking. It had rows of sharp spiked teeth like...like a piranha. Another had a bird beak and feathers. And they all had these *hairs* on their bellies that swelled, and then they stabbed them into Briz."

"At one time the Professor had spoken of making more Bellibones," Violet said as she hobbled out of her chair.

"They weren't Bellibones. And they weren't Mal Rous." Jaden reached her hand out to steady Violet.

"Let's put this here formula together." Isadora took the herb book over to Tamara, her subtle accent escalating with concern. "This one will pull out the toxins, and this one here, make it into a salve for the bites. I'm going to get him to drink some liquid bentonite."

Hubs came into the kitchen. He handed a piece of ceramic to Jaden. "I f-found this in th-the c-cave."

Jaden turned it over. Letters were carved into it. She read them aloud, "I-F-R-I-T-A-K-O-W-A..."

"*Ifrita kowaldi*," Hubs said in a clear voice. Everyone turned and looked at him. "It's a b-bird th-that eats b-blister beetles. It s-secretes a t-toxin through its s-skin into its f-feathers—makes ya n-numb if ya touch it."

"And how would *you* know that?" Ava stood in the kitchen doorway. It was the first thing she'd said since Jaden and Hubs had brought Briz home.

"Ava..." Jaden gritted her teeth, stopping herself from snapping, *Go away.*

Jaden waited for her sister to give her a deadly glare. But she didn't. Ava didn't even acknowledge Jaden—she just stared at Hubs.

"T-the Nature Ch-channel," Hubs answered.

Jaden could feel his frustration. Stuttering didn't mean he was ignorant. *Hubs is smart. Really smart,* Jaden thought, as she looked at Ava. *But you'd never take the time to find that out.*

"May I see that?" Taking the piece of ceramic, Isadora rubbed a finger over the letters. "It's real faded, but after kowaldi, it looks like there's a Q and a B."

"Q-B." Violet sounded surprised. "*Queller Bocanách.* I didn't think that they'd survived."

"So, what exactly are they?" Tamara asked. "What are we dealing with here?"

"I'm not really sure," replied Violet.

Isadora went into the living room and came back with her etymology book.

"How do you spell it?" Isadora set the book on the counter, opening it to the Q's.

"I believe it is spelled B-o-c-a-n-a-c-h," Violet said. "And Q-u-e-l—"

"...l-e-r," Isadora interrupted her. "Here it is. Queller, Old English, cwellere: 'killer;' Old Saxon, quellian: 'to torture, kill.'" Isadora's lips narrowed as she thumbed through the book. "And bo-ca-nah, the second 'c' is silent. It's Middle Irish for 'supernatural being.'"

"Oh, this just keeps getting better." Ava's tone was sour. "He was making supernatural killer beings?" She shook her head. "Of course. Why not? What better way to spend his time?" Ava kept her back to Jaden, her attention focused on Violet and Isadora. "So you're telling me that this idiot," Ava jerked her hand over her shoulder, her thumb directed at Jaden, "released some kind of flesh-eating flying monsters? Like releasing the Mal Rous wasn't bad enough!"

Ava paused as if she was waiting for someone to criticize her for insulting Jaden, then added, "Dekle was obsessed with making monsters."

"No," Violet said hesitantly, as if not wanting to upset Ava more. "That was not his original intent. He'd had so many failures. He'd started propagating the Queller Bocanáchs at the same time as me, while he was living in England, but my gestation period wasn't complete until he'd been in Louisiana for several months. It was my understanding that the Queller Bocanáchs weren't maturing. I thought he'd given up on them." Violet blinked. Her large blue eyes filled with sadness.

"You see, girls, there is a chance your grand-pere never planned on creating monsters." For some reason, Isadora had decided to defend the lunatic. "Most likely he felt he was making scientific history."

"Don't call that crazy man my grandpa," Ava snarled as she walked out of the room.

"It may have all been a mistake," Isadora said to the back of Ava's head. "He was probably clueless as to how they were going to turn out. And by then it was too late."

"Mistake? Clueless?" Jaden was taken aback by Isadora's comments. "Maybe the first time. But he didn't stop."

Olympe came hurrying into the kitchen. "There's a stinger in the side of Briz's neck. It's the size of a sewing needle. Jaden, what was it that stung him?"

"I don't know." Jaden's voice rose an octave. "*I don't know!*" She looked at Violet. "Did Dekle ever tell *you* what he'd made the Quellers from?"

Violet shook her head, her pampas grass hair swaying from side to side.

Jaden felt a hand on her shoulder. Looking up at Olympe, Jaden explained, "Two of the things were biting him and one, maybe two, were stinging him. One was sort of like a hornet. Everything happened so fast, and I only had my small flashlight...I just wanted them off Briz. That's all I was thinking about."

Olympe opened the freezer door. "We have to get the stinger out. We'll need some ice. And clay packs."

"Hornet? Are you sure it resembled a hornet, Jaden?" Isadora asked.

"I, I think so..." Jaden raised her shoulders while nodding.

Jaden thought Isadora and Tamara were looking at Olympe like she was overreacting, then realized it was concern creasing their faces as Isadora asked, "Has he gone into anaphylactic shock?"

"No," Olympe replied. "But his pulse was racing, and now it's slowed. His breathing is labored."

The triplets went into work mode—Jaden had witnessed it before—moving as if they were one, engrossed in a dialogue that only they could hear. Isadora sliced fresh ginger root, poking holes into it until it was juicy. Tamara filled a large pan with warm water, then took a jar of honey from the cupboard. Olympe grabbed a butter knife and a box of matchsticks.

"Jaden," Isadora paused before slicing the last of the ginger. "We'll need more light. Bring the reading lamp from my room and the large floor lamp from the living room."

The three sisters gathered up their remedies and hurried off, followed by Violet flying as fast as she could.

Jaden wasn't far behind. Plugging in the two lamps, she watched as Olympe and Brooke swabbed the blood from Briz's wounds and wiped the perspiration off his body. She blushed as she glanced at the towel being draped across Briz's lap. It wasn't like she'd never seen a naked male before.

They had cable TV at home. The Internet has everything. But this was Briz.

Jaden looked at Briz's bare chest. It was barely moving. Then it shuddered as if he were desperately trying to breathe. Jaden blinked back tears, her focus shifting to his face. "Is he conscious?"

"His mind seems to be drifting in and out," Violet said softly. "Jaden, do you think their blood mixed with his?"

"I don't think so." Jaden's uncertainty spiraled through her mind. There hadn't been much light. She thought they were only feeding on him but couldn't be certain. *Only feeding*...Jaden cringed.

"If that's the case, whatever is wrong should eventually pass," Violet replied.

Olympe had turned Briz's head to the side, revealing the hornet stinger wedged into his neck. How had Jaden not noticed the stinger before? His head had been resting in her arms on the boat ride—had she inadvertently pushed it in deeper?

Olympe pressed the butter knife's blunt edge around the stinger and worked at easing it out while Tamara and Violet washed the open sores on Briz's legs and arms. Isadora followed by rubbing fresh ginger juice over each of the punctures.

"Jaden, I forgot the dried mugwort leaves." Isadora didn't look up as she began applying a slice of ginger on top of each wound. "They're on the kitchen counter. Hurry up and get them for me."

When Jaden returned, Olympe was holding up the stinger. It was two inches long. Olympe applied drops of ginger juice to the larger hole and placed a piece of sliced ginger on top.

Isadora took the leaves from Jaden and handed some to Olympe. "Hold the lamp closer to Olympe, dear."

"I'm going to get out of your way," said Brooke as she moved toward the door. "If you need me, I'll be in the other room."

Jaden held the lamp closer, watching as Olympe crumbled a small amount of mugwort leaves onto the ginger slice on Briz's neck. Then, striking a match, she carefully ignited the dried leaves.

Jaden's eyes widened. Would burn marks scar Briz's beautiful body?

Isadora leaned toward Jaden. "It's all right, dear. The ginger root will act as a buffer, so the fire won't burn his skin."

The women repeated the process, covering every wound. Tamara followed behind, applying drops of honey around the bites, letting it slowly seep under the ginger slices and into the wounds to work as an antibiotic.

Tamara inhaled a deep breath. "You're right, Violet. He does smell like green tobacco. If that's the case, the nicotine would be releasing epinephrine into his system. That's why he hasn't gone into anaphylactic shock from the stinger. But the odor is strong. He could have nicotine poisoning. We best get some charcoal in him."

Violet studied an open sore encircled by a blister they hadn't seen earlier. She ever so gently touched the blister. It popped open and fluid leaked out. "Giant hogweed. I can smell it. I remember the professor bringing a plant back from the Carolinas. Look." Violet pointed to the area around the bite. "More blisters are forming."

"Jaden," Tamara's focus remained on Briz's arm. "Go tell Hubs to gather up some charcoal. He'll know what to look for. And have your mom bring in a bottle of lavender oil to put on these blisters. It's in the refrigerator with the other tinctures."

Jaden moved toward the door, pressing her hand to her chest to keep her breaking heart at bay.

CHAPTER 15

ESERE

Dwarfed by the weeds and dry stalks of cane, Esere and Anders stood in the middle of a field. The smell of home—Guyon Manor—wafted through the air, triggering recognition. Esere looked up at the evening sky—he was tired, his feet ached. Except for a few hours of sleep last night, he and Anders had been pursuing the fading scent of Jaden's mother and sister since yesterday.

"At least the rain has done stopped." Anders wiped at the fresh seepage of gunk that surrounded his pea-sized eyeball. "Esere, spit in my hand again. I think ya is right, the Calabar bean in ya spittle is helpin'."

Esere spit in Anders's palm, wondering if his friend's eye would ever grow back to its original size.

"Thank ya." Anders rubbed the salvia into his eye socket. "I sure is glad ya found me. I think Datura was gonna let me rot down in that hole." Anders reached his hand out for more of Esere's saliva. "If ya could 'a seen yer face yesterday, when ya came slidin' over the openin' of that cave, hangin' there upside down. I thought yer eyes was gonna pop out 'a yer head." Anders laughed.

Esere didn't see the humor in it. Dangling with one arm from a rotten hunk of cable that was stickin' outta the of ground; getting whopped in the head when Anders tossed the rope with the wood rung at him. But Esere had to admit, Anders's idea had been a good one. He did finally catch the rope and was able to loop it through the cable.

"I'm just happy ya climbed outta there before that cable snapped, or we'd both be stuck in the cave." Esere's beak-like nose rose into the air as he looked around. "Do ya smell that? I'm gettin' whiffs 'a Ivan and Tig, along with them women, right near."

Anders's long tongue swept out from his mouth, lapping up a scent. "Yep, Ivan and Tig. Let's go," he said, bounding forward.

Enthusiasm rejuvenated their tired bodies as they crawled under and over the weeds and cane plants...Until the chaotic sound of crows squawking filled the sky.

Their skin crept over their bones. They slowed their pace.

When they reached the edge of the field, they found themselves behind the Professor's garage. The roof was covered with crows, their dark bodies illuminated by the setting sun, as more settled on the house and perched in the trees.

Esere felt a tremble pulse through his fangs and the tips of his horns as his body prepared to defend itself. He and his siblings had a long-standing feud with Belle Fleur's crows, going back to when the Mal Rous had discovered and eaten a nest of crow chicks. Since then, every crow in Belle Fleur chased the

Mal Rous on sight, determined to peck them apart. The Professor had said crows were known to teach their young to go after an enemy. *For how many generations?* Esere wondered.

They stepped back, deeper into the cane.

"There is hundreds of 'em," Anders whispered. "Don't recall 'em doin' that this time a year." A few crows circled overhead. "We is so small, ya think they can see us? Smell us?"

"Yup." Esere knelt down, keeping his voice as quiet as Anders's. "Let's get into the cellar. Maybe Datura's in there."

Once all the crows had settled in, Esere and Anders high-tailed it over to the side of the garage and crept through the growth to the small painted window. Anders reached between the bars and pushed his hands against the muddy glass; poking his head inside, he looked in the cellar.

"It's empty. Tig and Ivan was supposed to hide that boy in the box." Anders flicked his tongue out. "How many days was I stuck in that cave? The room stinks of a human, but it ain't strong enough to be fresh."

"Let's look in the big house," Esere said, peering through the weeds.

"I say we go to the shack." Anders studied the birds in the nearby tree. "That's most likely where Datura and the other's is at. And 'sides, 'em birds are spookin' me."

"Anders, ya is bein' *capo*."

"I ain't no coward!"

"Then stop actin' it." Esere never knew his brother to be so chickenhearted. "We is here now. I say we go see if Datura's in the house. Maybe she already got rid 'a that boy and 'em women."

Without waiting for Anders to reply, Esere took off running across the yard, then waited for him in the shadows of the porch. A few curious crows flew from the trees onto the grass, watching as Esere and Anders checked the windows and doors. The place was sealed up tight.

"Told ya they is likely at the shack," Anders scoffed.

Esere ignored Anders's jibe as he dragged a paint can across the porch and over to the French door, as the crows inched closer. "Help me with this. We is stayin' here for the night."

They heaved the can against the lower pane, shattering the window. Stepping through the opening, shards of glass crackled under their feet. The house was stuffy. Quiet. No Datura and Ivan talking or arguing.

Esere took in a deep breath.

Anders's forked tongue licked at the air, then he mouthed the word, "Blood."

Esere nodded as they silently made their way to the kitchen. A trail of blood had dried on the floor. More was smudged across a sign taped on the refrigerator door, but neither of them knew how to read. Esere grabbed hold of the leg of a chair, dragged it to the refrigerator, and climbed on top. He opened the door and his heart sputtered as he looked at the gunny sacks stuffed inside, lumpy and smelling of Datura, Tig and Ivan.

He could feel the veins in his eyes thicken—anger had a way of tingeing them with blood. Misery blurred his vision; tears moistened his cheeks.

Anders choked out a gasp as he dropped to his knees.

"Let's get 'em out." Esere looked down at Anders. "Come on. Ya gotta help me."

They removed their family and freed their small bodies from the gunny sacks. Unwinding the coiled wire and ropes, they peeled off the electrical tape that bound their siblings' cold, inert forms. Blood covered their wounds like a moist gel.

Esere lightly stroked the tiny vines emerging from Datura's tentacles and the horns on Ivan's head. Plant roots were sprouting from a slash in Datura's spine and a hole in her chest, as well as from a slit in Ivan's throat and from Tig's ears and mouth. One at a time, Esere placed a hand on their chests, but there was no movement, no sound of a breath.

"Tig. Why would anyone do this to her?" Esere wondered aloud, running a claw gently over one of the horns on her jowls. Her skin was now a pasty white instead of a pretty salmon color, and her curly tendrils were pressed tight against her head. "We gotta bury 'em. It saved me."

"But ya was only run over. No one tried to cut yer head off. Look at 'em." Anders pointed at Ivan. "They is dead."

"Ya look at 'em. Their bodies is tryin' to sprout back to life. Maybe bein' in the 'frigerator was good for 'em. It preserved 'em. Like they was hibernatin'. We'll take 'em out behind the garage and bury 'em."

Anders folded his arms across his chest. "I ain't gonna be no bird food. We has to wait till tomorrow, when 'em crows is gone. Let's wrap 'em in some kinda blankets to warm 'em up, then hide 'em in case whoever done this comes back in the night."

CHAPTER 16

BRIZ

Throughout the night, Briz had stirred awake as hands roamed over his body, sponging his skin, applying herbs, forcing him to drink bentonite, to swallow charcoal. Each time, his mind had drifted back into darkness. He felt weak, fevered, damp with perspiration. His thoughts were disjointed. Briz knew he was at the triplets' house. He remembered going into the cave with Jaden. He didn't recall how he'd gotten out of the cave, or the journey back. He wondered how long he had been asleep. Had it been hours or days?

Briz struggled to sit up, but the weight of a blanket made him feel trapped.

No.

His hands and legs were tied to the bed. That's what the triplets had done to Jaden after she'd tried to suffocate Ava. Had he attempted to hurt someone, too?

A strange assortment of odors clung to his skin. Ginger, smoke...*tobacco?*

He could hear the sound of light, delicate breathing. Briz

raised his head and looked across the room. Ava. She was walking toward him, carrying a pan of water. *It must be her turn to care for me.*

She was wearing shorts and a tight low-cut shirt and smelled fresh and clean. She set the bowl onto the nightstand, then moved the mosquito net to the side. There was a hitch in his breath as she lowered his covers down to his hips. He could hear the water in the basin slosh as she dipped a towel into the liquid and was grateful as she sponged off his brow and face and throat, cooling his body. Dipping the towel again, she ran it down his chest, over his stomach.

Briz looked over at the closed bedroom door. A sultry grin inched across his face. He stretched his fingers out, the tips of them touching her bare leg. She didn't move away.

"Think I'll leave your legs tied." She smiled as she trailed her long fingernails over his arm and untied his hand. Leaning over him, she freed his other hand.

Briz wanted to pull her on top of him—wanted her to ease his pain—but thought even with Ava it might be wise not to rush. He didn't want her to run away.

Ava bent down, and her lips played with his. Briz closed his eyes as her tongue slipped into his mouth. He felt like he was falling into an altered state of mind—one where bitchy women were in control of men's bodies.

Briz moaned as her mouth moved away from his. He ran his fingers over her thighs as she reached for a glass.

"You should drink some water." Her voice was seductive. Inviting.

"*Shh.* Not now." He had kept his voice soft, as not to irritate her. After all, this was Ava. At times, he'd thought she was bipolar or borderline schizophrenic. But she didn't react.

He raised his hand to the button on her shorts.

"I'm going to need some help," she teased as she started to take off her shirt.

Briz knew he was salivating. He was a guy...he was a guy and questioning the rationality and sanity of who he was about to have sex with wasn't in the forefront of his thoughts.

"Maybe we should wake Hubs to help us," she said, impersonating a southern Belle. Briz's hands froze. *What is she talking about? Is she into threesomes? I don't want Hubs here.* "No, we can do this ourselves," Ava decided with a firm voice.

Yeah. No joke.

"Come on, Briz, you have to help out." There was that Southern lilt again. "Come on, you can do it."

He furrowed his brow.

"He's still hallucinating," the firm voice said. "We should get him to drink some more bentonite and add some to his bath."

Hallucinating? Briz forced open his heavy, lidded eyes. Ava was gone. His legs were no longer tied to the bed. *Had he imagined that, too?*

Briz's muscles were like marshmallows as two of the triplets pulled him into an upright position. *Isadora and Tamara,* he realized, as Isadora's long, single braid and Tamara's maroon plaid blouse came into focus. They lifted the sheet from his naked body. As they pulled him upright, he glanced down, relieved there was no reason for him to feel embarrassed. He raised one arm and then the other as they helped him slip on Hubs's robe.

Something's wrong with me. I was fantasizing about Ava. The first time he'd gone to see Jaden, Ava had opened the front door and for a quick second he'd thought maybe he was pursuing the wrong sister. But when Ava spoke, the thought had vanished from his mind.

Briz sagged to the side. The triplets gripped his arms.

"Come on, son. Olympe's filled a nice tepid bath for you with ginger." Isadora's normal singsong cadence was taut. "This fever should have broke by now. The bath will help it move on out. We can't carry you, Briz; we can brace you, but you have to walk on your own."

The two women helped Briz to stand. The three of them shuffled out of the room and down the hall, as he thought about how different his dream was from his reality.

He flinched, his eyes narrowing in response to the bright bathroom light. Someone flipped the switch off, leaving only the glow of a flickering candle as he moved toward the open door. He saw Olympe set the candle onto the counter.

Any sense of modesty that he might have still had fell away as they removed his robe and lowered him into the tub.

CHAPTER 17

JADEN

Floorboards creaked and groaned. Jaden watched three shadowy figures emerge from Briz's room. A light from down the hall lit up Briz in a striped bathrobe, braced between two of the triplets. They staggered forward.

The light went out. A soft golden glow remained.

Jaden laid her head back on her pillow, but tired as she was, her agonizing over Briz pulled her upright. Coolness penetrated her skin as she lowered her feet onto the floor. She looked over at the cots where her mother and sister were sleeping.

While asleep, Ava's scowl was softer. Jaden knew it would reappear with the sunrise. Since Jaden had returned from the cave, Ava had avoided her, ignoring Jaden's attempts to speak to her, refusing to even look at Jaden.

She knows. She knows I tried to kill her.

Noiselessly moving down the hall, Jaden looked into the bathroom. Candlelight shimmered on the water as Tamara placed ice packs on the hornet wounds on Briz's arms and neck. The rest of his body was submerged, his head resting against the back of the tub.

Without saying a word, Jaden went into Briz's bedroom, removed her nightshirt and put on her clothes. Then she changed the sweaty, mud-covered sheets on Briz's bed. His bloody shirt and shorts had been tossed and forgotten in the corner of the room. She picked them up and headed out to the back porch to wash everything.

Emptying his pockets, she pulled out an envelope. With a raised eyebrow, Jaden read the outside:

For MY Briz.

From YOUR Abigail.

On the back of the envelope was written SWAK.

His ex-girlfriend sent him a letter that was *Sealed With A Kiss?* Maybe Abigail didn't mean anything by it. Maybe that's how you signed a letter if you were the girl Briz had gotten pregnant when he was fifteen. Jaden stuffed the crumpled letter into her pocket and started the washing machine; it clamored to life, upending the quiet. Quickly turning it off, she went to the front porch and curled up in a wicker chair.

SWAK. The letter taunted Jaden from her pocket. She couldn't contain her curiosity any longer. With barely enough daylight to read by, she opened Abigail's letter as if it were made from hazardous material.

Briz,

I don't know why you lied to me. I would never lie to you. I don't believe you're using these mushrooms to help one of your friends with a science project for summer school. I know kids who get high from them. But remember, they can also be deadly. Please, be careful. Don't do anything stupid.

You haven't called me lately. Please don't tell me you've

met someone? I love you so much. I just want us to be together again.

Please call me soon.

ALL MY LOVE, Your Abigail

There was a painful thud in Jaden's chest. She inhaled quick, short breaths, as if trying to jumpstart her heart. *It's just an organ,* she thought. *Pumping Mal Rou blood through me. A broken heart never killed anyone. Did it?*

Jaden sat there, watching the sky grow lighter. The sound of pots clanging and dishes clattering informed her it would be all right for her to turn the washing machine back on. Standing in front of the washer, she considered tossing Abigail's little love note in and drowning it.

Jaden wiped a trickle of sadness from her cheek as she went into the kitchen.

"Morning, dear," Isadora greeted Jaden from in front of the stove.

Jaden forced a half-smile as she took a bottle of her Envie Tea from the refrigerator—then chugged down half of it to ensure that her venomous and spiteful Mal Rou instincts would continue to be kept at bay. Walking down the hall, she saw the back of Briz's striped bathrobe and Olympe's blue bathrobe going into his room.

"Ah, how nice," she heard Olympe say. "Someone went and gave ya clean sheets. I'll get ya a pair of Hubs's pajamas to wear." Olympe helped Briz sit on the edge of the bed. "And then ya should get some more sleep."

Jaden stood in the doorway, eyes narrowed, staring at *Abigail's boyfriend.* The thought held a bitterness that Jaden knew wasn't valid. If it was true, Briz wouldn't be here with her. Risking his life, for her. She turned away, hearing her mom and sister arguing in the other room.

"I want to leave, *now*."

From the sound of it, Ava's scowl lines were back.

"I'm not abandoning Jaden. She needs us." Her mom's voice was a loud whisper.

"Needs us? Haven't you heard? She's like a killing machine. She doesn't need us! Have you not grasped that her dim-witted boyfriend freed more monsters? Flying ones with deadly, sharp teeth. They're on the loose and probably searching the bayou for him so they can finish him off. And we'll be next."

"We are not leaving!" Brooke's whisper was louder still.

"What the eff is wrong with you, Mom? Do you have some kind of a death wish?"

"Don't you eff me!" Brooke snapped. "The sun is barely up, and you've already started complaining."

"I don't always complain. I just want to go!" Ava sounded like a hyena trapped in a cage.

Jaden finished off her bottle of brew as she walked into the room. "Mom, Ava's right." The following silence made Jaden crack a smile. Ava's mouth had dropped open—had Jaden ever sided with her before?

"The two of you should go back to town," Jaden said, already feeling the benefits of the Envie Tea. "Hubs will take you. I'm going to be all right."

"*Town*...I don't want to go back to town, you moron." Ava's first words to her in a day and a half were sharp and crisp. "I want to go back to Colorado."

Chapter 18

Esere

Esere stared up at the ceiling from Dekle's old bed, listening to the crows' feet scratching on the roof. Hundreds of them. Finding comfort in being near the Professor's belongings, he and Anders had slept in his room last night. Jumping onto Dekle's desk, Esere looked out the window at the birds roosting in the trees. In the dawn light, their feathers glistened with a fine mist as they stretched their wings. Above him, the sound of scratching stopped.

En masse, the crows took flight, darkening the sky and filling the air with a storm of squawking. Esere leapt back onto the bed.

"Get up, Anders. How can ya even sleep with 'em birds screechin'?"

"What? Where are we?" Anders's voice cracked as he looked around the room.

"It's mornin'. The crows are leavin'. We can go outside now." Esere hurried over to the open bedroom door. "The sooner Datura and Ivan and Tig is in the ground, the sooner they'll come back to life."

Anders bolted past Esere, down the grand staircase to the entry closet, where they'd stashed their family for safekeeping through the night; opening the door, he eyed their wrapped bodies.

"When Tig comes to, she might want to keep this here lime green blanket. It's her favorite color," Anders remarked as they picked her up and rested her near the stairs.

Esere smiled at the thought as they returned to the closet, where his attention went to Datura. "Careful of the roots sproutin' from her tentacles," he warned as they unwrapped her cloaked body. "Let's bury her first—at the back of the garage, near the cane field. The ground there should have a full day of sun."

Together, they carried Datura to the back porch. Esere's ears curved forward, listening for any remaining crows, as they stepped onto the moist grass and looked up at the trees and the rooftops of the house and garage.

"It's all clear." Anders nodded at Esere in agreement.

At the back of the garage, they shoved their clawed fingers into the soft, spongy ground and dug a shallow hole.

"Do we say somthin'?" Esere asked, lowering Datura into the hole. "Ya knows, like some kind 'a prayer? Or a spell?" Seemed right, he thought while covering Datura with dirt. "What'd ya say when ya buried me?"

"Nothin'. We didn't say nothin'."

Esere felt drops of rain. "Let's get Ivan." He looked up at the dark clouds. "Gonna be a downpour soon."

They hurried back to the house and dragged Ivan from the closet.

"Look." Anders pointed at where the horn on Ivan's ear was poking through the crocheted blanket. "Gotta watch out;

the sprouts and roots comin' out of his horns is gonna break off."

With Ivan unwrapped, Esere took hold of Ivan's ankles while Anders gripped his arms. "Watch his head," Esere cautioned as they hauled him through the kitchen. "It ain't all that well attached."

No sooner had they made their way down the steps of the back porch when Esere heard a loud hum and flapping wings.

Anders froze, his mouth open, as he stared past Esere. Turning his head, Esere was face to face with a small bird with cloudy orbs where eyes should have been.

"What is it?" Anders asked. "It ain't got no feathers. Its skin is all shiny like a fish."

It moved like a hummingbird, up and down, back and forth, sniffing Esere. Anders lowered Ivan's upper body to the ground. Then, letting out a high-pitched screech and flinging his arms around, Anders swatted at the thing until it flew away. Before Anders could reach down for Ivan's arms, the strange bird had returned.

Esere dropped Ivan's feet as the bird hovered so close to his face that he could feel rain flicking off its wings. It opened its mouth and hissed—revealing row upon row of tiny sharp teeth—as three more of the strange birds soared down from the trees.

"Get off 'a him!" Anders kicked at the birds that were snuffling Ivan's clothes and the gelled blood on his throat.

Esere stood motionless as the one eyeing him turned away and latched onto Anders arm.

With a howl of pain, Anders yanked the thing off and hurled it at a tree, as two of the other strange birds started pecking the back of his head. Knocking them away, Anders took off zigzagging across the grass with three of the birds right behind. He pushed open the garage side door, disappeared inside and shut the door.

A gnawing sound pulled Esere from his trance. The remaining bird was chewing on Ivan's neck. It stopped, blindly looked up at Esere, snorting and sniffing the air.

Esere's feet reacted before his mind, propelling him to the porch and through the open door. He glanced back. The mutant bird hadn't followed him—it was too busy picking at Ivan's flesh. Esere pushed the door shut and climbed onto the kitchen counter; reaching over, he clicked the lock.

When he looked out the window, he saw there were now two birds feeding on Ivan.

Esere shifted his gaze toward the garage. The birds that chased Anders weren't giving up. One flew over the roof, while the other was striking its beak against the broken window on the side of the building; enlarging the hole, it disappeared inside.

A loud piercing shriek took hold of the stillness and didn't stop.

Esere jumped down on the floor and huddled near the pantry—putting his hands over his ears, he tried to stifle the sound of Anders's screams.

Soon after, Anders went silent.

Esere heard a tapping. He looked up.

A bird was knocking its head against the kitchen window, getting closer to breaking the pane of glass with each rap.

"What are ya? Where'd ya come from?"

Two more of the strange creatures appeared at the

window, their unseeing eyes staring at Esere. One flew away. Esere heard a noise in the dining room. He inched back into the pantry.

"No!"

He drew in his last breath.

CHAPTER 19

BRIZ

Rain pelted the roof, making it impossible for Briz to sleep. Moaning, he crawled from the bed that he'd rarely left since soaking in the tub two nights ago. His body ached like it belonged to a ninety-year-old man. His hand was sore, but healing. He rolled up the sleeves of the lightweight pajamas Olympe had given him to wear and looked at the bites on his arms. They were no longer screaming red marks. Perhaps he wouldn't have scars.

He needed a shower. He could smell nicotine on his skin. And something musty...earthy. Briz opened the door and glanced at the living room where Ava was sound asleep on her cot. He glided his hand along the wall to keep his balance as walked toward the kitchen.

"There's a good chance that Briz will crave cigarettes," he heard Isadora say. "He still has signs of nicotine poisoning: headaches, dizziness. That's why we've been giving him so much charcoal, to help pull the nicotine out of his system."

"Couldn't those symptoms be from anything?" Jaden

asked. "The hogweed, the hornet stings. I mean, couldn't the stress of what he's been through cause headaches?"

"Let's not forget that musky scent seeping from his pores. It may affect his...*urges.*" There was an edge to the voice. He figured it was Tamara.

The floorboards murmured under Briz's feet, announcing his approach, causing an abrupt change of conversation. He paused in the doorway.

"If the sun doesn't come out soon and charge the solar panels, how much longer will we have electricity?" Brooke tuned toward Briz as he leaned against the threshold, steadying himself.

"For the rain it raineth every day...*The Taming of the Shrew.*" Violet, sitting prim and proper on her stool on the table, smiled at Briz, enjoying their Shakespearean connection.

Briz smiled back as he took in the homey kitchen scene. Hubs was in the antique recliner; the triplets were making breakfast. A small bouquet of pink flowers sat in the middle of the table, surrounded by mismatched dishes and silverware.

Briz ran his hand through his hair; a nervous habit that he believed helped him gather his thoughts. He looked at the three sisters. "May I help with anything?"

"Just sit yourself down." With a grin, Tamara looked at him—her hair was twisted into its signature bun.

Bundles of herbs hung above the counter. Every so often, drafts from the ceiling fan caused flakes of dried leaves to drift down and adorn the triplets' hair.

The splatter of pancake batter hit the skillet.

"Smells good." Briz smiled, sitting next to Jaden.

Breakfast was the first actual food Briz had eaten in days.

He wondered what Tamara had put in the pancake batter. After eating, he felt less queasy as well as stronger. His sense of balance had returned.

It was as if a shift had happened, sending a surge of energy through him—he could feel it as clearly as he could smell the sharp, woody fragrance of musk, the traces of nicotine permeating from his skin. He headed to his room, gathered his clothes, and went to take a shower. With only the catchment tank for fresh water, and so many people in the house, he kept his shower brief. Careful of his wounds, he dried off, got dressed, and swaggered into the kitchen.

What's up with that? Briz considered the fact that he'd never swaggered in his life. He smiled broadly, seeing Jaden all alone, perched on the kitchen counter, glugging down her Envie Tea.

"Do you have to drink so much of that stuff?" Briz took the bottle from her and set it on the counter.

"I kind of like it." She sat up straight, eyes level with his. "It helps me chill out."

He couldn't stop staring at her mouth. Over the past week he'd almost been killed, twice, and right now, he wasn't feeling hung up on taking things slow with her. Running his fingers over the stubble on his face, Briz considered turning around and going into the living room—that would be the smart thing to do.

Who cares about doing the smart thing?

Briz lightly touched her collarbone. He could feel her quiver under his touch. "It's just that sometimes you're more fun when you haven't been drinking that stuff." He kept his eyes on Jaden's as he placed his hands on her knees and slowly pulled her legs apart, then pressed his hips forward as he slid her to the edge of the counter.

For a fleeting moment, Briz wondered if his actions were due to the venom in his system. With a devilish grin, he recalled overhearing Tamara's comment that the musk in his system would affect his *urges*.

The reason was irrelevant. He wanted Jaden. He immediately heard his dad belting out the words to the Rolling Stones song, "You can't always get what you want. But if you try sometimes, well, you might find, you get what you need." Raising Jaden's chin, Briz kissed her.

Jaden's lips melted into his. And her mouth...*her mouth*... Their kisses deepened. He held her face in his hands; the smell of nicotine and musk on his skin grew stronger, taunting him. He was going to lose control.

Briz slowed their kisses until their lips were barely touching. He was so light-headed; maybe he wasn't as well as he'd thought. Bracing his hands on the counter, he lowered his forehead against Jaden's.

"Briz, I found Abigail's letter...accidentally." Jaden's breath held the fragrance of her herbal drink as it touched his face.

He looked at Jaden. Her lips slightly swollen, the skin around her mouth pink from the stubble on his chin. He wasn't a smooth-faced kid anymore—right now, it was obvious in a number of ways.

"What...?" He wasn't paying attention to her words. He had one desire, and it wasn't to talk.

"Abigail's letter," Jaden repeated. "I read it."

"Yeah..." The word was muffled as he focused on tenderly kissing Jaden's cheek.

"It was in your pocket."

"So?" His lips slowly glided down the side of her neck.

A pleased moan escaped from Jaden before she pulled back. "Abigail loves you."

"I know," Briz said flatly.

Jaden's expression went from concerned to perturbed. "Do you love her?"

Briz let out an irritated sigh. "No."

He should have said it with a semblance of sincerity, but he wasn't interested in having this little chat. Especially not now.

Aware of her stitches, he slid his hand under her shirt, grinning at the sound of her quick inhalation as his fingers trailed over her skin. He watched her eyes widen as he slowly raised his hand higher. Jaden thought of him as being a good guy, trustworthy. That was about to all change.

He heard a sound and paused, then looked over his shoulder. Ava was watching them through the window. He gave Ava a sly grin before bothering to meet Violet's gaze.

The Bellibone was hovering just beyond his reach, her wings flapping rapidly.

"You do realize you're not the only ones in the house." Irritation permeated Violet's normally sweet voice. "And that this is the counter our food is prepared on."

Briz took a step back, not leaving Jaden much room as she slid off the counter, her body pressing against his.

"Humph," Violet grunted.

Briz took another step back.

"Sorry, Violet." Jaden picked up her bottle of Envie Tea. "I'll just keep drinking this."

"Maybe Briz should have some, too." Violet's eyes never left Briz. "I'm assuming that whatever is in your system right now has altered your hormones, causing you to be...unruly! You should be resting in bed. Alone!"

"Unruly." Briz chuckled as he looked at Jaden. Her cheeks were pink with embarrassment—while his were colored from excitement.

With a cocky grin, he looked at Violet. "As William Shakespeare would say, 'Tis one thing to be tempted, another thing to fall.' Relax, Violet. We were only making out."

"Don't you William Shakespeare me. Just go to your room."

"Go to my room?" Briz laughed as he watched Jaden sheepishly follow Violet.

He didn't blame Violet for being upset with them. Jaden's mom and the triplets were in the living room, and some things should be done in private. Maybe later tonight, when everyone was asleep, he and Jaden could be the hormone-driven teenagers they were meant to be.

Frustrated, with a loud huff and shake of his head, Briz went out the back door, past Ava; not stopping until he reached the chicken coop, where he watched the roosters prancing around the hens.

He raked his fingers through his hair and gave it a tug.

Jaden deserves better. Keep your act together.

CHAPTER 20

AVA

Tucked in a wicker chair, Ava watched as the kitchen door swung open. Briz didn't pay any attention to her; he just stomped past, his pent-up frustrations causing his nostrils to flare. Ava pressed her lips together, trying not to chuckle. Once again, the porch had proven to be a most advantageous place to sit.

It wasn't like she was being a Peeping Tom or anything. She'd been sitting here, minding her own business, when she saw Jaden and Briz going at it through the window. Ava couldn't help but move to the chair next to the window for a better view. She loved it when Briz caught her watching them—and he'd smiled at her.

Those little bird monsters changed him for the better. What does he see in my sister? The dweeb has a poster of Boyan Slat on her wall. Boyan Slat! I mean he's cute, but who puts up posters of a guy who's trying to save the planet from plastic?

A rumble sent her flying out of her seat.

"Hubs is here!" Limping over to the front door Ava flung it open, repeating the words to anyone who would listen. "Hubs is here! I can hear his boat. I won't have to die in this hellhole after all!"

Ava hurried off the porch, cheerfully exclaiming, "I'm so out of here!"

She'd never thought of herself as a gleeful person, yet she couldn't stop smiling and waving at Hubs. As the boat came near, she could see his perplexed expression, which made her smile grow wider.

"*Huuubs...*" she drew out his name as he stepped off the boat and tied it to the dock. "Hubs, will you take me to town? I want to go right now." Ava could feel her grin extending from ear to ear.

"I j-just g-got here."

"Yeah. I can see that." She hooked her arm in his. "Come on in and have something to eat. Then we can leave."

The fine lines around Hubs's eyes creased as he rigidly removed her arm from his. "I h-have s-supplies." He stepped back onto the boat and handed her a box.

"Okay," she said, taking the box. "I don't mind helping." Ava paraded into the house, announcing, "Hubs needs something to eat. Then he's taking me back to town. As soon as I get there, I'm booking a flight home to Colorado."

Ava's eyes skipped from one triplet to the next, aware that they were all merely tolerating her presence in their home. The three of them, along with Violet, looked like they were stifling grins.

She kept walking. Her mother followed.

"Mom, I've been stuck in this house for a month. You can't stop me from leaving!"

"Stop exaggerating, Ava. It's been a little over a week. And we aren't going back to Colorado until we're certain that the Mal Rous are dead...really dead."

Ava set the box on the kitchen counter, pointedly ignoring her mom.

"Ava, are you listening to me?"

"It's hard not to, Mom. You're practically yelling in my ear."

"You aren't leaving," her mom continued. "Your grandfather created this mess, and we are not making the triplets and Hubs deal with cleaning it up! Getting rid of the Quellers and Mal Rous is our problem, not theirs."

"You've got to be kidding. I never even met the guy, and you expect me to deal with destroying his monsters." Ava motioned toward the living room, where she assumed the three women were fawning over Hubs. "They knew Dekle. Let them do it! I'm sure they have all sorts of witchy tricks up their sleeves. They can do some kind of a Voodoo dance and incinerate them. Or let Jaden do it. I understand she's quite capable of homicide."

Ava pursed her lips, her eyes challenging her mom to ask her what she was talking about.

"Either Hubs takes me to town..." Ava paused as the back door opened and Briz came in. "Or I'm taking the boat and going on my own. Just because Jaden screwed up everyone's lives doesn't mean I should have to suffer! Or die!"

"Go for it!" Briz said with a smug expression. "You'll never make it on your own. You'd be lost in the bayou in ten minutes flat."

"Fine! Then you take me!"

Briz looked less frustrated than when he'd stomped out of the house earlier. With a crooked smile, he chuckled. "Okay."

Surprised, Ava stood up straighter, waiting for him to make a snide comment.

"Briz, you are not helping the situation. I want Ava here with me." Brooke was standing so close to Ava that Ava could literally feel her mom breathing down her neck.

"Well, to be honest, ma'am..."

Yep, here it comes, Ava thought as she drew her shoulders back, glaring at Briz.

"She's only in the way," Briz smirked. "There's nothing she can do to help, and she wouldn't try even if she could."

Ava was about to argue when Briz leaned on the counter and gave her a wink. Or had his eye just twitched. She couldn't decide. Was he on her side or not?

Why not? He was probably tired of acting all brave. Maybe he understood she was just as tired of hiding behind a tough exterior. Ava looked at her mom, who was staring at Briz, shaking her head.

"Tomorrow, Ava," her mom said with a huff. "I'll ask Hubs to take us back to town tomorrow. Then I'll decide if you stay or go back to Colorado."

Ava's shoulders dropped as she whined, "Mom...those flying fiends could be heading here right now, scavenging for food—human food! Let's get out of town while we can."

Brooke turned and walked away as Ava added, "Tomorrow, Mom. I mean it! One more night and then, with or without you, I'm leaving."

Ava's attention settled on the box of food she'd set on the counter. On top were three pairs of drugstore reading glasses

*—of course the old biddies wouldn't go to town to get an eye exam—*and nicotine patches. She picked up the box of patches and tossed it to Briz.

"These must be for you. You stink of tobacco."

CHAPTER 21

DATURA

The sound of scales slithered over the ground above Datura, causing her mouth to twitch, her tentacles to pulse. She thrust one hand up through a layer of fresh soil and grabbed the snake. Raising her head from her shallow grave, she coughed up hunks of dirt, wiped off her face, then bit into the snake. After a few more bites, she tossed its remains aside and crawled out of the hole.

Datura's body was curved and bent, her bones stiff. Vines dangled from the ends of Datura's tentacles. Tiny leaves reached out beyond her toenails. She felt roots growing from her spine, wrapping around threads of clothing that had been wedged between her vertebrae when Briz thrust a machete into her back. A small root had sprouted from the hole in her chest and pushed its way through the tear in her shirt.

She remembered stabbing Jaden in the stomach. She remembered Jaden stabbing her in the chest.

Her beady eyes took in the sight of the Professor's old garage. Late afternoon shadows stretched across the yard.

Datura scanned the grounds for more graves but saw no other fresh mounds of dirt.

"What happened to Tig and Ivan? Why wasn't they buried?" Her words sounded loud in the quiet that surrounded her—no birds, no insects. Only mosquitoes.

Always mosquitoes, she thought as a distorted grin formed on her face. Her Professor Dekle Thatcher had been brilliant to make her with the DNA from those intrepid survivors, along with his own DNA, and that of rats, newt, tardigrade, and the datura plant.

Datura limped to the cellar window on the side of the garage. Wheezing, she placed her hand over a print on the muddy glass. *Mal Rou.*

Her tentacles stretched, sniffing the foliage, recognizing the scents. "Anders. Esere." Her severed nerves tingled. "No..."

Anders is in Dekle's cave. Esere is dead. Datura's nostrils flared as she inhaled another deep breath of air, knowing she was right the first time. *It is them. Esere came back to life.* "Did the professor know stickin' us in the ground would heal us? Did Jaden know...so she buried me?"

Datura looked over her shoulder, expecting to see Esere and Anders behind her as she made her way to the side of the garage—pushing on the door, she felt a slight resistance. She peered into the dark space and saw a small pile of bones. Stripped clean. Someone had devoured the flesh right off of them. Cautiously, Datura inched her way in. Shredded bits of orange-colored clothes were mixed in with the bones. She picked up a piece of the fabric; next to it was a dragon-like jawbone.

*Anders...*Closing the door, Datura sank against the wall, her mind a muddled mess, her emotions scratching her throat. She spat out muddy phlegm, then moved unsteadily toward the house. Near the porch were more bones, along with Ivan's blue shirt, torn to pieces.

A jagged chill moved up Datura's fractured spine. Her words were tender. "My brothers. What happened?"

A few feet from Ivan's remains were the bones and feathers of two crows. Had Ivan survived his throat being sliced by Jaden only to be pecked clean by vengeful crows?

Don't make sense. Then what ate the crows?

Datura tried to stand tall, bolstering her resolve as she ascended the stairs to the veranda and discovered a broken windowpane on the French door. She climbed through the opening, over the shattered glass, and paused, listening for any noise. All she heard was the hum of the refrigerator in the kitchen.

Her tentacles pulsed, detecting the aroma of blood. Several of her tentacles straightened, absorbing another odor. *Feathers...?* she wondered with a quiet breath. *No. Fish...?*

She crept over to the doorway and looked toward the stairs. A small leg bone was sticking out of a lime green crocheted blanket. Next to it were more bones. Datura sidled over to them. Tig's yellow-colored clothes were torn apart, and like Ivan and Anders, her bones had been pecked clean.

"Tig," Datura muttered as she turned away.

With a slow, uneven gait, she followed the smell of blood through the swinging kitchen door. Three gunny sacks caked with blood were under the table. Red streaks crisscrossed the floor, punctuated by more bones, pieces of Esere's red clothes, his beak-like nose.

This ain't right. Why would Jaden bring Esere and Anders back here to do this to 'em?

Her head dipped forward from the weight of her anger.

"I pumped too much 'a my blood into the girl. My last bite made her feral!"

Why didn't Jaden devour me like she did the others?

Datura picked up a scrap of Esere's clothing and bunched it up in her hand. Her tentacles fell limp. "Because she has my blood in her veins."

For a long moment, Datura stared at Esere's remains, as she ran her tongue over her protruding fangs. *I'm the only one left.*

Her sadness she ignored. It was not an emotion she cared for.

Revenge. Now that was worth nurturing. Datura straightened up, brushed her tentacles from her face and made her way through the lower rooms of the house, searching for traces of Jaden. Finding none, she ascended the stairs slowly, each step a painful reminder of the damage done to her body.

The first door opened into Amelia's bedroom. A box of old dolls sat in the corner. Datura removed a dingy white doll's shift from the box, held it up to herself, then took it with her to Dekle's room.

"Dekle... *My* love. *My* professor. *My* Dekle. Not Elvina's. *Mine!*"

Grief finally broke through Datura's heart.

My siblings is gone. Dekle is gone. Cool, moist drops of sorrow fell from her eyes. Other than feelings of anger, Datura had never been emotional. She blamed Jaden. When she bit Jaden, not only had her blood mixed with that girl's, but it also seemed Jaden's had entered her system.

Datura cried until her tears felt like fiery embers of spite.

She returned to the kitchen, climbed onto the counter, then stood in the sink, and turned on the faucet. Mud and blood swirled down the drain as water loosened the fabric of her clothes from the deep gash in her back. Shutting off the water, she peeled her clothes off, careful not to disturb any of her newly grown roots—choosing to let them wither away in due time—she slipped on the doll's shift.

"This place ain't safe," she said to Esere's bones. "The bayou?" Datura looked out the kitchen window. "The Professor wouldn't like it, but I could try to find 'em other three Mal Rous. Them ones he buried a long time ago. After all, I ain't so different from 'em."

Now that she was alone, the idea of finding them felt appealing. Even necessary for her own survival.

"He told me where they was at. They might not hurt me." Datura rubbed her pointed chin, then continued to talk to Esere as if he had sprouted back to life. "I could let 'em slaughter Jaden to gain their trust. If she's this feral, she has to be put down, killed off."

Datura considered the way the Professor had worked diligently, perfecting cloning for what he liked to refer to as his *Divine Retribution.*

"I always liked the sound 'a that." She picked a knife up from the counter. "For now, it's best if Jaden and her kin think I'm dead, too."

Datura steadied herself and then swung the knife onto the counter, chopping off the ring finger on her left hand. She held it up, taking in what she'd done. "It'll do."

Her body swayed as she wrapped her hand in a dishcloth, then lowered herself off the counter and hobbled outside. At the edge of the cane field, she tore apart her old wet clothes and scattered them around. Then, plucking a handful of squirming tentacles from her head, she placed them on top of her shredded clothes along with her finger—all in clear sight.

"Make Jaden think somthin' dug up my body and dragged it off."

She watched as her tentacles thrashed and squirmed, dying a slow death.

CHAPTER 22

BRIZ

Half-awake, Briz sat in the oversized chair, his legs stretched out in front of him. With his shirtsleeve rolled up, he applied a tobacco patch to his upper arm, grateful Hubs had thought to bring a box of them with the triplets' supplies. Ava came into the living room, her slender body moving with ease and self-assurance. Briz scooted back, sat up straight, and ran his fingers through his uncombed morning hair.

Violet was behind Ava, chattering. Neither one of them acknowledged him. He watched them with a blank expression, unaffected by the sight of a fairy-like entity having a discussion with a human. It felt normal, right-on par with the fact that he was about to head out to pick up refrigerated monsters. Just another typical day.

Violet flopped onto the desk, then fluttered back up so she was eye-level with Ava. Her leg wasn't healing as well as the triplets had hoped; flying was still a challenge for her.

"I'm nothing like my grandfather." Ava looked ready to swat Violet away. "Not only was he demented, he ruined my life."

"You do understand he was also a very brilliant man," Violet said, flapping her wings harder.

"That's what I've heard, and I'm smart enough to know that's not what you're referring to." Ava reached over and poked Violet's shoulder with her finger, causing Violet to teeter in midair. "I'm just high-strung when it comes to *things* and *people* trying to kill me. That's a far cry from being a mastermind of evil."

"I never said that. I didn't mean to upset you."

"No, you just wanted to make a point, and I get it." Ava eyed Violet's pampas grass hair, adding, "Don't get your dander all up. I *can* be nice."

Violet gave a wary smile as she nodded.

"Stop smiling at me, you little pixie," Ava snapped.

Briz stifled a laugh. Ava had her moments of being funny, even if it was harsh and cruel.

"I get it, Tinker Bell!" Ava was on a roll. "I almost lost my family *and my life*. If anything's going to kill them, I will —*with kindness*."

The conversation abruptly stopped when a rush of warm morning air ushered Jaden in through the front door. The two sisters silently dismantled the cots their mom and Ava had been using for the past week without making eye contact with each other or Briz.

So, this was Ava killing her sister with kindness, Briz thought to himself, amused.

With his elbows resting on the arms of the chair, he folded his hands, his lips pressing against his index fingers as his eyes took in Jaden and Ava, their curves, the arch of their backs. For a moment, Jaden's eyes met his, and the corners of his mouth curled up. In his mind, they were back in the kitchen, his fingers longing to explore her body as she sat on the counter. He released a slow breath as he lowered his hands and rubbed his palms over the smooth fabric of the chair's arms.

The lectures on "mindfulness" and ethics his mother had crammed down his throat appeared to be useless when nicotine and giant hogweed were flowing through Briz's system. One minute he was sensible and mature—the next he wanted a girl that would be his *bebelle,* his own little plaything.

Another gust of warm air entered the room. Briz looked over at the front door; Hubs was standing there watching him. As if Hubs knew what Briz was thinking, he shook his head and gestured for Briz to get up.

"C-come on. Ya c-can help on the b-boat."

Briz glanced at the two sisters before picking up his backpack and following Hubs outside.

"Ya is a g-good kid, B-Briz. Don't b-be st-stupid." Hubs strode ahead of Briz on the walkway to the dock.

"What are you talking about? I wasn't doing anything. Your mama told me to just sit. So I was."

"P-plain as day, w-what ya was th-thinkin' 'bout. It's t-time to g-get ya home." At the boathouse, Hubs pointed to a couple of gas cans. "F-fill up the t-tank for m-me."

Briz stashed his pack under the front seat on the boat. While hauling the gas cans and filling up the tank, he considered his plans for the day. Drop the girls at their rental apartment. Go to Guyon Manor with Hubs to help him load the refrigerated Mal Rous into his car. Then, go home and see his folks.

"W-when ya is d-done," Hubs interrupted Briz's rambling thoughts, "g-get my b-bag from the k-kitchen."

Briz finished filling the tank, bungeed the empty gas cans

in place on the boat and returned to the house, using the back door hoping to avoid any sisterly riffs. After making a quick bathroom stop, he returned to the dock with Hubs's bag.

The Lisette ladies weren't far behind.

Briz dragged his hand across his mouth as he watched Ava and Jaden coming toward him, followed by their mom. Briz glanced at Hubs. Hubs's eyes narrowed. *Is the guy a mind reader like the triplets? Or are my thoughts that obvious?*

CHAPTER 23

—

AVA

With a flirtatious pout, Ava walked toward Briz. He looked straight at her, then ran his hand across his mouth. She knew it—*he wanted her*; smiling, she stepped onto the boat. Then his attention shifted to Jaden. Ava put her hand on Briz's arm, feigning a need to steady herself.

"You, okay?" he asked, looking down at her foot wrapped in gauze. His sweet smile seemed mischievous as he took her arm and guided her down on the seat before turning to help Jaden and Brooke on board.

Ava flicked her teeth with her tongue as she watched her two-faced sister. She wanted to yell at Jaden, "You little bitch! You tried to suffocate me!" Ava flicked her teeth with her tongue again. She couldn't care less that Jaden "wasn't herself" at the time. *It was because of her brew...yeah right!*

From now on, Briz was fair game.

Briz sat next to Jaden, directly across from Ava. Ava stretched her legs out in front of her, sliding them between Briz's feet and grinning as Briz's gaze traveled the length of her legs.

Yep, fair game.

Ava glanced at Jaden, holding her ever-present bottle of tea. Her idiot sister's attention was on the triplets.

"Here, Briz." Olympe handed Briz a linen long-sleeved shirt. "It's one of Hubs's." Briz looked at Hubs as Olympe asked her son, "Ya don't mind, do ya, Hubs?" Briz held the shirt as if wondering what to do with it. "I just thought ya might want to keep the marks on yer arms hidden from yer folks. If ya keep them out of the sun, the scars will fade over time." She glanced down at his calves. "They aren't so noticeable on yer legs."

Briz glanced at his scars, then back at Olympe. "Thanks."

Ava watched as he pulled his T-shirt off and stuffed it into his backpack. Her boyfriend, Albert, was seven months older than Briz. Albert had the narrow-chested physique of a teenage boy, while Briz appeared to be on the verge of being buff. His abs showed the beginnings of a six-pack. She glanced at Jaden, who was also appreciating a shirtless Briz, as he pulled on Hubs's long-sleeved shirt, not bothering to button it up.

"Be safe," Olympe and Isadora chimed in unison while Tamara and Violet nodded in agreement.

Ava shifted her attention to the triplets. They were wearing large-brimmed straw hats, with their hands raised to shield their limpid blue eyes from the sun. Their paper-white skin glistened, giving them an otherworldly appearance as they waved goodbye, and Hubs motored the boat away.

Her mom turned toward Hubs and raised her voice over the noise of the engine. "Hubs, do you think Dekle Thatcher is still alive?" Hubs gave her mom a slow shrug. "Is there anyone we could ask? To find out?"

Moments passed before Hubs offered, "I c-can ask m-my grand-pere."

The backs of Ava's legs felt moist and were sticking to the skiff's aluminum seat. She willed the boat to go faster as they wove through the never-ending maze of inlets; her mind numbing to the sound of the motor. Since she had no intention of ever returning to the bayou, she took in the scenery.

She found the landscape pretty, peaceful and, after a while, boring. Blotting the perspiration from her brow and tying her hair into a knot, she looked at Briz; he reminded her of a bird of prey, his eyes piercing, as he looked at the shore. She tapped her foot against his, but he didn't notice. She followed his gaze.

"SHIT!" Ava stared at a group of fish skeletons floating in the water as they bumped against a huge carcass, half-in and half-out of the water. Moist flesh hung from its bones. "Is that...was that...an alligator?" Ava pointed at the shredded reptile. "Hubs. Have you ever seen anything like that before? It's those flying things, isn't it? Th-they ate a goddamn alligator!"

"Ava..." Her mom said her name, then nothing else as she spotted the remains.

"They're close!" Ava covered her mouth as she turned away from the gruesome sight clinging to the shore. "I know those flying piranhas are close."

Briz leaned forward and caressed her arm as if to comfort her. She studied the wounds on his neck. He knew better than any of them of the pain the Quellers could inflict.

"Shh. Shh." Her mother sounded like she was calming an infant. "You don't want to attract them if they're around."

"Right, Mom! 'Cos they can't hear the boat." Ava gripped the edge of the metal seat. "If they don't kill us before we get back to town, you can forget about me helping you clean up that old house. I'm not going back there!"

Her mom's attention moved from the shore to Ava.

"I mean it, Mom. I'm not going back to that place." A shiver streaked up Ava's spine. "It's cursed and should be burned down."

"It's not cursed," her mom replied, though doubt was in her voice. With an expression of disbelief, Brooke looked at the remains of the alligator. "Well…if it is, we can get it uncursed. This *is* the land of Voodoo queens and rituals."

Ava raised an eyebrow.

"Fine," her mom conceded. "You don't have to go to the estate."

"And *he's* taking me to the airport!" Ava locked her eyes on Briz until he nodded in agreement. "I'm getting out of this town!"

"We'll talk about it when we get home." As Brooke spoke, Briz stopped nodding.

"Hubs, can't we go any faster?" Jaden pressed her palms against her temples.

"You okay, babe?" Briz turned toward Jaden.

"No, she's not okay," Ava answered for her sister. "Those things could show up any second." Ava watched Briz's hand as he moved it away from her and reached over to Jaden, stroking her sister's hair, babying her.

Ava clamped her mouth shut. *What about me? I'm freaked out. I need someone to stroke my hair. To make everything seem all right!*

Hubs tapped Brooke on the shoulder, handed her a gun, and gestured for her to pass it over to Briz.

"J-just in c-case," Hubs said as Briz took the gun.

"I feel so much better now," Ava scoffed as she stared at the gun in Briz's hand. "Do you even know how to use it?"

Briz didn't respond. No one did. Ava felt her words tumble onto the floor of the boat, weighed down by the humidity, her anger, and everyone's fears. She glanced at her mom, at Jaden, Briz and Hubs. Like her, each of them held their jaws tight as they strained to hear the sound of wings flapping over the noise of the motor, their eyes focused on the trees.

A half hour later, the waterway opened onto a marshy wetland, leaving the unnerving shadows of the forested swamp behind. The tension in the air did not lift as Hubs's boat skipped across the water. Everyone remained quiet. Ava watched as a heron took flight, wishing she could sprout her own set of wings and escape this place. Violet flashed into her mind—*be careful what you wish for, especially when you're related to a mad scientist.*

"Briz." Brooke leaned forward and repeated Briz's name as Hubs's boathouse came into view.

Ava nudged him with her foot. Briz had been staring at the gun in his hand for the past ten minutes. When he looked up, Ava tilted her head toward her mother.

Briz straightened up and looked at Brooke. "Sorry. What?"

"When you and Hubs drive to Guyon Manor, would you...? Well, just let me know if Rick's truck has been towed away."

Or if he's still slumped over the steering wheel,

decomposing like when we last saw him? Ava thought with a shudder.

"Mom." Jaden touched Brooke's knee. "I'm going with Hubs and Briz to get the Mal Rous's bodies. And I'll get your purse, too."

"Your purse. That's what got us dragged into this mess!" Ava elbowed her mom. "If you hadn't insisted on going to get it, we wouldn't have found Rick dead in his truck, and we wouldn't have been attacked by the Mal Rous."

Her mom ignored her. Instead, Brooke reached over and squeezed her sister's hand.

"No, Jaden. You're coming to the apartment with us. If we're not going to Guyon Manor, neither are you! I want you where I can keep an eye on you."

"I'll be all right, Mom." Jaden pulled her hand free. "The Mal Rous are dead."

Ava looked at Briz, who was wagging his head as if he couldn't decide if it was true. *Were the Mal Rous dead or not?*

"I'm just going to help Hubs and Briz take the bodies back to the boat." Jaden sounded bent on having her way.

"We own an entire dead sugar cane plantation you can bury them on," Ava pointed out, her eyes on Briz.

"No..." Jaden winced as Ava gave her an I-wasn't-talking-to-you look. "Violet's worried they might regenerate."

Briz jumped in, looking back and forth between Ava and Jaden. "The triplets want to boil them until they've disintegrated."

"And then what?" Ava asked.

"We don't know..." Briz trailed off with a shrug of his shoulders, as if she'd asked if it was going to rain today.

"Mom, I need to be there. It's important to me." Jaden

glanced at Ava. "It's my mess." Jaden paused, then exhaled a frustrated breath. "When we're done, I'll have Briz bring me back to the apartment."

"Let her go, Mom," Ava said, looking past her mom and surveying the grass and reeds for predators. "It's not like she couldn't just as easily get killed by one of those flying beasts while she's with us."

Brooke gave Jaden a reluctant nod.

Chapter 24

Jaden

The ornate gates of Guyon Manor appeared both rigid and weary from decades of standing guard. Hubs stopped his car, and Jaden watched as Briz got out to open the gates. Though tense and cautious, Jaden also felt brave, no longer the spineless girl her sister claimed her to be. Still, she pressed her thumb between her eyes, an old trick her grandmother Jin had taught her years ago to stop from crying.

In the past, Jaden had associated tears with weakness. Now, she understood it was a way for her to release her emotions—it was better than yelling, better than arguing. Only this was not the time to cry. *Please, not now*, she begged herself. *Wait until I'm alone.*

Briz returned, with the long-sleeved shirt he was wearing buttoned all the way up, as if it would protect him from hungry Quellers. Hubs pushed on the gas pedal and the old Chevy Impala rolled forward a few feet, then stalled.

An omen? A warning not to enter? Jaden looked at the back of Briz's head. *Nothing happens by accident.* Was he thinking about his mom's words, too?

Her eyes met Hubs's in the rearview mirror. Turning the key again, the car changed its mind, agreeing to deliver them to their task at hand. Hubs drove around to the back of the house and parked close to the porch. The detached garage leered at them, its warped door resembling a sinister smile.

Oddly, the property looked peaceful to Jaden, unlike the day her mother and sister lay wounded on the ground, their blood soaking into the grass along with Tig's and Ivan's. She and Briz had been barely alive themselves as they killed Datura.

Hubs jumped back as he stepped out of the car. "C-crow's b-b-bones." He gestured toward the glove box. "My g-gun."

Briz handed the gun to Hubs, then exited the car.

"There are two more." Biz was pointing about seven feet away when Jaden came up next to him. The bones were stripped bare—the wings chewed off, feathers intact.

Jaden felt her cautious bravery waver. "Let's hurry."

Hubs popped the trunk and handed the same rusted machete Jaden had used to kill Datura, to Briz. Then gave Jaden a newer machete. The three of them studied the yard, the buildings, the sky, each silently looking for flying Quellers.

"Ready?" Jaden looked at Hubs and Briz as the three of them stepped onto the porch. Hubs stood at the door as Jaden grabbed the key her mother had hidden under one of the paint cans—handing it to him, he slipped it into the lock. The hinges uttered a raspy screech as Hubs inched the door open and peeked inside.

Quickly shutting the door, Hubs looked at Jaden. Her skin prickled at the alarm in Hubs's eyes. Briz put his hand on her shoulder. She turned to him; he wasn't looking at her; he was scanning the trees.

Smart. They shouldn't all turn their backs. That would leave them vulnerable to attack.

Drops of perspiration—from nerves as much as from humidity—made their way into Jaden's eyes. She wiped them away and nodded at Hubs. He opened the door, revealing dried blood, bones, and pieces of red clothing torn into shreds trailing out from the pantry.

"Esere. Esere's clothes were red," Jaden whispered. She wiped her eyes again. This time it wasn't perspiration. Had Esere dug himself out of his grave for this? Why did she care *this* was all that remained of him? Isn't this what she'd wanted?

Hubs stepped inside, followed by Jaden and Briz. They stood huddled near the doorway, so close that Jaden could feel the hair on Hubs's arm, on her other side, the fabric of Briz's shirt.

Jaden inhaled sharply, then covered her nose. The smell of death lingered in the room.

"Quellers," Briz said in a nervous voice. "They've consumed his flesh, like the alligator we saw earlier."

Anders too? Jaden scanned the room but saw no traces of his remains.

The wire, tape, and rope Hubs had tied the Mal Rous's bodies with were in pieces near the gunny sacks he'd wrapped them in. Still, when Hubs opened the refrigerator, its emptiness shoved them back a step.

The silence in the house herded them swiftly from room to room, fear binding the three of them together so they moved as one, making silent gestures to communicate. In the dining room they saw a paint can and the shattered window.

At the bottom of the stairs, they found a green blanket piled in a heap. Next to it, more bones. Jaden recognized the yellow shade of the shredded fabric.

"Tig," Jaden mouthed.

Near the closet were two more crocheted blankets. Jaden used her machete to spread them open. "Nothing," she said in a low voice.

She glanced back at the kitchen. Had Esere carefully removed his siblings from the refrigerator, only to be butchered by the Quellers.

Hubs aimed his gun toward the top of the grand staircase as he led the way up. The three of them hurriedly moved from Amelia's room to Dekle's but didn't find any bones or bits of clothing.

Elvina's bedroom door was open. Jaden stopped at the doorway and stared at the red stain on the floor, remembering when they had found her mother lying there in a pool of blood, her head cut open and punctures in her calves where Anders had dug in his tentacles. Her mother had been painting the walls. The open paint can and dried-up paintbrush lay near where her mother had fallen.

Jaden turned and looked down the hall, succumbing to a sudden wave of panic that a Mal Rou was sneaking up on them. "If Anders was with Esere, do you think he got away?"

Briz arched an eyebrow. "It would be a lot easier to gather up his bones than capture him."

"M-maybe his b-body is outside. D-datura and Ivan, too."

Hubs was right, but there were acres of land. Dead or alive, how would they find them?

Hubs dumped out a large box of Elvina's old clothes and handed the box to Briz. "F-for the b-bones," Hubs whispered. Downstairs, Hubs found a couple of cleaning rags and handed one each to Jaden and Briz. "To p-pick up th-their remains."

They gathered up Tig's and Esere's bones and shreds of clothing, the gunny sacks, even the bits of rope and wire.

Jaden heard Hubs take in a deep breath as they stepped outside. Briz set the box on the hood of the car as they scanned the yard.

"T-three m-more to find." Hubs marched toward the garage, clutching his gun.

Jaden hurried next to him, machete in hand. Hubs pushed open the door and they looked inside. Pieces of orange clothing surrounded what Jaden knew had once been Anders. She turned, watching Hubs. His attention was fixed on the trees as he retrieved the box.

She looked across the yard at Briz. He was standing where the lawn butted up against the cane field. His eyes met hers and he pointed toward the ground.

Jaden and Hubs placed Anders's remains in the box, then carried it to where Briz was staring at the acres of dried cane. Jaden looked down to see teal-colored bits of clothes and strands of shriveled up tentacles. Briz used the tip of his machete to point at a finger.

"Datura." With a sharp inhalation, Jaden turned away, feeling an irrational sense of loss. "We have to find the rest of her. The triplets are counting on destroying the Mal Rous—every last particle of them so they can't ever reseed themselves."

"Jade, the Quellers carried her away. There's not a chance in hell we'd find all of her bones. They could be anywhere." Jaden followed Briz's gaze across the vastness of the plantation. "Besides, we might find more than her bones out there."

Like the Quellers, Jaden thought.

"Let's just get out of here," Briz sighed.

"Ivan," Jaden said, glancing around the yard. "We have to find Ivan."

"I think he's under Hubs's car." Briz's tone was as rigid as his expression. "I saw some blue material near the back tire."

They placed what remained of Datura in the box, then Hubs stepped toward the field. Jaden thought he was going to urge them to look for the rest of her. Instead, he shook his head in a sign of defeat, walked to his car, and pulled it forward. The three of them gathered up Ivan's bones and scraps of clothing.

"I forgot my mom's purse. It's on the buffet in the dining room." As Jaden entered the house, Briz stayed at her side. She wondered if it was because of his desire to keep her safe or was he afraid, too? Jaden looked toward the broken window on the French door. "We should put something over that. To keep out raccoons, rats..."

"And Quellers," Briz added under his breath as he went into the kitchen and grabbed a large cutting board to cover the hole.

They shoved Elvina's antique buffet against the cutting board to hold it in place. Then, with her mom's purse on her arm and her machete in her hand, Jaden and Briz hurried back to the porch.

"Since the Quellers ingested the Mal Rous, will they take on the Mal Rous traits?" Jaden wondered aloud as she locked the back door and re-hid the key. She knew Briz had heard her, but he didn't respond.

As the car pulled away from the house, Jaden turned and looked out the back window. They still had to capture the Quellers. But she felt one step closer to being free of her lunatic grandfather Dekle's experiments. Jaden looked up at the second story window. An image stared back. *Datura? That's impossible. She's dead.*

She has to be dead!

The small Mal Rous's hands were pressed against the glass. Jaden squinted as sunlight glared off the window, erasing the image of Datura as quickly as it had appeared.

It's her ghost, intent on haunting me for the rest of my life.

CHAPTER 25

BRIZ

When Briz pulled up, he saw Brooke standing in a patch of shade in front of the rental house. She waved at him, then went back to swatting at mosquitoes and talking with her landlady. Briz got out of his car but kept his distance, not wanting to interrupt their conversation. Instead, he gave a smile and nod of greeting to the two women.

"Right now, I'm low on cash," he heard Brooke say to her landlady. "Will you take the money for the cost of repairing the window out of my deposit? Again, I'm truly sorry we weren't here to keep an eye on things while you were in New Orleans."

"That's nice of ya, dear, but I don't think it was yer fault that someone broke into the house. I'm just grateful they didn't take anythin'—they were just bein' nasty." The landlady patted Brooke on her shoulder. "Don't ya worry, it'll all work out. I'm sure the police will find yer car."

Despite knowing her car was stuck in a dried-up cane field, Briz observed Brooke nodding in agreement.

Brooke thanked her landlady, then walked over to Briz and, keeping her voice low, asked, "Where's Jaden?"

Without answering her question, Briz handed Brooke her purse and cell phone. Then he pulled a small key from his pocket. "She wanted me to give you this. She found it in with the inheritance papers Amelia's lawyer sent you."

"Briz. Where's Jaden?" Brooke asked again, taking the key.

"Uh, she said you knew." Briz opened his hands as if pleading his innocence.

"Knew what?" Brooke demanded.

"That you'd agreed that, of all people, Hubs shouldn't be on the boat alone with the Mal Rous, even if they are dead." He debated whether to tell her that all they found were their bones.

"She's going back to the triplets, isn't she? And then the cave?" Brooke shook her head. "To look for the rest of Dekle's journals!" Brooke's nostrils flared as she exhaled.

Briz shrugged his shoulders as he opened his car door. He had no interest in standing there in the heat defending Jaden's actions. Or his actions—he'd figured Jaden had lied to him, that her mom never would have allowed her to go back to the triplets or the cave. He'd tried to talk Jaden out of going, but she had made up her mind.

Briz was about to tell Brooke that Hubs would go to the cave with Jaden, knowing it had somewhat eased his own feelings of trepidation, when Brooke walked to the passenger side of the car and opened the door.

"Get in. Please," she said as she slid into the seat.

"What?" Briz frowned as he leaned down and looked at Brooke fastening her seatbelt.

"I need a ride. I want to talk with the triplets' stepfather,

Dr. Whiting. I know you've been there. You took Jaden to see him."

"Yeah, but don't you think it would be better to have Hubs take you?" Briz stalled. Right now, he just wanted to go home and make sure his family was all right, take a shower, and wash off the rank images of the Mal Rous remains that were stuck in his head.

"I don't want to wait." Brooke's voice cracked. "I can't sit around doing nothing. I've been doing nothing for days. I want to get some answers about Dekle—find out if Dr. Whiting knows what happened to him."

Briz was listening, but as he got in the car, his focus was on Ava standing at the front door, wearing a short bathrobe, her hair dripping wet.

"Briz, I'm struggling here, trying to figure things out," Brooke was saying. "I don't know what else to do. I have to start somewhere. My daughters are in danger..." The sound of her voice shifted toward the car's front window. "You're in danger."

"Hey, Mom," Ava called out. "Did he get your purse? Are you going to the market?"

Brooke held up her purse.

"Briz, take my mom to the market," Ava demanded when neither of them answered, then closed the door.

"Dr. Whiting's first," Brooke requested, giving Briz a beseeching smile.

Briz backed out of the driveway and gave a wave to the landlady, watching them from her porch.

"She wasn't too happy with us." Brooke's words pushed past the fake grin she was bestowing on her landlady. "Coming home from her trip and finding the apartment window broken, and us gone when we'd promised to keep an eye on the place."

"What did you tell her?" Briz asked as he pulled into the street.

"That the Mal Rous did it." A meek grin flitted across Brooke's face. "What *could* I tell her? I lied. I said that the girls and I thought we were just taking a day trip to Lafayette to pick up supplies for Carl, and I got sick and ended up in the hospital, and then my car was stolen. I told her this was our first day back, and I was shocked to learn the place had been broken into."

"Ah, no wonder she seemed sympathetic. If she only knew your week was so much shittier than that." Briz glanced at Brooke. "Sorry."

"No, I think saying I've had a shitty week is an understatement." Brooke gave a laugh that sounded a bit unhinged.

Briz stared at the road, feeling completely unqualified to help her keep her sanity.

"So..." Brooke turned toward him. "Are you having sex with my daughter?"

The car swerved as Briz looked over at Brooke. He quickly jerked the wheel, bringing them back into the lane.

"I didn't mean for my question to upset you." Brooke chuckled. It was less unhinged, but still a bit loopy.

"No." Briz sounded like he was being choked. He cleared his throat. "No, I'm not having sex with either one of them."

"Either one of them?" A hint of amusement flickered in Brooke's voice.

Briz could feel a flush of heat brighten his cheeks.

"Jaden's too young." Now, all traces of humor were

gone, making Brooke seem totally unbalanced. "And Ava has a boyfriend—though sometimes I think she likes to forget that fact. But she does, and they've been together for over a year."

"Jade didn't think you'd—" Briz stopped mid-sentence, thinking, *You'd what? Mind if he deflowered her daughter?* He thought about how embarrassed he'd felt during the whole sex talk his dad had given him when puberty first hit. But this...this was worse.

"You're the first boy she's ever shown any serious interest in. With all she's been through, I don't want her to leave town with a broken heart, too." Briz knew Brooke was staring at him, but he kept his eyes on the road. "She's only fifteen, and you're eighteen."

"I just turned eighteen two weeks ago, and Jaden will be sixteen in a couple of weeks." Briz pressed his lips together as soon as the words were out, wishing he hadn't just said that.

"And sixteen's the magic number, is it?" Brooke countered with attitude.

"I...I didn't mean it like that. But Jade's really bright. She wouldn't let anyone talk her into doing something that she didn't feel was right for her. She thinks things through."

"She used to." Brooke inhaled slowly, then released a deep breath. "I'm not so sure now that she's not *completely* herself."

"Mrs. Lisette, I wouldn't do anything to hurt Jade."

Brooke turned away from him and looked out the passenger window. To Briz's relief, she changed the subject and asked, "Back at Guyon Manor...the Mal Rous were dead. They hadn't survived?"

"They're definitely dead," Briz answered, gripping the

steering wheel tighter. "And Rick's truck wasn't on the side of the road."

"Rick." Brooke said his name with a sigh. "While I was waiting for you, I called Carl. When Rick didn't show up at home, his wife went looking for him." Brooke choked on her words. "The poor woman was alone when she found him. I hope she's all right...and her family. I know how hard it is for kids to lose their father, for a wife to lose her husband." Briz felt her summoning up the painful memories of her own husband's passing. "Rick's funeral is in two days. I want to go, and Jade and Ava should come with."

"Mrs. Lisette, I have to tell you, you're handling all of this really well."

"No, I'm not. Inside, I'm losing it—I just don't want my daughters to know. I need to be strong for them."

Briz stopped as a traffic light turned red.

"Briz, with all we've been through, please call me Brooke."

"Okay." He dipped his head forward in understanding.

"Why did your parents choose to move to Belle Fleur?" Brooke asked, looking at the tattered awnings on the stores that lined the old part of town.

"To be near my grandparents," Briz replied. "They're retired veterinarians and moved here after a huge storm swept through Southern Louisiana. They set up a kennel to take care of the abandoned and hurt pets."

"Very noble of them."

"I suppose so." The light turned green, and Briz steered the Prius through town. "I was a little kid and didn't really think about what they were doing. When I was fifteen, my grandpa had some health issues, and my folks wanted to be near him."

Briz turned onto a two-lane highway, and they rode in silence until the Meadow Seniors' Facility came into view.

"Mrs. Lisette...Brooke, what's the point of visiting Dr. Whiting?" Before she could answer, he continued, "I don't think the triplets will like it. I think his health is pretty fragile. How's telling him what's been happening going to help?"

Brooke replied urgently and without hesitation, like she'd been thinking obsessively about the stakes of the meeting for the past few days. "Violet believes there's a possibility that the Mal Rous can regenerate. What if she's right? Dekle had Mal Rou blood, so he could still be alive. I need to know what Jade's chances of survival are. Will Datura's DNA damage Jade's organs, shorten her life, lengthen her life?" Brooke's voice constricted as she whispered, "I can't imagine my life without her."

She's right. Datura's DNA had hyped up all of Jaden's senses and played with her hormones, but Briz hadn't considered that Datura's blood could cause serious damage to Jaden's body, or worse. That it could kill her.

Briz couldn't, wouldn't, imagine Jade gone.

Parking in the shade of a tree, Briz observed Brooke, who was gripping the door handle tightly. He wondered if she was having second thoughts about confronting the elderly man. But she was right. What Dr. Whiting knew could help Jaden.

"Let's do this," Briz said, getting out of his car.

CHAPTER 26

BRIZ

Briz held the door to The Meadow Seniors' Facility open for Brooke. She stepped past him and walked over to the receptionist's desk.

"Hello," the receptionist greeted them with a chipper Southern twang.

"Hi," Brooke replied sweetly. "We're here to visit with Dr. Whiting."

The woman reached to the back of her long neck, tidying the loose strands of hair that had escaped from her bun, as she said, "Dr. Whiting is in room twenty-two. Just down that hall there, and to the right."

As they walked down the corridor, Briz noted that with each step, Brooke stood up straighter, as if she were filling herself with the resolve to accomplish her goal. She knocked once on the door, and without waiting for an answer, she went inside.

Propped up in the hospital bed, Dr. Whiting reminded Briz of an old wooden puppet. The doctor smiled at Brooke as she went over to him. Briz closed the door while glancing around the room. Opposite the bed were two recliner chairs, a bookcase, and a painting on the wall depicting an old-style Southern home, not as large as Guyon Manor, but just as impressive.

Briz shifted his attention to Brooke. She was looking at a photograph that was sitting on the nightstand next to the doctor's bed.

"Elvina…" Brooke said, surprised.

"Why, yes. And who might you-all be…?" Dr. Whiting's aged voice still held the rhythm of his Southern roots. "Ah, perhaps you're Jaden's sister. She recognized Elvina's photograph, too."

"I'm her mother." Brooke flashed an appreciative smile.

Dr. Whiting smiled. Then, in a heartbeat, his mouth curved down. "Is Jaden all right?"

Not answering his question, Brooke motioned for Briz to come closer. "I'm Brooke Lisette, and this is Jaden's friend, Brisbane Nolan."

"Hello, sir." Briz stepped next to the bed, reaching out to shake Dr. Whiting's hand. The skin covering the doctor's fingers felt cool to the touch. Instead, Briz gave his hand a light squeeze before lowering it onto the blanket. Hoping to put the man at ease, Briz pointed at the painting on the wall. "Did Olympe's husband, Billie, paint that?"

"Yes. It was my family's estate. It belongs to my girls and Hubs, and my son now."

Dr. Whiting's fingers trembled as he asked Brooke again, "Is Jaden all right?"

Brooke stared at the whirring air conditioner; it appeared to be distracting her from her mission. Briz remembered how unwavering, how positive she had been during the drive that coming to see Dr. Whiting was the right thing to do. Was seeing the doctor's feeble state giving her second thoughts?

"Jaden's fine, sir," Briz spoke the words the doctor was waiting for Brooke to say.

"She's with Hubs," Brooke added, barely finding her voice. "They're on their way to visit your daughters."

Good answer, Briz thought. *Polite. Vague.*

"Well then," said Dr. Whiting, "to what do I owe this pleasure?"

Briz was suddenly grateful that Ava wasn't there. She would have made some inappropriate comment like, "Cough it up old man. What happened to Dekle?"

Again, Brooke appeared to be losing her train of thought, as well as her balance. Her expression was blank as her body swayed slightly. Briz wondered when she had last eaten. He saw a metal chair pushed up against the wall and moved it behind Brooke.

"Here, Mrs. Lisette," Briz offered. "Why don't you sit down?"

Brooke pulled the chair closer. She reached over and sandwiched the doctor's hand between hers. "I wanted to ask you about Dekle Thatcher." As Dr. Whiting looked at Brooke's hands, his eyes widened with clarity, his mouth trembled.

"And the loup garou," the doctor's voice quivered. The aged, loose skin covering his throat moved over his Adam's apple as he swallowed. "Rougarous," he whispered.

Briz saw Brooke's puzzled expression and explained, "Cajun folklore, about creatures with a human body, similar to a werewolf."

"Yes, loup garou. Rougarous..." Then Brooke softly added, "Mal Rous..." Briz felt relieved that she didn't mention the Quellers, or that Jaden now carried traces of Mal Rou DNA in her veins. "I'm sorry, Dr. Whiting. On so many levels, for so many reasons."

"You shouldn't blame yourself." Hate resonated in the doctor's Southern accent. "Dekle Thatcher had a way of ruining people's lives." The doctor's hand went limp in Brooke's hand. "My, my family...?"

"They're fine, Dr. Whiting. Everyone is fine." Brooke patted the doctor's hand before letting it go.

"The Mal Rous are dead," Briz said with confidence, having just boxed up their bones. Though they had only found Datura's finger, he assumed there was nothing else left of her; he added, "All of them. They won't be able to hurt anyone ever again." The doctor didn't move. He just stared at Briz. "We thought you would want to know."

Brooke cleared her throat. "Dr. Whiting, I was hoping you could tell me what happened to Dekle." She folded her hands in her lap. Briz imagined this was how she conducted herself when questioning one of her disorderly fifth grade students. "If you think he's still alive. Where I might be able to find him?"

The doctor looked straight ahead. Then, without the blink of an eye, the words spilled from his mouth.

"I killed him."

Briz's eyebrows rose. Thinking he'd misunderstood what the doctor said, Briz hesitantly asked, "You...you killed him?"

Dr. Whiting nodded his head.

"*You* killed him?" Brooke repeated Briz's words as she slouched down in her chair.

Dr. Whiting raised a crooked finger to his lips, as if he were deciding what words he was going to let spill out next.

"Forgive me," Brooke prodded, "but how? Why?"

The doctor lowered his hand, his chest rising and falling with quick, jagged movements. Briz realized Dr. Whiting was too old, too frail. What had they been thinking, coming here, pressing him for answers like this?

Dr. Whiting looked over at Elvina's photo, then at Brooke. "I injected a rabies virus into him. I've always told myself it was an accident. Self-defense. Elvina and I didn't tell anyone. Not even my wife, Sara."

Dr. Whiting coughed, as if his guilt was choking him. Brooke handed the doctor a glass of water that was next to his bed. After a few drawn-out sips, he continued, "Elvina had come to our home that night, asking if Amelia could stay with Sara and me. Elvina was so afraid of Dekle, who he had become."

The doctor held the half-empty glass in his lap, both hands gripping it tightly, as if to stop his hands from shaking. "She asked for my help. I agreed to follow her home but was delayed. She had arrived at Guyon Manor probably twenty minutes before me. I'd parked at the head of the driveway. Dekle didn't hear me until I was opening the backdoor."

Dr. Whiting's southern accent ebbed and flowed like the murkier waters of the bayou as his memories rose to the surface. "I walked in to find Elvina tied to a kitchen chair, Dekle next to her with a sharp knife, the sleeves of her blouse and hunks of her hair lying on the floor and a half-empty vial sitting next to a full hypodermic needle on the kitchen table. Dekle stopped chopping off her hair and laughed when he saw me."

The doctor's shoulders hunched forward, as if he could no longer carry the burden of what he had done.

"I'll never forget the depraved joy in Dekle's laugh. He had always been jealous of Elvina's and my friendship. He said he was happy to see me and that he had enough of the rabies virus to inject in the both of us." Dr. Whiting released his hold on the water glass as Brooke reached over to take it. "Then he came at me. I'd never been in a fistfight in my entire life. He punched me a couple of times...he was bouncing around like a prizefighter. When I regained my balance, I charged into him, knocking him to the ground. The needle was on the table next to me. I grabbed it. I did what I had to. To save Elvina. To save myself."

"You...you had to," Brooke agreed, her voice filled with a longing to console him. "You had to do it."

Dr. Whiting took in her words with a slight nod of his head.

"Afterward, I sedated Dekle, and we kept him tied up in the garage for a few days. Once the rabies virus had consumed his body, I had the local police drive him to the hospital in New Orleans—the town didn't have an ambulance back then. By that time, Dekle was mentally unstable, delusional—"

"Wasn't he always," Briz broke in sarcastically.

"There was a time when I thought he was worthy of Elvina's love." Dr. Whiting's breathing was uneven. He leaned his head back against the pillow. "There were no bite marks on Dekle, no way for the doctors to know that he had rabies. I told them he needed to be put in a mental ward for evaluation. That was the last time I saw him."

"And the hospital staff just believed you?" Brooke asked.

"Things were different in those days. They had no reason not to believe me. A doctor's word was as good as a preacher's." Dr. Whiting rubbed his brow.

"Aww...." The abrupt sound rumbled from the doctor's chest as he lowered his hand and shrank back in his bed.

Briz was about to go for help, but it quickly became clear the doctor's pain wasn't physical. The doctor's emotions were written in every line on his old face. He had spent his entire life keeping his and Elvina's secret trapped in his soul. Now he had handed his secret over to Briz and Brooke. Briz could feel the weight of it lurking in the room.

"Should I get a nurse?" Brooke asked.

A hushed "no" passed over Dr. Whiting's lips.

"You did what you had to do to survive." Brooke's voice wore the fabric of understanding—a fabric woven by a woman who had been married to a military man. "If you hadn't, Dekle may have destroyed hundreds of lives."

Thousands, Briz thought.

Dr. Whiting pushed his hands against his mattress to raise himself up. Brooke stood and helped him. As she adjusted his pillow, the doctor continued, "There's something else you should know."

Brooke sank back onto the chair. Briz drew a hand through his hair, steadying his overtaxed mind, thinking he'd already heard enough.

"A month after Elvina and Amelia had left town, this woman came to my office, wanting to know Dekle's whereabouts. I think the woman's name was..." He paused, searching for the name. "...Mae. Or maybe it was Margie. Anyway, she was six months pregnant—with Dekle's child. Obviously, Dekle had mentioned me to her; there was no other reason she'd just show up. She said that she lived in Houma. I told her Dekle had fallen ill and that I'd had him taken to the hospital in New Orleans."

"Dekle was messing around on Elvina?" Briz's normally low, mellow voice squeaked. "He had another wife? He has another kid out there?"

"She didn't say they were married. She implied that she knew about Elvina. I can only assume she was telling me the truth about the child being Dekle's. She said she was going to find him. Then she exited my office as quickly as she had appeared. I never told Elvina. I didn't see any reason to upset her more. I never told anyone. Until now."

"If Dekle did die from rabies—" Brooke started to say.

"Without being given the vaccine, there is no *if*," Dr. Whiting stated.

"Okay, so...if this woman claimed his body, he might be buried in Houma?"

"Perhaps." Dr. Whiting reached for his water.

"Here." Brooke handed Dr. Whiting the glass, holding it with him as he steadied his hand. "I'm sorry to have upset you."

"Don't blame yourself for things that happened a long time ago. Before you were even born." The doctor looked as if he'd mustered all his remaining strength to comfort her even though Brooke had come here ready to demand information from him.

Brooke rose and gave Dr. Whiting a gentle hug as she thanked him, and they said their goodbyes.

Briz and Brooke were silent as they walked through the parking lot. When Briz started the car, he glanced at Brooke. "Wow, that's a lot to digest."

"How has Jaden been keeping it so together?" Brooke's voice cracked. "She's been going through this for a month—and you. Neither one of you ever complaining, just persevering."

When Briz turned onto the highway, he heard a sharp inhalation, then another.

"Jade." Brooke's voice was plaintive and hopeless, heavy

with tears. "What's going to happen to my girl? I wish I knew how to help her."

Briz pulled the car to the side of the road. As Brooke's crying turned into sobs, Briz reached across the center console and put an arm around her shoulders, doing his best to comfort her.

BRIZ

Briz opened the backdoor of his car and removed a bag of groceries; handing it to Brooke, her voice faltered, "Thank you, Briz. For everything. For taking me to Dr. Whiting. To the store. You're a good kid." While at the market, she'd kept her sunglasses on, hiding her red, puffy eyes. With a forced smile, she added, "But I still don't want you to be *intimate* with either of my daughters."

Right on cue, Ava came sauntering out of their apartment. "What took you so long? I thought you were just going to the market."

"We did a number of things." Brooke glanced at Briz, her expression confirming she didn't want to elaborate.

"Here." Briz grabbed the other bag of groceries and handed it to Ava.

"Aren't you coming in?" Ava asked.

"No. I need to see my parents. Let them know I'm back from my *camping trip*."

"That's right." Brooke grimaced. "They think you've

been camping all this time. Not being the town superhero, killing monsters and cleaning up their remains."

"Let's not forget getting brutally attacked by a pod of flying demons," Ava added, moving closer to Briz as her mom headed to the house. With the grocery bag in one arm, Ava gave him a drawn-out kiss on his cheek, slowly gliding her lips toward his mouth.

Briz was aware that it didn't feel like an *oh, you're so brave* type of kiss. His head seemed to involuntarily tilt, his lips meeting hers. Straightening up, he took a step back. What was it with her? What was it with him? *This is messed up*, he thought. *I'm still messed up.* He ran his hand over the nicotine patch on his arm, as if it would stop him from being attracted to her, even if he didn't particularly like her.

"I love it when you're naughty," Ava said, her lips teasing at his ear.

Brooke paused at the front door, turning around as her daughter stepped away from Briz. "Tomorrow, what time did you want to leave for New Orleans?"

"New Orleans?" Ava chirped. "Is he taking me to the airport?"

"No. He's taking me to rent a car." Ava gave her mom a raised eyebrow. "Don't start, Ava. I'm really tired."

"Mrs. Lisette...*Brooke*," Briz interrupted before Ava had the chance to say anything, "I've been thinking. My grandpa has a pickup truck I used to drive before I got my car. It's an old half-ton, but it runs. I'm sure he'd let you borrow it. He has a newer truck he drives."

Ava answered first. "Say yes, Mom," she implored. "Not that I'm into dumpy old trucks, but it would save us money."

Brooke's eyes shifted to Ava and then back to Briz. "That

would be nice. Thank you. But if your grandfather isn't comfortable with it, I'll understand. After all, I am a stranger to him." Brooke returned her gaze to Ava. "Let him know that I *will* pay him. Otherwise, I'll rent a car for the next couple of weeks."

"Thank you, Briz." Backing away, Ava blew him a kiss.

On the drive home, Briz ran his hand over his mouth, wanting to get rid of the sensation of Ava's lips on his. "Jade," he sighed, "I *need* to see you again."

Briz parked in front of his house and looked at his calves. Olympe was right; the marks weren't as pronounced as the scars on his arms. If anyone noticed, he could say he'd stumbled into a thorn bush.

"G'day mum," Briz said, mimicking his mother's fading Aussie accent as he walked into the kitchen.

"You're home." His mom greeted him cheerfully. "And just in time for tea."

Tea. Briz smiled hearing his mom use the Aussie term for supper. He looked to see what she was making. The food at the triplets' was good, but his mom...his mom was the best cook. There were times that his friends, who couldn't grasp the concept of being a vegetarian, had offered to pay to eat at his house.

"Is that new?" she asked, glancing at his shirt before opening her arms for a hug.

"It's Grover's." Briz hesitantly hugged her, knowing he reeked of nicotine. He was ready to embellish the lie and tell her Grover smoked cigarettes.

His mom leaned back, her eyes taking him in as if noting something was different with her boy. Briz rubbed his neck, covering the spot where Olympe had removed the Queller's stinger. She didn't push for more info—raising four teenagers had enough challenges. She was good at letting some things slide.

"How was your trip?" she asked, turning back to the stove.

"Not bad." Briz shrugged, having already decided what fabricated story he was going to tell her. "On the way home, I stopped by to see Jaden. Do you think Grandpa would let her mom use his old truck? Their car was stolen."

"Their car was *stolen*. Here in town?"

"No. They had gone to Lafayette to pick up supplies for the electrician." *Lie. Lie. Lie.* "I know Grandpa doesn't know them, but it would be nice to help them out."

"Give him a call. It won't hurt to ask," his mom said, looking over her shoulder at him. "Oh, and call Abigail. She called here when she couldn't reach you on your mobile."

"Okay." Briz paused, sussing out his next tall tale. "I have to head out again tomorrow. Think Dad will mind if I'm gone a few more days? I promise when I get back, I'll help him with work every day until I leave for Europe."

"I'm sure it's fine—he's programmed computers for years without your help. Where're you going?"

"Grover found out his friend's uncle is in the hospital up in Monroe. He was close to the man and wants to go see him, but his car is at the mechanics. He asked if I could give him a ride."

"I hope Grover realizes what a good friend you are." Briz's mom gave him a sidelong glance, doubtful of Grover's ability to appreciate her son's good deeds.

Briz stared down at the floor, knowing it was Grover who was saving his butt right now.

"Uh, do I have time to call Grandpa before tea?"

"Twenty minutes, give or take."

Briz closed his bedroom door and exhaled. It felt good to be home, in his own room. After he called his grandfather and proficiently lied to him about Brooke's car being stolen, then to Abigail as to why he hadn't gotten her calls, he punched in Grover's number.

"Hey bro, how was your camping trip?" Grover asked with a snicker.

"Good." A cheerful tone covered Briz's deception. "I, uh, need another favor. Can you cover for me for a few more days? Told my folks I'm driving you up to Monroe to visit a sick friend's uncle."

"All right! I guess your little *bebelle* Jaden dished out some *gogo* and you're wanting more?" Grover's enthusiasm felt like slime seeping into Briz's phone.

"No. It's not what you think."

"Bro, when you're a guy, it's always about the *gogo*," Grover confidently declared.

Briz swore to himself. Jaden wasn't a plaything. He cared about her. More than cared. On the day Ivan and Tig had abducted him, hadn't he told himself he loved her? On the other hand, he *wanted* her...and sadly, sometimes her sister. Maybe Grover was right. With a guy, it is always about sex.

"Did your brother Cylis ever fix the motor on his skiff?" Briz asked.

"Yeah, but ya know, he's out of town for another ten days. His apartment's empty if ya want to use it." Briz could hear Grover practically salivating as he spoke. "*Gogo* is a lot better in a bed than a crappy boat or a sleeping bag. The spare key is stuck in the plant by the front door."

"Thanks. I'll think about it," Briz said, scrunching his eyes shut. "Think he'd mind if I use the skiff?"

"Naw, he won't care. He likes you better than me, and I

can use it whenever I want. You know where the key is in the boathouse?"

"Ya." The sound of female voices drifted from the kitchen. Briz inhaled the aroma of dinner. "Thanks, buddy. I'll call you when I get back."

Surrounded by his family at the dinner table, Briz rattled off a couple of fabricated stories about his *camping trip*. The entire time, beneath the lies, he felt the ache of the truth wanting to be told. Words like *Mal Rous, Quellers,* and *albino triplets* were eager to escape from his mouth. He looked around the table at his parents and sisters. He wanted to warn them. If the Quellers found their way to town, his family would be in danger—especially if, like the Mal Rous, they could follow his scent.

At the same time, he knew if he told them about Dekle's mutant creations, his sisters would laugh it off and tell him they were too old to fall for his stupid made-up stories. Briz sipped his glass of water, remembering it had been a little over a week ago that he was sitting in this exact seat, eating dinner with his family, wondering if it would be the last time he'd see them, worrying that the Mal Rous were going to kill him. And here he was again.

Same worries. New monsters.

"...and so, he ran away," his sister Roma said, snorting as she laughed.

Briz looked at Roma. She was a year younger than him, and the two of them resembled their dad, while his older sister, Hartley, and Airlie, the youngest, were spitting images of their mom. Like Briz, his mom had named the three of them after towns and cities in Australia—it was her way of staying connected to her homeland.

Briz had no idea of what had been so funny, but everyone was laughing over Roma's story, so he joined in.

It was near eight o'clock by the time his dad took him to pick up his grandpa's truck. When Briz returned home, the fullness of the day hit him. He was ready for a shower, and then he wanted to sleep.

As the warm water streamed over Briz's back, he thought about Jaden sitting on the triplets' kitchen counter, his fingers gliding over her bare skin, about Ava's lips on his cheek moving toward his mouth and what it would be like to get lost in her kisses. His brain continued to be consumed by the Lisette sisters until the sound of knocking on the bathroom door ended his euphoria.

"Hurry up, you've been in there forever," Roma called out. "I want to shower, too."

Chapter 28

Jaden

The morning light filtered through the trees, not yet filling the shadows. Jaden looked out the bedroom window, straining to see what might be skulking in the yard. She didn't see anything, but the act left her unsettled. It reminded her she was stuck somewhere between the worlds of fact, fantasy, and horror. Her hand hovered over where Isadora had removed the stitches from her stomach the night before.

There was a tapping on her door. Jaden pulled the curtain closed.

"You'll need protection," Tamara said, carrying a bright yellow rain jacket with matching pants and plopping them onto the chair next to Jaden.

Jaden drew her head back, a small double chin forming as a testament to her doubt.

"Protection?" She didn't mean to sound ungrateful, but it seemed a rifle would be more appropriate...or at least a stun gun. "They're made from plastic and polyester. I'll die from heat exhaustion if I wear them. We have knives for protection, and Hubs still has the gun he borrowed from his friend Stella."

"You won't be wearing them long enough to die from hyperthermia. Either way, you'll be sweating. It feels like a damn oven, and it's not even six o'clock in the morning. Tamara's short stature appeared to grow taller. She had a way of doing that when she was intent on making a point. "There's a good chance the Quellers have returned to the cave. It's home to them. The place where they first fed..."

Tamara's words brought vivid memories of Briz being attacked to the forefront of Jaden's mind. Maybe they didn't really need to look for Dekle's lab records. Or make certain there weren't more containers in the cave incubating with his experiments.

"You wear these, and if the Quellers do show up," Tamara continued, oblivious to Jaden's panicked musings, "you may have a chance of getting away from them before they can chew through the material. Or don't wear them, and the little beasts can start right in on eating your flesh."

Jaden picked up the plastic pants.

If the Quellers *were* there, with luck, she and Hubs could trap them back in the secret room. Eventually, the creatures would die. And that would be the end of them. At least until the day came that someone found their remains and harvested their DNA. Jaden didn't want to think about that.

She also didn't want to consider what awaited her today.

"Here's a duffle bag for any sealed-up containers you might find. Make sure you douse everything with Non-Odeur. Your skin and clothes, too."

An hour and a half later, the sound of Velcro ripped through the silence as Hubs removed Stella's gun from his cargo pocket. Jaden glanced behind her. In the pitch-black tunnel of the cave, all she could see was Hubs's flashlight floating in midair, reassuring her that Hubs was still there. Entering Dekle's laboratory, Jaden and Hubs scanned the cavern in search of Quellers. The creatures hadn't returned.

Hubs lowered the duffel bag to the ground as Jaden stepped past the toppled refrigerator. With Hubs right behind her, they entered Dekle's secret room. Their lights shone across the floor, illuminating the broken ceramic vessels the Quellers had been stored in for decades, and the patches of Briz's dried blood that stained the ground.

Chicken skin bloomed on Jaden's arms. The water container she had left behind was lying empty on the other side of the room. Had it been kicked over there when they were picking up Briz?

Hubs stepped into the middle of the chamber. His flashlight fell to the ground as he made a gurgling sound, like he was sucking in his very last breath.

Jaden's light went from the gun in Hubs's hand to where it was pointed.

An ear-piercing screech filled the small cavern as her flashlight lit up a tiny creature wrapped in Briz's bloody bandana that had been left behind. The *thing* covered its eyes from the light as it huddled next to one of Dekle's unopened jugs. It stood only six inches tall, with human facial features, brown tangled hair that resembled fur, and oversized, pointed ears. Its skin, having never seen the light of day, appeared translucent.

"What is it?" Jaden gasped. She heard the click of Hubs cocking his pistol.

"Wait!" Jaden shifted her flashlight to the ceiling, diffusing the light. Shaking, the creature uncovered its enormous eyes, its screeching subsiding. "It might be a Bellibone, like Violet."

Jaden approached the small creature. It immediately resumed screeching and pressed itself against the cavern wall.

Jaden stepped back.

The creature dropped Briz's bandana, revealing its female, human-like body. It started flapping its wings. The effect was like a nestling learning to fly, rising a foot off the floor before plopping back down. Unlike Violet's damselfly wings, this creature had two sets: the tops were curved, colorful like a butterfly's, the bottom webbed like a bat's.

"Roses...Can you smell it, Hubs?" Jaden breathed in the scent as she watched it struggling to fly. "The more she tries to fly, the stronger the fragrance."

Jaden looked over at Hubs. He was standing there with his mouth open.

"Look at her feet," Jaden added. "They're human, but the toes are long with claws, like a bat."

The creature tried again to take flight but was too weak.

"We can't leave her here," Jaden said, wondering how they would accomplish the task.

"C-close the d-door, so s-she c-can't get out."

Jaden moved slowly, trying not to frighten the creature more. When she turned back around, Hubs was crouched down, his gun at his feet next to his flashlight.

"It's m-more s-scared t-than we are." Hubs took a sealed package of sunflower seeds from his pack and tore it open before tossing several seeds toward the creature. It sniffed the offering, then consumed them, shells and all.

Jaden aimed her light into all the room's nooks and

crannies, wanting to be certain another one of Dekle's experiments wasn't hiding.

Hubs pulled out a flask of water from his pack, filled the top, and set it on the ground. The small creature resembled Violet enough that he didn't seem to be afraid. Jaden came up behind Hubs and put her hand on his shoulder. The creature growled at her.

"S-she don't like ya. Ya s-should w-wait in the other r-room."

"Are you certain?"

"Yup. I g-got the g-gun."

Jaden stepped away from Hubs, opening the door wide enough that she could slip through. He was right; her presence was only making the creature more nervous. She left the door open a hair, then sat on the floor of Dekle's laboratory to wait.

Surrounded by darkness, Jaden felt small and alone, even with Hubs so near. She wanted to call out to him, hear his voice, know that he was all right, but she stopped herself. Leaning against the wall, she removed Briz's hunting knife from her pack. Grateful he'd left it with her, Jaden sighed his name.

When they'd parted ways yesterday, Hubs had left them standing behind the boathouse while he waited on his boat. Briz had promised to write to her from every town he visited in Europe. Then he'd tipped her head up, and their lips had merged, despair filling their kisses. She'd reached behind him, gripping his shirt, pulling him closer, wanting to eliminate any remaining space between them.

From that point on, *space* was all that would be between them. It was the last kiss she'd ever share with him. She had sent him home. She didn't want him to get hurt again. He'd promised he wouldn't come back to the triplets', that he wouldn't be involved with capturing the Quellers.

Jaden's focus moved past her thoughts of Briz, to where her flashlight was pointing. Its circle of light glistened on a barely noticeable bulge on the wall. She walked over and ran her hand across the outline of the swollen area. It was no more than ten inches wide by one foot high; so subtle it was no wonder she and Briz hadn't noticed it before. Thankfully, it seemed too small to hide a container with some new mutant horror.

With her flashlight in one hand and Briz's hunting knife in the other, Jaden picked and scraped at the coating of salt. Large chunks broke off as she jammed the knife along the edges of what felt like a cubbyhole.

Jaden smiled, wishing Briz were here, knowing how much he'd love one-upping Dekle by finding his lab reports.

"This is for you, Briz." Jaden wedged the knife into the side of the corroded hinges that had emerged and broke the cover free.

The success of finding a tarnished silver box rushed through her.

Jaden swore she could hear a demented laugh. She imagined seeing her insane grandfather smirk at her as she looked into the empty cabinet.

"Shut up, Dekle!" Jaden snapped at her dead grandfather, refusing defeat. "You had to have stashed your records in here somewhere! If you had one cabinet carved into the wall, you probably had another."

She moved around the room, washing her light over the walls, talking to herself. "Look for the obvious. In Dekle's mind he wasn't hiding anything...Yeah...okay, he was hiding everything."

The door to the second chamber creaked open.

"Ya is *aaall* right," Hubs cooed.

Jaden turned to find Hubs standing in the doorway with the creature, her tiny body wrapped in his clean handkerchief, perched on his wrist like a bird. Hubs stroked the fur on her head.

The creature's strange, Martian-like eyes widened, taking Jaden in. Jaden didn't dare move or speak.

"I'm *caaalling* her Rosie," Hubs informed Jaden, drawing out his words. "I *diidn't* see any *mmmetal* boxes. But *thhere* are *twoo* sealed jugs in *thhere*."

Jaden's lips parted in surprise. Hubs hadn't stuttered.

"I'll get them." Jaden moved in Hubs's direction, then stopped when Rosie squawked, and her wings started to flap. Jaden kept her voice soft. "Maybe you should wait for me in the main cavern. I want to look around some more."

"Ya ain't *affraid* to b-be in here alone?"

"No more than usual."

How sad, Jaden thought. Fear had become second nature to her.

"Don't you want to put Rosie *in* your backpack?" Jaden asked, seeing he was wearing his pack.

"Rosie's *fiine*," Hubs whispered.

Jaden wondered how he was going to get Rosie out of the cave, into the light of day, then onto the noisy boat. "But won't she fly away?" she asked.

"I got it *alll* f-figured out." With the gun in one hand, Rosie in the other, and his flashlight held in place under his arm, Hubs moved toward the tunnel. "Re-remember to p-put the new padlock on the *dooor*. It's in the *duuffle*."

"Okay." Jaden trusted he knew what he was doing. She

didn't move until the light from Hubs's flashlight had faded down the tunnel.

Alone in the pitch-black chamber, Jaden's slender flashlight suddenly seemed nothing more than a pinprick of light. "There's nothing else in here. Only me," she reassured herself, shoving aside an urge to run as she continued scanning the walls.

"It doesn't make sense. Why would Dekle hide his lab records but leave his journals in the metal box Briz and I found? Unless...he believed he'd be back after he'd killed Elvina." Jaden shivered. If his plan had worked, Jaden's dad would never have been born. She would never have been born.

Jaden grabbed the duffle bag and headed into the other room. The fact that she was deep in a cave, and all alone, hit her. She hurriedly ran her hands over every area of the walls that she could reach. But nothing stood out.

"There's no way I'm coming back here again," she spoke loudly, as if to abate the silence that was breathing noisily in her ears. "Maybe he's hidden his records at Guyon Manor."

As she stepped away from the wall, her foot hit a jug. Jaden froze as the clunking of ceramic hitting ceramic sent a chill up her spine. She aimed her flashlight down and saw the container had collided with the one Rosie had been huddled next to.

Jaden studied the two containers from where she stood. Had she just released another Rosie? More Quellers? Nothing was leaking out, the way it had when she'd inadvertently freed Tig weeks earlier.

She stepped closer and looked at the roughly carved letters on the rounder jug. "QB," she read quietly, as if anything louder might awaken what lived within it. "Queller." Using her foot, Jaden rolled the second container over. It looked to be twenty inches long and was cylindrical in shape. A large piece of ceramic broke off, and she stumbled back. "Crap!"

Jaden no longer heard silence breathing in her ears. Now it was the sound of her heart thumping in her chest. Her light lit up the hole and she waited for something to crawl out—then glanced at the jug with the QB staring at her. It was close enough that she could grab it and run; close the doors behind her. She wouldn't have to tell anyone. In time, whatever was in the cylinder would die...*wouldn't it?*

Nothing appeared. The cylinder seemed empty. *Or whatever was in it was already dead.*

"I can't stand here all day..."

Jaden exhaled as she looked at the door, wishing Hubs would come in and tell her not to worry, that he'd *take care of it.*

"Right...Take care of it."

Jaden picked up the round jug so she could make a mad dash out of the room if necessary. Then she stomped her foot down, smashing the cylindrical container.

A musty odor floated up.

"Paper...?" she whispered as she aimed her flashlight at the hole—where what looked like a roll of yellowed papers had been hidden inside. With the toe of her shoe, she pushed aside ceramic chips. Confident the cylinder held only paper, she squatted down. Shaking off the ceramic shards, she leafed through the pages.

The decomposing papers were filled with sketches of grotesque shapes. They weren't exact likenesses, but Jaden recognized the Mal Rous and Violet. Next to each drawing were notes scribbled in English and... *Latin?* Jaden carefully slipped the roll of papers into the duffle bag and the jug labeled "QB" in her pack. She stood and turned in a circle, checking the room one last time for any remaining containers.

"Nothing," she said with relief, stepping into the main laboratory.

Jaden surveyed the salt-covered, corroded remains of Dekle's entire life's work. As far as she was concerned, there was nothing else worth gathering up. Nothing to salvage. She gave a slight nod, silently saying goodbye and good riddance, before closing the door and slipping the new padlock in place.

CHAPTER 29

AVA

With her feet propped on the coffee table, Ava sat on the sofa, admiring her ruby red fingernails; giving herself a manicure was one of the first things she'd done when she and her mother returned to the rental yesterday. She looked over at the clock. *Eleven-forty.*

She had plans, and Briz was messing them up. Ava picked up her hairbrush—rapidly tapping it against the side of her knee as she waited for him to drop off his grandfather's truck.

"Finally," she huffed as a noisy engine brought her to her feet.

It'll be fine, she thought, striding over to the front door and flinging it open. She'd still have plenty of time to accomplish her tasks and make her great escape.

"What took you so long? You only live ten minutes from here." Briz stood there, looking at her with a dumbfounded expression. "Well, move it! Come on, get in here."

Ava shut the door behind him, cutting off the ever-invasive heat.

Her mom greeted Briz, and he gave the two of them the rundown on the truck's assortment of idiosyncrasies—the oil had to be checked every few days; the shocks weren't so good; the air conditioner, Ava wasn't happy to hear, ran more lukewarm than cold.

"What are the chances that Hubs will bring Jaden back to town by tomorrow afternoon?" her mom asked Briz. "I'd like her to come with us to Rick's—"

A grin spread over Briz's face as he interrupted Brooke. "I found a boat I can borrow. I can go get her for you."

Ava knew her mom asked because she wanted Jaden to attend Rick's funeral with them. Irked by Briz's *oh-so-cheerful* tone and elation about seeing Jaden, which Ava still didn't understand, she opened the front door and stepped outside into the wall of humidity. Slinking over to the shed, she snatched up the bag of clothes she'd hidden last night while her mom was asleep.

She had also raided her mom's secret stash of money and used her mom's cell to call her boyfriend, Albert, in Colorado. If Albert did what Ava had asked, there would be a ticket home waiting for her at the airport in New Orleans. Now she just had to find their car and get her driver's license so she could get on the plane.

Ava stuffed her hairbrush in with her clothes next to her phone charger, a bottle of Non-Odeur she'd taken from the triplets' house and a medium-sized butcher knife. She opened the truck's door, releasing a gush of hot air, then slipped the bag behind the passenger seat.

"Let's go," Ava said, walking back into the house, interrupting Briz and Brooke's conversation. "I'll give you a ride home." Ava fixed her gaze on Briz. "I'm sure you have better things to do...like toddling back to your precious little Jaden."

"Ava, be nice." Her mom gave Ava a stern look. "And I'll take Briz home. I don't want you driving without your license."

Ava laughed. "Mom, I really don't think it matters. Besides, if I get pulled over, I'll just tell the officers that deadly mutant rodents hijacked our car, kidnapped us, and poisoned us, and I haven't had time to find our car or my purse with my license. I'm sure they'll understand. Especially if they grew up in this town."

Ava held back more of her biting words, realizing that like her, Brooke had been through hell and back. The only difference was that Ava was done! She had spent the night planning her escape. If her mom drove Briz home, it would ruin everything.

Brooke crossed her arms as she stared at Ava. Ava mirrored her mom's stance.

A few moments passed. Then Brooke gave Briz the slightest head nod, surrendering as usual. Ava held back a grin as she reached out her hand, and Briz relinquished the keys to the truck.

Beads of perspiration spread over her skin as she and Briz slid onto their seats. She put the key in the ignition, turned the air on high, and waited for the steamed-up windows to clear. When they didn't, Ava opened the window and saw her mom watching them from the doorway.

Her mom gave a small wave goodbye.

Goodbye, Ava thought. As her eyes met her mom's, guilt pooled around her heart. She considered changing her mind. Either way, she'd have to give Briz a ride home. She swallowed the lump of indecision that was growing in her throat as she backed out of the driveway.

"Yesterday at the manor, did you see any sign of the Quellers?" Ava asked as casually as she could. She might be desperate, but she wasn't stupid. She wasn't about to drive into a cane field and be ambushed.

"No. We didn't *see* any Quellers. But we saw..." Briz paused and looked out the side window. "To be honest, they could be anywhere."

It wasn't what she'd wanted to hear.

"So, are we or aren't we safe?" Her words were clipped as she turned into Briz's subdivision. "Here, in Belle Fleur? At Guyon Manor? The Quellers could be in another town by now, right?"

"Sure. Why not?" Briz's tone was flat as he dragged his fingers through his hair.

Ava twisted her mouth to the side. She wasn't willing to let her plans be derailed by Briz's sarcasm. She was doing what was best for her! She longed for the safety of home; to achieve her goal, she'd have to take a chance. Everything would be fine. She had the Non-Ordeur so the Quellers wouldn't be able to smell her, and she had a knife for protection.

"Tell your granddad thanks for the loan." Ava stopped the truck in front of Briz's house. She couldn't look at him as he got out. By stealing the truck, she was on the verge of becoming a criminal. "We'll get it back to him in one piece." Then she added, "By the way, I know what Jaden did."

Without saying a word, Briz closed the door. Ava wondered if he'd heard her. Did he know what she'd meant? That she knew everyone's little secret, that Jaden had tried to kill her.

Ava turned the radio on and cranked up the volume as she drove down the street, the pickup bouncing over every bump. The truck was old, but it still had some kick. Once she reached the dirt road that led to Guyon Manor, Ava sped up, leaving a whirling dust storm trailing behind.

"I'm going home," she sang out over the music.

Happily, she reviewed her plans: she'd get her purse, drive to New Orleans, then before boarding the plane, she'd call her mom and tell her where to find the truck.

Her sparkly attitude dissipated as she drove past the crushed growth where Rick's truck had crashed. Green sprigs were rising, reaching toward the sun. Life had continued, oblivious of the Mal Rous, oblivious that they had killed Rick. As if none of what they'd all been through had ever happened.

Ava looked in the rearview mirror and touched the fading scars on her neck, remembering the sensation of tentacles slithering over her skin; her mother slumped in the seat next to her, unconscious; and the two of them being slapped awake by the pack of Mal Rous in the middle of the cane field.

What was she thinking, leaving her mom to fend for herself?

"Screw it! Mom made her decision." Ava jabbed at the radio, shutting it off. *She doesn't have to stick around here any more than I do.*

Without glancing in its direction, Ava passed Guyon Manor. *We should sell the Mal Rous's bodies and Dekle's journals. We'd make millions. Way more than we'll ever get selling that dump.*

Ava scrutinized the ground that bordered the field along the road, looking for tire tracks or any other sign of their car.

"It has to be around here somewhere," she muttered with frustration.

At the end of the road, she found the slightest sign of tracks in a patch of flattened weeds and brush. It led toward the bayou, which fit with Ava's memories of sitting on a boat soon after being abducted. She turned into the field, drove a short distance, then stopped and climbed into the back of the pickup; raising her hand to block the sun from her eyes, she searched for their expired car.

"Wahoo!" Ava smiled as she spied the car roof, visible above the dead cane that stretched between her and her chance to fly home. She jumped down from the truck bed, removed the Non-Odeur from her bag and slathered it over her skin and clothes, then grabbed the knife and patted the hood of the pickup. "Can't take you any farther. I'll be right back."

Ava stepped through the foliage, holding the knife tighter as she looked toward the sky for Quellers. *I'm going home*, she repeated over and over in her head as branches scratched her legs and sweat dripped from every pore on her body.

When she reached the car, the front doors were wide open. Her sunglasses were on the console, broken.

Ava put her hand to her mouth, muffling a gasp as she spied a snake coiled up on the floor in front of the passenger seat—hopefully asleep. She looked in the back seat at her purse. Slowly opening the back door, she looped the butcher knife through the straps of her purse and tiptoed away from the car.

I'm in hell! Snakes, alligators...deviant monsters. My sister wanting to murder me. With her purse hanging from the knife, she gave it a shake. Nothing emerged.

Ava held her arm out, putting as much distance between herself and the purse as possible, as she hurried back to the truck. Dropping her purse in the truck bed, she used the knife to peek inside. She saw her wallet, her cell phone, and what she considered to be two mouse-sized cockroaches, which promptly flew in her direction.

"Get away from me," Ava snarled, ducking, and swatting with the butcher knife as if she were samurai ninja. "If I didn't need my license, I wouldn't have bothered you in your new home!

"Ow!" Ava jumped back as a stabbing pain pierced her ankle. She looked down to see two thin lines of blood dribbling onto her sneaker. "What the hell bit me?" Ava hurried into the hot cab, opened the window, and cranked the truck to life. Her foot felt as if it was swelling. "Is it snake bite?" Untying her shoe, she whimpered, "I just want to go home!"

CHAPTER 30

JADEN

"Did ya find anything in the cave?" Olympe called out as Hubs motored up to the dock. Her two long braids and blue blouse gave her identity away.

"Yeah," Jaden jumped onto the dock, handing Olympe their "protective" gear, then tied off the pirogue. "Some of Dekle's notes."

Jaden decided it was best not to elaborate as she glanced at Hubs, who was needlessly puttering around on the boat until his mama turned and headed back to the house.

"I'll take the bags," Jaden offered as she stepped back onto the boat. She hung the strap of the duffle bag over her shoulder and nestled the backpack with the ceramic jug close to her chest.

Hubs bent down to where Rosie was hidden from view under one of the seats. "I'll be a *mminute. Mmmaybe* ya can d-distract everyone."

Jaden understood. Hubs wasn't ready to expose Rosie to more humans. In the house, Jaden followed the sound of voices coming from the kitchen. Isadora was at the sink, while Violet and Tamara were seated at the table.

"Olympe told us you found Dekle's records," Tamara said as Jaden gently set her pack and the duffle bag on the kitchen table.

"I found something. But it's not his lab records."

"Well, let's have it." Tamara reached hastily for the pack.

"No!" Jaden's eyes met Tamara's, and she spoke in a kinder tone, "That one's a container...with QB carved on the side."

Tamara's shoulders drooped forward.

That's me...always the bearer of good news, Jaden thought as she unzipped the pack and lifted out the jug.

Tamara ran her fingers over the letters on the jug. "At least it wasn't released like the others." She glanced up as Isadora came and stood behind her.

Jaden opened the bag and lifted out the notes. Flakes of aged, yellowed paper sprinkled onto the table as she set them down. "I looked all over for his lab records. But these are all I found. They were sealed in a ceramic cylinder."

Tamara reached over and gently lifted one page after the other. "It's all drawings. His notes are written in..." Tamara put on the glasses that were on a chain around her neck, "...in Latin. Nearly all of them."

"We'll have to try to decipher them." Isadora leaned closer as Tamara gave her a dismayed look. "Don't look at me like that. It's doable. Every one of our books here on herbs gives both their common and their Latin names. I've never paid much attention, but our gardening books about insects state their Latin names, too. Besides, what other options do we have?"

"Jaden, is Hubs still on the dock?" Olympe asked, standing in the doorway.

Rigidly, Jaden turned toward Olympe and felt a little fib tying up her tongue as she stammered, "Ah, yeah...I, I think he was, was going to hose off the boat...or something." Jaden shifted her attention to Isadora. "You want me to get some of your herb and gardening books for you?"

"Thank you, dear." Isadora had slid several of the pages closer and was studying them. "You best bring my etymology book, too."

Jaden scooted past Olympe and down the hall, right into Hubs as he slinked out of her bedroom. "Your mama's wondering where you are," Jaden whispered.

Hubs sauntered into the kitchen as Jaden headed to the bookshelves.

"This one here sort of reminds me of you, Violet," Olympe was saying as Jaden came in with a stack of books in her arms. "But from the sketches drawn near it, it looks like he used bat and butterfly DNA. See, its wings...and its eyes, definitely butterfly."

Yep, bat and butterfly...that would be Rosie, Jaden thought as she watched Hubs sit up straight in his old wooden recliner, his neck stretched out to see the drawing.

"Oh my," Olympe declared after turning to another page. "I think he chose insects that are good at breeding."

"Breeding. Are you sure?" Alarmed and disgusted, Jaden plunked Isadora's books on the table.

"I daresay that is what it looks like." Olympe blew out a loud breath of air.

"Those are Quellers," Jaden identified the creatures in the drawings. "He made them...*cute.* I promise you, they aren't. We... I mean, *I* have to capture them before they reproduce!'"

Olympe shook her head as she said, "*We* have to."

"But..." Jaden wanted to insist that the triplets wouldn't be a part of this when Isadora interrupted her. She'd argue her point later.

"Not only procreate, it seems Dekle's goal was for them to survive on land and in the water. He combined fish and bird DNA, along with insect and plant. Here he's written, '*Fleogan Bocanáchs.*'" Isadora held the book on etymology and flipped through the pages. Then her thin finger followed the words as she read aloud. "*Fleogan* is Old English for 'move through the air with wings.'"

Jaden gave a shudder. "The other day you read bocanáchs means 'supernatural beings. So, fleogan bocanáchs means flying supernatural beings." Jaden pointed to a drawing. "Violet, look at these...are they drawings of the first Mal Rous? The ones Dekle took away?"

"They must be," Violet said, moving closer. "I don't recall them looking exactly like that, but look...that word, 'tardigrade.' Remember, I told you he used the DNA of tardigrade when creating the Mal Rous? He chose them because they can survive in very severe living conditions for decades."

"Yeah, I remember," Jaden sighed, rankled once again that this insane man was related to her.

Tamara was looking back and forth between one of the herb books and notes next to Dekle's drawings of plants.

"*Heracleum mantegazzianum.*" Tamara peered over the top of her glasses at Violet. "Just as you thought, its giant hogweed. It's what caused the blisters on Briz's arms." Tamara turned to another page in her book. "*Kalmia latifolia*, mountain laurel. Poisonous. Can cause vomiting, paralysis of arms and legs, coma, possible death within twelve to fourteen hours." Exhaling, she added, "And he has written here, 'green tobacco,' and 'tongkat'...whatever that is."

Tamara's head snapped up as a screech came from down the hall.

The triplets and Violet looked at each other. Then at Jaden.

"What's in your room, Jaden?" Tamara asked.

Jaden glanced at Hubs. After all, it was his room.

"M-maybe a B-bellibone." Hubs jumped up and strode across the kitchen.

"Another Bellibone?" Violet squeaked with surprise. "Like me?"

"N-not exactly." Hubs gave Jaden a quick glance as he started down the hall. "Wh-where are the cats?"

"In the garden house," Olympe responded, curiosity creasing the corners of her eyes.

"Let's stand over here." Jaden ushered the triplets and Violet to the opposite side of the island counter, dividing the onlookers from Hubs as he came back into the room holding Rosie close to his chest.

"Sh-she likes the *sssound* of my heartbeat."

"She's the one from the drawing." As Olympe's words of awe glided across the counter, Rosie cowered closer to Hubs.

After a few moments, Rosie's oversized, light-sensitive eyes peeked over at her audience. She focused on Violet, her eyes opening wider. Rosie looked up at Hubs, grinning. Then she looked at the others, revealing her full set of sharp, pointed teeth.

"Oh!" Isadora exclaimed. "Do you think she'll let us file those?"

"Shhh, shhh, Rosie, *yaaa* is okay," Hubs comforted, as Rosie began to screech. "D-don't look at her. It *friightens* her."

Everyone averted their eyes to the floor as Hubs stroked Rosie's fury head to calm her and took her back to the bedroom.

"Isn't that something...?" Isadora spoke softly, "Hubs hardly stuttered."

Jaden had to laugh. Hubs not stuttering was more amazing to the triplets than the sight of Rosie, a genetically engineered creature. Science and fantasy had officially become their reality.

"Was she hard to catch?" Tamara walked to the table and looked at the drawing Dekle had done of Rosie.

"She j-just came closer and closer..." They all turned toward Hubs, who had quietly returned. "She climbed *riiight* on my w-wrist. I was *sscared* as she c-crawled up my arm. I thought she was gonna b-bite me, but she *nuzzzled* my neck and purred. She n-needs food...Violet..."

Jaden thought it might have been the first time Hubs had ever started a conversation with the Bellibone.

"W-what do ya think I should *feeed* her?"

Violet's shock was apparent as her balance faltered in midair. "Well, Hubs," Violet said, as she made a less-than-smooth landing on the counter. "I'm not sure. If she's part bat, I suppose she's going to want to eat bugs. Some bats eat rodents, but she's also part human, so maybe some fruit."

Hubs gave Violet a nod and opened the refrigerator.

CHAPTER 31

JADEN

Jaden looked over at Hubs sitting in his recliner and Olympe at the kitchen table as she dried the last of the dishes from lunch. Hubs wore a tired but pleased expression as he held Rosie in his arms. The dainty creature was wearing a makeshift dress Hubs had fashioned for her out of a sock. Next time Jaden was in town, she'd buy Violet and Rosie some doll clothes to wear.

"Hubs, I'll sleep on the sofa tonight. You and Rosie can have the bedroom," Jaden said with a yawn.

"No. It's yer *rooom* f-for now. We'll be f-fine in the living *rooom*."

Tamara and Isadora came in carrying Dekle's journals that Jaden and Briz had found weeks before. Jaden yawned again as she dried the last of the lunch dishes.

"You're going to hurt yourself, yawning like that. Dislodge your jaw," Tamara said as she set the journals on the kitchen table next to the fragile stack of Dekle's drawings.

"Let her be." Isadora's gaze shifted from her sister to the

drawings. "Up at dawn, roaming the bayou, dealing with all this…"

"So has Hubs. So have we," replied Tamara with a salty tone.

"Yes, but we all had a nap while they were out and about, so quit your bellyaching." Isadora looked at Jaden and gave her a wink.

Jaden bit her lower lip, trying to hide her smile as she came around the island counter.

"We thought we should read through these again." Unfazed by her sisters' remarks, Tamara picked up a journal dated 1947 and handed it to Jaden. "When we read them before, we were concentrating on finding the mushroom formula. Maybe Dekle mentioned the Quellers and Rosie, and we missed it."

Jaden opened to a random page in the journal and read Dekle's meticulous handwriting aloud: "'I worry that they will be *lethalis*.'" Jaden paused. "*Lethalis?*"

"Lethal. Deadly. Fatal," Tamara answered in a blustery voice.

"So, there was a time when Dekle had a kinder heart," Isadora reflected.

"A kinder heart?" Jaden tried to buffer her annoyance. "Isadora, you're doing it again…defending this egomaniac whose life goal was to create an entirely new species."

"Why, yes, child…You yourself just read that he was *worried* they would be deadly. Which means it wasn't his original intent." Isadora focused on Violet. "Violet, dear, didn't you say that Dekle told you he'd tried to create others like you, only it wasn't until he'd added DNA from more aggressive species of plants, insects, and animals, ones that had better survival abilities, that his experiments were more successful?"

"Yes," Violet replied. "He also found that their feral instincts intensified after being combined."

"My point exactly," Jaden griped. "Even after the first 'batch,' he kept doing it. And combining them with human DNA? What was that about? It's not like humans are the most non-violent, non-destructive species on the planet."

Isadora peeked over the rim of her glasses at Jaden. "My dear girl, I know you want to think he was born abominable. And having known the man, I agree that in the end, he was. All I'm saying is that I don't believe he started out that way. He was a visionary. He created hybrid creatures with the intent of proving his theories about DNA and cloning, not harming people."

"Visionary?" Jaden exhaled her frustration. "If he were alive today, he would probably run one of those corporations that make genetically modified seeds. They don't seem to care that what they're doing might adversely affect humans over time, or even now. The GMO corporations could be genetically modifying humans to be cruel; evil like the Mal Rous and the Quellers...and the companies don't know it. Or like Dekle, they know and don't care."

A soft chirping came from Rosie. Jaden saw her eyes were open wider than normal.

Jaden lowered her voice. "Sorry. I shouldn't have been so loud."

"It's *okaay*. I'll t-take her into the living *rooom*."

Ah-ah-awwwah-ha-awwwah. Jaden yawned again.

"Wore yourself out, did you? Snapping at Isadora and defending your opinion," Tamara guffawed as she walked over to the refrigerator. "Did you ever think that her intention was to comfort you, knowing you're related to the man?"

Jaden looked from Tamara to Isadora and Olympe. As blunt and rude as Tamara could be toward her sisters, she was also protective of them.

"I'm sorry, Isadora," Jaden offered sheepishly. "I guess I just didn't want to think that Dekle was ever a good person."

Tamara placed a bottle of Envie Tea in front of Jaden. "Drink some of this to calm yourself down."

"O-o—," Jaden covered her mouth as another yawn interrupted her reply, "k-k-kay."

Tamara's eyes fixed on Jaden's. "If you're so tired, go in your room and take a nap."

"Jaden," Olympe said with a smile, countering her sister's tone. "I wanted to say how grateful I am that Hubs and ya found Rosie. It's wonderful! He's stuttering less and less, pausing, trying to enunciate his words. I think it's 'cos of Rosie's fragrance. We never tried using aromatherapy to help him. We tried herbs and homeopathic formulas. And drugs for stuttering, which he reacted badly to."

It was half-past two, but Jaden's eyes felt as heavy as if the clock had struck midnight as she carried her tea and Dekle's 1947 journal to her room. She sat on the bed and looked out the window. The clouds had stalled in the sky, covering the sun. Adjusting the mosquito netting around her, she realized that with Violet being part damselfly, she had seldom found a mosquito in the house.

Jaden leaned back on her pillow and opened Dekle's journal. A third of the way through, tucked into the binding, she found two black and white photographs, old and worn, as if handled too many times.

One photo looked like it had been taken in Dekle's cellar

laboratory at Guyon Manor—it definitely wasn't in the salt cave. Dated 1952, it showed a lab table with Violet standing next to a group of test tubes and jars. Plants hung down from the low ceiling behind the table. In the corner of the photo, she could make out a part of the crate that had imprisoned Briz.

The second photo was of Dekle holding a toddler. Next to him was a very pregnant Elvina. Jaden turned over the photo. Neatly written was: *The child was a stillbirth. A son ~ 1946.*

"A year before they moved from England to Louisiana," Jaden said to the empty room. "Well, you did have a son."

Jaden stared at the two photos until her eyes became bleary.

"Don't lie to me." The sound of a British accent sent a jolt through Jaden.

She looked toward the closet as Dekle stepped from the shadows, moving aside hanging plants like the ones in the photo—plants that moments ago hadn't existed. Jaden reached to pull the mosquito netting aside, then stopped, as if the sheer fabric would keep her safe from her illusions? Dekle studied Jaden as she studied him.

"I'm not lying. You did have a son, my dad. I am your granddaughter."

"You certainly don't look like any grandchild I'd have."

Jaden considered how she resembled her mother's side of the family; her Asian ancestry was ever-apparent in her dark eyes and hair.

"Well, I am. My sister, Ava, resembles Elvina."

"Mmm, my sweet, darling Elvina. I do miss her."

"Miss her? In your journal, you wrote you were going to kill her with the rabies virus."

Dekle moved closer, stopping when Jaden drew back.

"That wasn't me," he sighed. Then his voice grew louder. "It wasn't me. I worshiped Elvina. Datura's blood changed me. She's the one that wanted Elvina dead."

"Evidently you loved Datura more than Elvina," Jaden said with disgust.

Dekle lowered his head. "At first Datura's blood emboldened me. Then it controlled me."

"And now Datura's blood is in me." Jaden sat taller as Dekle raised his eyes to meet hers. "So, what now? Am I going to end up like you?"

"I am sorry. I truly am...I..." Dekle slipped into silence as he took a step back into the hanging plants. And then he was gone.

The journal fell onto the floor. Jaden's head popped up. The clouds had moved on, and the afternoon glow of sunlight lit the room.

"I dreamt it." She looked toward the closet. "Or am I losing my mind like he did?" Jaden picked up the journal, tucked the photos back in the binding, then closed her eyes and fell into a deep sleep.

Chapter 32

Briz

The box of nicotine patches sitting on Briz's desk challenged his better judgement. He'd never smoked in his life, but right now, he craved a cigarette. He hoped the nicotine, and other assorted poisons from the Quellers, would pass through his system in another day or two. His hormones were hyped up and out of whack. He felt emotionally unstable.

Briz turned the box over to read the patches' potential side effects: dizziness, headaches, nausea, abnormal or vivid dreams. He reluctantly applied a patch, thinking that he didn't want any more abnormal and vivid anything in his life.

His printer was pumping out pages of info about hornets, green tobacco poisoning, blue-hooded ifrita birds—everything Jaden and the triplets suspected Dekle had used in creating the Quellers—when his cell rang. "Hey, Brooke, what's up?"

"I'm really sorry..."

The hairs on the back of Briz's neck rose.

"What? Did something happen to Jade?"

"No...no," Brooke said, then fell silent.

So, what could be wrong now? Ava had just dropped him off a couple of hours ago. "Are you having a problem with the truck?"

"No. Well, yes. Ava's driven off with it. She's taken it to New Orleans."

"Seriously?"

"Sadly, yes." Exasperation strained Brooke's voice. "She never came back after taking you home. I saw she'd used my cell to talk with Albert yesterday, so I called him. Ava told him I had approved him booking her a flight and that I'd reimburse him. She's flying out of New Orleans this evening and arriving in Denver late tonight."

"She can't get on the plane without her driver's license," Briz stated.

"I know. I assume she went to find our car. Last night she asked me what I remembered about the day we were attacked...where I thought the car was. When I get back to Colorado, I'm going to..." Brooke released a loud huff, leaving Ava's punishment hanging in the ethers—to be decided at a later time.

"Do you want me to give you a ride to New Orleans and find her?" Briz asked.

"No. At least I know she'll be safe in Colorado. But your grandfather's truck...?"

Briz looked at the clock next to his bed. "I want to get to the triplets while there's daylight. The truck should be safe in the airport parking lot. It's pretty old. I doubt anyone would steal it."

"Ya. Hopefully you're right." Brooke paused before

asking, "Briz, when you see the triplets, please, don't mention that we went to see Dr. Whiting. Next time I see them, I'd like to tell them myself."

"No problem." Though Briz doubted there would be a next time. "Uh, Brooke, why don't I pick you up in, say, twenty minutes? You can ride with me to my friend's boat, then you can take my car to use." There was no reply. "You know, in case I don't get Jade back in time for the funeral tomorrow."

"I'd appreciate that. Thank you...for everything." Brooke sounded ready to cry. "I will get your grandfather's truck back."

"Don't worry. There's nothing we can do about it right now. By the time I bring Jade back, you'll have *talked* with Ava, and you'll know where she left the truck, and the three of us can go get it. I have to get ready. I'll see you soon." Without saying goodbye, he ended the call.

When Briz arrived at the triplets' house, Hubs was standing on the dock, looking to see who was making such a noisy entrance. Briz doubted they ever had visitors. He had planned to leave earlier in the day but had been waylaid researching Queller information. And helping Brooke had been more of a time-suck than he'd expected.

Briz killed the engine and tossed a line to Hubs.

"A friend of mine loaned his boat to me," Briz explained, slipping his backpack over his shoulder as Hubs tied the line to the dock. "Brooke sent along some food supplies and clothes for Jaden." Briz jumped from the boat, carrying two canvas bags.

"It's Briz," Hubs announced as he walked toward the garden.

Briz smiled at Isadora as she stepped from the screened enclosure—then something darted past her. It hovered in front of Briz with sharp teeth exposed, growling.

"A Queller!" Briz shouted.

Briz stumbled backward, his eyes wide as he swung the canvas bags through the air. The creature didn't look like the ones Jaden had described to him. But those teeth! What else could it be?

It moved quickly, and Briz started to swing again.

"No, Briz! Rosie!" Hubs shouted.

The thing's lip lowered over its teeth as it positioned itself two feet above Briz. It reminded him of Violet...Yet, it was nothing like her.

"It's *ookay*. He's a *frriend*." Rosie flew down and landed on Hubs's outstretched arm.

Briz watched Hubs bring his arm close to his chest and stroke the thing's furry hair. He wasn't stuttering. Was it because of her?

"Jaden and I *fouund* her in Dekle's *caave*."

Of course, where else would you find something as strange as that?

"Did you find Dekle's reports?" Briz asked, nervously watching Rosie.

"No *repoorts*. Just *nootes*." Hubs stepped back, putting some space between him and Briz.

Briz took notice of how protective Hubs and the creature were of each other. Looking past Hubs, Briz gave a slight nod of hello to Olympe and Tamara, who were watching from within the screened garden.

"I brought some clothes for Jaden." He held the bags steady, not wanting to make any sudden movements and set Rosie off.

"Jaden's in the shower, dear," said Isadora.

Jaden naked.

An impish expression exposed Briz's desires as he hurried toward the house.

CHAPTER 33

JADEN

Jaden stepped out of the shower, wrapped her bath towel around her, and peeked out the bathroom door. The house appeared to be empty. She pattered barefoot into the kitchen, where the wall clock informed her she'd napped for two hours. Opening the refrigerator, Jaden let the cool air embrace her as she reached for a bottle of water. Then she inhaled a quick breath—a familiar scent mingled with the fragrance of herbs drying in the kitchen.

Jaden smiled.

Warm hands embraced her waist.

"Briz..." she sighed. Her knees felt weak as she turned to face him, and he pulled her close. "You aren't supposed to be here. You promised you wouldn't come back."

"I didn't technically agree. I just sort of nodded." Briz leaned back, looking at her with smiling eyes. "Do you want me to leave?"

"No. I'm glad you're here."

"Your mom sent a change of clothes for you. They're on your bed. She wants me to bring you back to town tomorrow morning." Briz let his fingers trail over Jaden's skin as he moved her wet hair aside. "My grandpa loaned his truck to your mom to use."

Jaden giggled from his touch. "That was nice of him."

"Ava thought it was nice, too." Briz leaned down, placing his lips on her neck, as he murmured, "She's used the truck to sneak off to New Orleans."

"She did what?" Jaden shifted away from him, disrupting his kisses.

"She called Albert and had him buy her a plane ticket home." Briz pressed his hand against Jaden's lower back, guiding her closer to him. "Your mom was pretty upset, but decided at least she wouldn't have to worry about her."

"Hu-hum." The sound ended their conversation. "Jaden, grab your brew, then go get dressed," Tamara said in a scolding tone. "There's some of *your* drink left in there, too, Briz. Maybe you should have some. *Now*."

"We weren't even kissing," Briz groaned.

Tamara flicked her wrist, gesturing for them to stand farther apart. Briz didn't move.

"No, but I bet you were going to be puckering up any second. Weren't you?" Tamara smirked. "Like our papa used to say, you are living in the dreamland of adolescent love."

Jaden slouched as she reached for her bottle of Envie Tea. She and Briz would never have a private moment together as long as she was being guarded by the triplets and Violet.

"My sisters and I have been discussing a new formula for you, Briz." Tamara sat her basket of vegetables on the kitchen counter, then reached between the two of them and removed a small bottle from the refrigerator. "Seems it had better include a lot of hops." Pushing the refrigerator door closed, Tamara handed the bottle to Briz. "Here. For now, inhale this."

Briz opened the bottle and choked on the smell. "It's camphor."

"That's right. It's good for a lot of things. Congestion, arthritic pain…" She gave him the once-over as she slowly enunciated, "Libido."

Jaden waited for Tamara to insist that she take a whiff of the camphor, too. But for now, the woman's attention remained on Briz.

"My libido has been messed with enough," Briz protested as he set the bottle on the counter. "The Quellers beat you to it."

"Briz, I think Jaden's mama would like you to take the time to breathe some of that in." Tamara put her hands on Jaden's shoulders and aimed her toward the hallway. "Go get some clothes on."

Jaden paused at the door as Tamara said, "Not you." Jaden turned, seeing Briz had started to follow her. "Jaden doesn't need your help." Tamara took hold of his arm, stopping him in his tracks.

"I was just going to wait for her in the living room."

"You can stay right here and start washing the vegetables for dinner." With a bit of attitude, Tamara released his arm. "If Jaden didn't have Datura's blood in her veins and you hadn't recently been injected with large amounts of tobacco and tongkat toxins—making you a tom cat—the two of you would behave like most kids in your situation."

"That's exactly what we were behaving like," Briz interrupted as he looked at Jaden, holding her bath towel in place.

"I didn't mean *teenagers*." Tamara shook her head. "I

meant you'd be feeling afraid for your lives…that your fear and the need to survive would kick in and override your *cravings* for each other. It's plain to see that's not the case. You're too doped up on tongkat."

"Okay." Briz drew his hands through his hair and looked down at the small woman. "I give. What's this tongkat you keep mentioning?"

"Along with being a teenage boy, tongkat is why you're on the prowl," Tamara snickered.

And probably why he has such a healthy ego right now, Jaden thought.

"I found some of Dekle's papers," Jaden said. "Tongkat is one of the plant sources of DNA that Dekle used in the Quellers."

"He also added drops of cobra blood." Like a snake, Tamara didn't blink as she looked at Briz. "Both of the ingredients were meant to increase the creatures' testosterone levels and their desires to procreate. No doubt the green tobacco is doing a number on your hormones, too."

With that bit of information, Briz lowered his hands and stopped looking down his nose at her.

"At least they will all pass through your system." Tamara raised her eyebrow. "While Jaden will more than likely be drinking her tea for the rest of her life."

Briz's attention went from Jaden to the bottle of camphor sitting on the counter.

Jaden went to get dressed.

She spread her clothes out on the bed, elated to have something else to wear. She selected a knit T-shirt and regular shorts, opting to save a pair of knee length cargo pants for later.

When Jaden came back into the kitchen, the basket of

vegetables hadn't been touched; the entire household was thumbing through a stack of papers. Briz looked up at her from the table. She felt a shy grin spread across her face as he picked up his bottle of camphor and breathed it in. What she was wearing was a big change from the bloodstained capris and baggy T-shirt he was used to seeing her wear.

"I, uh, I printed these out from the Internet," he said to Jaden as she sat down between Olympe and Isadora. "You thought it was a hornet's stinger in my neck?" Olympe gave Briz a slight nod. "I think we'll be able to catch it. If the Quellers are in a pack, we could capture all of them. Hornets are attracted to pheromones, sweet things...lights..."

Briz held up a page as if he was at school doing a show-and-tell. "This page talks about ground hornets. It says they're pure evil when antagonized. I printed info on as many types of hornets as I could find."

"Do you have anything on the Japanese giant hornet?" Isadora asked.

"Yeah, right here." Briz handed her the pages. "And the bald-faced hornets that are found in Louisiana."

Isadora reached for her glasses and read, "The Japanese giant hornets' venom has an enzyme so strong it can dissolve human tissue. When pursuing prey, they can travel a range of sixty miles or ninety-six kilometers at speeds reaching twenty-five miles per hour."

"Check this out." Briz picked up another page. "I found this on Africanized bees, also known as 'killer bees'. They're a hybrid—right up Dekle's alley—they were developed at the same time he was working on his DNA experiments. Back in 1957, the bees escaped from their quarantined area in Brazil." Briz looked at Jaden. "Didn't you say one looked like a bee?"

"Dekle's drawings more or less confirmed it," Isadora answered before Jaden could reply. "Along with bee and hornet, he used sea lamprey, ifrita bird, piranha, cobra. Plus, mountain laurel, tongkat, tobacco, and giant hogweed. He wanted the Quellers to be sturdy...survivors."

"Sea lamprey?" Briz asked.

Isadora carefully leafed through Dekle's brittle drawings. "It's like an eel, son. But with a suction cup mouth full of tiny sharp teeth. They suck the blood out of their victims."

Jaden watched Briz as he looked at the drawings and listened to Isadora describe the disgusting parasites. Briz's head swayed back as disbelief widened his eyes. Jaden understood. It was bad enough being attacked by Dekle's monsters. But it was worse when you learned their full capabilities. No doubt they would be swarming in Briz's dreams tonight.

CHAPTER 34

BRIZ

Sounds of fear. Sounds of terror—shattered the stillness of the night. Briz's eyes sprang open. Shrill squawking pierced the air, silencing the high-pitched hum of insects. From the hammock where he'd been sleeping, Briz stared into the darkness and saw...nothing.

Then he heard the sounds of death. Briz rolled out of the hammock and moved quietly to the back of the porch. Dark shadows distorted his vision. He turned on his flashlight, aiming the beam of light at the chicken coop.

His heart raced into his throat where it felt stuck, stopping him from getting air into his lungs. The Quellers had found their way to the triplets' house. They were as Jaden had described them, but no longer the size of doves. At least four times larger now; they'd been eating well.

One was in the coop. The other three were chewing through the wire cage. Every wound the Quellers had inflicted on Briz flared with pain.

The triplets' two hound dogs rubbed against Briz's legs, whimpering. The Quellers stilled, hovering in place, listening, sniffing the air. Then they turned toward the house.

Toward Briz.

The Quellers outside of the chicken coop flew over to the porch. He wondered if he smelled familiar to them—after all, he was their first meal when they were initially freed.

Briz's light lit up their eyes. He could see a cloudy gray spot in each of them, like a cataract, the size of a pea, right where their pupils would be. *They aren't completely blind anymore.*

Briz slowly stepped all the way back to the front door, his chest pounding. The Quellers followed, pushing against the old screen, determined to get in.

Where are the cats? Briz scanned the porch but didn't see them.

The remaining chickens went silent. The insects were silent. The fourth Queller appeared. With their faces pressed against the screen, the Quellers bit at the flimsy barrier. Briz turned off the flashlight, hurried into the house with the dogs, and slammed the door shut, waking Hubs and Rosie, who were asleep on the couch.

Hubs turned on a lamp.

"NO. Turn off the light!" Briz shouted.

Hubs looked confused, then afraid for his life. He glanced at his gun on the table next to him, as Rosie flew to the window, making a high-pitched sound.

"Hubs! Turn off the light."

Briz rushed over to the window where Rosie was hovering and growling. He reached in front of her, closed the window, then hurried over to the window facing the bayou and pulled it shut. "Hubs, make sure the windows in the triplets' rooms are closed."

Before Hubs could move, the three sisters came out of their rooms, switched on the hall light, and entered the living room.

"What's all the commotion?" Tamara asked, slipping into her bathrobe. "It's one o'clock in the morning."

"Close all the windows, and the curtains." Briz demanded.

"Close the windows?" Tamara questioned, half asleep. "It's already too warm in here."

"Quellers. Turn off the lights!" All the lights immediately went out.

Briz opened Jaden's bedroom door. "Jaden close your window." Jaden turned on her bedside lamp. "Turn off the light. The Quellers are here."

Moments later, every window in the house was shut, every curtain closed, and the cats and dogs were sequestered in Jaden's room. Everyone gathered in the living room, their heartbeats filling in the silence as they waited. Their bodies were dark shadows huddled together in pairs: Violet and Rosie on the arm of the sofa next to Hubs, his arm around his mama; Tamara and Isadora next to them; Jaden snuggled close to Briz in the oversized chair.

Even over the clanking of the ceiling fan, Briz could hear Jaden's shallow breaths keeping time with his.

He heard Violet gasp and Rosie make a mewling sound. Then...

Tap.

Tap.

Briz held Jaden closer to his sweaty body as they looked toward the window by the front door.

TAP-TAP-TAP-TAP.

"They're going to break through," Jaden said in a frightened whisper.

TAP-TAP-TAP.

TAP-TAP-TAP.

Briz listened as more tapping sounds rattled the other windows.

Hubs stood and went to the window by the door. "B-Briz, if ya o-open the w-window and sh-shine a light in its eyes, I'll sh-shoot it." His stutter was back. Briz wondered if it would lessen again...if they survived tonight.

Briz nodded to Hubs, even though no one could see him. "Okay. But I want everyone else to go into Jaden's room, and no matter what, don't open the door." No one argued with him.

Jaden slipped out of his arms. "Give me your flashlight. I'm going to get us some knives. The rest of us should have weapons, too."

"Bring one for me," Briz said, releasing her hand.

"What about Rosie and me?" Violet asked. "I think we should stay in here in case you need help."

"N-no!" The word erupted from Hubs's chest. "N-no," he said quieter. "G-go w-with mama."

"Hubs, if you miss," Briz grabbed an afghan from the back of the sofa, "or if the other Quellers follow this one into the house before we can close the window, I'll turn on the light, maybe I can throw this over one or two of them and you can shoot them." Briz gulped in a breath of air. "Just don't shoot me."

The flashlight glowed down the hall, and the tapping moved to the kitchen window. The light went out.

Jaden came up behind Briz in the darkness and whispered, "Here's a knife."

The women followed Jaden into her bedroom, clicking the door closed behind them.

Briz stepped next to Hubs at the window and turned on the flashlight. The tapping returned, louder, faster, matching the sound and beat of Briz's heart. Opening the curtain, Briz quickly raised the window. With the shaft of the gun inches from the Queller, Hubs pulled the trigger.

The bullet tore a hole in the window screen, and the Queller dropped to the ground. Briz had heard people describe the sound of a gunshot like a car backfiring. Being so close to it, he thought it sounded deadly, like it had pierced into his heart as well as his eardrums.

Briz flashed his light toward the end of the porch. He didn't see the remaining Quellers, and the tapping at the other windows had stopped. He hurriedly closed the window, figuring the gunshot had scared them away. Hubs turned on a lamp as the bedroom door inched open.

"We're coming out," Jaden said, her voice strained.

The triplets squinted at the light as they came into the room; then sitting side by side on the sofa, they stared at Briz as if asking, *now what?*

Briz sat with Jaden, staring at the wall clock. Five, ten, fifteen minutes passed—sleeping no longer seemed like an option—they needed one of Olympe's calming brews. Before he could make the suggestion, Rosie flew toward Hubs, then darted away, shrieking and flying from window to window.

"Listen!" Violet hissed. "Rosie. Stop. Be quiet."

Still shrieking, Rosie flew into Jaden's bedroom, then into the kitchen.

"Rosie!" Violet hissed again. "Listen, everyone. Do you hear that?"

"Hear what?" Tamara asked. "I only hear the fan."

Violet pulled the chain hanging down from the ceiling fan, turning it off.

"I hear it," Jaden said. "It's growing louder. Whatever it is, it's coming closer."

Violet flew to the large bay window and peeked through the curtain into the dark night.

"V-Violet, get away from the w-window." Hubs walked over and took her in his arms. "It's not safe."

Chapter 35

Jaden

The humming resonated through Jaden's veins, then throbbed in her head. "That Queller that you shot..." Jaden covered her mouth as if to stop her words. "It must have been the one with hornet DNA." She went to the desk where Isadora had left the stack of papers Briz had printed.

"Don't you remember?" Jaden asked, thumbing through the pages. "Its pheromones must be attracting other hornets. Right here." She pointed at a paragraph. "It says, 'If a hornet is killed near a nest, the pheromones will cause the other hornets to attack the quarry, intent on revenge, willing to destroy themselves for the good of the all, to keep their nests safe. They will come out at night. They will repeatedly smash into windows. They are attracted to light.'"

Before Jaden could read another word, Hubs turned off the lamp, but it was too late. The flurrying sound of a thousand wings grew into a wailing as the insects settled upon the house.

"From the size of the Queller, the smell of its

pheromones must have attracted hornets from further away," Violet said over the noise.

Jaden rubbed her brow. The stagnant air in the room seemed both heavier and warmer as the hornets found their way through the opening the Quellers had made in the porch screen. She covered her ears, not wanting to hear the hornets chewing through the window screens or the thwacking of their bodies hitting the windowpanes.

Jaden's words were clipped. "They. Can't. Break. The. Windows. Can. They?" She uncovered her ears—lowering her hands, she waited for a reply.

The lack of an answer—from anyone—caused her to feel short of breath. Her hands and feet tingled, then became numb. *Ava was right. Everything that has happened...is happening, is because of my stupidity.* She hadn't stopped reminding herself of that since the day she'd first released the Mal Rous.

She felt starved for air. Her mouth was dry.

Briz stroked her back, trying to calm her. Jaden pushed him away. She didn't want to be comforted. She wanted to be punished. She wanted to run onto the porch and let the hornets sting her over and over in exchange for forgiveness. Sting her until she fell into a coma so deep that all of her guilt and thoughts and memories were erased.

Her breathing quickened.

A flashlight glowed, flitting around her head. Then the light bobbled down the hall. It returned moments later and flickered over Jaden's face as Olympe handed it to Tamara.

"It's all right, Jaden." Olympe's Southern accent was soft as she placed a small paper bag over Jaden's mouth and nose. "Ya is hyperventilating. I want ya to just breathe into the bag, dear. Calmly. Can ya do that for me?"

Jaden's eyes widened as she complied with Olympe's request.

"One. Two. Three..." Briz counted each breath.

Jaden tried to turn her head away, but Olympe held the bag firmly in place.

"Come on," Briz encouraged. "Three more breaths." Jaden inhaled. Briz continued to count aloud. "Four. Five. Six."

Olympe lowered the bag. "Now dear, ya gonna breath in six breaths without the bag."

Jaden continued to hyperventilate.

Through the sound of her rapid breaths and the hornets' bodies striking the windows, Jaden heard Isadora's voice. "We have to change her breathing pattern or she's going to pass out."

Briz knelt in front of Jaden. Surprising her and everyone else, he leaned his head forward and kissed her, long and deep.

Tamara aimed her flashlight at the floor.

When Briz ended the kiss, Jaden took a deep breath and sank back in the chair.

"Well," Tamara remarked. "That was a lot more effective than breathing into a bag. You might want to stay close by, Briz. It's going to be a long night, and you may need to do that again."

Jaden wanted to smile at Tamara's joke, but she knew Tamara was right. That was one thing Jaden admired about the woman. She was honest. No matter how painful the truth, Tamara was always willing to rub it into your open wound—with a chuckle and a grin.

"I've always loved this house." Sorrow bathed Olympe's

words. "But right now, I feel trapped, and I'd like to be somewhere else."

"Trapped," Jaden exhaled the dreadful word.

With no way to escape.

They were trapped in the house that Olympe's husband, Billy, built for her and Hubs so long ago. Olympe had once told Jaden that before Billy died ten years ago, he'd told her how happy he was knowing she'd be safe in this home—her and Hubs and her sisters. It was their own little oasis. Jaden could feel Billy's spirit alive and well in this house. In its walls. He never truly left Olympe and Hubs.

Violet turned the ceiling fan back on. It clanked and clinked as it wrestled with the sticky air, trying to move it through the room, but it wasn't loud enough to buffer the sound of the hornets.

The group clustered together in the living room. Jaden, sitting in one of the wingback chairs, forced herself to stay awake as the night dragged on, to keep watch as the others nodded off one by one. Her eyes grew heavy, but she couldn't sleep.

Wouldn't sleep.

She was committed to keeping them safe, the way Billy would have wanted.

Or if not safe, she would be awake to strike back if the Quellers returned. She could at least sacrifice herself to save everyone else. In her mind, Jaden could see the write-up Briz had brought: *The hornets will sting their quarry, bite it with their powerful mandibles until there are no more signs of life in the victim.*

Hours later, whether chased away by the first light of day or from sheer exhaustion, the droning noise from the hornets that had vibrated deep into the core of the house subsided.

Minutes passed before the sound finally stopped in Jaden's head.

She watched as everyone was stirred awake by the silence that now blanketed the bayou.

Relief. It was almost tangible. A silky presence that spread through the room.

"Sh-should we b-bring the dead thing in?" Hubs asked.

"Goodness gracious, yes," Tamara said, her words pushing Hubs to the door. "We don't want the hornets smelling its pheromones anymore. We can put it in the freezer for now with the Mal Rou bones. When the time comes, we'll boil them all together."

"Do you think they'll be back?" Jaden asked as Hubs opened the front door. "The hornets? The Quellers?"

Hubs peered through the screened door before stepping onto the porch.

Violet cleared her throat. "I think that where the Mal Rous were misguided souls who enjoyed feeding off of people's fears, the Quellers are like deadly bacteria that want to consume flesh and blood," Violet said as brusquely as Tamara would have. "So, yes, I believe the Quellers will be back." Hovering at the window, Violet drew the curtain aside and gasped. "There are dead hornets...everywhere. The screens on the porch look like they've been shredded."

Tamara joined Violet to see the night's leftovers for herself. "Everything will have to be washed with ammonia," Tamara observed. "The scent of the pheromones will be on the wood planks and could trigger another attack," she added, walking down the hall.

Jaden stood next to Violet. They watched from the window as Hubs used a rag to pick up the dead Queller and wrapped it around the Queller's belly where drops of sap were leaking from its ringlet-like hairs. It was a cross between a bird and a Japanese giant hornet with a brown and yellow body and sheer wings, but no stinger.

Jaden's hand went to her neck, remembering when Olympe had removed the two-inch stinger from Briz.

"We has to *kiill* the rest of the Qu-quellers," Hubs said, coming into the house.

"The other three probably aren't far away." Briz's voice was somber as he followed Hubs into the kitchen. Jaden walked behind Briz—reaching out, she took his hand. His fingers wrapped around hers. They felt strong and reassuring. For a moment, Jaden indulged in the thought that everything was going to be all right.

Isadora was standing near the refrigerator. She opened a trash bag, and Hubs deposited the dead Queller inside. "We're going to need something to use as bait to attract the remaining Quellers," Isadora stated as she secured the bag and put it in the freezer. "Then Hubs can shoot them."

"What about the chickens?" Tamara looked out the kitchen window at the chicken coop. "The Quellers went after them last night. We could make a door in the top of the cage—leave it open so the Quellers can fly right in—if we attach a wire, we can pull the door shut and trap them inside." She turned back and looked at Hubs. "You'd have to be quick, Hubs. Shoot all of them before they could kill the chickens."

"Or b-bite through the c-cage and escape."

"You've really thought this through." Briz walked to the window and viewed the coop, with Jaden still at his side.

Tamara gave a curt nod. "Wasn't much else to do last night but come up with a plan."

"Let's do it. We can't drag this out another day. We

might miss our opportunity." Briz squeezed Jaden's hand. "We need a backup plan. I don't want those things heading to town. In case they don't go for the chickens, I think I should be the bait."

"NO!" Jaden pulled her hand free from his. "I'll be the bait!"

"Jade, this isn't open to debate. I'm not letting the Quellers come near you."

"NO!" Jaden snapped again. "I won't go along with another one of your asinine plans. Back at the cave, I shouldn't have let you ram down that door. That's how you got attacked by the Quellers the first time."

"Would you at least hear me out?" Briz looked around the room. "I'm it...I'm the best option. Think about it. I've already survived one attack from them, so I might be immune to whatever toxins they'll inject into me. Besides, Hubs and I will kill them before they can do any actual harm."

Jaden crossed her arms over her chest and glowered at him.

"Yes, son..." Isadora stepped between the two of them. "That's what we'll all do—think on it. For now," Isadora pointed at Jaden, then Briz, then at Hubs, "the three of you can clean up all the hornet bodies. Cleaning supplies are out on the porch by the washing machine. We'll talk more when you're done."

"Do ya *thiink* the Qu-quellers hunt du-during the *daay*, too?" Hubs asked.

"Let's hope not," Briz replied, opening the back door.

CHAPTER 36

BRIZ

The last remnants of sunlight colored the bayou with a dull orange glow, announcing the end of a long day and declaring the start of an even longer night. As Briz and Hubs walked toward the house, the savory aroma of dinner quickened their pace. Briz wondered if the Quellers liked cooked food. Or did they only eat fresh, raw meat?

"I doubt the death of that Queller sent the other three flying off to safety," Briz commented.

Hubs didn't respond. But it had been on Briz's mind all day as he and Jaden and Hubs cleaned up the dead hornets from the porch, gutters and roof. Every little sound had him jumping and swinging the broom through the air.

Everyone had come to the conclusion that the Quellers were nocturnal. Why else would they have been hunting at night? Perhaps sunlight was too harsh on their undeveloped eyes, and dusk to dawn was when they thrived.

Still, Briz had imagined that the Quellers were watching them as they rigged the chicken coop with a trap door, as they patched the screened porch as best they could.

He thought he'd seen the Quellers in the trees when he and Hubs had smeared honey and tied pieces of fruit around the trunk of an old persimmon tree a half mile from the house, hoping another swarm of hornets might find the sweet treats distracting. He had sworn he could feel the Quellers watching as he and Hubs piled rocks and the dead hornets in a sheet and sunk it a mile from the house in the deepest part of the bayou, following Olympe's theory that doing so would rid the area of the insects' scent.

Upon entering the house, Hubs went to shower while Briz walked over to the large bay window that faced the bayou. Unlike Jaden, the triplets had surrendered to Briz's backup plan and didn't want Briz to clean up. They wanted his odor strong.

"The moon will rise around eleven o'clock," Briz said to Violet, who had flown up next to him. They expected that the remaining Quellers would be hunting for food well before then.

Or for revenge.

"The moon's an arrant thief, and her pale fire she snatches from the sun," Violet recited with a dash of dramatic flair.

Briz glanced at her hovering at his side. His brow furrowed.

"William Shakespeare," Violet said before he could ask. "From *Timon of Athens*."

"Never read it."

"Oh." Violet sounded surprised by his answer. Every other time she'd quoted Shakespeare, he'd responded in kind. Then again, maybe his mom had made him read the story, but right now his thoughts were on surviving, not poetic words.

"I don't think the hornets are going to be a problem tonight." Briz focused on Violet's reflection in the window as she settled on the back of the wingback chair. "But, if we kill the Queller that was created with Africanized bee DNA, there's a chance a swarm of killer bees will attack us." Violet's reflected eyes met his. "The Internet write-up said, 'Africanized bees deploy in great numbers'...*Deploy*..." Briz ran his fingers through his hair, "like the military. It also said, 'They'll pursue perceived threats over long distances from the hive.'"

"We're as ready as we can be." Violet's voice was soft, as if she wanted to be comforting. "The back door hinges are oiled, so you won't be heard when you sneak out. The triplets have spent the day studying Dekle's lab reports and preparing poultices and herbal remedies—everything they could think of if things go badly tonight."

Briz gave her a slight nod. "Prepared as we can be." His words were barely audible. He knew he was in over his head. "There must be some secret government agency that could deal with this mess...or even the National Fish and Wildlife Service."

"Really...?" Violet squeaked.

"Wishful thinking. I know you're right. If the government got ahold of Dekle's experiments, they'd be used for—"

"It's time to eat," Jaden said, walking up to them.

A half hour later, dinner was done. But like hearing Violet's poetic words earlier, Briz's thoughts hadn't been on the meal.

"Why don't the two of you go into the other room," Isadora offered as Jaden and Briz started to clear the table. "We'll take care of the dishes."

Hand in hand, they went into the living room. Briz sat in Hubs's oversized chair, and he guided Jaden into his lap. He held her, letting the weight of her body and the feel of her skin distract him from more unwanted thoughts.

Hubs came in and looked at Jaden and Briz snug in his chair. Without a word, Hubs picked up his mandolin, then sat in a wingback chair. Violet and Rosie landed on the chair's arm, Rosie doing her best to copy Violet's facial expressions and the way Violet was sitting. Hubs strummed a melody, which normally would have been soothing. Due to the circumstances, *haunting* was the word that came to Briz's mind.

When the dishes were done, the triplets joined them and settled in to wait. Olympe went to her piano, her fingers following along with Hubs's melody.

Part of the act, Briz thought. Everyone hoped, with all the lights on and the sounds of everyday life, their contrived show of feeling safe would lure in the Quellers. Briz noted that what was missing was the normal murmur of conversation. He wasn't alone in having nothing to say.

Jaden leaned her head on Briz's shoulder, caressing his hand and toying with his fingers while they listened to the music. Briz glanced at Isadora and Tamara sitting next to each other on the sofa. Worn out from the lack of sleep and preparing for tonight, both of the women appeared to be struggling to stay awake.

At long last the moon made its appearance, its silvery threads of light shimmering through the trees and yard.

It was beautiful. Peaceful.

Until they heard the chickens.

The sound of cackling was the distress signal everyone

had been waiting for. Briz kissed Jaden on the side of her head, then slid her off his lap.

Tamara and Violet stole into the moonlit kitchen; following them, Briz stood in the shadows looking out the window.

"There..." Violet spoke softly. "Do you see them?" A touch of moonlight glinted off the one with eel-like skin. "That must be the one derived from sea lamprey DNA."

The Quellers hovered in front of the chicken coop, taking turns darting around the cage, looking at the trap door Hubs had made. Tamara picked up the thin wire they'd run from the cage onto the screened porch and in through the cracked-open kitchen window. They'd tested it a dozen times today, and each time it had worked.

One queller looked at the wire.

"I think they know it's a trap," Tamara whispered. "Have they been watching the house all day? Saw what you and Hubs were up to?"

The Quellers turned and flew toward the screened porch, then up to the roof.

Seconds later Rosie was squealing, and Jaden called from the other room, "They're watching us through the large window."

Briz hurried into the living room, Tamara and Violet close behind.

Rosie was flying around Isadora and Hubs as if to keep them safe. "Shh, shh, Rosie." Hubs cupped his hand and Rosie settled in. Stroking her head, Hubs lowered Rosie onto a chair.

"They're just watching us," Jaden repeated. "They haven't looked for a way onto the porch."

The lamplight shone out the window and across the

narrow section of the screened porch, exposing traces of the Quellers' dull gray pupils.

"They want us," Violet said as she fluttered up behind Briz. "They want us for killing their sibling."

"The chickens were a lame idea," Tamara muttered.

Jaden looked at Tamara, realizing the woman judged herself as harshly as she judged others. "Tamara, even if it didn't work, it was a good idea. They're just smarter than we thought."

Briz felt a firm hand on his shoulder. He turned, standing eye-to-eye with Hubs. "Y-ya *suure* 'bout d-doing this?"

"I think Violet's right." Briz looked back at the Quellers. "They want revenge."

"B-but I k-killed t-that one, not you."

Briz glanced at Olympe, who was still sitting at the piano. Her concern for her son was apparent in her face.

"Hubs, we've already been over this. They know the smell of my blood." Briz saw Olympe's relief as the woman's tense shoulders relaxed. Then his eyes met Jaden's. "It's going to be okay, Jade...I'll be okay." Briz knew he sounded like he was trying to convince himself as well as everyone else.

Rosie began to squeal.

"V-Violet, s-sit with Rosie." Before Violet could join her, Rosie took off, screeching and flying from one side of the room to the other. Pausing in front of the window, she stared at the Quellers, curling back her lips and baring her sharp teeth.

"Thatta girl, Rosie. Give 'em hell." Tamara stepped over to the window. "We want to keep them distracted."

The light in the hallway flowed through the door as Briz,

Hubs, Jaden and Olympe filed into the kitchen. Everything Briz and Hubs needed had already been laid out on the table.

"Hubs..." Briz paused, watching as Hubs hugged his mama. "If they come onto the porch instead of going after me, get in the house as fast as you can. Once I've lured them into the yard, sneak back out and shoot them."

Hubs applied a fresh layer of Non-Odeur formula to his face, over the sleeves of his shirt and to his pants. He picked up a sharp knife and looked at Briz. Briz gave a nod, flinching as the sting of the blade cut into his calf. Blood dripped down his leg. Briz hoped it would be enough to attract the Quellers.

"A Queller just flew over the house," Isadora called out. "Turn off the hall light."

Jaden reached around the corner and flipped off the switch. Briz was grateful the dimly lit room concealed his concerns for what he was about to do. It was his plan, and he wanted to project complete confidence, even if inside he felt completely unnerved that it could all go horribly wrong.

All too soon, Olympe was helping him put on Hubs's raincoat for protection. Briz raised the hood, pulling the drawstring tight, until it pinched the outer edges of his eyes and cheeks. The less skin exposed, the less flesh for the Quellers to bite. Picking up the hammer, he slid the handle up his sleeve, holding its cold metal head in his hand.

"So, Hubs, when one comes at me, I'll try to whack it with the hammer," Briz whispered. "You can shoot it once it hits the ground."

Some of the tension in Briz's shoulders relax as Jaden came over and took his free hand in hers.

"I still think this is a stupid idea." Jaden's touch was

gentle, though her hushed voice conveyed her lingering disapproval. "There's no way you can kill all three of them. You'll be lucky if you kill one before the others attack you."

"O-one l-less to w-worry about," Hubs said to Jaden. "I'll sh-shoot it w-when it's on the g-ground," he confirmed to Briz.

Since Rosie's arrival, Hubs's stutter came and went with his level of stress. *Hubs is really nervous,* Briz thought, hearing his halting words. *No telling what his aim will be like.*

The keys on the piano played a more upbeat tune than Briz had expected to hear. As he closed the backdoor, Jaden sung a series of off-key notes: "La, la, la...All three Quellers are here watching us through the window...La, la...let us know when Hubs is safely situated on the porch."

Once Hubs was hidden in the shadows, Briz tapped lightly on the front door.

The music stopped. Briz opened the porch screen door and let it bang closed, inviting the Quellers to investigate. He walked into the yard over to the screened-in garden—not too close to the house, yet near enough that Hubs would reach him in time.

Sweat dripped into his eyes. Insects chirring around him reminded him of the hornets that had attacked the house last night. The hood on his rain jacket pressed against his ears, causing his breathing to sound how he felt—like he was swimming underwater.

The sound of wings brought him to the surface. Flying in formation, the three Quellers' shadowy forms were coming right toward him, the beating of their wings growing louder, like the drone of a bagpipe. The hairs on Briz's arms rose straight up. Earlier, he'd considered tying himself to a tree in the yard, so he couldn't run away and mess up his entire plan. But messing up his plan might just save his life.

The Quellers appeared entirely engrossed with Briz—they hadn't smelled Hubs. Briz refrained from looking over to Hubs's hiding spot on the screened porch. Instead, Briz wrapped his fingers around the head of the hammer.

His feet cramped, aching with the desire to run, as he forced himself to stand still while the Quellers hovered only three feet from him. They studied Briz as he studied them.

Each was different, yet somehow similar in shape and size. One had bird feathers, while its body was shaped like a fish—ifrita kowaldi and piranha, judging by what Briz had seen of Dekle's sketches. Briz's printouts said the bird's skin and feathers had some kind of neurotoxic alkaloid that caused numbness in your hands if you touched them, even paralysis.

Another Queller had the shape and color of a bee, but with scales and a two-inch-long stinger. *Killer bee and piranha*, Briz thought.

The third Queller had fish fins shaped like a bird's wings that flapped rapidly up and down. Its torso was smooth like an eel. Briz could see gills on its long neck. It opened its large oval mouth, which resembled a suction cup filled with row after row of sharp teeth. *Sea lamprey.* This one sent fear rushing through Briz's veins as he recalled that the eel-like fish sucked blood out of its victims.

The triplets suspected that the scattering of hair-like tendrils on the Quellers' bellies released their plant toxins.

The Quellers circled Briz, making strange snorting

sounds as if excited that their first real meal had returned as easy and tasty prey.

In unison, they came closer, stopping inches from his face, their pallid eyes staring directly into Briz's eyes.

No, not my face...or my eyes. Go for the blood on my leg!

The killer bee Queller turned away from Briz and began flying to and fro as if keeping guard or looking for predators...*or Hubs.*

"Me..." Briz pushed the raspy word from his throat, wanting to distract the bee Queller, hoping it hadn't picked up Hubs's scent. "You want me." But the bee Queller continued flying to and fro while staring at the house.

Briz watched as the ifrita Queller's belly hairs swelled in circumference and extended to about five inches in length. *Poisons.*

Jaden was right, this was a lame-ass plan. Briz held his breath, dreading what was to come. The creature dove to his leg. Briz made a choking noise as its sharp beak jabbed into the cut on his calf. He choked again as the tips of the now fat tendrils pierced his skin. Briz could feel a pulsing sensation as toxins pumped into his body. He locked his knees to stop from sinking to the ground.

The sea lamprey Queller was in front of Briz. Its wide-open mouth with rows of teeth stopped Briz from removing the hammer from his sleeve and striking it. He worried that if he missed, the mutant devil would latch onto his face. Suddenly the sea lamprey Queller shrieked; the ifrita Queller stopped pecking at Briz's leg, pulled its tendrils free and switched places with the sea lamprey Queller.

They have learned to work as a team. But it was more than teamwork—it was as if they had a strategy for getting revenge.

A biting cold moved through Briz. Dekle's notes hadn't mentioned their ability to develop reasoning skills, of being intelligent or vindictive. *He probably didn't know it was possible. He didn't know what he was creating.*

Briz gripped the hammer and waited for the sea lamprey Queller's teeth to penetrate his flesh. Once it was attached to his leg, Briz would pull the hammer from the sleeve of his jacket and slay the ifrita Queller that was in front of his face.

Instead of biting Briz, the sea lamprey Queller's sharp, probing tongue pushed deep into his leg, causing his knees to buckle. Briz worked to steady himself as its swollen tendrils slid over his leg, as if searching for the best area to penetrate.

The ifrita Queller remained in front of Briz as it sniffed the air. Then it began to squeal.

The glow of a flashlight swept over the Quellers as Hubs stepped into the yard. The ifrita Queller continued to squeal as the bee Queller launched itself toward Hubs.

It was time. Briz pulled out the hammer.

A gunshot ripped through the air.

The bee Queller dropped to the ground. The sea lamprey Queller released its hold from Briz's leg and bolted into the trees. Briz swung the hammer at the ifrita Queller as it flew toward Hubs but missed. Reaching for it, Briz's fingers skimmed over its feathers. His hand went numb as the Queller darted away.

Hubs's flashlight searched the darkness, his other arm outstretched, ready to fire the gun again.

The ifrita Queller's poisons reached Briz's bloodstream; he fell to the ground, feeling cold and weak. He heard the front door bang open. Jaden ran into the yard, carrying a garbage bag and a jug of ammonia. Calling Briz's name, her light flickered across the ground, over Briz and into the trees, her words coming between her sobs.

"I'm sorry."

He didn't want to hear her say it anymore. Those two words had become Jaden's mantra. Bending down, she reached for his hands, trying to help him up.

"J-Jaden, pour the am-monia over the d-dead Queller." Hubs moved Jaden aside. "Then p-put it in the bag. D-don't get the ph-pheromones on yer skin. P-pour am-monia on the ground, too." Hubs slid his hands under Briz's arms, raising him to his feet. "Be quick J-Jaden. The other two m-might come b-back. S-sorry, B-Briz. I sh-should have w-waited for you to use the h-hammer."

Briz wanted to tell Hubs that wasn't true. He had to shoot the Queller while he had the chance. When he knew the bullet wouldn't hit him. But saliva was pooling up in Briz's mouth, and he couldn't speak. He swallowed, and his mouth filled again. In slow motion, his head drifted to the side. He could feel drool dribbling over his lower lip.

As Hubs hurried Briz onto the porch, the house went dark.

Olympe's voice met them as she held open the porch door. "The lights don't work. Do ya think the two remaining critters were smart enough to chew through the electric line to the solar batteries?"

"M-most likely," Hubs said as he hauled Briz into the house.

The glow of flashlights flickered around the room, one lighting up Briz's face. A string of words that made no sense moved past the saliva in Briz's mouth. His words felt as tangled as his feet became when he tried to walk.

"Oh, my..." Olympe took a hanky from her pocket and

cleaned the drool off Briz's chin. Then she hurried into the bedroom.

"Does it have a stinger?" Isadora asked as Jaden handed her flashlight and the bag with the Queller to Tamara.

"Yes." Jaden replied. "It's the one with bee DNA."

Briz raised his head and saw Isadora lighting candles and lanterns. He could see Jaden's dark silhouette pacing back and forth, hear her talking to herself as Hubs maneuvered him into the bedroom.

"Jaden," Tamara called as she carried the bag into the kitchen. "Make yourself useful and find out what Olympe is going to need."

Jaden marched into the room past Hubs and Briz and pulled the mosquito net to the side of the bed. The flame from a candle glistened and blurred as sweat trickled into Briz's eyes. He wanted to wipe away the moisture—like the saliva in his mouth, his perspiration was profuse—but was unable to move his now numb arm.

"Hubs, could ya tell which one of them bit him?" Olympe asked as Hubs eased Briz onto the bed. "So I know what toxins I need to be treating him for."

"If-ifrita." Hubs gripped Briz's shoulders, holding him upright as Jaden untied Briz's hood and removed his rain jacket, then peeled off his moist shirt. "L-lamprey, too," Hubs added. "D-don't know if its f-feelers got him...It was h-hard to see."

"All right then, in case it did, I'm gonna need the pouch for mountain laurel poisoning," Olympe muttered to herself. "Jaden, hand me the pouch I put together for the sea lamprey. It's right there on the chest-a-drawers. And horse chestnut..." Olympe trailed off, as if trying to remember which cures did what. "Yes, hand me that pouch, too. That ifrita Queller has horse chestnut DNA…Its poisons aren't normally fatal. He may vomit. Fetch a bucket, and a couple of towels. He can't stop drooling."

Jaden was already down the hall when Olympe called out to her, "And Jaden, bring a lantern."

"Now, Briz," Olympe said softly, "besides having lost yer coordination, ya may start to feel like ya is in a stupor. But we are gonna get ya through this."

Briz made out the blurry image of Jaden carrying the lantern as she barreled back into the room, followed by Isadora carrying a pan of water and Tamara with a stack of towels. Then Jaden and Hubs were gone.

The triplets' voices were like leaves rustling through the room. Random words like "mountain laurel," "difficulty breathing" and "watery eyes and nose" reached Briz's ears and the edges of his mind as the women removed his damp shorts and cleaned and tended to his leg wound. He was thankful they'd had the foresight to prepare for the worst in advance.

CHAPTER 38

BRIZ

The bedroom door creaked, and Briz opened his eyes. "Ya has been asleep for some hours now," Olympe said, setting her flashlight on the nightstand. Placing her wrist on Briz's forehead, she smiled. "Yer not so feverish anymore. Let's have a look at yer leg."

Briz raised himself up and moved the sheet aside.

"Thank goodness them monsters did little damage to ya." Olympe unwrapped the bandage that held the herbs and slices of ginger in place on his calf. "Do ya think ya is strong enough to get in the tub?"

"I think so. I feel like I had the flu." Briz gestured toward his shorts, wondering why he felt modest—he was wearing his briefs, and the woman had already seen him naked.

"Couldn't wash them for ya." Olympe handed Briz his shorts. "No solar power."

"Did bees swarm the house?" He pulled on his shorts—they felt heavy on his achy body.

"I reckon, unlike the hornets, the bees don't like to come

out at night. And the ammonia worked on getting rid of the smell of its pheromones right quick."

The house was lit with a scattering of candles and lanterns. Briz slowly made his way to the bathroom. The triplets had filled the tub with herbs and left a candle nearby, along with a cup of broth. Briz lowered himself into the water, grateful that the temperature wasn't as warm as the air in the house. No electricity meant no fans and no air movement. He raised his calf above the water and looked at the thin slice Hubs had cut into his leg; beneath it was a nickel-sized hole and three punctures.

Olympe's right, the Quellers didn't do much damage.

Briz drank the broth, then sank down in the tub, lowering his head under the water. His mind became quiet—no thoughts, no bayou noises of crickets chirping, frogs croaking, or the alligators growling and hissing. Just silence.

He felt lightheaded when he got out of the tub and headed into the kitchen for another cup of broth. He looked at the clock—it was four-thirty in the morning.

From the other room, he heard the triplets discussing their options.

Tamara's words carried through the house. "If Briz is strong enough, we should all head out today."

"What? Ya want us to leave our home?" Olympe asked, her sweet voice sounding wounded. "Maybe the rest of the Quellers got frightened off. They could be long gone by now."

"It's just not safe for us here, Olympe," Isadora agreed with Tamara, though she spoke with a kinder tone. "If they haven't left, Briz can't keep being a lure while we try to catch the last two."

"*Thhe* Qu-Quellers is smart now, mama. Bet *thhey* is thinking of a *waaay* to get into the *houuse* right now."

Briz drank the last of his broth; brushed his teeth, hoping to kiss Jaden; then went into the living room. He leaned his shoulder against the wall to brace his weary body. "I think Tamara is right."

He had kept his voice soft, but from the way everyone looked in his direction, he knew he had startled them. Their faces were lined with exhaustion, even Violet's and Rosie's. Briz's eyes settled on Olympe and Hubs, sitting side by side. Briz felt bad for Olympe—she was outnumbered.

"Briz..." Jaden hurried over to him. "How are you feeling?" She wrapped her arms around him, her hands caressing the bare skin on his back.

"I'm doing all right." He rested his chin on top of her head as he looked at everyone. "All of you are probably more tired than I am. Have any of you had any sleep?"

"We've been taking turns napping," Isadora said, leaning back on the sofa like she'd just woken from one.

"So, do ya agree with the others?" Olympe asked. "We should leave our home?"

Briz nodded. "It's like we thought. The Quellers seem to be nocturnal, so if we leave here around noon, there's a good chance that they wouldn't even know we left."

Jaden shifted to his side, her fingernails trailing over his skin, stopping on his waist as she turned to face the others. Goosebumps and tingles caused his stomach muscles to contract.

"We could go to Guyon Manor," Jaden suggested with a cringe. "I know it's not the best place, but it would be large enough for all of us." Briz noticed that Jaden pointedly did not look up at him when she said "all of us"—without a doubt she was sending him home again.

"Well, all right then. We'll have to lock things up real tight." Olympe's head bobbed up and down as she patted Hubs's knee. For a moment, she regarded the photos and paintings on the walls, then stood and looked at her sisters. "We'd better all get some sleep for a couple of hours. Jaden, ya can sleep with me. By no means is my son sleeping out in the hammock. He'll be sleeping on the sofa."

"No, thank you," Jaden said matter-of-factly. "Briz is hurt. I'm putting a clean bandage with ointment on his leg. *And...* I'm sleeping in his room. In case he has a...relapse..." This time Jaden looked at Briz. "This is the last time we'll get to be together." She looked back at the triplets and softened her stance. "Please don't argue with me. I said sleep. Don't worry your little white-haired heads off, we're not going to have sex! I won't even get under the covers."

Briz grinned as he turned and went into his bedroom and lit the lantern.

"Look," Jaden stood in the hall, talking to everyone. "I'm leaving the door open. Violet can sleep in here, too, if she thinks we need a chaperone."

Briz paused, waiting to hear if Violet would agree to this. Surprisingly, no one objected. Taking off his shorts and leaving on his briefs, he slipped into bed. He doubted he'd have a relapse, and since he'd returned, the triplets had been filling him with a concoction that had megadoses of hops. He was still a teenage guy, but his hormones weren't as whacked out as they had been after the first Queller attack.

Jaden came into the room quietly grumbling, "Did you see their expressions? With everything I've been through, they still treat me like I'm a little kid. I've survived the Mal Rous. I'm sixteen…Well, close enough."

Briz lay back, watching as Jaden applied a salve and clean bandage to his leg wounds.

When she was done, Jaden whispered, "I'll be right back. I want to get my drink and brush my teeth and put on my nightshirt."

Briz grinned as he scooted over to make room in the small bed for Jaden. *Could she be any sweeter? Makes me want her even more.*

When Jaden returned, she turned out the lantern and lay down next to him. A golden glow continued to grow in the room as the sun broke the horizon.

Briz waited until the rustling of the triplets' slippers disappeared into their bedrooms before looking towards the door. No one had come into their room to check on them, though no one's bedroom door had closed, either. Briz assumed every ear was focused on them.

"You want to get under the sheet?" he asked.

"Yes. But I guarantee that if I do, Violet will flutter in here. By the way," Jaden leaned closer, her lips next to Briz's ear. "I didn't say we weren't going to make out."

Careful of his bandaged leg, she lowered herself on top of him.

"I love that you're not as innocent as you appear," Briz said, focused on the pleasure of her body.

Jaden's slender arms held her above him, and her long dark hair draped around their heads like a curtain of privacy. The beat of his heart quickened as Jaden lowered her mouth to his, and he realized he wasn't as tired as he'd thought.

Her lips were warm, her kisses tender. Briz slid his hands over the contours of Jaden's body, resting them on the hem of her nightshirt. Their kisses grew deeper, and he let his fingers trail across the backs of her thighs, longing to pull the sheet aside and her nightshirt off, to feel her skin against his. It was obvious he wanted her. He moved his hands to safer ground, weaving his fingers through her hair.

She whispered against his mouth, "I'm sure Violet and Rosie can smell our pheromones. I can. Any minute Olympe will bring us bottles of our drinks."

Briz knew she was right, but he didn't care. Jaden raised her head higher. He reached up and moved her hair to the side so he could better see her face.

"This is the beginning...and the end of our relationship... isn't it?" Jaden said with a sigh of sadness.

He understood what she meant. Once at Guyon Manor, she'd send him away again. He knew she wouldn't let him be the decoy to capture the remaining Quellers—and for that, he was grateful. And in less than two weeks, he'd be leaving on his trip.

He cupped her face in his hands, raised his head and pressed his lips to hers, wondering how this mere sylph of a girl had had captured his heart.

CHAPTER 39

JADEN

Jaden felt the comfort of Briz's arm draped over her waist. His body, separated by the fabric of the bedsheet, nestled against her. Her nightshirt was sticking to her skin—she stared at the ceiling fan, willing it to work. It was midday, and the warmth of the bayou had settled in. With a soft moan, Briz nuzzled her hair, then rolled onto his other side.

The events of last night seemed like nothing more than a bad dream. One more Queller was dead, and Briz was all right. Jaden could hear the triplets shuffling around the house, preparing to flee.

She glanced at the open bedroom door. Violet wasn't in the room—everyone had trusted them to sleep, and only sleep, in the same bed after all. Someone had placed a glass of her Envie Tea and a glass of Briz's elixir on the nightstand. Jaden slipped from the bed, grabbed her drink and her clothes, and looked over at Briz before closing the door.

Then her attention went to the pile of items in the middle of the living room. *How long did the triplets think they would be gone?*

The three cats were eyeing their makeshift cages, the triplets' suitcases, a wooden box filled with healing tonics and supplies and boxes of food. Jaden guessed the triplets didn't realize that Hubs could drive to the store from Guyon Manor.

There was a box of old photos and Billy's paintings.

In case they decide not to return?

For the first time in decades, they were leaving their home, their sanctuary. Jaden wondered if Isadora and Tamara had ever been to Guyon Manor; she knew Olympe had been there when Hubs was three and again when he was six and had been attacked by the Mal Rous. She and Billy had hoped Dekle could heal him.

Like that scumbag would ever do the right thing. Sure, he'd developed cures for the various ailments the Mal Rous had inflicted on their victims, but Jaden couldn't get past the fact that his "help" was for a problem he'd created.

Near the front door was the jug with QB carved on its side that Jaden had brought back from the cave, and she wondered if it contained an incubating Queller. Jaden knew she couldn't have left it there for someone to find years from now—though a part of her wished she had. Now, it was their responsibility. No. *Her* responsibility.

Jaden retreated to the bathroom to get ready for the day. When she came out, Briz was in the kitchen with the triplets.

"This is plenty, thank you, Isadora," Briz was saying while eating an apple. "Sorry we slept so long."

Briz smiled at Jaden as she came into the room. A warmth spread across Jaden's face, as if they'd done more than just sleep together.

"I'm good with an apple, too," Jaden said. "Or whatever

is handy." When she opened the refrigerator, it was empty and warm. Which explained the ice cooler sitting on the counter filled with the Mal Rous and Queller remains.

"I have some bread and jam for ya here." Olympe patted her on the shoulder as Jaden closed the refrigerator door.

"If everyone's ready," Briz said, "when you're done eating, we should head out."

Breakfast was quick. Locking up the house was easy. Loading the two boats was like putting together a three-dimensional jigsaw puzzle.

They worked with as little commotion and talking as possible. Everyone was aware that the Quellers could be nearby. Hopefully not watching them. Hopefully asleep. And not following them.

Jaden settled herself among the triplets' two dogs, the boxes of food and the cooler on the boat Briz had borrowed from Cylis. Briz and Hubs used long poles to guide the boats away from the dock and along the shore of the bayou, unwilling to start their motors and draw attention to their great escape.

Jaden looked back at the house. The roof appeared to be smoldering. Steam rose from the ground and off the dock as the midday sun struggled to burn the clouds away. The clouds won.

The triplets sat in Hubs's boat across the water from Jaden and the dogs. Holding open umbrellas and wearing lightweight clothing that covered their white skin from head to toe, large floppy hats, and sunglasses, the three sisters looked as if they were posing for a modern-day version of a painting by the artist Claude Monet.

Jaden couldn't see Violet and Rosie; she assumed the Bellibones were tucked under one of the seats.

As they glided past the cypress trees, the dogs lay down at Jaden's feet. The only sounds to be heard were the ever-present drone of insects and the water rippling over the sides of the boats. From time to time, a carp splashed out of the water, or a bird called. Hubs nodded to Briz when the channel widened, and the noise of the motors soon filled the bayou.

Jaden faced straight ahead, thinking of her friends back in Colorado. Her life in Louisiana had been so all-consuming that she hadn't thought about them in weeks. She wondered what they had been up to lately. What movies had they seen? How many of their soccer games had they won? What boys were they crushing on? Or were they falling in love...*like her?*

She gave her head a slight shake. Briz was nothing more than a crush. Their bond was intense because it was based on fear...well, fear and lust. Not love.

It made sense that after weeks of thinking you might die, all of your senses—appreciation, infatuation, passion—would be heightened...*but love?* Can you fall in love with someone after knowing him for a little over a month?

Why not? Her grandma Jin had told Jaden that desiring someone emotionally, mentally, and physically was a powerful, heady experience and that she'd fallen in love with Jaden's grandpa after just three dates.

Jaden turned back toward Briz. He smiled at her. She continued to face in his direction, taking in the landscape between sneaking peeks at him—allowing herself a few moments to feel the fullness in her heart. Soon Briz would be out of her life forever. Maybe that was why she hadn't let herself admit she loved him.

She looked at Briz again. He was scanning the shore. She

knew he was keeping an eye out for the Quellers. Her attention went skyward and to the upper branches of the trees—she continued peeking at Briz as she watched for Dekle's flying beasts.

Briz sped up so their boat was parallel with Hubs's, causing Jaden's hair to blow across her face; she quickly knotted it into a bun as they headed onto the open waters of the wetlands. The two dogs sat resting their chins on the side of the boat as they peered over at their mistresses. Jaden followed their gaze.

The triples' umbrellas were tipped forward, butting the impact of the wind. Though protected by dark sunglasses, their pale eyes were probably wide open with the anticipation of returning to the town they had renounced so long ago.

Hubs's boathouse came into view, and Jaden's stomach became a tight mess of emotions. She took in a deep breath. *One step at a time*, she reminded herself. First, make sure the triplets are safe. Second, call her mom—who would threaten to ground her until she was old enough to vote. Third, fourth, fifth...her list continued to grow, along with all the reasons that she despised herself.

The boat slowed. It was time to accomplish step number one.

Seated at the front of Hubs's boat, Tamara stood with less than steady legs. Violet and Rosie fluttered up, one on each side of Tamara, their tiny hands gripping the fabric of her maroon-colored blouse, as if to help balance her, as she leaned forward and slid the boathouse door open. The three of them sat back down as Hubs guided the boat in.

The dogs were up and ready to jump onto land. Jaden held them by their collars.

"I'm going to pull up right behind Hubs's boat," Briz raised his voice over the sputtering motor. His boat kissed the back of Hubs's, and in unison the motors shut off. Briz slipped past Jaden and stepped onto Hubs's boat to help the triplets onto the dock, while Jaden ushered the dogs ashore.

Once she was on dry land, Jaden moved to pick up a suitcase when she caught a glance of Olympe staring in the direction they'd just come, her lips taut. The triplets had been so calm while loading the boat, never shedding a tear even though they were leaving their home. Now Jaden wondered if it had all been an act.

"Where's the garage?" Isadora asked, less nostalgic than surprised. "Hubs," she said, turning back to him. "What happened to the other building? The one where I kept my car?"

"It f-fell *doown* a long *tiime* ago."

"Isadora had a car?" Jaden hadn't intended to say it out loud.

It was Tamara who answered. "We might live in the backwoods, but we aren't backwards!"

"Of course not. That's not what I meant..." Jaden was glad Tamara's eyes were trapped behind the dark glasses. She could feel them chastising her.

"Thank you, son," Isadora said to Briz as he handed her one of the caged cats. She joined Jaden, and together they walked to the back of the boathouse, where Hubs's car was parked.

"Our papa used to drive Tamara and me up to this little herb shop in Lafayette," Isadora reminisced. "Harriet, the woman who ran it, didn't mind the way we looked. She was very helpful."

"Helpful..." Olympe said, coming up behind them with

another caged cat, the two dogs following her. "From what I remember, you and Miss Harriet—"

Isadora stifled a grin as she interrupted her sister, "One day papa bought me a car so I could drive there on my own. I didn't have a license; I reckon he figured no police officer would want to stop me. They were most likely too afraid of me, 'cause of my skin color—worried I would put a curse on them."

"There's a lot more to unload, girls. You can gab when we get to the house," Tamara urged, striding past the others carrying the third caged cat. She opened the car door. "Briz wants you to call your mama, Jaden. Have her meet the two of you at his friend Cylis's boathouse. He said she knows where it's at." Tamara handed Jaden Briz's cell. "You might not want to share all the details as to why we're going to be staying at Guyon Manor. Just skim over things for now. You can fill her in later when she can see for herself that everyone's all right."

Chapter 40

Jaden

Jaden waved to her mom as Briz steered the boat up to Cylis's boathouse. She watched as Brooke got out of the car, her clothes hanging on her frame like they were a size too big. Jaden wondered when her mother last ate—stress had a way of filling her up, leaving no room for food. Jaden had barely stepped onto the dock when her mom was in front of her.

"I'm never letting you or your sister out of my sight again," Brooke said, wrapping her arms around Jaden.

Jaden hugged her mom back. "I'm okay, Mom. We're all okay. And Ava's safe with Albert now."

Her mom squeezed her tighter as she choked out her words, "No, she's not. I don't know where she is."

"What?" Jaden gasped, her breath lodging painfully in her chest. "Briz told me Ava was flying home."

Jaden pulled free from her mother's grip as Briz came up next to her. The once fine lines on her mother's face now resembled the distress marks added to new furniture to make it look old.

"She wasn't on the flight." Her mom reached over and caressed Jaden's cheek. "Albert and I thought since she missed her flight she might be driving to Colorado, but she hasn't shown up yet...and we haven't heard a word from her."

Jaden's thoughts immediately went to the Quellers. Had they attacked her sister? "Did you look for her? Did you check at Guyon Manor? The hospital?" Jaden didn't mean to sound as if she were chastising her mom. Behind her questions, Jaden was condemning herself.

"Yes. Everywhere...." Her mother's voice competed with her worried expression. "I even drove to the airport in New Orleans and checked the hospitals there and the one in Belle Fleur. Albert keeps threatening to fly here to look for her himself."

"No way. Albert can't come here!" Jaden felt as if she was going to hyperventilate.

"I apologize for driving your car all the way to New Orleans, Briz...and about your grandfather's truck," Brooke said as Briz carried the cooler to his car. "I'll pay him for it."

Briz shook his head. "I'm not worried about it. Let's just find Ava."

Jaden rode in the back seat; reaching up, she placed her hand on her mom's shoulder. "I'm sorry I wasn't here yesterday for Rick's funeral."

Brooke patted Jaden's hand, accepting her apology without comment. Surely her mom's thoughts were on Ava.

When the trees that loomed over the shack where Jaden had released the Mal Rou Tig came into view, the hair on her arms rose. She flashed back to when she thought she saw Datura in the window after helping Briz and Hubs gather the Mal Rous' bones. What if Datura was alive?

"Stop the car!" Jaden yelled.

"The last time you insisted I *stop the car* on this road, you ended up getting bitten by Datura," Briz said, accelerating.

"Stop the car now!" Jaden insisted, unbuckling her seatbelt. "I want to look for Ava at the shack."

"The shack?" her mom questioned, turning back toward Jaden.

"The shack, Mom. Where I first found the Mal Rous." Jaden kept her voice even, wondering how her mother could forget. The day and place would be etched in Jaden's memory forever. "Maybe Datura tricked us into thinking she was dead. Maybe she has Ava." Briz slowed the car; Jaden knew her words had resonated.

"But Datura's dead." A nervous rise in Brooke's voice filled the car. "Briz said you have her body."

"No. We don't." Unlike her mom, Jaden's voice deepened. "All we found was one of Datura's fingers. And now Ava's missing. If Datura *is* alive, she might have taken Ava there." Jaden pointed in the direction of the shack.

"Then I'll go. The two of you can wait in the car," Briz announced as he put his car in reverse. "I'll take the machete. I'll be fine."

Irritation creased Jaden's eyes as she blurted, "No way, Mr. Macho with the I'll-take-care-of-the-little-women attitude! I'm going!"

"Briz, Jade's right. You wait in the car. I'm already carrying enough guilt about all you've been through. I will not allow you to put yourself in harm's way anymore! I'll go with Jaden."

"NO!" the word exploded from Jaden and Briz at the same time.

"Jaden, I'm not letting you go without me!" Brooke glared at the two of them as Briz pulled to the side of the road. "Besides, Ava's my daughter, and I have as much right as anyone to look for her! I can't wait around doing nothing when...when Ava might be hurt."

"Well, I'm not letting either of you go without me!" Briz argued. "Datura could be waiting to ambush you. We'll all go. We've got one machete, and I have my hunting knife."

Returning to where it all began, Jaden thought as her mom jumped out of the car.

Briz had his hand on his door handle when Jaden said, "Briz, the other day when we were leaving Guyon Manor with the Mal Rous bones..." She looked out the window to make certain her mom wouldn't hear. "I thought I saw Datura watching us, but then I figured it was just a glare on the window."

"Why didn't you say something?" Briz's tone was less than kind. "Hubs and the triplets are there all alone." With a shake of his head, Briz got out of the car.

I'm the world's biggest idiot. Briz was right. Not telling them was putting all of them in more danger. But Hubs had his gun and the other machete...there were plenty of butcher knives in the kitchen that could be used as weapons. *They'll be all right. They have to be.*

Briz opened the back of the car and handed Jaden the machete, then pulled his hunting knife from its sheath. All Jaden could think as she led the way through the foliage was that they looked like one sorry-ass trio going to do battle. Mosquitoes stuck to the sweat on her arms as she used her machete to clear away cobwebs on the overgrown path. Her moist shirt clung to her. Jaden glanced back at her mom. Beads of perspiration trickled down Brooke's face, dampening her blouse.

They approached the shack and peeked through the foliage.

Watching. Listening.

The place looked worse than Jaden remembered. The three of them inched up the mold-covered stairs and paused. Peering through the vacant space where the front door had been, Jaden's mind spun back to the moment she'd flung the door open so hard it had crumbled apart, the day Datura had bitten her and changed her into a Mal Rou.

The spongy floor buffered the sounds of their footsteps as they moved through the main room. Briz kept watch while Jaden and her mom crept into the bedroom, hoping to find Ava. Perhaps poisoned, gagged, and tied up—but alive.

The room was empty. Together they entered the kitchen. Spider webs, resembled sheer tulle fabric, draped over the massive fallen tree that had demolished the room. Briz walked out onto the back porch and into the yard. Moments later he returned, shaking his head.

Maybe her mom was right, and Ava was driving to Colorado. After all, she was determined to get out of this town. With a feeling of unease, Jaden took her mom's hand. "Let's go."

Where else could Datura have taken her? Jaden wondered as they made their way back to the car.

Jaden had just finished telling her mom about the Quellers finding the triplets' house—conveniently leaving out the part about the thousands of swarming hornets—as Briz pulled next to Hubs's Chevy and the front door of the manor opened.

Olympe stood in the entrance, watching as Jaden, Briz, and Brooke exited the car. "We were getting worried. What took ya so long to get here?"

Jaden did her best to smile. Olympe was at least eighty, and the woman had just left the only home she'd known since she was a young girl...because monsters were in the woods. As far as Jaden was concerned, there was no need to upset her more. Olympe could continue to think that Ava was safe in Colorado.

"My mom got lost trying to find Cylis's boat house." Next to Jaden, her mom supported the lie with a shrug along with the sound of strained laughter.

Jaden's mind flooded with visions of Datura as she asked, "Did Hubs search the house...*for Quellers?* Did he look in the garage? The cellar?"

"Yes, dear. He did. Before he'd even let us get out of the car." Olympe took hold of Brooke's arm as they walked into the house. "Did Jaden tell ya about Rosie?"

"No, she didn't." Brooke glanced over her shoulder at Jaden, her expression clearly wondering what other secrets Jaden was keeping from her.

Jaden gave her mom a thin smile. Truth was, she had forgotten all about Rosie. Her focus had been on getting the triplets to a safe place, and now finding Ava.

Olympe made the introductions while Jaden went from room to room on a mission to find evidence that Datura was alive. Jaden saw that near the stairs, Tig's blood had been cleaned off the hardwood floor, and in the kitchen, Esere's blood was no longer smeared across the kitchen tiles—something she should have done, not the triplets.

After searching the house, Jaden checked the garage, the cellar, even the yard, retracing Hubs's steps, wanting to be certain that there wasn't a clue that only she would recognize.

When the clouds were fiery streaks of orange and red,

and the mosquitoes were swarming for their evening meal, Jaden gave up and went back into the house. The triplets and Brooke were preparing dinner, but Jaden's stomach felt like a solid mass of knots. The aroma alone was too much for her.

She found Briz and Hubs in the sitting room arranging mattresses they'd hauled down from the upstairs bedrooms. No one wanted to sleep where they would feel trapped.

Everyone wanted to be in a room where they could easily escape.

CHAPTER 41

JADEN

My life before Mal Rous. My life after.
My life before Quellers. My life after.
My life before Briz. My life after.
My life before Ava was killed. My life after.

Jaden stared into the darkness. Unable to sleep, she'd been writing the words over and over on a chalkboard in her mind. Her thoughts clung to visions of her sister. Jaden was ready for daylight to arrive so she could begin her search again.

She sat up on the mattress she was sharing with her mom and looked around the room. The light of the moon kept its distance from the porch and windows, leaving the parlor a befitting gray.

Her skin felt clammy. Everyone was crowded together, sleeping as best they could, fully clothed in case they had to escape. Briz was asleep on the small Queen Anne sofa; Hubs shared one of the musty mattresses with his mama; Tamara and Isadora were on another mattress; Violet and Rosie were curled up in a moth-eaten chair. All the doors and windows were locked. The triplets' old dogs lay sprawled in the entry as if guarding the front door.

Jaden listened to the creaking bones of the house and to the fans oscillating back and forth, sending a slight breeze through the muggy room. Slipping off the mattress, she stood over Briz. In the dim light, she could make out his flashlight and sheathed hunting knife next to his pillow, his machete on the floor within easy reach. She shook her head.

She should have told him to go home yesterday. But her selfish desire to be near him overrode all *shoulds*.

Jaden wanted to wake him and steal him away for some time alone, make certain everything was good between the two of them before she made him leave. Last night he'd reassured her he wasn't upset with her for not telling him she may have seen Datura in the window, that he was just tired. But she didn't believe him.

Most of all, she wanted to tell him she loved him. Only, what was the point? He didn't need to know. They'd be parting ways soon.

A scurrying jolted her attention from Briz to the stairs. A dark form streaked down the grand staircase and hid under the sofa below Briz. Jaden tilted her head and saw one of the triplets' cats. Her heart quickened as she squinted at the stairs, trying to see what had been chasing it. *One of the other cats*, she hoped. They were always running around, teasing each other.

"Everything's fine." Her mouth formed the words, but her voice was muted. She looked at Briz, her mom, the triplets and Hubs. If harm came to any of them...*Keep them safe. Better I get hurt. Not them.*

Jaden felt in her pocket for her dad's small knife, then opted for Briz's hunting knife. She slipped it into her cargo pocket, straining to hear any unusual noises over the sounds of the fans. But the house was old. She couldn't make out much beyond the groans of pipes and scampering of mice in the walls. Jaden picked up her flashlight and machete next to her bed and quietly went up the stairs.

She flashed her light toward Amelia's bedroom door. It was closed, just as they had left it. As was Elvina's bedroom door. The hairs on Jaden's arms rose as the light met Dekle's door. It was ajar.

She listened for the flapping of wings as she crept down the hall. Then, reaching out with the machete, she pushed the door open wider.

No Quellers. She blew out a breath.

The south-facing window ushered in silver beams of moonlight. Jaden scanned the room with her flashlight. Nothing looked disturbed. Most of Dekle's belongings had been packed into boxes and shoved against the antique bed frame along with paint cans, brushes and rollers. The bed and her grandfather's desk beneath the window were covered with drop cloths protecting them from the splattering of paint.

Jaden went over to the desk. Moonlight revealed a gap in the windowsill. Claw-shaped handprints were smudged on the glass. Jaden inhaled a slow deep breath, paying attention to every nuance of every smell in the room, finding her burgeoning Mal Rou capability an asset.

Datura's scent filled her nostrils.

Jaden turned slowly. Datura stood on the corner of the bed, wearing a dirty white shift, her hands behind her back. She kept her eyes on Datura, braced herself on the side of Dekle's desk, and stood straighter. Datura attempted to mirror Jaden's stance, but the small Mal Rou's body was crooked, her spine badly damaged from their last encounter. They looked at one another with bitter animosity.

In that moment, Jaden knew Ava was alive. Why else would Datura show herself? She wanted Jaden...and Ava was the bait.

Datura's eyes widened with delight as she brought her hands out from behind her back and twirled the ring on Briz's car key around her index finger. Jaden winced, seeing where Datura was missing a finger. In her other hand, she held Hubs's gun; it was just a pistol, but it looked large in proportion to Datura's small bony grasp. More deadly.

Hubs's gun had been next to his bed. Briz's keys on the table near the sofa. Jaden felt a chill that started deep in her belly, then crawled across her skin. Datura had snuck into the room while they were asleep.

"Where's my sister?" Jaden's words came out strained. Not good. With Datura, she could not appear meek. Nor could she afford to be hostile. That would upset Datura, and the house was filled with everyone Jaden cared about.

Jaden tried to calculate her options. She could see that Datura had already released the gun's safety lock. If she threw herself at Datura and stabbed her, would Datura be stunned enough that Jaden could take the gun away from her?

But...Ava. First, she had to find out where Ava was.

"Put that machete down." Datura raised her chin. Her voice was cocky. "If ya play nice, I'll let ya see yer sister."

Jaden set the machete on the desk.

"Naw. Put it on the ground." Jaden placed the machete on the floor. "Now, kick it under the bed."

Jaden lightly pushed the machete with her foot.

"That's a good girl," Datura purred.

"What did you do to my sister?" Jaden demanded, gritting her teeth.

"Aw, ya say that like ya think I'm evil. Ya know, when Dekle created us, he thought we might be able to help people. To heal 'em."

"Sure he did."

"Come on, Jaden, ya has to know that our plant DNA can be healin'. The thornapple in my system...*in your system*...is right good for asthma patients. Why, since ya and me shares Dekle's DNA, we is like sisters. We is like—"

"I'm nothing like you!" Jaden looked toward the door, realizing the possible consequences of her loudness. Waking everyone could cause their deaths. Or their changes if Datura fancied adding to her collection of Mal Rou zombies.

"Hah." Datura's voice was slow and steady. "This here drama ya is goin' through, worryin' 'bout yer sister; it's all nourishment to ya now. Yer boyfriend's pain, yer mama's anxiety, 'em other people's fears. It's energizin' ya, just like it's energizin' me. I can feel it... It's like a *high* hummin' through me." An icy chuckle escaped from Datura. "Don't go foolin' yerself into thinkin' it's only a Mal Rou trait. It might be stronger in us, but I think we got it from our human DNA." Datura grinned, exposing her canine teeth. "You and me, we is just alike."

Jaden's hands clenched as she took in a sharp breath. She didn't want to hear anymore.

"Ya gonna tell me ya don't feel it, too? I know ya can. That's why ya can't sleep." Datura nodded her head toward the door. "Yer cells want to feed off 'a all 'a the fears of 'em people downstairs." Datura inhaled as she ran her tongue over her lips. "Go on girl... Ya can taste it in the air. *Mmm.* I know ya wants to."

Jaden's tastebuds swelled with the bitter taste that Datura might be right.

"Don't it make ya wonder if yer fear is feedin' off 'a yer thoughts, or if yer thoughts is feedin' off 'a yer fears?"

"I'm not like you," Jaden said again.

"Ya don't sound so sure." Datura's eyes narrowed. "Ya should be thankin' me for makin' ya a stronger person. Ya ain't no mousey little girl no more."

"Where is Ava?" Jaden asked.

"We is gonna go see her right now. Ya can drive, can't ya?"

"Ya, I can drive." As soon as she said it, Jaden regretted letting Datura know.

"I've been walkin' enough." Datura gestured toward the door. "Get movin'. And if ya is smart, ya won't alert the others, or ya might never see yer sister."

Hubs's gun. I have to get the gun away from her.

JADEN

Jaden's bare feet pressed into the gravel as she pushed Briz's Prius away from the house. Each sharp stone was worth the pain; if she'd gone back for her shoes, she could have woken someone and given Datura a reason to attack or use the gun. At a safe distance from the manor, Jaden got into the driver's seat and started the car. The clock on the dash read three-ten A.M. She looked in the rearview mirror. No one appeared. Grateful hybrid cars were quiet, Jaden waited to turn on the headlights until she'd driven well past the ornate wrought-iron gate and was heading down the road.

Jaden glanced over at Datura in the passenger seat. As much as Jaden didn't want to be a Mal Rou or to think like a Mal Rou, right now she needed to draw upon her newly acquired genetic abilities. She wished she hadn't been consuming so much of her Envie Tea.

"Stop the car at that there trail." Datura's voice was soft as several of the tentacles on her head latched onto Jaden's upper arm, tightening to make certain Jaden did as she was told; releasing their grip when Jaden parked the car and opened the door.

As if echoing Jaden's pounding heart, thunder rumbled in the distance.

Datura climbed out of the car right behind Jaden. A cloud settled beneath the moon, turning the landscape into layers of dark images. Jaden turned on her flashlight, wondering how many more times she would have to walk on this path that had destroyed her life.

"No, this here way." Datura waved the gun toward the darkness that reached out beyond the front of the car. "The car's just a little decoy for when they come lookin' for ya."

Jaden followed Datura, striking her feet solidly against the ground, hoping someone would see her footprints when daylight came.

"Damn bugs." Jaden swatted in the air while walking past the car. "They're attracted to the light." Jaden switched off the flashlight as she bent down and slapped her legs, quietly setting Briz's key ring on the road. After another thirty steps, Jaden slipped her hand into her pocket. She let Datura get a few feet ahead of her before removing her pocketknife.

"There's nothing out here. Where are we headed?" Jaden asked, covering the sound of her knife hitting the ground.

Datura turned and Jaden placed her foot on the knife. The knife was small; she hoped Datura wouldn't notice it... but that whoever came looking for her would find it.

Jaden reached up and tied her hair into a knot. "What?" she asked with attitude. "I'm hot."

Datura continued to walk. "Stop ya jabberin' and move faster."

Jaden released a sly grin at Datura's complaint—knowing her maneuverings had gone unnoticed. "I can't go any faster; the pebbles hurt my feet. I'm walking on the side of the road."

"Ya princess!"

Jaden picked up her pace. It was too dark to know if her footprints showed up, but she continued walking with heavy steps on the softer ground.

A quarter mile up the road, Datura stopped.

"Here!" Datura pointed at the cane field that bordered the water. "I covered up the tire marks." She laughed proudly.

Tire marks? Jaden didn't ask Datura what she meant— then she flashed on Briz's grandpa's truck. She turned on her flashlight back on. Dead branches were stuck upright in the soil, more were strewn around to blend in with the rest of the dead foliage. They hadn't given the area a second thought when they had driven past it yesterday.

"Go ahead 'a me." Datura pushed on Jaden's calf.

Jaden plowed forward, knocking down as much of the barricade as she could.

"Stop right there," Datura snapped. "I ain't no dummy. I know what ya is doin'."

Datura stuck the branches back into the ground. "Don't ya go pissin' me off again, girl. Now get goin'."

Jaden walked on the tire tracks, her feet sinking into the ground. More thunder informed her that her ploy of leaving a trail could be washed away well before sunrise.

She felt the weight of Briz's hunting knife in her pocket —it would be her last resort. If she couldn't take the gun from Datura and kill her, Jaden would at the very least maim

Datura. Even if it meant in the process that Jaden was going to die, too. As long as Ava lived!

Jaden's sweaty clothes felt glued to her body as she continued to trudge past the walls of dried-up cane on either side. She kept her light aimed down, keeping an eye out for nocturnal reptiles that might be slithering near her feet. Though crossing paths with a deadly snake might be another solution—if she could get it to bite Datura.

More likely, Datura would eat the snake.

Jaden knew they weren't far from the water. She could smell it. Mud squished up between her toes; the air was thick with mosquitoes. She untied her hair, so it hung down, protecting her face.

"We is here," Datura croaked like a bayou bullfrog.

Jaden raised the flashlight to point straight ahead. The light reflected off a dirty bumper with a sticker that read "Adopt A Pet."

The gun. Jaden turned back toward Datura, ready to kick the gun from Datura's hands.

Datura had the gun aimed at Jaden's knee. Her finger was on the trigger.

"Don't ya even think 'bout it, or it'll be pretty hard for ya to walk." Datura gestured the gun toward the truck. "Get ya sister."

Jaden proceeded to the cab of the truck. Shining her flashlight through the open window, she found Ava's body tipped to the side in the driver's seat. Her skin was covered with hundreds of red welts from mosquito bites. Futilely, Jaden swatted at the hungry mosquitoes buzzing around Ava.

"She's dead!" Jaden swung back toward Datura, ready to pummel the murderer. Datura wasn't there.

"Close," Datura smirked as she clambered onto the hood of the truck. "But not yet. Now get her out."

Jaden opened the door. Grasping Ava's arm, Jaden shook her sister. Ava didn't respond. She could see punctures on Ava's arms and neck. Jaden inhaled sharply. She had to stay focused, to be strong. She had to come up with a plan to get Ava out of here. To get her some place safe.

Jaden shook her sister harder this time. Then slapped her, expecting Ava to reach up and slap her back. But there was no response. Jaden raised Ava's eyelids. Ava's pupils constricted from the light. Such a little movement meant so much.

"Don't make me say it again, girl. Get her outta there!"

Get her out yourself, Jaden wanted to snap back. "How much poison did you pump into her? She's practically a corpse. I can't get her to move. Or did you..."

"I thought 'bout it, lots. But I didn't make her one 'a *us*." Datura laughed.

Jaden flinched. *One 'a us.*

Even with the triplets' Envie Tea, Jaden would forever carry a part of Datura in her blood.

"This here sister 'a yers is way feistier than ya ever was! I had to keep givin' her thornapple juice. But she was worth it. Now I got you."

Juice. It was an interesting choice of words to describe Datura's toxic sap. For all the healing capabilities thornapple possessed, Datura always preferred to administer amounts that were just shy of deadly.

"She ain't gonna remember nothin' that's happened to her." Datura sounded disappointed. "Nothin' that I did to her anyhows."

"Why not leave her?" Jaden asked. "What good is she to you? Like you said, you have me now. I'm the one you want."

"With her along, I know ya is gonna behave yerself. Ya won't try doin' anythin' stupid." Datura scrambled up the front window onto the roof of the truck, then looked down her long nose at Jaden. "Besides, she's my backup. In case ya mess up...and I decide to change her." Datura's nostrils flared. "Or if I need *bait*. Now hurry up!"

"Bait?" The word quietly trembled past Jaden's lips as it blared in her head. "What do you need bait for? You have me."

"Just get her out."

Jaden propped Ava up and pulled her toward the door. "She's too heavy. Too drugged. I can't lift her." Her flashlight lit up Datura's bitter expression. And the gun. It was so close Jaden could reach out and grab it.

Datura held the gun steady with both hands and took a step back. "For all I care, ya can drag her. Just do it!"

Jaden inched Ava out of the truck and braced her sister against her own smaller frame. As Jaden glanced at Datura, she experienced a sensation of a noose tightening around her heart. The Mal Rou was scraping her gums with her claws, making them bleed, getting herself ready to mix her blood with Ava's with just one bite.

"A little insurance, so ya do what I tell ya."

"I thought the gun was your insurance." Jaden felt the noose tightening more.

"It don't hurt to remind ya what I can do to her." Datura pointed the gun at Ava. "She'd make one fine Mal Rou. Then again, I can just shoot her. Let her die in yer arms."

Jaden tried to back her sister away from the truck, away

from Datura. Stumbling, Jaden struggled to keep herself and Ava upright.

"Now let's get goin' or I might just decide to change her right now." Datura grinned, blood dripping from her mouth. "Turn her into a savage, like I did to you. So she'll skin and debone yer mama alive like ya did to Ivan and the others."

"I didn't skin and debone them!"

"Ya expects me to believe ya, when ya sliced Ivan's throat and watched that boy kill Tig. And ya tried to kill *me*." The sound of thunder emphasized Datura's words.

"I never would have hurt any of you if you hadn't attacked my mom and sister." Jaden wondered if this was the truth or a lie. Hadn't she wanted all the Mal Rous dead? Then again, hadn't she also bonded with Datura? "And *you* tried to kill me, and Briz."

"Don't whine. I just gave ya a little gut wound."

"Gut wound? I thought I was going to die. If you were so concerned about Tig and Ivan, why didn't you try to stop us? You just stood by and watched."

"Admit it! Datura licked the blood from her lips. "Ya went and skinned 'em alive, stripped 'em down to nothin' but their bones."

"I didn't. Datura, I have your blood in me! Your DNA! They were my family, too! It horrified me when I saw what had happened to them." It was true. But Jaden knew they were a family that she never wanted to see again. That she was glad were dead.

"Why didn't ya bury the others like ya buried me? They just needed to be given a chance to heal." Datura lowered the gun for a moment.

"Bury you...I didn't—"

"I know I'm to blame, too," Datura interrupted Jaden. "I was so angry with ya that day when ya and that boy hacked Ivan and Tig up. When I bit into ya again, I went and made ya too feral."

"It wasn't me! I didn't skin anything! It was the Quellers —another one of your psycho Professor Dekle's creations."

Datura raised the gun, aiming the barrel at Ava. "I've told ya before, don't ya ever talk bad 'bout him."

"Fine." Jaden said in a flat tone as she protectively moved in front of her sister. "I've never met the man, but I'll love him as if he was the grandfather I'd always wanted."

Datura snorted her annoyance, then sprang from the roof of the truck.

Jaden recoiled as Datura latched onto her shoulder with one hand before moving onto Ava's back. Jaden steadied her legs as she raised her voice. "I'm willing to go with you, but wherever we're going, we'll make better time without Ava. Let me stick her back in the truck and leave her here."

Datura spit on the ground at Jaden's feet. "Naw...I think it's best if I have the both 'a ya."

"You were ready to shoot her a second ago. She'll be a pain in the butt when she's not in this stupor." Jaden's mind was scrambling to find the words that would convince Datura to leave Ava behind. "I care about my human family, but I love you, Datura."

Datura grunted with disbelief as she dug her claws into Ava's shoulder, her tentacles burrowing into Ava's matted hair and around her neck.

"Get movin'." Datura pressed the barrel of the gun against Ava's head.

The discussion was over.

With Datura still clinging to her sister, Jaden draped one of Ava's arms over her shoulders and wrapped one of her own arms around Ava's waist. With the flashlight aimed at the tire tracks, she dragged Ava forward.

"Not the way we came, ya idiot." Datura jerked her head in the direction of the bayou. "That way. We is takin' the Professor's boat."

The growth was dense, the ground mushy. Jaden struggled to pull her sister through the foliage as thorns scraped Jaden's calves and cut into her bare feet. She was numb to the pain. Over the past few weeks, she'd learned that fear had a way of doing that to a person. You didn't feel anything once survival mode kicked in.

She considered letting Ava fall to the ground, taking Datura with her. But she'd have only seconds to remove Briz's hunting knife from her pocket and from its sheath and stab Datura. By then, Datura could shoot them both. Or chomp her bloody teeth and gums into Ava...changing her forever.

When we're on the boat, Jaden thought, *that'll be my best chance to get rid of Datura. If nothing else, I'll grab her tentacles and fling her into the water.*

Plants reached up around them, thicker in some spots than others. The closer they moved toward the water, the muddier the ground became. Jaden's feet were near ankle-deep in bog. She tugged her sister forward, the force causing her to drop her flashlight.

"Leave it," Datura spat. "I can see just fine in the dark. Keep movin'."

Jaden looked down and saw Ava's bare feet in the flashlight's beam. Her sister's shoes had come off. If they didn't disappear into the thick mud, along with the flashlight, they'd marked the trail.

She glanced up at the sky, wishing the clouds would set the moon free so she could see, too. But maybe it was better this way. Being abducted by a mutant with a gun was bad enough. She'd rather not know if they were about to be bitten by a deadly snake or attacked by a gator.

CHAPTER 43

DATURA

Datura held the gun in one hand as she dug the claws of her other hand deeper into Ava's flesh, steadying herself on the girl's back. Jaden's efforts to maneuver her sister through the growth had become increasingly jolting. Datura wondered if Jaden had been right. Maybe she had been overly zealous when injecting Ava with her poison. As her tentacles wrapped themselves around clumps of Ava's hair, several tentacles drew in a deep breath.

"Mmm," Datura sighed and nestled her nose into Ava's hair, savoring the fragrance of Ava's scent. She stayed that way for some time, raising her head only when Jaden stopped walking.

"I have to take a break." Jaden sounded short of breath.

"Then I'm gonna have somethin' to drink." Datura leaned over Ava's shoulder and let one of her tentacles pierce Jaden's neck. Jaden didn't even flinch as the tentacle's mosquito-like mouth pierced her skin and fed on her blood. A second tentacle, this one swollen with poison, rested near Ava's throat.

"I ain't given yer sister no thornapple since last night. Try anythin', and I'll pump enough in her to kill her."

"I thought she was your backup plan!"

"Don't mock me, girl. She is my backup. Unless ya do somethin' stupid."

When satiated, Datura's tentacle retracted from Jaden's neck. "Break's over. We is almost there."

Datura secured the claws on her feet in the fabric of Ava's shirt as Jaden continued dragging and jerking her sister through the shrubs and reeds.

Dekle's pirogue was nestled in a patch of marshy grass. Half-hidden, the boat was just shy of being rubble. But it functioned—and it was one of the few things Datura had left of Dekle. She looked at Jaden and considered that the young girl was her last remaining kin.

Datura raised an eyebrow. *No.* Even if it was true, and Jaden is Dekle's granddaughter, Datura wouldn't be dumb enough to think of Jaden as family again. The girl would have to prove herself first. Or be put down after she helped her find the other Mal Rous. The craggy lines in Datura's face deepened as she considered what Jaden had said earlier, how she had been *horrified* when she'd seen what had happened to Tig and the others. That they were her family, too. That she loved Datura.

Her musings were interrupted when Jaden lurched to the side, almost making Datura drop the gun. *It weren't intentional,* Datura thought, not smelling an odor of deceit. The girl's strength was waning as she pushed through the cattails and bulrush plants that cradled Dekle's pirogue.

Jaden held Ava against the boat, and Datura climbed onto the gunwale to check for any stowaway alligators.

"All right." Datura moved to the bow of the pirogue.

"Get yer sister in the boat before some gator feeds on the two 'a ya."

She watched as Jaden struggled to lift her sister. Finally, Ava's body came sliding on her back across the bench, her arms flopping limply on either side. For days mosquitoes had been feeding on Ava. Datura thought it was a shame that the girl's creamy complexion was covered in red welts. Jaden wasn't looking much better.

"Push us into the water, then hurry on up and get in." Datura glanced up and sniffed the air. "It's gonna rain soon. I can smell it."

The boat jerked up and down, then back and forth. Datura teetered on the bow. "Don't be stupid. I thought ya was smarter than that," Datura snarled, regaining her balance as the boat stopped rocking. Jumping down next to Ava, she reached up and rested the gun on Ava's neck.

"I was just trying to get the boat clear of the plants, Datura."

"Sure ya was." Datura wondered if, like a Mal Rou, Jaden no longer released the scent of anger, or fear...or deception.

"Hold on." Jaden pushed the boat again while stepping into the waist-high water. Clutching the gunwale, Jaden raised herself up, flung her leg over the edge and dragged her soaked body into the boat.

Datura kept her eyes on Jaden as she sat herself on the middle bench and reached for an oar. She didn't think Jaden was dumb enough to whack her with it, not with the gun resting against Ava's neck.

"Head in the direction 'a the salt cave."

"The salt cave?" Jaden looked back at Datura.

"We's goin' to find the Professor's first Mal Rous. He told me 'bout 'em. They're so nasty that even someone as feral as you won't be able to get near 'em. He used to say I'm a bloody miracle. So are they. Just like my sister and brothers were."

"I told you. I'm not feral! And I. Didn't. Kill. Them."

Visions of Jaden stripping the flesh from her siblings' bones came to Datura's mind. "Shut yerself up and start rowin'."

Datura didn't know the exact spot the Professor had stashed the other Mal Rous, only the general location, but now that she had Jaden back, things were looking up. Even if they didn't find Dekle's other Mal Rous, Datura wouldn't have to spend the rest of her life alone. Maybe one day, she would forgive Jaden for killing her siblings, and Datura could think of her as family again.

A couple of Datura's tentacles stroked Ava's skin; changing Ava was feeling more and more like the right thing to do. Then there would be six of them once they found the other three Mal Rous.

The boat was wider than most; difficult for only one person to maneuver. With the gun aimed at Jaden's back, Datura watched as Jaden slid from side to side on the bench, dipping the oar on one side of the pirogue, then the other, in her efforts to steer the boat into the bayou.

Datura looked up at the sky. It would be daylight soon. She'd hoped they'd be farther away from the plantation by now. Thunder still called from the distance as clouds filled the sky—in the dim light, their blurred reflections glided over the water as the boat moved closer to a channel overgrown with bald cypress trees.

Datura's attention went back to Jaden as the girl pulled

something from her pocket. Jaden quickly moved her hands so Datura couldn't see what she was doing.

"Ya best drop it! Whatever ya got there, drop it over the side 'a the boat."

"It's nothing." Jaden turned and tossed a leather case onto the hull. "It was in my pocket...It was poking me."

Datura picked the case up. It was empty. She looked up just as Jaden lunged at her with a knife. Datura knocked it from her hand, then waved the gun at Jaden. The girl shrank back.

"Ya just run outta luck, ya dummy!" Datura punctured a fresh hole in her gums, letting the blood run down her chin, before picking up the knife and slashing Ava's arm.

"I done told ya not to try anythin'." Datura set the knife beside her as she inhaled the aroma of Ava's blood.

She knew no matter how much of her DNA she injected into Ava, the girl would never be nice to her, not the way Jaden once had been, but she had to show Jaden who was in charge if she wanted to keep her under her control. With her mouth open, Datura tipped her head towards Ava's arm.

The boat rocked. Datura ducked as the oar came toward her head. Jaden was preparing to swing the oar again as Datura aimed the gun at Jaden and pulled the trigger.

A moan came from Ava as the sound of the gunshot reverberated across the bayou, sending birds scattering from the trees, fleeing for their lives.

Jaden hadn't screamed. Datura figured the bullet hadn't found its target. Then Jaden wrenched to the side, her body leaning against the gunwale. Her face paled as she cupped her hand just below her shoulder, blood seeping through her fingers.

"You hate me so much that you want me dead?" Jaden sounded as if the wind were knocked out of her.

"Naw. I don't want ya dead." Datura paused, sensing an unfamiliar feeling. *Sorrow.* It surprised her that it had such a rancid taste. "What I wanted was for ya to choose *us*...the Mal Rous...To choose *me*, like Dekle did."

With knee-jerk reaction, Datura took a step closer to Jaden. She hadn't meant to hurt the girl. Not really. If Jaden died right now, she wouldn't have anyone in her life that cared about her.

"I swear, I'll choose you, Datura, if you leave Ava alone," Jaden said, her chest sinking lower onto her body.

"Don't be givin' me no ultimatums. I'm gonna do what I has to do. Ya shouldn't have come at me with that oar!"

Jaden's eyes grew wide as she looked past Datura.

"*No!*" Jaden yelled as a bird dove from the sky toward her.

"What is it?" Datura bellowed as the strange creature flew away. "I ain't never seen no bird like that."

"A Queller! It can smell our blood. It'll eat us alive, like it did Esere and the others."

Datura inhaled the tangy aroma of Jaden's blood. "Ya sayin' that's what killed my siblin's?"

Datura turned to see where the Queller had gone when a second one dropped out of the sky, swooping so close to Ava, Datura could see the hairs on its belly skim over the blood on Ava's arm.

"It's the one that's part sea lamprey! Keep it away from my sister!" Jaden shouted.

The Queller retreated to where the first one hovered near the trees.

"Datura, give me the gun," Jaden implored as she stood up and moved closer to Datura.

Datura's eyes met Jaden's. Was the girl going to shoot her? Or was she choosing to keep her safe like the Professor would have? Before Datura could hand Jaden the gun, the sea lamprey Queller was back, its spiny tongue reaching out through rows of pointed teeth as it flew straight for Ava.

Jaden stumbled forward, twisting her body so she landed sprawled face-up over her sister, shielding her. The Queller attached its mouth to the open wound on Jaden's shoulder. Jaden screamed in anguish, the sound vibrating like shock waves through Datura. For a moment, Ava raised her head as if to see what the noise was all about.

"Get off 'a her!" Datura yelled at the creature as its swollen hairs fastened to Jaden's skin and began making a pumping motion.

Dropping the gun, Datura grabbed the knife, climbed on top of Jaden and held the blade against the Queller's throat. She was ready to plunge the knife into its slick eel-like skin when she was hit from behind. The knife slipped from Datura's hands as she fell onto the deck.

Ava's eyes blinked open. Her vacant stare met Datura's.

The bird-like Queller came at her again. Datura sprang up, grabbing onto her assailant as it reached the boat, not letting go as the two of them plunged into the green waters of the bayou.

BRIZ

A twinge of pain shot up Briz's neck. His whole body was stiff from sleeping all night on the small sofa. He automatically reached for his knife, aware that this was a sign that his life had moved well beyond what was considered normal and into the realm of phantasmagoric horror.

The knife wasn't there. Briz flicked on his flashlight, looked under his pillow and on the floor. There was no sign of it. As he picked up his machete, his eyes went to Jaden, asleep in her bed.

Then he realized it wasn't Jaden. It was her mom.

The hardwood floors were cool against his bare feet as he made his way from room to room in search of Jaden. At the top of the stairs Briz looked down the hallway at Dekle's open bedroom door.

"Jade?" he said her name softly as he approached. "Jade..."

He peered into the room, but she wasn't there. Disappointed, he went over to Dekle's desk and leaned toward the window to see if he could spot her in the yard.

The Professor had had a perfect view of the garage and cellar.

Of course, Briz thought, *so he could keep an eye on his laboratory.*

Briz's gaze shifted lower. The window was ajar. His eyes creased as he drew his finger around the small, rodent-like handprint on the dirty glass. As he turned and stepped away from the desk, his foot pressed down on a plastic hilt. He aimed his light to the floor, saw the handle of a machete sticking out from under the Professor's bed. Jaden's machete.

Muddy imprints of Datura's small feet were on the drop cloth covering the mattress.

"Jade was right." Alarm swelled in his throat, choking him. "Datura's alive." He picked up the machete and slipped its strap over his shoulder.

"Aww, Jade..." His voice trembled from the ache in his heart. "Where are you? What did Datura do to you?"

Briz clutched his machete as he walked over to the closet and opened the door. He swallowed hard, uncertain if he was feeling relief that the closet was empty or anguish that Jaden wasn't in it. His feet slammed against the floor as he rushed to Elvina's bedroom, then Amelia's room, the guest room, and the bathroom.

Then he flashed on the day Tig and Ivan tortured him and forced him into the wood crate. He raced down the stairs, through the kitchen, out the back door and across the stretch of grass to the garage. Bits of stone and dirt stuck to his damp feet as he ran to the garage's cellar door. He paused, then spun around with his machete raised, expecting to see Datura hiding in the shadows. The shadows held nothing but his fears.

He opened the cellar door—a murky light clung to the

room's small window. His breath stalled in his lungs as he hurried down the stairs, over to the crate. A guttural sound escaped from his chest as he opened the lid. No Jaden.

A hand squeezed his shoulder. Briz pulled away, ready to fight. Hubs jumped back, and Briz lowered his machete.

"Jade's gone." His words felt like jagged pieces of shrapnel scraping his tongue.

"We'll f-find her," Hubs reassured him. "My g-gun is missing, too. She's pr-probably looking for her sister."

The early morning sun filtered through the trees as they headed back to the house. Briz could see Brooke standing at the kitchen window, watching him. He wasn't ready to talk to her. Or to believe that Datura or any other monstrosity Dekle might have conjured had abducted Jaden.

Briz walked away from Hubs and made his way around the yard, looking for Jaden, wishing she would suddenly appear from the cane grass calling his name. When he came to the front of the house, he stopped and stared at where he had parked his car. Long strides took him to the front door—pounding on it, the lock clicked, and the door opened.

He brushed past Olympe, announcing, "My car's gone! Hubs, can I take your car? I have to look for her. I have to look for Jade." His hands shook as he struggled to put on his tennis shoes.

"Do you think Jade was right? Datura's alive?" Not waiting for a reply, Brooke slipped on her shoes. "I'm coming, too."

Minutes later, Briz was turning the key in Hubs's Chevy Impala.

"Where are we going?" Brooke slipped bottles of water and a couple of granola bars into her purse.

"I guess the shack." Briz glanced at her purse. Food and

water were the furthest things from his mind. Maybe it was a mom thing—always being prepared.

"We were just at the shack yesterday," Brooke said. "It was empty."

Briz refrained from glaring at her. "Do you have any other suggestions?" He didn't bother hiding his annoyance.

Well past the Guyon Manor gates, Briz looked at Brooke from the corner of his eye. Her lips were pressed together as she wiped her eyes.

For him, his girlfriend of the past, what...five, six weeks?...was missing. For Brooke, both of her daughters had vanished.

Where's my compassion? he wondered.

Possibly lying dead on the banks of the bayou, in the form of Jaden.

AVA

Agitated by the feeling of water running down her neck, Ava stirred awake. Thunder rumbled as she tried to roll onto her side, but the weight of her blanket was so heavy that she couldn't move. She moaned as rain pelted her face and more thunder cracked overhead. Her eyes opened. She stared up at the clouds until the rain forced her eyes to close.

"Where am I?" Her throat and her mouth were dry. She licked rainwater from her lips.

Ava's sharp, quick mind felt as if it was a lump of sludge. She was thirsty, tired. Disoriented. *I must be dreaming.* Wasn't she supposed to be home? Albert had paid for her flight back to Colorado.

She rolled her head to the side and blinked. Slowly, her reality came into focus.

"I'm on a frickin' boat?" she rasped.

"What the...? Jaden? Get off of me. You weigh a ton." Ava pushed against her sister. "What's wrong with you? Why are you making that noise?"

Ava raised her head and leaned to the side. The noise

was coming from what must be a Queller. At least four times larger than Jaden had described, it was draped over Jaden's chest with its mouth attached to her shoulder. Confusion skittered through Ava's mind.

"*Shiiit!*" Ava squeezed her eyes shut as her breathing came in painful fits and spasms. "This isn't happening." As if responding to Ava's doubt, the slurping and grunting grew louder. "Stop it," she demanded in a hoarse voice. "Stop it!"

Ava forced her mind to work. Her body to move. Sliding Jaden off her and onto the boat deck, the Queller was oblivious to the movement. It continued to drain Jaden's blood while its tendrils pulsed, pumping her with toxins. Ava reached for an oar, then spotted what she was certain was Hubs's gun. Near it was Briz's hunting knife.

"Get off of her!" Clutching the knife, Ava repeatedly stabbed the Queller, watching as blood seeped from the hideous creature's swollen body.

"Jaden's blood," Ava gasped. "You're killing her!" Her voice cracked as the words rang out over the sound of the downpour. "You're killing her!" Sobbing, Ava continued to stab the Queller again and again, until it fell off Jaden.

The sounds of Ava's hysteria were absorbed by the cypress trees, by the torrent of rain that washed the blood from Jaden's skin and clothes, from Ava's hands. When a bloody pool of water collected around Ava's bare feet and claimed the bottom of the boat, she dropped the knife.

Ava worked to steady her breathing, to control her panic. She stared at her sister, willing Jaden's chest to rise and fall. She took Jaden's hand to feel for a pulse. Only it was impossible to tell if there was one.

"Don't you die on me!" Ava shrieked. "I'm going to get

you help." She looked around. She had no idea where they were.

"When we get to land, it's not like I can carry you, or even drag you through the mud while I look for someone to help us," she said to Jaden, as if her sister could hear her. "I'll have to leave you in the boat." As she spoke, raindrops found their way into her mouth, teasing her dry throat.

Ava grabbed the oar and sat on the bench at the bow of the boat. They were in open water, but she could see narrow channels nearby. Her arms felt painfully weak; as she rowed toward the shore, she looked at the hundreds of welts that covered her arms and legs.

"Blasted mosquitoes. How long have we been here?" Then she saw the cut on her upper arm. "What happened to me?" she whispered tearfully. "All I remember is driving into the cane field to get my purse from our car...and then I got bit by a snake."

Her eyes grew wide, but Ava's voice remained quiet. "No. No, it wasn't a snake. I got bit by that Mal Rou, Datura. Yeah...she smacked me awake, then what?" Ava glanced back at her sister. "That's all I remember until I heard you...I heard you screaming." Ava blanched, looking around the bayou as if the sound of Jaden's painful scream was clinging to the trees. "And I...I saw Datura fall into the water with a Queller. I thought I was dreaming."

Ava stood up—gripping the oar like a weapon, she looked over the side of the pirogue to see if Datura or the Queller were hanging onto the hull; hoping the bayou had held them in its watery grip until they'd drowned.

Small waves rocked the pirogue. Nausea coursed through her, forcing her to sit. Ava looked across the bayou— a boat was barreling through the water. She raised the oar and waved it through the air, thankful that some crazy alligator hunter was out this early in the morning.

"Help is here!" Ava watched as the boat veered in their direction. She set down the oar and wiped her tears and the rain from her face. "We're going to be okay. You're going to be all right, Jade."

As the boat came closer, the bobbing of the pirogue intensified. Ava held onto the edge of the gunwale, holding herself steady. The rain subsided and she could see a woman sitting at the bow. It was her mom...her mom was here! Her amazing, wonderful mom holding a machete, ready to fight. And Briz.

The boat slowed as Briz guided it closer.

"It's just us," Ava called out as Briz killed the motor. "Jaden and me." Her mother didn't lower the machete. "It's just Jaden and me..."

Briz tossed Ava the end of a rope. As soon as Ava tied it to the cleat, Briz pulled the rope, dragging the pirogue closer.

"Your arm. Is the wound deep?" Briz reached over to help Ava onto their boat.

"I don't know." Ava looked at the loose flap of skin on her arm, then back at Briz. His face wore a pained expression as he stared at Jaden. Briz climbed onto the blood-covered pirogue, mumbling *sea lamprey* as he stood over the Queller. "I did my best to kill it. There was another one—it drowned with Datura."

"Both Datura and the last Queller are dead...?" She could hear hope in Briz's voice.

"I think so." Before Ava could say anything more, her mother's arms were around her.

The two of them stood there crying as they watched Briz lift Jaden into his arms. Balancing himself against the rocking of the pirogue, he carried Jaden onto the boat and placed her on the deck near the bow.

Ava squeezed her mother, then released her, letting her go to Jaden. Tears streamed from Ava's eyes as Briz took her in his arms and held her close.

"You're all right, Ava," he whispered. "You're all right."

What did he know? Ava didn't feel all right. And Jaden. Jaden looked anything but all right. Then Ava realized Briz was quietly weeping. She hugged him tightly, her emotions crashing through her. What was wrong with the world? With her? So much anger and violence and abuse. She inhaled a ragged breath. *Kinder. If Jaden survives, I'll be a better sister. A kinder person.*

Briz released his hold on her. Ava knew Jaden was his priority. Right now, getting her to the hospital was their only hope. This time, the triplets wouldn't be able to help.

Ava's attention went to her mother sitting on the floor of the boat with Jaden limp in her arms.

"Here." Briz handed Ava a small pouch. Ava stared at the fat cross on top of it. "It's a first aid kit. Cylis keeps it on the boat. Maybe there's something that'll stop the bleeding."

Briz stepped back onto the pirogue with a bucket, causing Ava's body to jolt forward as the boat bobbed. Finding his knife and case, he hooked it to his belt.

Ava slicked back her wet hair, then knelt next to her mom. She couldn't imagine what her mother was feeling right now.

"Sweetie, help me raise Jade up so we can slow the bleeding." Her mother's voice was calm as they carefully moved Jaden.

"That's a good sign...Right, Mom? That Jade's still bleeding? Her body's flushing out the poisons."

"I don't know," Brooke said, running her hands over her rain-soaked shorts before opening the first aid kit.

Ava looked over at Briz as he slipped Hubs's gun into his cargo pocket, stepped back into the boat and set the bucket with the dead Queller at the stern. The motor rumbled and Ava braced her sister as they began to move through the water, pulling Dekle's pirogue behind.

Brooke tore open an antiseptic pad, rubbed it over her hands, then opening a second antiseptic packet, she gently cleaned around the hole in Jaden's shoulder.

"Ava, was Jaden shot?" The motor nearly drowned out her mother's voice. "I see the Queller's teeth marks, but this puncture isn't like the ones they inflicted on Briz." Brooke glanced at Briz before applying antibiotic ointment to a wad of gauze pads.

Ava didn't answer. Her mind was scavenging through all that had transpired, trying to recall the sound that brought her out of her paralytic state. She'd heard Jaden scream. Hubs's gun was on the boat. Had there been a gunshot, too?

"I need more gauze." Brooke pressed what gauze she had against the wound trying to stop the bleeding.

"Use this," Briz offered, removing his damp shirt and handing it to Brooke. "It's better than nothing."

Ava hadn't realized that while steering the boat, he'd been keeping an eye on what they were doing...on Jaden. Of course he would.

Her mother placed Briz's balled-up shirt over the gauze covering the wound. "It's all we can do for now." Brooke leaned closer to Ava. "Now, you. Keep pressure on this while I clean the cut on your arm."

"My arm can wait. I'm just really thirsty."

"There's water in my purse." Brooke gestured with her

head toward the bench. Ava reached under it for the purse and took out the container. "Sip it slowly."

Easier said than done, Ava thought as she flipped the lid and took a large gulp.

"How did you find us?" Ava knew she sounded like a vulnerable little girl.

"Jaden did her best to leave a trail. We found Briz's car key on the road, and her pocketknife and footprints. Briz's grandfather's truck was near the water; we remembered about Dekle's boat. We hoped that since you'd have to row, we'd be able to catch up to you."

"Ah," Ava uttered. "Daddy's trusty pocketknife." Ava pictured the knife. It was Jaden's now. The same knife Ava had used to cut the ropes when the Mal Rous had left her mom and her tied up in the salt cave. The same knife Ava had used to stab Anders and Tig. "It's like Dad's ghost is here in Louisiana, trying to keep us safe."

Brooke inclined her head toward Ava. "He loved you girls with all his heart. I'm not surprised that even as a spirit, he'd choose to stay close to the two of you."

"The three of us, Mom. He's staying close to the three of us." Ava reached over Jaden and took hold of her mother's hand.

"Oh, baby. I love you." Her mom kissed her hand.

"Mom." Ava looked at Jaden. "Do you think she's going to make it? That she'll be all right?"

"I hope so." Her mom's voice conveyed more sorrow than hope. "And you? Are you going to be okay?"

"Yeah—" Ava choked on the word, then spluttered, "No...I don't think I'll ever be okay. Especially if Jaden dies." She began sobbing. "I...I think sh-she tried to s-save m-my life. Sh-she was on t-top of me, li-like she was pr-protecting me from the Qu-queller. S-so it w-wouldn't suck out *my* bl-blood."

Ava cried for everything she'd been through. For Jaden. For her dad dying when she was so young.

"I'm s-sorry. Mom. I sh-shouldn't have taken the t-truck and snuck off like that." Ava pointed at the first aid kit. "Is there any tissue in there?"

"No," Brooke said, shaking her head.

"Sorry..." Ava blew her nose into the bottom of her shirt.

Brooke shifted Jaden in her arms as Ava stood.

"Look—a boathouse." Ava pointed toward the shore. "I thought we were farther away." She stepped over to Briz and sat next to him.

Briz angled his head to Ava's ear, to avoid shouting over the engine. "I'll call Hubs as soon as we reach the dock. Have him call his aunt, Dr. Schilling, to meet us at the hospital. Hopefully, she won't ask too many questions."

They gave each other a look of doubt, then stared straight ahead as the boat sped closer to shore.

After Briz guided the boat to the dock and secured the lines, Ava helped him lift Jaden into his arms and to keep his balance as he maneuvered himself and Jaden onto the dock.

Ava turned back toward her mom. Brooke had moved onto the bench—staring at the three of them, with her elbows on her knees, her chin resting on top of her folded fingers.

Her mother looked like she was praying. With all that was happening, it would be the smart thing to do. Call on a higher being to help to save Jaden.

"Mom, you can get off the boat now."

Brooke looked at Ava. Her mother's expression revealed her sadness, her breaking heart. Ava reached toward her.

"Mom..." Ava's voice was tender. "Mom, we should hurry. We have to get Jade to the hospital."

Her mom inhaled a shallow breath, as if that was all that her lungs would allow. Then she reached up and took Ava's hand.

Chapter 46

Briz

Determined to make the thirty-five-minute drive to the hospital in twenty, Briz pressed down harder on the Impala's gas pedal. He glanced in the mirror at the three Lisette women in the back seat of the car as he passed the town entrance. Brooke was cradling Jaden's head in her arm while keeping Briz's shirt pressed against the wound. Ava held Jaden's elbow, keeping her sister's arm raised. Anxiety hung in the air.

Dr. Shilling arrived as Briz was opening the back door of the Impala. She eyed the blood smeared over his bare chest, then focused on his face once she was certain it wasn't his blood.

"Thank you for coming," Briz greeted her somberly. Then he leaned into the car as Brooke and Ava guided Jaden closer to him.

"I'll get a wheelchair," Dr. Schilling offered.

"It's okay. I'll carry her." Briz stood and adjusted Jaden in his arms.

"We need to get our story straight before we go inside,"

Dr. Schilling said hurriedly as she took in Jaden's limp body. "I don't want to give the staff any reason to make a police report. Just go along with what I tell them. It won't be pleasant, but if I'm harsh and annoyed, they won't ask questions."

Briz started walking toward the building. As Ava and Brooke got out of the car, he heard Brooke say hesitantly, "I... I already went to the police. When I couldn't find Ava. They pretty much laughed me off when they recognized me as the woman who had reported a missing daughter a few weeks ago and they found Jaden at the manor. Since Ava had made arrangements to go to Colorado, they didn't write up a report. They wanted me to give it a few days before they'd issue an APB."

"Good, then we don't need to bother them again," quipped Dr. Schilling.

"When Hubs called you, what did he say?" Briz inquired, his pace quickening as Dr. Schilling came up behind him. He doubted Hubs would have mentioned Jaden had been attacked by a mutant sea lamprey.

Dr. Shilling released a puff of air. "He wanted to know if his grand-pere ever told me what had happened to him when he was a little boy."

"Had he?" Brooke asked as she and Ava caught up to the doctor. "Had Dr. Whiting told you?"

"More or less," Dr. Schilling replied.

"Did you believe him?" Briz questioned, wondering why a doctor, all science and fact, would believe such a wild story.

"Not really. Over the years I'd heard stories from the old-timers that Rougarous were real—not just a folk tale. From time to time, my father-in-law would make a comment about Dekle Thatcher's experiments. The day after I saw *you* in here," Dr. Schilling looked at Brooke, "and we found traces of oleander and thornapple in your system, I had other patients that claimed they'd been attacked by Rougarous, and I thought about things he had told me. A week later, when Hubs brought Jaden to my house and asked me to stitch her up, I started going through old hospital records from years ago. I still don't know what to make of it all."

"I thought it was made up, too," Brooke admitted. "I didn't believe Jaden. If I had, she wouldn't be half-dead now."

The hospital doors were sliding open when Ava started to sink to the ground. Briz stopped walking as Dr. Schilling and Brooke caught Ava.

Dr. Schilling studied Ava's face. "Your daughter's dehydrated. How long was she lost?"

Briz did a quick mental calculation. "Three days." But he knew those three days Ava had been with Datura—dehydration wouldn't be the only reason Ava was weak and her eyes sunken.

"Thornapple," Briz added. "You should check Ava for thornapple poisoning. Jade, too, plus ifrita toxins, mountain laurel..." Briz paused, trying to remember all he knew about the makeup of the Quellers. "Uh, horse chestnut."

With Ava braced between Dr. Schilling and Brooke, they followed Briz into the hospital.

Dr. Schilling immediately went into commander mode. "Jezebel, these are the *city girls* I called you about." Dr. Shilling directed her tirade at the nurse, who jumped up from behind the front desk. "Did you get things ready in the OR?" Jezebel took Ava from the doctor and guided her into a wheelchair. Dr. Schilling ushered everyone into the emergency room.

The doctor turned to Briz. "Put her on that gurney."

Briz did as he was told, then was pushed out of the way by another nurse.

"The stupid fools. Wandering around alone on the bayou." Dr. Schilling spoke to the nurse while gesturing at Jaden. "This one's lucky she's not dead." Her voice rose as she snapped at Brooke, "What type of blood does she have?"

"O," Brooke sputtered.

Briz wondered if the doctor's abruptness was part of her act. Or did she honestly think Brooke was an unfit mother?

"Get her into the OR. We have to start the blood transfusion right away." When the nurse didn't move fast enough, Dr. Schilling barked, "Did you hear me? She needs a transfusion *now*. Hurry up!" The nurse jumped into action, and Jaden's bed was rolled down the hall into the operating room.

Dr. Schilling looked at the nurse standing next to Ava. "Jezebel, she's severely dehydrated. Get her situated in room one. Set her up with intravenous fluids; clean the flesh wound on her arm. Let me know if it needs stitches."

Jezebel eyed Ava and Brooke like she recognized them.

"Find this boy a shirt to wear," Dr. Schilling snapped at the remaining staff. She placed her hand on Brooke's shoulder, her voice sympathetic. "I know you want to be near your girls, but right now, I need the two of you out of the way. You can sit over there."

Someone stuck a nurse's scrub in Briz's hand. He slipped the shirt over his head as the doctor hurried to the OR. Then he and Brooke stared at the two closed doors that separated them from Jaden and Ava.

When the nurse had finished tending to Ava, Dr.

Schilling went into the room to stitch up the cut in Ava's arm. Afterward, Briz and Brooke were allowed into her room. Silently they waited for Ava to wake up, even though the nurse had told them she'd probably sleep through the night.

An hour later, Dr. Schilling returned to Ava's room. Briz felt his body tense—the doctor approached as if she was going to be the bearer of bad news.

"Please." The doctor gestured that she wanted to speak to Brooke privately in the outer room.

Briz touched Brooke's hand. She looked into his eyes and gave a nod.

"Whatever you have to say, you can say in front of Briz."

Brooke and Briz followed the doctor.

"I'm transferring Jaden to the Intensive Care Unit at the Ochsner Medical Center in New Orleans." Dr. Schilling paused, then as if wanting to be certain they understood her words, she continued in a soft, precise manner, "Did you know Jaden had been shot?"

Briz remained quiet, aware of the weight of Hubs's gun in his pocket—not wanting Hubs or his friend Stella to be wrongly accused of aggravated assault.

"Jaden has lost more blood than what we have in stock to replace." The doctor's eyes shifted from Brooke to Briz, then back to Brooke. "She has slipped into a coma."

A coma. Briz put his hand on his forehead, pressing against the words. But they only grew louder. *A COMA. A COMA.*

The nerve endings in his head pulsed with the sensation of millions of tiny needles; his chest felt as if it had swelled to twice its size, trying to buffer his bleeding heart. Was he having a stroke? Going into shock?

Briz looked at Brooke. How was she handling the news?

She was still standing, still conscious. Her fingers were covering her mouth. The blood appeared to have drained from her face.

Coma. The word only had four letters. Two syllables. Yet it had the ability to destroy lives. Briz wondered if he was as ghostly white as Brooke.

"Mrs. Lisette." Dr. Schilling's voice resounded with authority. "We must leave *now*. You can ride in the ambulance."

"Can I come?" Briz could hear the pleading in his words.

"No. There won't be room."

The doctor's response hit him like a punch to his stomach. "I'll follow in Hubs's car," Briz said quickly.

Dr. Schilling glanced at the closed door separating them from Ava. Then she looked at Brooke; with a nearly imperceptible shake of her head, she walked away.

"Briz." Brooke took Briz by the arm and turned him, so they faced each other, her countenance stoic. "I know you want to be with Jaden, but right now, I need you to be here for Ava. She's been through a lot, too...and I can't be in both places. Please, stay with Ava. She's going to need you." Brooke's last words were choked off as she stopped herself from crying. "I promise I'll call you as soon as we get to the hospital in New Orleans."

"Here," a nurse interrupted as she handed Brooke a plastic bag, along with Jaden's small pocketknife.

Briz glared at the nurse as he reached over and took the bag of Jaden's blood-soaked clothes and knife from Brooke's trembling hands. Setting the bag on the table next to the chairs they'd been sitting in earlier, he saw the food he'd run out and picked up for Brooke and him to eat. It was still on the table. Untouched.

"Okay." Briz turned back to Brooke. "I'll stay with Ava." Though he wanted to go with Jaden, the girl that he loved. "I'll have to leave for a bit. Return Hubs's car and get mine."

"Ava will need this." Brooke's brave expression faltered as she handed him the key to their rental house. "For when she's released. She doesn't have a key."

"Don't worry, Brooke. I'll be here for Ava."

Brooke gave him a hug. Then she was gone.

CHAPTER 47

BRIZ

Moisture wept from Briz's soggy tennis shoes with each step he took through the hospital, leaving a trail on the vinyl floor, out to the parking lot. The sun's rays moved through the remaining clouds like liquid heat, saturating Hubs's car. Hot air penetrated Briz as he slid into the driver's seat.

He felt his mind snap like a rubber band stretched to its limit as he sucked in a breath, his nostrils flaring from the smell of his blood-soaked shirt crumpled on the floor behind him. Slamming the door shut, he cranked the air on high, balled his hands into tight fists, and pounded out his anger and grief on the steering wheel. With each strike he cussed and swore, yelling until his throat was so dry he couldn't yell or swear any more, and silence filled the interior of the car.

With empty eyes, he stared out the front window and whispered, "Please let me die."

It seemed like a more peaceful option than living this nightmare. Then he thought of his family—how much he loved them. How much they loved him. Shame flooded his being. *Idiot. Why would I ever think dying was the solution?*

Briz dragged his hands through his hair, slower than normal. *Situations change. People change. Life goes on, ebbing and flowing.* Fate has a way of twisting and turning a person's life around in a matter of seconds, filling it with joy, just as easily as with despair. With his hands resting on his lap, he felt his breathing slow. He closed his eyes and tried to enter a more mindful state.

Soon, calm overtook his despair. After everything that had happened in the last few weeks, life felt more precious than ever. *It's not something you just throw away. Jade and I will come out on the other side of this!*

"Jade's going to pull through," Briz reassured himself as he drove out of the parking lot and headed to Guyon Manor. He hoped the fragile sliver of calm he'd created would stay with him.

When he spotted his Prius, parked on the side of the dirt road where Jaden had left it in the wee hours of the morning, Briz realized he had been in a daze. He hadn't been mindful of anything; he had driven through Belle Fleur without noticing the stop signs, let alone other cars and pedestrians. He wondered if anyone had honked at him. He was lucky he hadn't run someone over.

In the distance, Briz saw the shack. As he neared his car, the head of the trail appeared like a parasitic amoeba, creeping out from the dead cane in search of a new victim. He sped past it, reminding himself they had won their battle with the Mal Rous. With the Quellers. With Dekle.

He hadn't driven fast enough. The vision of amoeba slip sliding closer attached itself to his thoughts. There would be no victory if Jaden died. *Jaden's in a coma. If she lives, how long will she be paying the price for the mistake she made?*

Briz slowed the car as he drove down the driveway

toward the house. Isadora greeted him at the oversized front door, wearing her signature color of lavender, her pale eyes framed by her white eyelashes, her pale skin framed by her long, white hair, not yet plaited into a single braid. Her sweet smile was nowhere to be seen. He looked down at her as she reached up and hugged him—the weariness of his mind and body settled in.

"Hubs told us everything. You should be getting some rest now, son."

Briz bowed into her embrace. "There's too much to do." His voice was heavy with fatigue. "I have to get my car, find someone to tow my grandpa's truck out of the cane field. Take care of Ava."

"In a bit. You've had a full day. Up at dawn, and it's not yet noon. Right now, you need to rest."

Isadora took his hand and led him into the sitting room. "You sit here. I'll be right back. I'm gonna make you some tea and something to eat. Then you will take a nap. When you wake, you can fill us in on how the girls are. Hubs will help you with the truck and whatever else you need."

Briz leaned back on the sofa. He pulled at the bottom of the hospital scrub, aware that underneath the garment, he was covered with Jaden's blood. Violet and Rosie sat across from him. Rosie smiled her pointed, toothy grin before the two of them flew into the kitchen.

"My life is so bizarre," he muttered under his breath.

What seemed like only moments later, his cell rang. When he opened his eyes, he saw the plate of cold vegetables and a cold cup of tea sitting on the end table next to him. How long had he been asleep? As he pulled his cell from his pocket, he saw the time—three o'clock—and accepted the call.

"Hello," he said drowsily.

"Briz...?" Brooke asked.

Briz held the phone closer to his mouth. "Yes."

"It didn't sound like you." The timbre of Brooke's words was tight, jumpy.

Briz ran a hand over his face to wake himself more, then said one word. "Jade?"

"She's in the ICU. She's still in a coma. They're giving her more blood." Brooke paused as if waiting for Briz to respond—but he didn't know what to say. The silence was brief. "The doctors are hopeful. Since she's young and healthy, she should come out of this and be all right."

Jade's alive. Briz wanted to smile but had forgotten how.

He went to the window and looked out at the yard. "Why didn't you call sooner?"

"Briz, I'm sorry. It took over an hour to get here; then Jaden was rushed into the ICU. It took me awhile to get my bearings and connect with the new doctor and staff." Briz could hear the exhaustion in Brooke's voice. "She's being well cared for."

"Are you okay? Have you eaten?" Briz knew he sounded like his grandmother. "Is there any place you can get some rest?"

"I...I don't know. I doubt I'd get any sleep anyway. Right now, I just want to be close to Jade."

Briz nodded, wishing he were there, too.

"I went to the cafeteria, but I couldn't eat...Have you eaten?"

"Yeah." He glanced at the plate of untouched food on the end table. "The triplets made me something."

"Are you with Ava now?"

"I'll be there in a couple of hours. I asked the nurse to call if Ava woke, and I haven't heard anything."

"Okay. Good." Brooke's voice faltered as she repeated, "Good...good."

"Brooke...don't worry about Ava. I'll take care of her."

"Thank you, Briz." Brooke's voice sounded slightly steadier. "Dr. Schilling's on her way back to Belle Fleur. She thinks Ava could be released from the hospital in a day or two. I assume Ava will want to come to New Orleans. Will you make sure she brings a couple of changes of clothes for me?" Brooke went silent as the muffled sound of voices carried through the receiver. "Briz, I need to go. I can't thank you enough...."

Briz wanted to say, "No problem." But nothing came out.

CHAPTER 48

BRIZ

Briz ran his thumb over the pearl-inlaid handle of Jaden's pocketknife as he stared at Ava asleep in the hospital bed. Upon returning to the hospital yesterday, he attended to Ava's injuries from the mosquito bites, knife wound, and Datura's tentacles; applying lavender oil and Isadora's ointment, but Ava had remained motionless. Last night, he'd stayed well past visiting hours, waiting for her to wake up, but she never did. He only left when the nurses prodded him out the door.

The triplets assured him the lavender oil would work fast —as usual, they were right. Most of the red welts had already started to fade.

As if the sound of his thumb rubbing over Jaden's knife was too loud, Ava lifted her head. Her wide eyes scanned the room before settling on Briz. Her expression was one of confusion. Then recognition.

"Hey, sleepyhead," Briz said as he slipped the knife back into his pocket. "How are you feeling today?"

Ava looked around the room again.

"You know where you are?" Briz asked.

She nodded once. "Is my mom here?" Her voice was hoarse. "Is Jaden...?"

He wanted to answer her. But what could he say? He refrained from telling her Jaden was in a coma to avoid upsetting her.

"Briz..."

He stared into her eyes as he reached over and gently held her hand. "Uh...Jade was taken to a hospital in New Orleans, and your mom is with her. So, you're stuck with me." There was a quirk to his mouth as he tried to smile. It was the best he could do right now.

Ava raised herself and glanced at a pitcher next to the bed.

"Here..." Briz poured her a glass of water.

She sipped it slowly, then said, "I want to go see them."

That's what he'd been dying to do. *Dying*. Couldn't he have thought of a better word?

"Me, too," Briz agreed. "If Dr. Schilling gives the okay, we'll go tomorrow."

"No. Today." Ava handed him back the glass. "Today," she repeated, flicking the blanket off and swinging her feet off the bed.

Briz chuckled as her body flopped sideways back onto the bed.

"Today," Ava insisted again as she reached her hands out for Briz to help her sit up. "Find the doctor. I want to go see my mom and sister."

"Ava, you've been through an ordeal! You have to take it slow. We'll go to New Orleans tomorrow." Briz set the glass down, then helped Ava to sit upright. He sat on the bed next to her, holding her steady.

"Just go ask the doctor." Ava nudged him to make him get up. "It's my body. It should be my choice. I want to leave. Hospitals freak me out."

"I'll tell you what." Briz didn't get up. "When you can sit without falling over and are able to walk around the room, I'll ask if you can be released. Then I'll take you to your place. We aren't going to New Orleans until tomorrow. I don't want you relapsing or passing out on the way there."

Ava rested her head on his shoulder. "No. No way. I don't want to stay at the rental alone."

Briz considered all she had been through. Of course she wouldn't want to be alone. He didn't want to stay there either—not surrounded by Jaden's belongings. Every little thing would cut into his heart.

"Yeah, I understand." He squeezed her shoulder. "I have a place where we can stay. My friend's brother is out of town. I crashed at his apartment last night."

"We?" Ava sat up straighter and looked into his eyes. "You're not going to just leave me there all alone, are you?"

"No. We'll both stay there." Briz met her gaze, then her head sank back to his shoulder. "My family thinks I'm up in Monroe. Besides, I don't think your mom would appreciate it if I just dumped you at some stranger's house. We'll have to stop by your place to get some things for your mom. And clothes for you." He could feel her head nod in agreement.

"Slide back." Briz stood as she scooted back and raised her legs onto the bed. "You hungry? I'll have the nurse bring you something to eat."

"Thank you."

Briz tilted his head as if he hadn't heard her right. Had Ava ever said "thank you" to him...or for that matter, to anyone?

"Please, look for the doctor," Ava added. "I *am* checking out today!"

"Fine." Briz chuckled. Even weak and weary and somehow more polite, Ava was Ava. "But I told Hubs I'd help him take the triplets and all their stuff back to their house today—it'll take two skiffs. They don't want to stay at Guyon Manor any longer. If Datura didn't drown, they think it would be the first place she'd go. Datura doesn't know where their home is on the bayou. They'll feel safer there."

Briz pulled the blanket over Ava's bare legs, as she asked, "What if the Queller didn't drown with Datura?"

"Hubs is going to stay with them. He was pretty confident that if the Queller survived, he'd be able to kill it, since there's only one."

"He's not afraid?"

"I didn't say that," Briz replied. "I'll be gone for a couple hours. You should stay here while I'm away."

"I don't want to."

"Okay...Then do you want to come with?" Briz assumed she'd never want to go near the bayou again.

She gave him a feeble glare. "Your friend's place would be good."

Several hours later, after Ava had eaten a few bites of food and walked around her room on her own, the nurse returned with the release forms, a wheelchair, and Ava's clothes.

Ava recoiled at the sight of them, as if the fabric was woven with sinister memories. "You can toss those," she commanded in a tone sharp enough to snip through the material.

"I understand, dear." Without fuss, the nurse retrieved another hospital gown from a cabinet. "Let's put this here gown on over the one ya is wearin', but with the openin' in the front. That way yer little fanny will be covered." Ava slipped her arms through the armholes. "There, see, that'll work." The nurse sounded pleased with herself as she motioned for Briz to roll the wheelchair up to the bed.

"I don't need that." Ava pushed the chair away with her foot.

"Course not," the nurse replied, looking at Briz. He gave her a slight shrug. "But it's hospital regulations, so why don't ya just sit on down in it." Intent on doing her job, the nurse wheeled Ava out to Briz's car.

When Briz opened the passenger door, Ava smiled. "My purse!" she exclaimed as she slid into the car. "Where did you find it?"

Briz wasn't surprised Ava didn't remember. "My grandpa's pickup," he reminded her, as he turned to the nurse and gave her a wave goodbye. "I grabbed it when Hubs and I towed the truck out of the cane field." Briz could see a spark of memory light up in her eyes.

"Oh. Yeah…" Ava's voice was kind, almost sweet. "I'm really sorry, Briz." She held her purse out the door and gave it a jiggle. "It's not full of cockroaches, is it?"

"It shouldn't be." He smiled. "I shook it out pretty good."

Briz found Ava's words of apology, along with her unexpected thank you earlier, encouraging. Ava's eyes were misty. *Soulful*, Briz thought. He had never seen this side of her.

His parents always told him it was important to take responsibility for your actions—the good and bad. It was part of his mom's whole "everything happens for a reason" philosophy. Maybe Ava understood that if she hadn't run off to find her purse and flee town, she wouldn't have ended up in the hospital.

And Jaden wouldn't be in a coma.

But then, if Datura hadn't captured Ava, would she have come after him...or Brooke?

On the short drive from the hospital to Ava's house, Ava nodded out. Briz let her sleep as he drove around the block three times waiting for her landlady to finish unloading her groceries and packages from her car, not wanting to be the one to explain the whereabouts of Brooke and Jaden or make up another lie as to why Ava was wearing the hospital gowns.

When he pulled into the driveway, he woke Ava up and they hurried in and out of the rental house so fast that Ava hadn't even taken the time to change into street clothes.

Briz and Ava didn't talk on the way to Cylis's apartment. She didn't ask any questions as he showed her around the place. Briz had expected her to insist on calling her mom, but she didn't. When he was leaving, Ava was about to take a shower. He still hadn't told her Jaden was in a coma.

Later. I can't just blurt it out and leave. He'd tell her when he got back from helping Hubs and the triplets.

CHAPTER 49

BRIZ

Briz rapped lightly on the apartment door, not wanting to wake Ava if she was asleep. Helping Hubs and the triplets had taken longer than he had expected. He turned the key and knocked again before opening the door. He was about to say hello, but no sound came out as he looked at Grover and Ava sitting next to each other on the sofa, passing a bottle of liquor between them.

Briz stomped into the apartment. "What the hell are you doing?"

"Drinkin'," Grover said it like the clown that he was.

Briz went over and took the bottle from Ava. "Absinthe... 171-proof!"

The bottle was half empty. Briz looked back and forth from Ava to Grover. "How much of this did you drink?" he snapped.

"The half that's missin'," Grover laughed.

"Great!" Briz looked at Ava. She'd just spent the night in the hospital for dehydration after being injected with toxins from Datura for three days. And now she'd consumed a pint of alcohol.

"Why are you even here?" Briz snarled at Grover. "I didn't see your car out front."

"I walked," Grover slurred, the effects of the absinthe apparent. "I snuck away. My ma's been raggin' on me all day. I didn't expect to find *her* here." He smiled at Ava. "She wanted to talk with her mom, but her phone was dead, so I let her use mine."

"I told my mom I made the hospital let me go, and I was at your friend's place." Ava sounded like she had a mouth full of stones.

"Geez, her sister's in a coma." Grover reached over and put his hand on Ava's thigh. "Wow man, a coma. That's heavy. I mean, she could die." He stroked Ava's leg as if to comfort her. "She started crying and wouldn't stop. She was like majorly depressed...and scared."

Briz looked back at Ava and realized her eyes were puffy and red.

"I was depressed...and scared," she repeated Grover's words. "You didn't tell me about Jade."

"Oh, and like alcohol's going to help!" He glared back at Grover. "It's a depressant, you moron!"

"I don't feel depressed anymore," Ava slurred. "Besides, I'm not driving. I'd never drink and drive." She raised her hand and made a sloppy grab for the bottle in Briz's hand. "In fact, I never drink! Albert's dad is a drunk, so he gets uptight about it whenever anyone drinks alcohol. Can't even stand the smell of it." She leaned into Grover's face. "Ya know, Albert can be a real prude, but I love him!"

Briz felt like a peeping Tom watching the two of them.

Grover was licking his lips as his eyes lowered to take in Ava's cleavage. Ava glanced down at the lacey bra peeking out over the low neckline of her shirt before sinking back on the sofa.

Briz's fingers skimmed over his forehead and through his hair.

"Grover!" Briz kicked his *friend's* foot. "Stand up."

Grover didn't move. Briz kicked Grover's foot again. This time Grover gave Briz an indignant look.

"Stand up, *buddy*!"

Grover wobbled to his feet. Ava grinned at Grover as if she were proud of his impressive feat. Then her head bobbed forward as her eyes followed him dropping to the ground.

Briz looked down at Grover. "That's what I thought."

"What did you do that for?" Ava continued to slur her words. "We were having fun. F-u-" She paused to give Briz stink eye. "N."

Grover propped himself up against the sofa.

"Yeah, fun." Briz eyed Grover, then with a wave of exasperation scrutinized Ava's outfit. "Why do you do that? Why do you dress like a reality star desperate for attention? Give guys a chance to look at your eyes for a change."

"Leave me alone." Ava's words were garbled. "I wasn't ex-expecting company...Only you."

"Only me? Great." Briz gave her the once-over again.

Ava pulled herself upright, stood, and tripped over Grover.

"Whoops," she mumbled.

Grover didn't seem to notice.

"So you dressed like that for me?" Briz's voice had an edge to it as he went into the kitchen and set the bottle of absinthe on the table.

"Listen, buddy, I dress this way *for me!*" Ava stumbled in behind him. "I like it! It works for me."

"Yeah. Right." Briz looked over at her with a raised eyebrow before opening the refrigerator. "Have you eaten? I have some leftovers in here from last night."

Ava stepped behind him as he reached for a container of food.

"Don't change the subject. You're being a dick." Ava rubbed her mouth as if it would help her stop slurring. "You...you can't judge me! You know nothing about me." Ava sniffed as she pushed the refrigerator door into him.

"I know you've had too much to drink!"

Ava shoved the door into him again. Annoyed, Briz set the leftovers on the counter and closed the refrigerator door.

"You, you...you don't know anything you...you a-hole." Ava swayed as she went to punch Briz in his arm and missed. "You think you're so smart." Briz caught hold of her arm just above her stitches and steadied her.

"Don't touch me!" Ava jerked away from him. "No one touches me unless I let them! Our neighbor learned that one when I was nine years old, and he molested me." Ava sounded near tears. "But I showed him. I spray-painted the windows on his new red car and scratched PERV on all the doors."

Briz felt a wave of shock move through him. He'd had no idea. Of course he wouldn't—why would he?

She was only nine! If that had happened to one of his sisters and he found out, he would have chopped the F-ing predator's hands and dick off.

"He wasn't the only one." She continued to sway as she vented, "By the time I was fourteen, two other men and," she raised her hands and made quotation marks, 'a family friend' had tried to molest me too. But I'd wised up, grew my fingernails out nice and long and strong." She held up her fingers in Briz's face. "I pretended to go along with them. Even asked if I could 'touch' them first." She gave a tearful laugh as she slurred, "Oh, I touched them all right. In a matter of seconds they were screaming as they dropped to the ground."

She dabbed her nose with the back of her hand, then plopped down in a kitchen chair. Briz handed her a paper towel, and she blew her nose.

Wow, this explains a lot, Briz thought. *Her anger and her high-and-mighty, piss-off attitude is her form of protection.*

"Albert's the only other person I've told that to."

Briz pulled out a chair; moving it closer to her, he sat down and earnestly said, "Not all guys are like that, Ava." The corner of her mouth pinched as she shrugged a shoulder. "When it happened, did you tell your mom?"

"Noooo," she exaggerated with an annoyed expression. "I thought she'd be mad at me. I felt like it was *my* fault those jackasses tried to take advantage of me. Like I'd done something wrong."

"Ava, I know I haven't known your mom long, but I think she would have believed you. And I don't think it's too late to tell her." Briz wanted to reach over to comfort her, but he didn't want to upset her more—and he didn't want to experience the pain of those long, sharp fingernails if she took it the wrong way.

Ava released an alcohol-scented heavy sigh. "I have an IQ of 127. The only guy that appreciates it is Albert."

"Maybe if you dressed less...more..." Briz didn't finish his sentence.

"It em-...*em-POWERS* me," the word ripped from her

mouth, heavily doused with essence of absinthe, "...to shove my sexy butt in men's faces." She blew her nose again and let the paper towel drop on the ground. "Then ignore them. Make them feel beneath me, like they're worthless pieces of shit. Like the way those men made me feel about myself."

Briz thought about his sisters, the way they dressed once they'd reached puberty, enticing guys to come on to them. And about himself...the way he'd changed with puberty and started coming on to girls. After all, he had gotten his girlfriend back in Seattle pregnant. *A dad. I was almost a dad when I was fifteen.*

For a few minutes neither Briz nor Ava spoke. Briz stared at the floor, processing what he'd just heard. Ava must have been twelve the last time she saw her dad. She'd been molested by, as far as Briz knew, four different assholes, and since being in Louisiana she'd been attacked numerous times by monsters her grandfather had created.

He raised his gaze to Ava, wishing he could offer her words of comfort. But she was too intoxicated for his words to register, so he got up, took a pan out of the cupboard, and dumped in his leftovers. Ava needed food in her stomach. So did he.

Briz glanced back at Ava. She was chug-a-lugging down the bottle of absinthe.

"Nope.... Not cool. You've already had more than you can handle." Briz moved toward her, ready to take it out of her hands.

"Yes." Ava clutched the bottle close to her chest. "Grover said it would help me not be depressed." She jumped up from the chair and held the bottle behind her back. "And you...you depress me."

"Yeah, well, Grover says a lot of things to hot-looking girls that aren't true."

Briz reached behind her and took hold of the bottle. She gripped it tighter as she stepped back, slipped, and landed on the floor. With a laugh, she waved the bottle over her head.

Briz snatched the bottle away from her. There was only a quarter of the absinthe left. He set the bottle on the counter, reached out his hands and helped her up.

"You think I'm hot?" Ava smiled. "I didn't think you liked me."

"Man, your moods are all over the place. The last thing you need is alcohol." Briz's cell rang. He pulled it from his pocket and looked at the caller ID. "It's your mom."

"Hi, Brooke. Has Jade made any improvements?"

"No, she's the same," Brooke replied. "But the doctors have remained hopeful."

"Are you all right?" Briz asked.

"I'm just tired." Brooke cleared her throat. "Jade lost so much blood that they're giving her a complete transfusion. They're almost halfway through, and she's had no negative reactions to the new blood. Wouldn't it be great if when they're done she no longer had Datura's DNA in her system?"

Ava grabbed the phone from Briz. "Mom. Mom, I'm so sorry," Ava babbled as she started crying. "I'm so sorry that I was going to run away. This never would have happened. I didn't want Jade to die. I love her. I've always loved her. I never really hated her. I'm..." Ava's crying turned into sobs.

Briz took the phone from Ava. "Sorry, Brooke. She's pretty *upset*."

"I want to go see my mom!" Ava cried out loud enough for Brooke to hear.

A moan came from the other room. Briz put his hand over the mouthpiece as Grover's head snapped up and just as quickly dropped back against the sofa.

"How long has she been like this?" Brooke asked. "When we spoke earlier, she was pretty calm."

"Uh...I'm not sure. I was gone for a couple of hours. Had to help Hubs. Since I got back, she's been..." *drunk,* he thought, as he said, "emotional." Briz shook his head. This whole lying thing was just coming way too easy for him these days. "I'm making her something to eat right now."

"She saved me," Ava blubbered. "Jaden. Last week, she tried to suffocate me, and yesterday she saved my life."

"I better get going." Briz was trying to stop Ava from glomming onto the phone again. "She needs to eat. Then I'll get her to take a calming remedy the triplets sent for all of us."

"You'd better give it to her right now. Tell her I love her." Brooke's voice quavered. "What time will you be here tomorrow?"

"I'm not sure." Briz looked at the inebriated mess that was Ava. "I'll call you before we leave. If there are any changes with Jade, call me! No matter what time it is."

"Absolutely, Briz. And thank you for helping Ava. Thank your friend, too, for letting the two of you stay at his place."

Briz had put his phone back in his pocket when Ava clutched onto his arm.

"Grover said Jaden was dying. Now, she's dead. That's why you wouldn't let me talk to my mom." Sniveling, Ava kept talking. "Jaden was always so sweet. Her whole goodie-two-shoes thing made me sick. The Mal Rous...they did what

I couldn't. They destroyed her sweetness. I hate that I ever tried."

Ava shook her head. "I heard that thing sucking out her blood." She leaned her head against Briz's chest. "I-I'm so s-sorry J-Jade. A-and n-n-now you're d-d-ead."

"Ava, Jade's not dead. She's not dead. She's in a coma."

Coma. A wave of sadness hit Briz. He thought he'd moved past it.

Ava reached up and kissed the tear on his cheek. Then the corner of his mouth. Then she kissed his lips, and Briz realized grief can make you do crazy things.

CHAPTER 50

AVA

Ava's head was pounding. She wanted to throw up—her mouth tasted like she already had. Shielding her eyes from the morning sun that was assaulting her through the gap in the curtain, she looked around the room, wondering why she was in a strange bed in a strange apartment. And why her clothes were tossed on the floor.

She heard a door open; peeking through slits in her eyes, she watched as Briz came out of the bathroom with nothing on but a bath towel wrapped around his waist. He tiptoed over to a chair where he grabbed some clothes from his backpack, then tiptoed back into the bathroom.

What have I done? Ava's thoughts caused her head to pound harder.

Moments later, the door opened again. She pretended to be asleep until she heard the bedroom door close.

Did he have sex with the wrong sister? She swallowed back the puke that was inching up her throat. *No...if we had done it, I'd remember...wouldn't I?*

Woozily, Ava went into the bathroom; staring into the

mirror, she couldn't decide if she looked worse than she felt. She saw stitches in her arm and remembered being in the hospital. But then what happened?

"What's this doing here?" Her eyes widened at the sight of her toiletry bag propped open on the back of the toilet.

While she brushed her teeth, Ava scanned the bathroom for a clue to where she was—*dark blue towels and a brown rug. Not much to go on.* She rinsed her mouth and watched the water flow down the drain.

Her thoughts were slow. Her ability to speak even slower as her memory returned. "Briz brought me here...." She moaned. "Oh, there was alcohol. Lots of it. I was crying. And I kissed Briz—I mean, like really kissed him."

Panic stirred in her stomach. "Is Jaden dead?" Vomit met her lips as she leaned over and heaved into the toilet bowl.

After brushing her teeth again, Ava wrapped a hand towel around the stitches in her arm and stepped into the shower. The sound of the water was so loud she wanted to cover her ears, but the towel around her arm would have gotten soaked. The droplets felt like hail stinging her skin. It was a quick shower.

Ava took baby steps in an attempt to quell her nausea and throbbing head as she went back into the bedroom. Her suitcase was sitting on the floor near the bed. She got dressed and went into the kitchen, hoping she was ready to learn what had happened to her sister.

Color, light, and words yelled at her as she entered the bright room. The words came from Briz: "HOW ARE YOU FEELING?"

"You don't have to yell," she said, holding her ears.

He laughed so loud she held her head tighter. Then he smiled loudly.

"I'm not yelling, Ava. I'm practically whispering." She looked at him doubtfully as he screamed, "Sit down. I'll make you some toast. I spoke with your mom; told her I'd call before we leave for the hospital."

"The hospital?" Ava steadied herself against the refrigerator, more to balance her mind than her body. "Not the mortuary?"

"Mortuary?" Briz looked over at her. "Ava...Jade's in a coma. She's not dead. I kept telling you that last night. You were pretty out of it, but I thought I'd gotten you to understand."

Ava just stared at him. Coma...Hospital...Horrible as it was, it all sounded so much better than *dead* and *mortuary*.

"Good hangover?" Briz chuckled. Loudly.

In fact, everything he did was noisy—even putting the bread into the toaster. Ava pulled the chair from the kitchen table, grimacing as it scraped across the floor. When she sat down, her attention went to a framed poster. The picture was unsettling: a man similar to the grim reaper was standing over a dead green woman who had been stabbed.

"*La fin de la fee vorte*," Briz said, faking a French accent. "It means the end of the green fairy. This..." he tapped the bottle of absinthe on the counter, "is the green fairy."

The bottle was sealed, but she could smell it as if he were waving it opened under her nose. She wanted to puke right on the kitchen table.

"I bet Grover is in bad shape, too," Briz added. "The two of you drank half the bottle. Then you finished off another quarter of it."

Grover? Ava wondered why the name sounded familiar.

"I'm going to see if Hubs will buy another bottle to replace this one for Grover's brother, Cylis."

"Cylis?" This name she didn't recognize. Her brow pinched together as pieces of yesterday took shape in her mind. "Is this his place?"

Briz glanced over his shoulder at her as if to see if she was serious about not knowing where she was. Then it hit her.

"I got drunk with Grover. Eww," she muttered. "Grover! I don't even drink."

"The two of you were getting real *close* last night." Briz's comment made her feel like she might have to bond with the toilet bowl again. "I'm glad I showed up when I did."

"I owe you." Ava placed her elbows on the table and supported her head with her hands.

"No. I think we're good." Ava felt uncomfortable hearing his seductive tone. "Does Albert really wear a *purity* ring?" Briz asked out of the blue.

"Well...it resembles one." Ava looked at Briz. He was wearing a flirtatious grin.

Oh no...we did do IT. That's why he asked about Albert's ring. That's why he's being so nice to me.

"Augh," Ava croaked at the sound of a plate clattering onto the table, then stared at the dry toast and cup of peppermint tea Briz had set in front of her.

"You're going to want to drink a lot of water today." Briz leaned against the counter, watching her.

She bit into her toast, thinking how *low* she had gone. Briz was her sister's boyfriend. Teasing him, tempting him, luring him was one thing. But this was beneath even her moral standards. Then it dawned on her. Briz was just as much to blame.

"When you're done eating, I'll give your mom another

call, and we'll head out." Briz's voice was kind, brimming with eagerness. He wanted to see Jaden.

Ava nibbled on her toast as Briz straightened up his friend's place. Once they were on the road, she dozed, her head resting against the car window—a plastic container in her lap in case she had to throw up.

She opened her eyes as the car crossed over the raised lane markers as they entered New Orleans. After living in Belle Fleur for the past couple of months, New Orleans felt frantic, noisy. The traffic—like everything else today—was loud.

She glanced at Briz. His brow was tight as he focused on where he was going. He didn't say anything until he turned into the hospital's parking lot.

"You okay?" he asked as he parked the car.

Ava scowled in reply. She wasn't ready to speak. Her head was throbbing. Her mind was overwhelmed by what a horrible person she was. Her heart, which she had worked long and hard at keeping sequestered from the world, was beating with anguish over her sister.

When she stepped out of the car, the heat of the day slammed her back against the door.

Briz came up to her and slid an arm around her waist. "You're going to be fine. Your hangover will pass. Datura's poisons will move out of your system soon. But I doubt you'll want another drink of alcohol for a *long* time."

She thought about slugging him but didn't want to make any jarring movements.

Briz continued to hold her steady on the elevator ride, and as they walked through the Neuro-ICU ward. Then Ava saw her mom in the corridor, talking with a nurse.

Brooke turned as if Ava had called out her name. Her

mother's expression went from relief at seeing Ava to concern. *Or was it anger?* Ava wondered, feeling Briz's arm wrapped around her, keeping her upright.

Ava could feel her face redden. Did her mom know that she and Briz had done the deed? Was it that obvious? If her mom confronted her, she'd confess, but she was going to make sure that her mom understood that it was grief sex. Everyone knew it was a legitimate response to sorrow.

"Briz, move your arm! You're making it obvious that we had sex."

"We didn't...." Briz hissed in her ear. His fingers tightened around her waist as he drew them to a stop.

Ava exhaled as she leaned against him, teetering between relief, nausea and wonder. *Then what did we do?*

"Sweetie, look at you," Ava's mom said, hurrying over. Briz moved aside, and Brooke hugged Ava. "Are you all right? I can't believe the hospital released you when you're still so weak."

Ava expected Briz to laugh or make a snide comment about her hangover. But he wasn't paying attention. His eyes and thoughts were focused on Jaden.

Her mom took hold of Ava's hand, and the two of them stood next to Briz. Ava's nausea intensified at the sight of the ventilator breathing for her sister and the assortment of other machines surrounding Jaden.

"Briz." Keeping her voice quiet, Brooke glanced at the nurses' station. "I told the hospital staff that you're my son, so they will let you visit Jaden any time."

Briz raised his eyebrows. Ava figured, like her, he was wondering why the staff would believe her mom—he looked nothing like them. Did her mom also tell them he was adopted?

"What can they say?" her mom added, as if hearing Ava's thoughts. "That I'm lying, and they want to see your birth certificate as proof?" Brooke placed her hand on Ava's shoulder. "I booked you a flight, sweetie. You'll fly home tomorrow afternoon. Albert will pick you up. He's going to stay with you at our house, so you won't be alone."

"I'm not going back to Colorado without you and Jaden," Ava stated firmly. "We're a family. We'll get through this together. Besides, we still have work to do on that dump."

"No. I'm done." Brooke took hold of Ava's hand again. "We'll sell the place *as-is*; get whatever we can for it."

"Jaden's going to make it...right?" Briz's voice carried the anguish of a young boy in love.

"The nurses keep giving me words of encouragement." Brooke paused, then added, "They found traces of ifrita toxin and mountain laurel poison in her blood. Thank you for mentioning it to Dr. Schilling. She pushed them to check for it. They don't...don't know if she'll ever be a hundred percent." Brooke stopped again. Regrouping her emotions, she did her best to sound optimistic. "They've given her all new blood...I don't think she'll need to drink any more Envie Tea."

"Envie," Briz whispered so softly Ava barely heard it. Then he cleared his throat. "The triplets don't think it's just the loss of blood that caused the coma. They think it was the mountain laurel toxins, too."

Brooke, Ava, and Briz stood hand in hand, looking through the glass wall.

"I've got a call out to my cousin," Briz said after a few minutes, breaking their silence. "I'm canceling my trip."

"Briz, you know Jade wouldn't want you to do that." Brooke looked past Ava at Briz, but he continued to stare at

Jaden. "Unless you're still feeling ill from when *you* were attacked. Otherwise, Jade would want you to go. Besides, as soon as she can be moved, I'm taking her home."

Briz didn't respond. He was too fixated on Jaden's still form in the hospital bed.

CHAPTER 51

JADEN'S SOUL SELF

Jaden's Soul Self hovered above Jaden's body. Not long ago at Guyon Manor, Jaden's Soul Self had watched her from above, waiting to see if Jaden would leave her body behind. "But this time it is different," her Soul Self said to the machines keeping Jaden alive, to the walls surrounding Jaden like a disinfected womb. "Days have passed since she was brought to this room, and still she is not aware of herself —aware of me."

Jaden's Soul Self looked at Jaden, wondering if this was it, if it was time for the cord to be broken." Her Soul Self sighed, "I'm not ready for her to die."

The machines pulsed louder, but the walls did not respond.

"You have only known her a few short days," her Soul Self said to the room. "I know you have seen many people in here over the years. Have gotten to know them briefly. Cheered when they improved. Wept when they did not. But I have known this girl her entire young life. I am this girl. I know all that she has gone through. All that she is capable of doing. What her destiny can be. I am not ready to part ways with her body."

The glass door opened; Jaden's Soul Self glided to a corner of the ceiling, watching as a young man entered the room. She smiled down at the boy known as Briz. She had been taking great pleasure in his daily visits. With him came a spark of awareness in Jaden, a subtle pulse deep in Jaden's heart, giving her Soul Self hope that Jaden would pull through.

The boy sat next to the bed, his blue eyes glistening with emotion. "Your mom called me last night and told me they'd removed your ventilator." He inhaled a deep, uneven breath. "Jade...Jade, you're breathing on your own, babe." He wiped his eyes. "You're breathing on your own." His smile lit the room.

He took Jaden's hand. His touch was all at once painful, upsetting...and soothing, like a lyrical piece of music washing over Jaden, over her Soul Self. Her Soul Self watched the silver cord connecting her to Jaden vibrate lightly with love.

"Love." Her Soul Self beamed at the two of them, then at the walls and machines.

The boy known as Briz raised Jaden's hand and kissed her palm. The sensation caused the silver cord to quiver, tentatively at first, then faster and faster. Nothing but emptiness stirred in Jaden's mind.

The boy looked through the glass wall. The nurse on duty had her back to the room. He stood, leaned over, and pressed his lips to Jaden's.

Her Soul Self was jerked a few feet down toward Jaden's body, as if the silver cord was a fishing line that was trying to drag Jaden back from a distant place in the heavens where the stars could not be seen.

Still, Jaden's body laid motionless.

The boy turned and looked at the ceiling.

"Do you see me?" Jaden's Soul Self asked. "Or perhaps it is that you feel me?"

He didn't respond. Instead, his gaze shifted back toward the nurses' station. Jaden's soul looked, too. The nurse hadn't noticed his indiscretion, and though the woman thought Briz was Jaden's brother, he seemed to be weighing the risk of kissing Jaden again.

The boy known as Briz whispered in Jaden's ear, "If the nurse wasn't there, I'd climb into this bed and hold you… Maybe I should anyway."

"Maybe you should," Jaden's Soul Self said encouragingly.

Jaden's Soul Self longed to raise Jaden's arms, wrap them around the boy and hug him tightly. But the situation was not in her control. Like everyone else, all her Soul Self could do was wait for Jaden to decide.

Stay. Or go.

The boy called Briz sat back in his chair, keeping Jaden's hand in his. His voice was warm and rhythmic as it wove its way around the room with words of love, words of strength, words of forgiveness.

Then he left.

And Jaden's Soul Self resumed her place where Jaden now resided—drifting in darkness.

CHAPTER 52

AVA

Ava heard the sound of shoes declaring their awkward newness as they shuffled over the floor, up the linoleum-lined corridor, toward Jaden's room. Southern accents whispered against the walls. Ava heard the words "aunties," "Jaden," and "bayou." She looked down the hall and gave a soft gasp, stunned to see the triplets and Hubs.

"Mom," Ava said, "you better come here."

Olympe, Tamara, and Isadora waved at Ava and Brooke. Carried by their new shoes, they walked quickly down the hall in stylish outfits made of light, airy fabrics in their favorite colors of blue, lavender, and maroon—which Ava assumed had differentiated one sister from the other since birth. Ava wondered if the price tags were still attached. Hubs lengthened his stride to keep up with his quick-stepping mama and aunties.

"I didn't expect to see you here," Brooke greeted them with happy surprise.

"Th-they *waanted* to be *heere* for Jaden. Me, too." Hubs

surprised Ava by giving her a quick, somewhat wooden hug. "Is n-now okay?" he asked as he hugged Brooke, too.

"Yes," Brooke smiled. "Now is a great time. The other night, they took Jaden off the ventilator. She's breathing on her own now."

"They can't all go into the room at the same time," the nurse announced from behind her desk.

"Please," Brooke appealed, "just this once. They're sort of a package deal. They're my deceased husband's aunts; his only remaining living relatives." Ava took notice of the way her mother had nailed the deal with a lie about being related to the triplets. Brooke drove it home by continuing, "It might be helpful for Jaden...having the three of them with her at the same time. Their presence could bring her out of the coma."

"We won't stay long, dear," Olympe reassured the nurse.

"The rules say only two visitors at a time." The nurse pursed her lips, then added in a long, drawn-out Southern accent, "Now, with that said, I want to *see* only two of you in there..." Her stern expression broke as she flashed a grin at Brooke. "When the curtain is closed, I can only assume you're following the rules." The woman moved to the opposite side of the nurses' station. "Make certain that you speak quietly to the patient. And it's important to share only positive memories." The nurse turned her back to everyone and started thumbing through a stack of papers.

Positive memories? Ava wondered what positive memories the triplets could possibly have of Jaden. Ever since they'd all met, their lives had been in turmoil.

"Now, she's a fine woman," Olympe remarked, looking at the nurse. "Got a real understanding of healing." Then

Olympe patted her purse. "I brought an aromatherapy for Jaden. Do ya mind if I put some on her?"

"They don't allow perfumes in intensive care," Brooke replied.

"Hogwash," Tamara interjected. "It isn't perfume. It's therapy."

Olympe leaned closer to Brooke. "Thought ya might want to know that Hubs found a source for hydrofluoric acid. Don't worry, dear. We all will take care of *everything*."

Ava watched as her mom's eyes widened. It was good news—the hydrofluoric acid would dissolve the Mal Rous's and Queller's bones—but for the past week their thoughts had been on Jaden and nothing but Jaden. They had all but forgotten about what needed to be done with the remains of Dekle's creations.

Brooke opened the sliding glass door for the triplets and Hubs, pulled the curtain to cover the glass wall, then closed the door while stationing herself outside the room like a sentry keeping guard.

"What are you doing leaving them alone with Jade, Mom?" Ava asked under her breath.

"Ava, they'll be fine. Jaden will be fine," her mom whispered.

"I don't think so." Ava kept her voice low. "You heard Tamara. I bet you fifty bucks she's in there applying that aroma oil to Jade. I'm going in to keep an eye on our so-called aunts." Ava slipped past her mom and entered the room.

Ava found the triplets' colorful attire had brightened the heartbreaking décor of tubes and machines that were attached to her sister. Hubs had situated himself against the large window that overlooked the parking lot seven floors below, while his mama and aunties surrounded Jaden's bed.

Tamara looked over at Ava as she placed her wrinkled hand on Jaden's arm. "Not to worry," Tamara said. "We washed our hands in the lavatory when we got off the elevator."

Tamara's normally brusque cadence and manner were soft as she paused and ran the back of her other hand over her eyes. "Jaden, you've been in here sleeping nonstop for a good six days now. It's time to come back to this world. A lot of people that love you are missing you...me included."

Olympe stood shoulder to shoulder with Tamara as if holding one another up.

"Me, too," Olympe added. "All of us is missing ya." For a moment, Tamara leaned her head against Olympe's.

Then Tamara straightened herself and addressed Jaden. "We just came from seeing our papa at the seniors' home. The second time this week. I know...I know...it's a lot for bayou hermits like us." Tamara took Jaden's hand in hers. "Today, when we were leaving the home, my sisters and I insisted that Hubs take us to see you—I have to say New Orleans is nothing like we remember it. I haven't been here since the 1970s. When were you last here, Olympe? Isadora?"

The two sisters gave Tamara a funny look.

"What?" Tamara asked. "I'm trying to keep the conversation going. There's a good chance she'll come out of this if she hears familiar voices, but it's hard to know what to talk about. What we've all been through together would make me want to stay in a coma. So that leaves telling stories." Tamara looked at Isadora, who was standing on the opposite side of the bed. "Isadora, you want to go first?"

Isadora straightened Jaden's already straight blanket. "Hello, dear. We've been thinking about you every day;

praying, choosing that you come through this just fine... better than fine. Guess Briz told you we're back home now, and all is good. No more Quel—."

"No," Ava said, stuffing her annoyance into a pleasant tone. "Only talk about positive things."

Isadora's eyes widened in understanding. Quellers and positive memories did not go together.

"When was the last time you were in New Orleans?" Tamara asked, guiding Isadora to safer ground.

"That's right...New Orleans." Isadora paused as she ran a knuckle over her chin. "Well, the last time I was here was... umm...I think 1983. I came with my friend Harriet. She's the one I told you about who owned an herb shop over in Lafayette." Isadora's accent sweetly framed her thoughts. "Harriet was a beautiful mix of American Indian and African American. Anyway, one day Harriet asked me to come to New Orleans with her to pick up an order." Isadora's voice grew quiet. "Harriet passed away not long after. To this day, I miss her..." Isadora's eyes met Tamara's. "Oh my...that didn't sound like a happy thought, did it?"

Ava chose not to rebuke Isadora for her last comment. More trusting of the triplets, she positioned herself next to Hubs at the window and stared down at the cars driving through the parking lot, wondering if the drivers were dropping off ailing friends or taking them home.

"Guess it's my turn to share a memory with ya now," Olympe said as she looked around the sterile room. "I haven't been in New Orleans since my husband Billy and I got married. It was on June 29th, 1967." Olympe folded her hands in front of her as she collected her memories. "The Supreme Court had just ruled that prohibiting interracial marriage was unconstitutional, and Billy wanted to be wed in the city. All of us rode here in two cars—Isadora, Tamara, Hubs, our mama, and papa, and Isadora's friend Harriet."

Olympe turned toward the window where Hubs and Ava were standing.

"Ya remember, Hubs?" Hubs gave his mama a little smile. "Ya was fifteen and wanted to drive, but ya didn't have yer license yet. When we got to the church, the preacher man took one look at us and kicked us out. Thank goodness Harriet was with us. She had us go to the Ninth Ward, and we got married in a little church there. Enough of that for now. I'll tell ya more when ya wake up."

Olympe set a small bottle on the table next to the bed, then leaned close to Jaden's ear. "I've brought ya an aromatherapy oil. It has yer Colorado blue spruce in it to remind ya of yer home. But I'm not supposed to apply it to ya in here...rules and all. When ya is out of this here ICU, ya should keep a drop on yer temples. It'll help ya feel better."

Ava looked at Jaden. She imagined her sister wide-eyed, taking in the triplet's every word.

"I wanted to try to make you a mixture with Briz's pheromones," Isadora said. "Thought that would snap you out of this right away. Though he said you haven't reacted to him when he's been here. Hubs suggested we get you some rose oil since his stuttering has improved so much being around Rosie. Do you remember her?" Isadora took a bottle from her purse and placed it next to Olympe's blue spruce. "On the way here, we stopped and bought him a small bottle of rose oil for when Rosie can't be with him, and we got one for you, too. Thought the fragrance would soothe your heart."

Ava's attention went to Tamara. The woman had moved to the bottom of the hospital bed and gently taken hold of

Jaden's feet. She cradled them with her eyes closed, as if summoning Jaden's spirit to bring her back into consciousness. Tamara's expression grew more and more melancholy until she released her hands.

"You come back to us, dear," Isadora said.

"We're looking forward to seeing yer lovely smile." Olympe patted Jaden's hand. Then, arm in arm, the triplets went into the hall to talk to Brooke.

Ava was about to follow them when Hubs went over to Jaden and took hold of her hand.

"*Hellooo*, Miss J-Jaden. It's me, Hubs." His voice quivered. "V-violet wanted me to say *hellooo*. And Rosie nodded; I th-think she *knoows* something's wrong with ya." He glanced at Ava before continuing, "I'm sure Briz *toold* ya he is l-leaving in five more days. W-when he's gone, I'll *keeep* coming to see ya, till ya is all b-better."

Hubs walked out of the room, and Ava followed. Her mom was talking with the triplets when Hubs went over and wrapped his arms around Brooke. His sweet gesture reminded Ava of how her dad would have comforted her mom. Her mom returned his embrace.

CHAPTER 53

BRIZ

Briz set his backpack on the floor and glanced at Jaden's motionless body as he stepped over to the window. "Hey, babe. It's nine o'clock in the morning. You'd never know it being in here," he said as he opened the curtain, then turned back to Jaden.

"I wanted to see you before your mom and sister arrive, to have a few minutes alone with you before I have to catch my plane." He slid a chair next to the hospital bed and held Jaden's hand.

"So, yesterday was a long day. After leaving here, I borrowed Cylis's boat and went to the triplets' place. I didn't want to leave town without seeing them again. They send their love. I think I've convinced them to let Hubs install a satellite dish at their place. I'm not sure if it'll work, but there's only one way to find out. And Violet's trying to teach Rosie to talk." He chuckled. "I guess it's been a bit of a challenge."

Briz looked out the window. The sky was a clear, bright blue. Perfect weather for flying. His lips formed a hard line.

Why couldn't it be stormy with all flights canceled? He exhaled softly.

"I'm going to keep talking—I want you to hear my voice. So you'll imprint the sound of it." He lovingly squeezed Jaden's hand.

"It looks like Violet might have to have her leg amputated from the knee down. Dr. Schilling went over to Hubs's trailer and met her. Guess it went smoothly. At least Dr. Schilling didn't freak out at the sight of Violet. Everyone had warned her, you know, that Violet looks like a fairy. They're going to wait a month and then decide. If they do it, Dr. Schilling will perform the operation at her house. Everyone seems cool with it...Or, I don't know, maybe they're putting up a good front."

The beeping of the machines in the room felt like electronic needles piercing into his heart. He longed to lean down and kiss Jaden. Passionately. Taste her. Feel her skin against his.

"I think after the past ten days of driving here on Highway 90, I could do it in my sleep." He inhaled, then blew out a slow breath. "I'm really going to Europe. I'm really just going to leave you lying here. My folks are in the lobby downstairs. They're taking me to the airport."

Briz rubbed his brow and whispered, "Shit."

Frustrated, he shook his head. "You know, your mom insisted I go on this stupid trip. She says that I'm too young to put my plans on hold for someone I hardly know. I told her that I do know you...that you're a part of me. I can feel you. It's like...it's like our hearts beat to the same rhythm."

A faint smile snuck across Briz's face. "Do you remember the other day when Hubs and the triplets were here?" he asked, as if she'd answer him. "Olympe told me before leaving that she defended me? I wish I could have heard her telling your mom that we're *split-aparts* like Billy and her. Apparently, she went into Plato's whole theory about soulmates. I know it sounds crazy, but now and then, crazy just feels right."

He shrugged. "Maybe your mom's right. I'm just talking nonsense. You know she even called my mom, telling her I should keep my travel plans. My entire family has been going on and on how there's nothing I can do to help you right now. I need to give you time to heal."

Briz let his fingers trail over Jaden's hand.

"And I believe you will heal. You not only resemble your mom, you have her determination. I know when you're ready to come out of this, you will."

Briz softly laughed, remembering the way Jaden had come onto him once she had Datura's blood in her system. "No Mal Rous blood moving through you, no more whacked out emotions. Or, as Tamara would say, hyped-up *urges*." He linked his fingers in hers. "My system's clean now, too. Totally back to normal. No green tobacco poison or cravings for cigarettes." He paused before saying, "I don't know if Ava's mentioned anything, but the night we stayed at Cylis's, she..."

"Morning," a nurse said, walking into the room. "I'll just be a moment."

"No worries." Briz watched as the nurse checked the readings on the machines. Then he reached into his backpack. "Three more days and you'll be sixteen, Jade. I'm sorry I won't be here for your birthday." Moving aside the ever-present container of tissue, he set a small, gift-wrapped box on the table next to Jaden. "I bought you something. I hope you'll like it."

"You must be excited about your trip." The nurse smiled at Briz.

Briz cocked his head.

"Your mom told me about it. You're leaving today, right?"

*My mom...right...*he thought. *My mom, Brooke.*

"Yeah, I'm flying out in a couple of hours."

His attention went back to Jaden.

"Don't give up on her, Briz." The nurse looked at him, then at Jaden. "You know, she can probably hear you."

Briz tried to smile, but it felt more like a grimace.

"Guyon Manor's officially locked up, *sis*," he relayed, knowing the nurse could hear his every word. "Yesterday when I got back from the triplets', Hubs helped me do a few things at the manor for *mom*. We fixed that broken windowpane and made sure all the locks on the windows work. Turned off the water. The place is ready to be sold as-is by a realtor here in New Orleans."

The nurse left, and Briz turned to make sure she was out of hearing range.

"Did I tell you, the other day I stopped by your mom and sister's rent-by-the-week apartment? Ava hates it. She calls it the rent-a-wreck apartment. She misses staying next door to the hospital at the Brent House."

Briz leaned forward. He placed his elbows on the edge of the bed and clasped his hands together as he memorized her face.

After a few minutes, he whispered, "Wake up, Jade." Then resting his forehead against his hands, he stared down at the pattern in the blanket.

"Wake up so you and Ava and your mom can go home." He raised his head. "Ava's changed. She's still Ava, but seeing you like this...she's nicer. I don't think she'll be so hard on you anymore."

He took Jaden's hand in his. "Please, wake up. It's up to you..." Looking at her in the hospital bed, listening to the machines in the room, Briz wanted to scream.

All they had been through since they'd met and this...this was how it was going to end.

He gave his head a slight shake, thinking, *She might not even love me. Not the way I love her. I have to let her go.* Briz pulled his cell from his pocket—he scrolled to a photo of her laughing that he'd taken when they'd first met.

"I don't want to let you go," he whispered close to her ear. "Envie. Crave me. Desire me."

Something above him caught his eye. He looked at the ceiling but saw nothing.

"Remember me, Jade. Remember us. Remember the first time we met in Twyla Mae's bookstore. Remember our first kiss—the way you trembled when I touched you."

He slipped his phone back into his pocket. Then gently touching Jaden's arm, he cleared his throat and sat up straighter.

"You are my first love, Jade," he said softly. "'The more I give to thee, the more I have, for both are infinite.' That's a line from *Romeo and Juliet*. I looked it up last night. William Shakespeare was quite the romantic."

He exhaled another loud breath, then quietly begged, "Please live. Please survive this. I don't want your life's story to end in a tragedy."

He glanced at the nurses' station; at the clock on the wall tick, tick, ticking away at Jaden's life. Ticking forward to his new adventure.

"So...so this is it, then."

Briz picked up Jaden's hand in both of his and stroked her palm, running his thumb over the finger where her jade ring would normally have been.

His eyes brightened. "Did you just try to squeeze my hand?"

Her face was expressionless. He'd only imagined it.

"I'm going to write to you. Like I promised." He laid her hand down.

Briz stood. He studied her face, hoping that somehow she had heard him...felt him.

"It's been quite a ride, Ms. Jaden Olivia Lisette." He ran a finger over her cheek. "Maybe everyone's right, I'm not grownup enough to love someone the way that I love you. Wake up and be happy. May the rest of your life be smooth and easy. No more deadly adventures."

He bent down and kissed her forehead.

"Jade...*my* Jade..." His eyes were moist. An ache filled his body with a longing so intense it felt as if pieces of his heart had been pulled from his chest...the only way it would ever be whole again, was to be with her.

Someday.

He backed toward the door, his attention on her face, hoping that maybe, just maybe, she'd open her eyes and smile at him.

CHAPTER 54

AVA

Half asleep, Ava reached over and groped for her mom's buzzing cell in the dark. She picked up the phone and croaked, "Hel-lo?"

"Mrs. Lisette?" asked a woman's voice.

"Huh..." The word barely came out. Ava cleared her throat.

"This is nurse Caroline in ICU at Ochsner Medical Center..."

Ava's heart sped up. "Jaden. What's happened to Jaden?" Her words rush out.

The night lamp between the two twin beds clicked on. Ava pushed the speaker button; shielding her eyes from the light, she handed the phone to her mom. "It's the hospital."

"Yes," Brooke said breathlessly into the cell. "What is it?"

"Your daughter is awake. You should come to the hospital at once."

"We're on our way." Ending the call, Brooke looked at the time on her cell. "It's four-fifteen in the morning."

"It's tomorrow..." The hairs on the back of Ava's neck rose. "Weird. Jaden woke up on her birthday."

In silence, they dressed. In silence, they drove to the hospital.

In silence, they listened as the doctor explained, "Most coma patients are confused when they first awaken. Sometimes they're angry; not understanding where they are or how they got here. So speak softly. Don't make sudden movements, grabbing or hugging her until she lets you know that she's ready for physical contact. There's a chance that she won't know who you are. Be patient. If she sees that you're afraid, she will be, too."

The doctor put a hand on Brooke's elbow, guiding her as they walked down the corridor toward Jaden's room. "As she progresses with her recovery, she'll be moved from the ICU, and we'll have a physiotherapist work with her for a couple of weeks."

Ava and Brooke paused at the sliding glass door. All smiles, Brooke glanced at Ava as the two of them moved toward the bed, stopping a few feet from Jaden as she stared at them.

"Morning," Brooke said quietly. "Do you know who we are?"

Ava watched Jaden's eyes move slowly from their mom over to her. Then Jaden gave a slight nod. Ava didn't know if it meant Jaden knew who they were or if she was merely acknowledging them, but it didn't matter.

"Sweetie." Brooke sounded giddy. "I'm so happy you're awake."

"We both are." Ava took her mom's hand in hers.

Ava felt tears of happiness beginning to obscure her vision and saw mirroring droplets of joy in her mother's eyes.

Ava reached for the box of tissues as her and her mother's excitement spilled down their cheeks.

Jaden was awake. Alive! This was a birthday they'd never forget.

Ava and Brooke sat in Jaden's hospital room, waiting for her to be comfortable with them, worrying every time Jaden closed her eyes that she may not open them again. It was mid-morning when Jaden finally spoke. Her voice was a whisper, her words were few, but that she could articulate her thoughts so clearly gave Ava an adrenaline rush. Jaden was going to be all right.

***

Ava pushed her breakfast tray to the side, savoring the doctor's words: "Jaden can be released tomorrow."

After three extra days in ICU, and two weeks of physiotherapy, her little sister would be free to leave. An added bonus was this would be the last day Ava had to eat breakfast at the hospital cafeteria. Soon they would be heading home, and they would all be able to carry on with their lives.

Ava watched as her mom tried to type on her cell. "What are you going to say?"

Brooke held the phone so Ava could see.

"Hello Briz, Jade woke on her birthday," Ava read. Her eyes met her mom's. "You sure you want to tell him it's been almost three weeks since she woke, and you didn't bother sharing the good news with him sooner?"

Brooke gave her a nod, then set her phone on the table. "I can't do this right now."

"I'll do it." Ava picked up the cell. "You can't keep putting it off. He deserves to know."

Her mom took a napkin from her tray, dabbed her eyes, and blew her nose. No one in the cafeteria gave her any notice. After all, it was the hospital. People were always walking around in a daze or crying—either with happiness over healed loved ones or sadness for loved ones who couldn't be healed.

Ava understood why her mom was so emotional, overwhelmed by what she was going to tell Briz. They'd both procrastinated answering the texts and emails he'd sent them over the past couple of weeks, asking for news about Jaden.

Geez, the guy was in Europe. Europe! What Ava wouldn't give to have the chance to travel through France and Italy, and he was being all mopey about her sister. He was young. He needed to just move on with his life.

"What do you want to say to him?"

Her mom gave her shoulders a shrug. "I don't know. Whatever we tell him, he's going to wish he'd stayed here."

"Okay. I won't push send until you give me the go-ahead. I'm writing it as if it's from you."

Her mom nodded.

Ava typed, quietly saying each word aloud. *"Hello, Briz. Sorry I didn't contact you sooner. Things have been busy here. I have some great news. Jaden woke on the morning of her birthday. The doctors believe because she was in the coma for only fourteen days, there is a good chance she will have a full recovery. In a few days, the three of us are flying home to Colorado."*

Ava paused. "Do you want me to tell him the rest?"

Brooke nodded again. Ava continued.

"Jaden is physically weak, but getting stronger every day.

She is mentally alert, and all of her faculties are intact, with one exception. She has..."

Ava looked over at her mom. "What did the doctor call it?"

"Psychogenic amnesia," her mom spoke in a flat, android tone.

Ava spelled out the word as she resumed the email. *"P-s-y-c-h-o-g-e-n-i-c amnesia. The doctor said it occurs as a result of severe stress or psychological trauma. Jaden remembers her name and that we live in Colorado, though she doesn't remember the name of our town. She knows who I am, and Ava. Right now, she doesn't remember anything from the past few months. In fact, a large part of her life she can't recall. The doctors believe she will eventually regain all of her memories once she gets into a regular routine back home."*

Ava paused, stretching her fingers, contemplating how to say what had to come next. Then she started typing again. *"After all Jaden has been through, I think her having amnesia is a good thing. She has no recollection of the Mal Rous, Quellers, the triplets, or Hubs. She also has no memory of you. I know how much you care about Jaden, so this is difficult for me to ask, but I feel it would be best if you didn't write to her or try to contact her. She'd been living a nightmare...as had you! We all had. Some memories are best forgotten. Because of your help, we all survived. I will never be able to repay you for all that you have done. Thank you. And now, for respecting my wishes. All the best to you, Brooke."*

Ava let out a slow breath to release the intensity of the moment. "We should change Jaden's cell number and email in case he tries to reach her."

Her mother's sad expression was answer enough. Ava would take care of it later today.

"Should I push send?"

Ava knew her mom was anguished about what she was doing to Briz. In Brooke's mind, Briz was the boy who had been a wise-beyond-his-years savior to her and her family, the most caring, understanding, respectful boyfriend she could ever want for her youngest daughter.

Her mom looked at the ceiling. Then she nodded.

Ava pressed send.

CHAPTER 55

BRIZ

Briz was sitting at a restaurant in Sestri Levante, a little town on the Italian Riviera, when his cell vibrated in his pocket.

Finally, he thought when he saw the email from Brooke.

It was morning in Louisiana. He imagined Jaden's room at the hospital. It was worlds apart from the Mediterranean Sea glistening in front of him in the afternoon sun. Slowly, he read each word of the message.

Then he read the email two more times. It was short and painfully to the point.

When he looked up, he could no longer see the beauty of his surroundings.

"What's up?" his cousin asked. "Bad news?"

"Good, and bad."

Briz and his cousin still had ten days left of their trip. It wasn't enough time to come to terms with what Briz just read. He turned his head slightly, looking at his cousin from the corner of his eye. "When you and I are done traveling, I'm going to stay in Europe longer. Maybe spend a couple of months bumming around."

"Do you have enough money to do that?"
"I'll make it work. I'll find some odd jobs here and there."
Anything but going back to Belle Fleur.

CHAPTER 56

JADEN

Jaden gave Albert a tentative smile as she watched him hug Ava. Jaden didn't recognize Albert, but she knew she should. He stood about three inches taller than her sister's five feet, six-inch frame, with copper hair and smoky-blue eyes. Jaden flashed on eyes the color of the sky, smiling at her—nothing like Albert's. The image faltered before scattering across the floor of the Denver airport's baggage claim area.

When Albert and Ava ended their embrace, Albert shook Brooke's hand. "Welcome home, Mrs. Lisette." Keeping his distance, Albert said, "Hello, Jaden."

Jaden gave Albert a single nod of her head. He had an accent. She had forgotten on the flight home, Ava had reminded her that Albert was from Sweden—or was it Norway? He was a year older than Ava; the two of them had met when he was at Ava's high school as an exchange student. Now he was starting college at CU Boulder with a student visa. But what was he majoring in? Ava had told her as they were exiting the plane. But now Jaden's mind was blank.

Her mind was blank about a lot of things. The only memory she had of the past few months was waking up in the hospital, totally freaked out and alone.

Parts of her entire life were sketchy. It was as if her brain was feeding her bits and pieces of her memories with no sense of order.

She clutched the strap of the daypack hanging from her shoulder. Her mom bought it for her the day she left the hospital. It contained her wallet, a brush, pen, and small tablet in case a memory revealed itself and she wanted to jot it down.

"Albert's getting the car," Ava said as Albert walked away. "We'll meet him downstairs at passenger pickup. Now, stay put." Ava looked at Jaden like she thought Jaden might wander off. "Mom and I are going to get the luggage. We'll be right back."

Dazed, Jaden watched the people around her collect their baggage. The smells, hustle, and noise at the airport terminal had joined forces, taking turns at bombarding her nerves and thumping against her skull. Had airports always been overwhelming to her, or was it a side effect of having been in a coma? Right now, she just wanted to go home.

Home. She wondered where it was. What it was like. *When I see it, will it help me remember my past?*

Jaden gripped the handle of her carry-on, hoping it would ground her, as she watched her mom and sister pile their luggage onto a cart. Then her mom hurried over, took Jaden by the hand as if Jaden were a five-year-old that might get lost, and they followed Ava as she wove their cart through the crowds toward the elevator.

The cart clunked to a stop near the curb as Albert drove up; minutes later they were on the freeway—the four of them, their pile of luggage and an uncomfortable silence that seemed to propel the car faster.

"Albert, would you mind turning up the air?" Brooke asked. "It's a bit warm here in the back seat."

Albert turned up the air, giving the silence even more of a chill.

Nothing like an amnesia patient to take the joy out of a homecoming, Jaden thought while looking out the window. She stared at the Rocky Mountains, but her mind's eye saw the room she'd left behind at the hospital in New Orleans, where she'd spent the past two weeks under observation after leaving the ICU.

Every day she had asked her mom and sister what had happened, how...why she had been in a coma. Every day they had told her that she and Ava had been on a boat exploring the bayou, when Jaden had slipped, stumbled forward, hit her head, then landed on two sharp objects; one punctured her shoulder, the other her stomach. When she asked her mom why they were even in Louisiana, her mom had hemmed and hawed. Ava threw in the word vacation.

"Let's wait until you're stronger," her mom had said to her the first time Jaden brought it up. "Let's wait until we get home and you're settled in," she'd said to Jaden, their last night in New Orleans. "Let's wait" were now her mother's favorite words. Or perhaps they'd always been, and it was just one more thing Jaden couldn't remember.

Ava's answers had been even less informative. In fact, they were nonexistent. "Just focus on getting better." "Be thankful you're alive." "At least you remember how to hold a fork and can feed yourself. Some coma patients have to start from scratch, like a toddler. You can still read and write and do math. You'll be fine!"

Secrets. Jaden could tell her mom and Ava were keeping something from her. It was obvious from the way they snuck glances at each other before speaking to her with guarded words. Why didn't they didn't think she could handle the truth?

Someday I'll remember. I'll understand why I feel like I have a broken heart.

Albert flipped on the turn signal. Jaden glanced at the clock on the dashboard—they'd been driving for forty minutes. The car slowed as he took the exit to Louisville.

Louisville, Jaden thought. *Mom told me we moved here from Colorado Springs after Dad died. I remember parts of my life from then.* Jaden shifted her gaze to the back of the passenger seat where Ava sat. *Were we close?*

They reached a small, middle-class neighborhood. After a few blocks, Albert parked his car in front of a two-story, cream-colored house.

Albert and Ava unloaded the car as Brooke unlocked the front door. Standing behind her mom, Jaden felt hot stuffy air rush out the door as if escaping after months of solitary confinement.

Jaden paused at the threshold, waiting for a memory—any memory—to greet her. Instead, the clicking of luggage wheels on the walkway nudged her into the entryway.

Brooke set her purse on a table near the door as Ava and Albert came into the house. "Would the two of you mind running to the grocery store while Jaden and I settle in?"

"Sure, Mom. Anything special you want?" Ava asked, piling the luggage in the hallway.

Jaden saw her sister was all smiles, happy to be home, excited about being with Albert.

Envy shoved Jaden's sadness to the side.

"Something for dinner...and breakfast...some snacks," Brooke requested as she opened her wallet. "Whatever you want, Ava. We need everything."

"Mrs. Lisette—" Albert spoke his first words since leaving the airport.

"Albert," her mom cut in, "it's time you started calling me Brooke."

With a slight nod of agreement, Albert continued, "Brooke, before we go to the market, I'd like to hook up the cables on Ava's car battery. Make sure the car is running. In case you need it."

Albert avoided looking at Jaden, but she felt sure the "in case you need it" was all about her. Did they think she was going to suddenly wig out and have to be whisked off to a hospital and put in a straitjacket? It was a possibility—she still had to have follow-up appointments with a specialist now that she was home.

Jaden wandered into the living room and opened the curtains, sneezing as dust filled the air like...*fairy dust*, she thought. She watched the swirling particles and imagined a fairy with delicate damselfly wings fluttering through the room.

Then her attention settled on the fireplace mantel. She went over and picked up a photo of her mom and dad. "Dad," she whispered as she set it back down. Next to it was another photo, of an older woman and man.

"Do you remember them?" Ava asked, standing near Jaden.

Jaden regarded the framed picture and shook her head.

"They're Mom's parents." Then, as if Jaden wouldn't know what that meant, Ava added, "Our grandparents."

"Our grandma's Asian?" Jaden tried not to sound surprised.

"You couldn't figure that out by looking at Mom...or in the mirror?"

"What are their names?" Jaden ignored the snide tone of Ava's voice.

"Grandma Jin and Grandpa Bill. They live in San Jose...*California*." Ava said California like she wondered if Jaden knew where that was.

Jaden nodded, thinking she'd look at a map later, just to be certain.

"But they might be moving here."

"Because of me?" Jaden asked.

Ava shrugged as she went over to a window. "Let's air this place out."

"I'll do it. If Albert's ready, you should get going." Jaden turned toward Ava. "Hey, do I know how to drive?"

"Yeah. But you don't have a driver's license." Ava walked away, then paused. "Is there anything you want me to pick up for you?"

"I don't know. What do I like?"

"I'll ask Mom. She'll know."

Ava trotted off to the kitchen, and Jaden walked around the room muttering to herself, her words drifting as aimlessly as the dust. "I'm part Asian. I live in Louisville, Colorado. I woke up from a coma on my sixteenth birthday. I remember sky-blue eyes smiling at me."

The house needed to be cleaned, but Jaden thought it felt homey, comfortable. She turned the jade ring around on her finger, then looked at the ring and smiled.

"A habit." Her smile grew. "I think I do this a lot."

There was chatting and the sound of the front door closing.

Brooke appeared, wheeling two of the suitcases to the bottom of the stairs. "Let's unpack." Her voice carried the lingering emotions of the last month, weeks, and days—a swirl of exhaustion, weariness...and relief. At last, they were home.

Jaden took the handle of her suitcase and followed her mom upstairs.

"This is your room." Her mom stood watching her, wanting to see Jaden's reaction. Would Jaden's life come tumbling back into focus?

Or will it be like the remnants of fabric used to make a patchwork quilt that I'll piece together over time? Jaden wondered why the image of a handmade quilt would come into her mind. Was her grandmother Jin a quilter?

She glanced at the poster on the wall. "Boyan Slat, The Ocean Clean Up" was printed on it. She looked at his picture but didn't know who he was. Then, standing in front of the chest of drawers, she looked at a photo of her with two other girls her age.

"Those are your friends, Michelle and Beth."

Jaden looked at her mom blankly.

"I'm sure as soon as they know you're home, they'll want to come by to see you." Her mother's words were laced with hope.

Jaden's chest tightened. The girls in the photo were strangers to her.

"The doctors want you to take things slow, so what do you say, I homeschool you this semester? Once you feel ready, you can return to your regular school. Or I'll enroll you in online classes."

Jaden felt a sense of relief. She wasn't ready to face her *forgotten* world. She walked over to the desk and picked up a sketchbook. "I draw?"

Her mother smiled, as if thinking Jaden had recalled something that she enjoyed doing. But Jaden was merely trying to piece together information about herself.

Jaden flipped through the pages. "I'm not very good."

"You're better than most." Her mom had stepped closer to look at the drawings over Jaden's shoulder.

Jaden's brow furrowed as she set the book down.

"I'm going to unpack, sweetie."

Her mom left the room as Jaden went over to the window. The house across the street was painted a soft yellow with white trim. Its large, white double doors looked like buck teeth grinning at her. One tooth disappeared as the door opened and Jaden cried out with enough volume that her mom came running back in.

"What? What's wrong?" Brooke looked outside.

Jaden glanced at her mother, then out the window. "I, I thought...I thought..." Jaden stammered as she saw only a little boy playing with his dog. "Nothing. It's nothing."

Brooke ran her hand up and down Jaden's back to comfort her. Jaden wanted to tell her she thought the boy and his dog were monsters. Strange, little, humanoid monsters. *If I say anything, will Mom put me back in the hospital?*

"You okay?" her mom asked.

"Yeah. I'm all right." Jaden's voice carried a tremor of unease.

She took a step away, leaving her mom's hand to comfort nothing but air.

"As soon as Ava gets back, I'll make us something to eat.

You probably just need some nourishment." Brooke's eyes revealed a deeper concern. "It's been a long day."

Jaden waited for her mom to leave the room before she looked back out the window.

No monsters were in sight—only the little boy and his dog. Jaden checked under the bed and in the closet. No monsters there, either. She sat on the bed with crossed legs, unwilling to let her feet hang down.

Jaden scanned the room, hopeful she'd find something that would remind her of the missing parts of her life...that would let her know who she was.

"If I never regain my memory, who will I be? Will I be like I was before the coma, or will my personality be different?" she asked her reflection in the mirror on the closet door.

The image looking back at Jaden had hollow, drawn cheeks. *What happened to me?* She still appeared to be young and innocent—except for her eyes. They could not conceal the jumble of confusion in her mind, her bewildered soul, the ache in her heart and the one memory that remained: eyes blue as the sky looking at her with love.

THE EXPERIMENT,
A Violet Novella

PREQUEL TO THE SWEET DESIRE, WICKED FATE TRILOGY

Enjoy reading the first several chapters
of the prequel to the
Sweet Disire, Wick Fate Trilogy

Thrust into a world beyond the four walls Violet had always known as home, the fairy-like Bellibone must fend for herself. Staying out of sight is vital to her survival. If found, she would be killed and dissected.

WRAY ARDAN

The Experiment

A VIOLET NOVELLA

A Prequel to the YA Romance Horror Trilogy
Sweet Desire, Wicked Fate

Chapter 1

Louisiana – 1959

The cellar door creaked open. Violet gripped the bars of her small, bird-like cage as the sound of cautious footsteps faltered on the stairs. She peered into the shadows, troubled by the flowery perfume that drifted down into the musty, chemical-scented air of her laboratory home.

The flow of a knee-length skirt made its way into the room, its soft floral pattern a stark contrast to the dank environment.

Violet glanced over at the five compact cages stacked on the shelves next to hers. Within them, her so-called siblings were asleep.

She looked back at the skirt, now weaving through the vines that hung from the ceiling like serpents. A slender woman came into full view, her fingers trailing over the length of the lab table.

"Elvina, what are you doing here?" Violet whispered under her breath.

Though Elvina had no knowledge of Violet's existence,

Violet knew everything about her. Her favorite color, her favorite food, that a silver four-leaf clover was attached to her keychain.

Violet had spent her life observing Elvina from a distance, had strived to emulate her. After all, Elvina's husband, Professor Dekle Thatcher, had created Violet using his wife's DNA as one of the principal ingredients. Like Elvina, Violet had pleasing features and a pale complexion, though her miniature human physique stood only twelve inches tall. She also carried the DNA of damselfly, pampas grass, and violets—Elvina's favorite flower. With her wings and white tresses of hair, Violet resembled a fairy.

She had assumed it was only a matter of time before curiosity would tempt Elvina to disobey Dekle's wishes. Eventually she would want to see what her husband would not allow her to be a part of, to discover how he spent all those hours, years, hidden away in the cellar beneath the garage.

In the 1800s, the structure had been a kitchen, separate from the house; the room beneath had provided a cool place to store canned preserves and root vegetables. Now the cellar was the Professor's dungeon-like laboratory. And it stored monsters.

Not a soul was allowed inside. Ever. Including Elvina. In spite of the love Dekle had once felt for his wife, Violet knew the man would beat Elvina to an inch of her life if he discovered she had been inside the cellar.

Violet watched Elvina make her way through the room. At one time, Professor Thatcher's wife and daughter had been his pride and joy.

Aware that she herself was part of the problem, Violet felt heat rise up her neck and face. Eight years ago, when she had emerged from her gestation vessel, Dekle had spent his days obsessively teaching her to speak, cultivating her mind, educating her—entirely ignoring his family.

Dekle had deemed Violet a Bellibone, a variation of the long-forgotten French term *belle et bonne* that meant "a female excelling in beauty as well as goodness." He'd once told Violet he often called Elvina a Bellibone while courting her back in England.

Violet exhaled. Things had changed. Dekle had changed.

In the past, he'd declared Violet his experiment of a lifetime. Now he lavished his devotion upon his other genetic experiments: the Mal Rous.

Unlike Violet, they carried none of Elvina's DNA. Instead, the Professor had combined his own DNA with that of rats, lizards, snakes, poisonous plants, venomous insects, along with newt DNA—and the micro-animal tardigrade, to insure the Mal Rous were capable of surviving extreme conditions.

The Mal Rous physiques were a frightful combination of human and vermin; their faces and the curious shapes of their heads exposed the rest of their molecular makeup.

The Professor had assigned the Mal Rous the Latin name *Cerophagous Cautelosus*. *Cerophagous*, meaning flesh-eating, *Cautelosus*, meaning treacherous, cunning. But he preferred using the nickname he'd bestowed upon them: *Mal*, for evil, *Rou*, from a Cajun tale about rougarous; part human, part animal beasts.

Elvina gasped as she stopped in front of the small cages. The scent of her fear exploded into the air around her as she took in the sleeping Mal Rous; the horns on their hideous heads and faces, the fangs protruding from their mouths.

With a halting movement, Elvina turned away. She eyed the rows of test tubes on the lab table, following the upward movement of their swirling vapors that formed a burial shroud-like mist above her head.

Violet's damselfly wings flicked back and forth as she imagined the scenes of Dekle maniacally mixing lethal potions that must be churning through Elvina's mind.

Elvina turned; her gaze settled on Violet's enclosure. Violet wondered if Elvina would be charmed by her fairy-like appearance, notice that their faces looked vaguely alike, understand that Violet had human emotions and desires—all unfulfilled.

Or would Elvina only see her as a transgenesis—a strange genetic mutation—and think her abominable?

Elvina took a step back as she registered that, unlike the rest of the cages, Violet's was unlocked.

"I will not harm you," Violet's soft floral breath accompanied her words. "But they will."

Violet glanced at the Mal Rous. They'd been stalking the woman for years. Even now, while asleep, the tentacles that covered Datura's rodent-shaped head pulsed, breathing in Elvina's presence.

"Your scent, the smell of your perfume, will linger; they'll know you have been here. Dekle will know, too. You and your daughter should leave Belle Fleur before Dekle harms you." Violet gestured at the surrounding cages. "Or worse...before he allows them to attack you."

Next to Violet, Ivan stirred. The fragrance of Violet's breath was overpowered by the stench of his filthy cage.

Elvina made a choking sound, her body quivered like a locust ready to take flight. In a panic, the woman raced up the stairs. The cellar door banged closed, the key and lock rattling with Elvina's revulsion.

Violet shrank down to the bottom of her cage. The person she longed to emulate thought she was a monster.

She looked at Ivan as he stretched to the full length of his nineteen-inch body. His leathery skin, along with the scattering of horns on his head, chin, and tips of his ears, indicated the presence of his horned lizard DNA.

The Mal Rou yawned—Violet found herself enveloped in his breath, reeking of the poison ivy sap that flourished in his saliva. Ivan reached for a nearby rag and bit into it, releasing the excess of coral snake poisons that had accumulated in his fangs while he slept.

In the cage on the far side of Ivan's, Datura roused herself—standing, the influence of her rat and newt DNA were evident on her face and body. Pointed tentacles extended from her head, reaching up well beyond her sixteen-inch stature.

Datura's genetic makeup included a substantial amount of mosquito DNA, allowing some tentacles the ability to suck blood from prey, while others swelled with the poisonous sap of the thornapple plant. Several of them, that could detect odors, started investigated the scent in the air. Datura's long, bulbous nose pulsed at the information her tentacles relayed. "Elvina," she snarled. "That vile woman stinks like you, Violet."

Violet didn't respond. Datura's insults were nothing new.

After all, Violet was part damselfly. In nature, damselflies considered mosquitoes the tastiest of snacks. No matter how many times the Professor reassured Datura that Violet wouldn't harm her, Datura hated the Bellibone. That

Violet was articulate, proper, educated, didn't help—but it was her genetic link to Elvina that Datura couldn't tolerate.

Datura longed to replace Elvina; she often encouraged Dekle to get rid of her. In that respect, the professor was weak. He had Datura for companionship, but he would always need Elvina for releasing his sexual urges. And to raise their daughter, Amelia.

Datura rattled her cage door.

Violet glared at Datura, then at the occupants of the other cages. Elvina didn't understand. The Mal Rous were the monsters, not Violet.

Yes, she possessed the same ability as them, to breathe in a person's pheromones as they were released through the skin—the chemicals enabled Violet and the Mal Rous to detect the human emotions of fear, anger, joy, desire. Where the Mal Rous fed off the foul smell of fear as they inflicted pain on their unsuspecting victims, Violet found no joy in hurting humans.

The main thing she had in common with the Mal Rous was that they were all created in a test tube, incubated in a life-giving elixir.

All five of the Mal Rous were clever, but Violet regarded them as her intellectual inferiors. They refused to be educated; instead, they spent their time hunting, inflicting pain, preferring to prey on humans.

Yet, Dekle had made it clear to Violet that he considered the Mal Rous, not her, his ultimate achievement in genetic engineering.

"This is our chance," Datura said to Ivan, her shrill voice waking the remaining Mal Rous. "We could go after Elvina right now, tear into her like we did that-there boy at the cottage. Mess her up good. Maybe *accidentally* kill her.

Dekle would understand. We'd tell him it was self-defense. The woman snuck into the cellar and done come after us, intent on destroyin' us. We did the only thin' we could so she wouldn't be able to tell others 'bout us." Datura switched her attention to Violet.

"Violet, unlock our cages. Now!"

Violet knew Dekle loved the Mal Rous more than his wife. He would believe anything they told him once he realized Elvina had disobeyed him.

"Now!" Datura snapped again.

Violet looked toward the small cellar window, coated in a muddy brown paint so no one could see in; ignoring Datura's demands, she left her cage, opened the window, then flew toward the manor. Squinting in the bright sunlight, she went from window to window, looking for Elvina until she found her in her bedroom.

"Monsters...He's created monsters..." The tangy odor of Elvina's panic seeped from her pores, then slid out the open window as she gripped the bedpost to steady her trembling legs. "Dekle, you had such an extraordinary mind. Your aspirations were to break the code of life, to discover the information hidden in strands of DNA...not...not..." Elvina's words trailed off as she paced back and forth.

"He did," Violet whispered. Dekle often told her how his colleagues at Cambridge had only gained recognition for genetic manipulation after stealing his research findings, then dismissing him. Elvina's inheritance of Guyon Manor had allowed him to leave England and continue his research in secret.

From the day Violet drew her first breath, she could smell Dekle's longing to share his excitements with the world. But he couldn't, not without endangering her safety, and soon after, the Mal Rous. He was compelled to keep all of his scientific breakthroughs a secret.

For years Violet observed his frustration, wondered if he was conscious of the gradual changes in his personality. Did he know he'd stopped loving Elvina? Was his unbalanced mind aware of how he abused her?

"Dekle was a good man when he married you," Violet lamented. "He was a good man when he created me."

"I must be calm," Elvina began again, unknowingly interrupting Violet's hushed affirmation. "Give him no reason to suspect that I know. That horrible creature is wrong."

Violet cringed at the accusation. She wasn't horrible.

"Dekle won't let them hurt me," Elvina's tone carried a painful ache of uncertainty. "He's my husband. He loves me."

Violet had seen the dark bruises on the woman's arms, heard Dekle brag to the Mal Rous of his abuses toward his wife. *That isn't love!*

The rumble of a truck on the drive stopped any further speculations.

"Papa's home!" Amelia's gleeful voice echoed from down the hall. Violet hurried away, the beating of her wings muffling the twelve-year-old girl happily repeating her announcement. "Papa's home!"

By the time Dekle entered the cellar, Violet was back in her cage. Immediately, his body tensed, his tongue flicked out, lapping up the lingering fragrance of Elvina's perfume.

Datura caught Dekle's eye; she gave him a nod, confirming what he already knew. Grief flashed over Dekle's face, quickly replaced by an angry flush—a low guttural noise emerged from his chest as he went to his desk.

"Book 4: 1959 DNA/Genetic Testing, by Professor Dekle Thatcher," he read aloud the meticulously printed bold letters on his journal.

With the book cradled in his arms, he left. His truck groaned and rattled, then faded into the distance.

Chapter 2

The high-pitched trill of crickets filled the night air as Violet waited for Dekle's return. Hours passed, while the Mal Rous speculated in lurid detail about ways Dekle could punish Elvina. Violet longed to lash out at the cretins but knew better. If she did, they'd come after her when she'd least expect it. It was safer to keep quiet.

At the sound of Dekle's truck pulling into the garage overhead, the Mal Rous, along with the crickets, went silent.

The lock on the cellar door clicked, followed by a loud thud as the door was kicked open. With a groan, Dekle hauled a large container down the stairs. Violet wrinkled her nose at the fumes that seeped from it. The odor was familiar, but she couldn't place it.

One at a time, Dekle lugged down more containers, an ice cooler, and oversized stoneware jugs. The Mal Rous watched quietly, as if not wanting to distract their Professor. *Or agitate him*, Violet thought. He wasn't in the best of moods; he wouldn't hesitate to strike his beloved creatures.

Eventually, climbing from her cage, Violet fluttered closer to the Professor, determined to learn his intentions. His clothes held the musty aroma of a journey through the forested wetlands, combined with a strong chemical smell; telltale signs that he'd spent the last few hours in his primary laboratory, concealed in a salt cave in the bayou.

"What is this?" Violet hovered near the vessels. "What is it for?"

"The six of you are my greatest achievement," he replied, his brusqueness making his British accent more pronounced; hearing his declaration, the Mal Rous cooed with pride. "Now that you've been seen, I need to keep you safe." He skimmed through the handwritten pages of a notebook.

Violet considered the Professor's words; her wings contracted, forcing her to sink onto the table.

Safe. It was that same fear that followed her everywhere. Being discovered meant grievous harm, abduction from the only home she'd ever known. Even death.

She believed Dekle was also concerned about *his* safety. Knowledge of his experiments could lead to his being locked up for insanity or incarcerated for all the ills his vile creations had inflicted on the townspeople. The Professor's actions were as much for self-preservation as for his beloved Mal Rous.

He opened several of the containers—their pungent wafting's invaded the room. Violet found herself overcome not by the smell, but by the full memory that it unleashed. The germination formula he had developed, the one she had gestated in.

The elixir. Liquid placenta...liquid air.

Six years earlier, Dekle's genomic experiments had resulted in the first pack of Mal Rous. They were feral, uncontrollable. Unwilling to destroy them, Dekle had taken the same steps Violet had just observed—the same stoneware jugs, the same distinctive odor. One day he sealed the creatures in the jugs, declaring they could survive for years... possibly decades, while he discovered a way to humanize them.

Violet hadn't seen them since. She was certain he'd buried the loathsome things somewhere in the swamp. *For what purpose?* She wondered. *Those monsters attempted to feed on townspeople.* Violet looked over at the five caged Mal Rous. *These barbarians aren't much better! Not as deadly, but still vicious and conniving.*

"May I take notes for you?" Violet offered hoping to appear supportive, while considering her options. She wouldn't be forced into a jug—risk being stranded in perpetual hibernation.

In a gruff manner, he said, "No," then walked over to the ice cooler and removed several containers. His tone made her reconsider her approach. She retreated to the darkened stairwell to watch and think.

With intense focus, the Professor worked late into the night, accompanied by the soft strains of Rosemary Clooney albums. The singer's rich voice was bizarrely uplifting, considering the circumstances.

"You'll never know just how much I miss you, you'll never know just how much I care..." Tig, the more sadistic of the Mal Rous, with her black widow and spurges plant DNA, sang with the record in a series of vile screeches.

Alchemist that he was, Dekle heated and cooled substances, toying with them, transforming them into a clear, runny gel. Then a satisfied expression eased the lines on his face. He walked over to the Mal Rous's cages.

"Who wants to be first?" he asked in a soothing voice.

None of the little monsters replied.

With wings outstretched, Violet glided over to look into the jugs. Each was now half-full of the liquid placenta. Silently, she moved to the far end of the lab table.

"Don't be frightened, my little darlings," Dekle soothed. "You must have faith in me. After all, I am one of you."

Violet remembered the day Datura's blood entered Dekle's veins. Kindness left his soul; malevolence took root. It was the day the Mal Rous' desires became his desires, too.

Dekle reached into Anders's cage and removed the slim, seventeen-inch-tall creature. Anders's DNA also included strains of the poisonous oleander plant, centipede, and Komodo dragon. His powerful jaws could have easily bitten off the Professor's hand, but the Mal Rou completely trusted the man.

"Your new home," Dekle purred, as he lowered Anders into one of the large jugs—followed by Tig, and Ivan, then Datura, and Esere—each in their own stoneware vessel.

"Sit." The Professor motioned to the Mal Rous as they peered up at him. "Better yet, curl up in the fetal position. Get comfortable, so you can sleep soundly."

Esere remained standing as his siblings sank down, disappearing from view. He seemed suspicious. Violet wasn't sure if Esere's cautious nature came from his vulture or calabar bean DNA.

The Professor poured the solution over the curled Mal Rous, filling each jug near to the brim.

Then the Professor pressed on top of Esere's head, trying to force him down into the large container. Esere jerked back. Violet noticed the Professor kept his hand away from the horn on Esere's chin where Esere carried a paralyzing venom derived from his scorpion DNA.

"I'm going to put you in a place where you'll be safe," Dekle murmured, coaxing Esere into a fetal position. "You'll be fine."

The Professor poured more solution over Esere; he hacked and coughed as the dense liquid flowed into his beak-like nose.

"Everything will be all right, Esere. *You're* going to be all right."

Esere's body stilled.

The Professor gazed into each jug, studying the small, curled forms within before pressing the lids in place. "Now for you, Violet."

"I was hoping to talk with you first," Violet lied, moving from the table into the vines that hung from the ceiling.

"What about?" Dekle asked as he began to hermetically seal the five jugs housing the Mal Rous.

When Violet didn't respond, Dekle looked around for the small Bellibone. "Violet, I'm not in the mood for games. I promise you will only be in the container for a few weeks. Just until I clean out this room and eliminate Elvina."

Eliminate Elvina? He plans to kill her?

"You must trust me, Violet." His soothing tone belied a growing impatience.

Dekle stepped closer. Violet jerked back as he thrust his hand into the vines, his fingers inches from her. Panic sent heat rippling through Violet's wings, causing them to curl— losing her balance, she dropped toward the floor. She strained to force her wings to unfurl, struggled for them to beat before she hit the ground. Then Dekle's hand clamped around her, crushing her wings against her back.

"All right!" she shouted. "All right," she repeated more calmly. "I'll go willingly. I know you're doing this for my own good."

She relaxed in his grip, intent on gaining his trust as he placed her in the ceramic jug.

"I would never harm you," Dekle's voice was silvery smooth; though she detected a deceptive, caustic odor in his breath.

Violet inhaled deeply, worrying it might be her last. She released a convincing sigh of resignation as she raised her wings above the liquid and looked up at Dekle with a smile, her blue irises glimmering with the faith that he demanded.

He smiled back.

"Remove your necklace, Violet. I can't be certain that the solution won't damage it. Then curl up and get comfortable."

Violet nodded, her wild pampas grass hair bouncing as she unlatched the tiny clasp and placed the necklace in his hand. He had given her the heart-shaped pendant years before—she had never removed it.

Dekle picked up the container of the liquid air solution; using both hands, he tipped it forward until the thick fluid flowed out.

Violet crouched down as if to settle in, then sprang upward, her wings beating rapidly as she raced to the small window and stole into the dark night.

CHAPTER 3

The hinges on the side door of the garage screeched. The Professor stomped into the yard as Violet flew to the oak tree at the back of the house. Tucked behind the leaves, she stayed hidden from the beam of Dekle's flashlight as it darted through the trees like a miniature spotlight.

Abruptly, his search stopped. His attention shifted to Elvina, watching from the open kitchen window. The light above the sink illuminated her chestnut-colored hair while a dim glow crept out across the yard, not quite reaching Dekle as he muttered, "Don't even think about calling your precious Dr. Whiting, my *dear* little wife."

Dear. The word had passed over his lips with a snarl as he strode to the garden shed and returned with a rake gripped in his hands.

Violet flew from tree to tree, following Dekle to the side of the house. With his flashlight aimed at the eaves, he reached the rake into the air, hooked its long metal teeth onto the phone line and yanked it down, then tore the electric line free. The house went dark.

Through the open windows, Violet could hear Amelia call out to her mother.

"I'll light some candles, sweetheart. Just a minute," Elvina replied.

Dekle spun around, his flashlight skimming over the trees before capturing Violet in its accusatory glow. "And you, you bloody thing! You coward! I knew you were too mousey to fly off into the night; always worried a barn owl will pluck you from the sky. You've no backbone. Not like the Mal Rous."

Backbone has little to do with the Mal Rous's actions, Violet thought. Wreaking havoc and attacking people had nothing to do with courage. Their actions fed their biological needs. The scent of their victims' fears nurtured their chemical makeup.

"Blast you, Violet! You need me," Dekle continued in a threatening hiss. "Without my protection, you'll have to fend for yourself against predators, and the scalpels of scientist if you were caught. You'll never survive." Dekle's tone softened, while his expression remained hard. "I'm not going to hurt you. I care about you and just want you to be safe. You were my first successful experiment. Go back to the cellar. Please. I'll be there in a few minutes, and we can talk."

Dekle never said please. Violet wished she could believe him—she missed their time together before the Mal Rous, when she and Dekle were confidants.

"Please," he said again. But his attention was back on the house. "First, I must take care of Elvina. She can't tell anyone about you."

Take care of Elvina... Violet needed to warn her!

A soft drizzle of rain began to fall, as if Guyon Manor mourned Elvina's coming fate.

Violet broke a small branch from the tree and flew to Elvina's bedroom window; holding the branch like a jousting weapon, she rammed it through the screen and slipped inside.

She could hear Dekle charging up the stairs, his angry footsteps interspersed with the sound of Elvina trotting behind, as if she was being pulled along.

"What's wrong, Dekle?"

Violet grimaced; Elvina knew exactly what was wrong. At least the woman was trying to sound innocent.

"I want your keys!" Dekle snapped.

"My, my car keys?" Elvina asked as they made their way down the long hall. The narrow beam of Dekle's flashlight grew brighter as Violet hurried to the chest of drawers. She clutched Elvina's keys, thinking if ever a four-leaf clover could bring luck, now was the time.

Dekle roared into the room as Violet darted to the window and peeked out from behind the curtain. His light scanned the top of the chest of drawers—grabbing Elvina's purse, he dumped the contents onto her bed, then aimed his flashlight at Elvina, the light exposing the worry in her eyes while leaving his face a dark mask of anger.

"Where are they?" With his hand raised, Dekle advanced toward Elvina.

Run, Violet thought. *Run!*

Elvina cowered, waiting to be struck.

"Papa...?" Amelia stood watching from the doorway, a flashlight in her hand.

Dekle dropped his arm. His expression shifted to concern, though Violet thought guilt would have been more appropriate.

Without saying a word, he went to Amelia, placed his

hand on her shoulder, and guided her back down the hall. With timid steps, Elvina followed.

Violet had often wondered if Dekle would also harm their daughter. Thankfully, it appeared he would not.

When no one returned, Violet looked for somewhere to put the keys where Elvina would find them and Dekle would never think to look.

Violet inched open the closet door; Elvina's yellow bathrobe hung from a hook. She dropped the car keys into the robe's pocket, imagining Elvina trying to figure out how on Earth they had gotten there. Hopefully she'd find them tonight, take Amelia, and flee.

Chapter 4

Stars filled the sky as Violet flew the length of the sugar cane field. She scanned above her for hungry predators, then looked back at the silhouetted form of the manor dominating the solitary rise in the landscape.

Her gaze shifted to the group of tall trees at the far end of the property, to the cottage the caretaker had vacated. It would be a safe place to wait for Dekle to calm down. For him to forgive her for disobeying him. *For him to forgive Elvina,* Violet thought, hopeful that he'd find compassion in his heart.

Violet circled above the small dwelling before landing on the kitchen windowsill. "Rats," she muttered, seeing the screen of the open window had been chewed apart. She slipped inside, heard the soft tapping of claws scurry across the wood floor, spotted the dark shapes of rodents running off to hide.

The cottage was empty, except for a wooden rocking chair in the main room. On it sat a pillow, the cotton matting torn apart, no doubt used by the rodents for their nests.

Physically tired and emotionally drained, Violet settled on the remains of the pillow as the rats returned, squealing and scampering, deciding she wasn't a threat.

In the middle of the night, the rattle and clamor of a vehicle sent Violet rushing from the house; hovering above the trees, she peered across the acres of cane to where the lights on Dekle's pickup bounced down the dirt road toward town. She darted closer.

The truck was loaded with boxes, along with the cages, the Professor's lab table, his desk. He'd emptied his laboratory, just as he'd said he would.

What of Elvina? Would he murder her with Amelia so near?

Violet's stomach twisted with dread as she hurried to Guyon Manor. From Elvina's bedroom window, the golden glow of a candle lit Amelia cuddled in her mother's arms. Tension creased Elvina's eyes as she stared at the closed bedroom door. The pheromones that drifted out the window conveyed worry, panic, fear.

Violet retreated to the garage to wait for Dekle's return.

She awoke to the rumble of his truck pulling into the garage. Perched in the rafters, the truck's dashboard light revealed Dekle's demeanor was not of a man who carried forgiveness in his heart.

The bright headlights guided him as, one at a time, he hauled the five jugs housing the Mal Rous from the cellar and nestled them into the truck bed.

"You'll be safe." Dekle spoke to the ceramic containers as if the Mal Rous within could hear him. "I'll come back for you after Elvina's funeral." His tone was unemotional; a chill rippled over Violet's skin. "Amelia will go live with her grandmother. When I dig you up, you can all have the run of the house." Dekle patted a jug as he placed a shovel next to it, then climbed into the cab and drove off.

Violet flew high enough to see the truck's red taillights glowering at her. At the edge of the property, where the family graveyard had lain for two hundred years, was a low-lying mist; or were Elvina's buried ancestors rising up, preparing to welcome the sweet woman to join them? Violet blinked back tears as an ache stabbed at her heart.

The kitchen door opened, and Elvina ushered Amelia onto the back porch, an overnight case in the young girl's hand. Elvina paused, her head tilted, as if she were straining to hear the fading sound of Dekle's truck.

"Mama, how long will I be staying with Dr. and Mrs. Whiting?" Amelia's voice was groggy with sleep.

"Just a couple of days," her mother stated, guiding her daughter into the car.

With the headlights off, the car rolled down the driveway, then paused on the dirt road, until Dekle's truck was out of sight.

Violet watched his pickup turn on the path that wove through the cane field to the caretaker's house.

Elvina's funeral. The words propelled Violet through the night sky in pursuit of Dekle—determined to convince him to let Elvina live.

When she reached the cottage, the truck's headlights were illuminating Dekle's rigid movements as he dug a deep hole at the base of a large tree. Dropping the shovel, he placed one of the jugs into the hole.

Violet pounced on the hood of the truck. The slightness of her body made as much of an impact as a grasshopper. Still enough that Dekle turned in her direction.

He stepped from the glow of the light into the darkness.

His voice lashed out, "I knew you'd be back. Coward. Datura was right. What the blazes was I thinking when I created you? You're a worthless mistake. I'll deal with you later!"

The jug in the hole rolled onto its side. Violet thought it resembled a large, squat toad. Was the Mal Rou within Esere—conscious, struggling to get free?

Then she saw the head of Dekle's shovel swinging toward her.

CHAPTER 5

Violet came to as an engine sputtered to a stop and her body lurched forward. Straining to open her swollen eyes, she found herself crumpled behind the seat of what she believed was the cab of Dekle's pickup. The last thing she remembered was Dekle striking her with his shovel. She had viewed him as a father figure. He had created her, fed her, clothed her, nurtured her. Now she was nothing to him.

The truck door opened with a groan. Over the gusts of a hostile wind, she heard a man offer help with the shutters before leaving. It wasn't Dekle, though the voice was familiar. *Dr. Whiting...*

Violet inhaled a deep breath but couldn't detect the scent of Dr. Whiting's emotions; the organic decay of swamp that preceded a tropical storm tainted the air.

"Thank you." It was Elvina who replied, her voice quiet, mournful. "Thank you for everything. *Everything.*"

For a moment, relief buffered the pain in Violet's sore body. Elvina was alive. Dekle hadn't followed through with his dark deed. Perhaps taking his anger out on Violet had been enough revenge for him.

"Elvina...we did what we had to."

"I know." Her words carried a tremble of regret.

Violet heard the garage barn-like doors close, the lock shoved into place. Gingerly touching her bruised head, she wondered why Dekle had left her here. Why hadn't he bottled her up like the Mal Rous. Did he think he'd killed her?

Violet crawled under the seat and slid out the other side. Slowly, she moved one limp wing, then the other, feeling tenderness where they were attached to her back. She pulled herself onto the seat, saw the small wing window was open, and climbed out...

* * *

THE EXPERIMENT, A Violet Novella

ISBN 978-0-9914111-77

Copyright © 2020 by Wray Ardan & Steven Lee Smeltzer

ALSO BY WRAY ARDAN

Sweet Desire, Wicked Fate

Imagine Jade Gone

The Experiment, A Violet Novella

BOOKS CAN BE PURCHASED THROUGH

Amazon

Barnes & Noble

Kobo

Apple Books

Sign up for my newsletter to be notified of new releases, free short stories & pre-release specials.

wrayardan.com/newsletter/

Acknowledgments

To those of you who read book one of the trilogy Sweet Desire Wicked Fate, I want to say thank you for your reviews, suggestions, and enthusiasm. I have taken your words to heart, and I look forward to your feedback.

On a daily basis, I give thanks for my love, Steven L. Smeltzer, and his continued encouragement and belief in me.

Thank you to my editor, Meredith Narrowe, as well as Dr. Malik Cotter for his knowledge and advice on the healing remedies the triplets use throughout the story, and Lou Ann Arenz for her insights on nursing and hospital protocol.

Special thanks to Mr. Zack Lemann from the Audubon Butterfly Garden and Insectarium in New Orleans and Victoria Bayless, Curator at Louisiana State Arthropod Museum, for their information on hornets. My appreciation also goes out to William M. Goodman, Ph.D., P.G. Senior Staff Geologist with RESPEC Consulting and Services, and David Plumeau, Business Unit Sr. Mine Engineer at Cargill Deicing Technology, for sharing their knowledge about salt caves. And to everyone Steven and I met while visiting Louisiana. We found you all to be kind, gracious, and helpful.

Where writing Sweet Desire, Wicked Fate took me on a

journey of learning to face my fears and insecurities as an author, Imagine Jade Gone has taught me to believe in my inner voice. To trust the muse that speaks to me at the most unexpected times and the insights and advice of friends and reviewers.

As a side note, in chapter 11, Briz makes a reference to a book his sister Hartley had read. The book he is referring to is The Women's Encyclopedia of Myths and Secrets, by Barbara G. Walker.

Until Book 3,

Aloha

About the Author

WRAY ARDAN lives on an island in the middle of the Pacific Ocean with an artist, four cats, and a parrot. Her award-winning romance horror trilogy, Sweet Desire, Wicked Fate, was inspired by sculptures created by her partner, artist Steven Lee Smeltzer. In Steven's mind, the ceramic characters appeared mischievous; in Wray's novels they became the deadly Mal Rous. As well as being a writer, Wray, along with Steven, has set up a creature shop for a computer animation company, worked as associate producer and set designer on a television pilot, and had a series of their characters featured in a young children's animated movie. Imagine Jade Gone is the second book of the trilogy Sweet Desire, Wicked Fate.

To learn more about Wray Ardan, visit her website at
wrayardan.com